Accolades for America's greatest hero Mack Bolan

"Very, very action-oriented.... Highly successful, today's hottest books for men."
—*The New York Times*

"Anyone who stands against the civilized forces of truth and justice will sooner or later have to face the piercing blue eyes and cold Beretta steel of Mack Bolan, the lean, mean nightstalker, civilization's avenging angel."
—*San Francisco Examiner*

"Mack Bolan is a star. The Executioner is a beacon of hope for people with a sense of American justice."
—*Las Vegas Review Journal*

"In the beginning there was the Executioner—a publishing phenomenon. Mack Bolan remains a spiritual godfather to those who have followed."
—*San Jose Mercury News*

MANEUVERS

Libya's bid to oust a North African leader is calculated to turn world opinion against the U.S.—Khaddafi plans to field an American hit team to assassinate the ruler. Mack Bolan's mission to stop the hit seems doomed to failure—until he infiltrates the mercenary underworld and is chosen to be part of the hit team....

"Mack Bolan stabs right through the heart of the frustration and hopelessness the average person feels about crime running rampant in the streets."

—*Dallas Times Herald*

DON PENDLETON's
MACK BOLAN.

FLASH POINT

A GOLD EAGLE BOOK FROM
WORLDWIDE.

TORONTO · NEW YORK · LONDON · PARIS
AMSTERDAM · STOCKHOLM · HAMBURG
ATHENS · MILAN · TOKYO · SYDNEY

First edition July 1988

ISBN 0-373-61412-8

Special thanks and acknowledgment to
Charlie McDade for his contribution to this work.

Those who have been once intoxicated with
power . . . can never willingly abandon it.
—Edmund Burke

Unlimited power is apt to corrupt the minds of those
who possess it.
—William Pitt

I have no quarrel with a man whose skills and
ambition bring him a measure of power. But if he
steps over the line, I'll be there to stop him. Count
on it.
—Mack Bolan

To the men and women of the
American Armed Forces

PROLOGUE

He had never seen stars like this. They were hard points, so sharp they hurt his eyes. In the pure, smokeless air they burned brightly with a steady light that was almost devoid of the fainthearted flicker he was used to. He rolled onto his back and lay flat, staring up at the sky. After snapping the lens covers off his binoculars he brought the glasses to his eyes and scanned across the deep blue, twirling the focus knob with a single thumb. No matter where he turned, no matter how he fiddled with the knob, countless stars like clouds of sparks swam in and out of focus. The more he tried to single out an individual star the harder it became. There were too many clamoring for his attention. Finally he dropped the glasses on his chest and closed his eyes. He wondered whether he was as tired as he felt, or if the sheer immensity of the sky had simply overcome his senses.

He sat up, a slight hint of wind tugging at the loose sleeves of his shirt. It was cold, much colder than he had imagined. The edge of the world seemed sharply etched and just beyond the reach of his fingers. The horizon was almost brutal in its abrupt shift from the deep velvet blue of the sky to the hard blue-black of the land.

Narrowing his eyes to slits, he stared at the land sweeping off behind him, trying to force some definition on the smeared edge of the featureless world. Scanning from left to right and back, he covered the 180-degree sweep twice with no success. The midnight vastness of the sub-Saharan wilderness was as empty of landmarks as the inside of a tin can must seem to a trapped bug lost on its slippery surface, wandering in perpetual circles around and around the infinity of its cylindrical prison.

He shuddered at the image and realized for the first time that the limitless space had intimidated him. Used to a different kind of wilderness, where emptiness was regarded as a sin against progress and every square foot of earth was tarred or cemented, as if to prevent it from blowing away, and grass clung to the cracks in the hard shell smeared from one end of the city to the other, Leon Alvarez wondered what he was doing here.

The wind picked up a little and he could hear it hiss like a giant cobra as it swept across the barren sand. The fine dust began to sting his cheeks and he looked anxiously around, wondering if a sandstorm was coming. He'd read about them, even seen photos such as they were, but the storms were rare in this part of the world, more a figment of Hollywood's overactive imagination than a real threat. It was just one more example of the tricks solitude had been playing on him, screwing up his mind, teasing him with portents of disaster, then laughing at his groundless fears.

He took a large flashlight from the pouch slung over his shoulder and thumbed it on. The beam lanced out, then seemed to disappear, swallowed by the void. He pointed it down, slowly, watching the elongated oval of light finally appear and crawl slowly toward him, growing rounder as it came, like some giant amoeba in search of perfect symmetry. The beige color of the earth seemed almost translucent, small shadows of occasional stones the only blemishes on the smooth surface.

And then his feet appeared, the scarred suede of his desert boots nearly lost against the slightly lighter earth tones, their presence betrayed more by the shadowy outline of their thick soles than by any real sense of substance. Alvarez closed his eyes and shook his head, shuddering yet again, as if trying to shake off an unpleasant memory.

But when he opened his eyes again the vision was still there. He didn't like the way it made him feel, as if he were no more substantial than a ghost, a fading blip on a radar screen or a footprint rapidly filling in with snow. He tried to block out the thoughts, knowing that the last thing he could afford to do was doubt his own existence, his ability to move through the world and shape it.

He was out here to make a difference, to find something bad and make it better, to stop something evil from growing like a cancer and spreading faster and farther than even the men who planned it could imagine. That, he knew, was an overblown, more than slightly romanticized version of what he was there to do, but he had never pretended to be anything other than an idealist, adrift in a sea teeming with pragmatic sharks and realists by the school.

Tired and frightened by having looked too closely at his own inconsequentiality, he thumbed off the light and the desert boots disappeared. Alone in the darkness, unable to see just how small a thing he was, he felt a little better. He stood up and stuffed the light back into his pouch. About to snap it closed, he heard something and stopped, his fingers still on the cold, smooth metal. He strained his ears, but all he could hear was the wind and the rasp of the sand. His sleeves snapped once in the breeze, and the wind died.

He shuffled his feet, listening to the hard rubber soles grind the dry sand with a crunch like that of fresh snow, and he heard the sound again. It was distant, sounding like a cough, and stopped almost as soon as he realized he'd heard it. Then it came again, a low grinding. It was an engine, he was almost certain. But the source of the sound was too indeterminate.

Alvarez sprinted back to his jeep and tumbled into the front seat. He clicked on the range finder and watched as the soft green light of the display screen gradually brightened, bathing his hands with its sickly color. He threw the sweep toggle and watched as the slender baton of white began to rotate. On the first pass it left no trace, but on the second a small green bubble grew and burst almost immediately. On the third pass the bubble reappeared, joined by two more. He turned up the gain and listened to the metallic pings echo and die.

The small radar unit was limited but still useful. Short in range and relatively unsophisticated, it wasn't even government issue, having been lifted from a Soviet APC that had fallen into Company hands after the Yom Kippur War in 1973. The lab boys had played with it for a few weeks, satisfying everyone's curiosity and learning a little about the state of Soviet electronics art. Then, like so many of the spoils of war, it went on to a new career not so different from that for which it had been designed, just switching sides. The irony was compounded by the vehicle, an Egyptian jeep courtesy of Moscow. Alvarez knew that even in that respect machines were like the men who used them. Men, too, found new flags and switched sides more often than anyone wanted to believe. It was an irony no one cared to think too much about. Especially not his colleagues, whose stock-in-trade it was to assume defections were a disease of one side only.

But if that was true then what the hell was he doing here? Chad wasn't a place you went for rest and recreation. It sure as hell wasn't a vacation hot spot. It was a desolate wasteland where even a fistful of diamonds might not buy you a drink of water. There was no logical reason why anyone on Earth should want the place. But somebody did and, as in so much of human affairs, that desire had led another to the conclusion that he shouldn't have it.

Watching the blips grow and die, grow again and fade away a second time, Alvarez struggled against his own cynicism and disillusionment. He had been at his job too long, he thought. This was no way for a man to make a living. Like baseball, at which he had excelled when a much younger man, spying was a short-term career that left you ill prepared for the rest of your life, a part that came sooner than anyone wanted to believe and that more often than not ended in anger and frustration a hell of a lot sooner than anyone wanted. He was, he knew, doing it to himself again. Soon he would begin the litany of former friends and colleagues, and former enemies for that matter, who had stayed on a little too long, then found when they tried to walk away that they couldn't make it in the real world. There were too many bad habits learned, and too many social skills never learned.

Alvarez pushed the thought away, but it slipped through his mental fingers like a ball of mercury and kept coming back with a will of its own. He was on the downward roll now and he didn't like to think about it. His wave had crested and it wouldn't be long before it thundered to the beach where, if he was lucky, he would lie like a landed fish and, if he had enough time, would learn a new way to breathe.

But there was a bright side. At least his source had been on the money. Something was in fact happening in the desert. That was all the gnarled old Italian had been able to tell him, but even so small a gem had its own sparkle in a wasteland like this. Even intelligence needed a little more water and a little less sunlight, someplace to stick down a few wiry roots and hang on. The question still to be answered was what actually was going on.

The blips were growing larger as the three vehicles drew closer. The kilometer scale showed them inside the three-klick radius now, too close for him to risk starting his own engine. He would have to sit there like some weathered statue, Ozymandias the spy, the only vestige of a vanished civilization, and hope the newcomers didn't have him on their radar. He realized he was holding his breath, as if that too could be monitored, as the small column of electronic ants zigged their way across the desert. As nearly as he could figure they would pass within a few hundred meters of him. Their progress was steady, and so far had shown no hesitation. If they knew he was there, they had shown no sign of it.

While he waited he did some rough figures in his head. He had first heard them at about eight kilometers, but the sound had been faint. He could give them that much of a lead and then follow them unheard, even closer if he allowed for the sound of their own engines masking his. Once they stopped he would assume they had reached their destination and take precautions. That, of course, was assuming they didn't know he was there, an assumption he made with some reluctance.

The old Italian had been more than willing to share his information. Wouldn't he have been just as eager to tell someone else about the dark American? Or had he been instructed to tell Alvarez in the first place? Past master of the second guess, as any intelligence operative must be, Alvarez had long since gone on to deeper layers of the onion, peeling away skin after skin. It kept him sane and, he liked to believe, it kept him alive. Like those mathematicians who spent their recreational hours devising three-, four- and five-dimensional chess, Alvarez had always been interested in additional coordinates, trying to define his position as precisely as possible. That too kept him alive. Whether it also kept him sane was still before the jury.

Six dazzling swords flashed up over the crest of a small hill, bouncing in three pairs as the vehicles, still indeterminate, drew closer. They would pass by to his right. Alvarez threw the jeep into neutral and allowed it to roll back below the crest of the faint rise on which he sat. He kept his eyes glued to the screen.

The blips were even with him now. They seemed to float for an instant as Alvarez inhaled sharply and held it. Then, with a small glitch like a drunk stumbling over a threshold, they passed on, starting to widen the gap between themselves and the focus of their barren circle. The rising growl of the engines peaked and began to fall away.

The approach had seemed to take an eternity. The departure was faster than he wanted. At six klicks he kicked his engine over and jammed the gearshift into first. The snarl of the transmission seemed to slice open the night like an invisible buzzsaw and for an instant he was convinced they would hear him.

He left on the radar and began to follow. Matching speeds, he kept the blips at the six-kilometer range and rolled through the night. He had no idea where he was going.

But then, he almost never did.

After an hour the sky ahead began to glow faintly. Even a small fire out here would cut through the darkness, but this was considerably more than that. Five minutes later the blips stopped moving. He narrowed the gap to five kilometers and killed his engine. The rest of the way was on foot.

Alvarez stepped down from the jeep, strapped on a canteen and flipped the toggle on his directional beacon. He made sure the handset worked, then tucked it into his pocket. It wouldn't do to lose the jeep. There were far more pleasant ways to die than choking on your own swollen tongue in the desert.

He walked briskly, almost carelessly, until the glow ahead vanished abruptly. He slowed his pace, dropping instinctively into a crouch. Taking more care now, he stepped quietly, stopping to listen every few meters. There was no sound at all. Even the intermittent wind had died away. His feet seemed to thunder on the dry sand.

Alvarez worked his way toward the top of a small rise—a little rockier than the rest of the soil—and dropped to his belly just short of the crest. He squirmed the last ten meters, peering cautiously over the top.

What he saw took his breath away.

CHAPTER ONE

"Where the hell is Mitchell? I thought he was supposed to be here at eleven-thirty." The big man stood and began to pace back and forth. The hotel room was not that large, and the man's bulk made it seem even smaller to his companion.

"How the hell am I supposed to know? I'm not even sure where I am anymore. I'm getting sick of this creeping around, holing up in out-of-the-way places. I've seen more cities in the past six months than the whole rest of my life."

"McNally, you are the biggest bellyacher I ever met. You take the damn pay, don't you? And you never made half this much in your life. Who are you kidding? This is the softest gig you're likely to see."

The big man stopped pacing long enough to glare at his smaller colleague. At six-five, his head nearly scraped the bottom of a garish chandelier dangling from the ceiling, its phony gilt half peeled away, the rest flaking in small blisters. Pete Sadowski was notorious for his hot temper, and infamous for what happened to those who provoked it. His size had earned him the nickname Wide Load, but his colleagues had shortened it to Load. Affection had played no part in the process. McNally half closed his eyes to shut off the conversation before he said something he'd regret.

Sadowski resumed his pacing, hands clasped behind his back. McNally watched the play of muscles in the larger man's massive forearms, their rippling making the tangled tattooed cobras writhe as if alive. Suddenly, with a thunderous crash, Sadowski dropped into the musty armchair, obscuring its wing back with his broad shoulders and barrel chest.

"I'm a little tense, I guess," he said, sighing. It was as close as he would come to an apology, and McNally grabbed it eagerly, unwilling to provoke him further by continued silence.

"Flak is usually reliable. I'm sure he's just caught in traffic."

"We got just under two hours. If buddy boy doesn't show soon, he's in deep shit. And I don't want to be the one to explain why we missed the meet."

"We can go without him, can't we?"

"Hell no!"

"Why not?"

"Man makes connections like this, you got to wonder why he doesn't show up when the deal goes down. I do, anyhow."

"What are you suggesting?"

"I'm not suggesting anything. I'm just thinking out loud, that's all. I don't know if I trust the bastard. I got a funny feeling."

"Forget it, Load. You're just on edge, that's all. He'll show, and after tonight we can move on."

McNally stood and walked to the window. He pulled the dusty curtain aside and stared out into the street below. Traffic was still fairly heavy on Twenty-third Street. As one of the major crosstown thoroughfares, it carried a disproportionate share of traffic in the Chelsea area. It was cold and McNally's breath clouded the window, quickly freezing to a thin crust on the grubby glass. He scraped at the ice with his fingernails, raking it into small gray mounds, leaving the glass cleaner than it had been in months. "God, I hate New York," he said.

Sadowski grunted. It wasn't possible to tell whether he agreed or disagreed. McNally was about to flop back on the rumpled bed when a sharp rap on the door echoed through the cramped quarters.

"That must be Flak."

"Better be," Sadowski growled. "I ain't expecting anybody else."

McNally skipped to the door, skinning his left shin on the bed frame on the way. He looked through the peephole, bending to get his eye as close to the grimy glass as possible. Between the smeared lens and the fish-eye distortion, it was barely possible to identify Flak Mitchell in the dimly lit hallway.

McNally slid the chain free, cranked back the dead bolt and opened the door. He stepped back and let the visitor in, quickly closing the door and relocking it.

"What kept you, Mitchell?" Sadowski snarled. He ran a thick-fingered hand over his hairless scalp, which gleamed dully in the yellowish light from the chandelier.

"Traffic's still pretty heavy around here. It took me a while to find a parking place."

"Everything set?" McNally asked.

"Yeah. You got the money?"

"Don't worry about it," Sadowski snapped.

Mitchell shuffled his feet. Sadowski made him nervous. The big man, no doubt largely because of the huge bald head, reminded him of one of those cartoon bombs Wile E. Coyote used on the Roadrunner, a round ball with a short fuse. He seemed always to be seconds from going off, destroying everything except the appropriate target.

"I'm not worried. But I'm sticking my neck out pretty far here. These guys play hardball. We walk in without the cash, we're all in trouble."

Sadowski stood up, the ancient chair groaning as his weight shifted. As he regained his feet, the chair, finally free of its burden, sighed with relief. "Let's go." The big man grabbed a pea jacket from a hook on the open closet door and swung into it with a theatrical flourish.

McNally slipped into his own coat, a dark blue down parka, and checked the pockets for his mittens. Sadowski didn't bother with gloves, and didn't bother to disguise his contempt for those who felt a need for them.

He opened the door, forgetting the chain, which snapped taut with a clank. Sadowski cursed and pushed the door closed far enough to slip off the chain, then pulled it back to slam against the wall with a thump that echoed down the hall like a thunderclap.

McNally and Mitchell stepped out into the dim light, the former pausing long enough to put out the light before closing the door and locking it. By the time he finished Sadowski was at the other end of the hall impatiently stabbing the elevator call button. Mitchell was halfway between the two men, as if uncertain whether to align himself with one or the other, but certain that proximity would be seen by both as choosing sides.

The scarred mahogany of the elevator door was just beginning to roll back with a continuous groan when McNally reached it. All three men stepped inside, Sadowski rabbit-punching the down button with one stony knuckle. The door groaned closed, its electrical drain making the small interior light flicker until it eased home.

Nobody said a word as the elevator swayed eight floors down, hitting bottom with a thud and bouncing twice before it came to rest. The door opened, this time with no help from Sadowski, and the yellowish light of the lobby flooded the car. The light was nearly as dim as that of the eighth-floor hall, but after the gloom of the elevator car it seemed like bright sunshine. Mitchell looked around nervously as he crossed the lobby, and McNally noticed Sadowski watching the newcomer out of the corner of his eye.

They pushed through the revolving door out into the cold. The darkness made it seem even colder and all but swallowed the illumination from the few street lamps. Their breath crystallized in front of them, small clouds drifting a foot or two before disappearing. Mitchell led the way to his panel truck, walking the three blocks as if running from something. He kept glancing back over his shoulder at the two men behind him.

He stepped into the gutter behind the truck, yanking the keys from his pocket and fumbling with the lock. A small, awkward hand had painted Flotsam Inc. on both doors in a wavering black. Mitchell got the door open and climbed into the driver's seat, then leaned over to open the passenger door. The cracked leather of the bench seat creaked with the cold, catching one jacket cuff as he drew back.

McNally climbed in first, then Sadowski, the latter's bulk canting the truck slightly to the right. Mitchell shifted his jacket, tugging a bulky sweater down over his belt. When his passengers were settled he cranked the starter. The old truck protested noisily, then stuttered out into the street, lurching over the potholes and litter.

The ride took less than ten minutes. On the waterfront a huge warehouse, remarkable only for the amount of rust accumulated on its metal doors and window frames, loomed dark against the gray sky. Adjacent to it sat another building, apparently carved from the warehouse rather than separately constructed. Old lettering that had once identified the place had long since been buried under countless layers of graffiti. Mitchell coasted to the rear of the building, parking between it and a pier reeking of creosote and rotting garbage. Even in the cold air the scent of decay was sharp.

He jumped out of the truck and led the others to a sheet-metal door. A small bell button—recently mounted on the doorframe—gleamed dully, its brass already beginning to lose its luster. Mitchell stabbed the button once, paused, then stabbed it three times. The bell itself echoed distantly somewhere in the bowels of the building.

Mitchell shuffled his feet, his back to the others, while waiting for a response. It was getting colder by the minute and he wished he had brought gloves. He knew the building was unheated and, if anything, would be even colder. He blew on his hands to keep them warm and was about to reach for the bell a second time when staccato footsteps approached the door from inside.

A sharp scrape, which sounded like a bolt being drawn, alerted all three men that the door was about to open. It swung outward, the knob bumping Mitchell on his knuckles and making an already numb hand all the more numb. A bulky outline stood framed in the open doorway against a dim light deep in the building. To the right a rolling metal door exposed the interior of the warehouse. Mitchell stepped forward.

"You ready, Flak?" The shadow in the doorway asked the question without moving aside to let the three men in.

"Yeah. Come on, Randy, it's cold out here."

"Not much better in here. You bring the money?"

Sadowski stepped in front of Mitchell. "You want the money, get the hell out of the way and let us in. I'm tired and I'm hungry, and I've just about had it with all this bullshit. You want to make a deal, then do it. You want to play cloak and dagger, get somebody else."

Randy moved back and Sadowski brushed past him. McNally and Mitchell followed. The heavy door closed with a boom that reverberated throughout the warehouse for several seconds, then slowly died away with a rumble. The four men stood on a raised platform at the head of a flight of metal stairs.

Sadowski was the first one down, followed quickly by the other three. He strode into the center of the huge building, surrounded by towering columns of metal drums. Randy rushed to catch up, feeling as if Sadowski were taking control of the situation. He was concerned about keeping the upper hand, knowing that the kind of negotiations they were about to conduct swung on intangibles.

Two men stood at the far end of the aisle along which Sadowski had begun to move. Randy took the big man by the shoulder.

"Hold it, cowboy. You're a guest here. Ain't you got no manners?"

"Manners are for wimps and assholes. Which one are you?"

Randy reached for his hip, then, as if thinking better of it, laughed. "You got balls, buddy. I'll give you that."

"Don't matter to me." Sadowski shrugged. "I don't mind playing by your rules, but I do want to play. Let's get this over with. This place gives me the creeps."

Mitchell lagged a little behind the others, still fumbling with his sweater. Randy turned and stopped suddenly, but his features were obscured by shadow. Mitchell couldn't see clearly enough to gauge what might be on his mind.

"Come on, Flak. Haul ass. You're the one who put this thing together. Looks like you changed your mind."

Mitchell laughed. He heard his voice break, and the laugh seemed to die somewhere among the towers of drums. He wondered whether it sounded as bad to the others as it did to him. "I'm not feeling so hot, must be coming down with the flu or something."

"Where's the stuff?" Sadowski demanded.

"Where's the bread?" The voice was low, with the rasp of a buzzsaw on hardwood.

Sadowski turned to look at the speaker. The two men who had been waiting for them had moved forward and now stood about fifteen feet away.

"You first," Sadowski challenged. "Five hundred pounds of C-4, twenty-five blocks, twenty pounds each. And I want to see all twenty-five."

The one with the buzzsaw voice snapped his fingers and four more men stepped out into the aisle. "Tony, show the man the goods."

One of the new arrivals detached himself from the knot and vanished, reappearing a minute later pushing a hand truck. Five wooden boxes, each not much larger than a crate of fruit, were stacked on the truck.

"You want to see it?" Buzzsaw asked.

"Damn right!" Sadowski dropped to one knee, ignoring the others. The man pushing the hand truck offered him a small crowbar, but Sadowski shook his head. He hefted one of the cartons and squeezed it in his huge hands. With a shriek of resistant nails the lid popped up on the wooden box. Sadowski grabbed the half-open lid and yanked it off. He turned the crate top down, then lifted it carefully, leaving on the concrete floor a slightly smaller oblong of indeterminate color and composed of five smaller blocks. They were wrapped in plastic. He slit the covering of one with a thumbnail, pinching off a small wad of the explosive at the same time.

He rolled the C-4 into a ball, brought it to his nose and sniffed. The sharp chemical bite made him shudder.

"Looks good. Now, we agreed on five grand a block, right?"

Buzzsaw nodded. Sadowski slipped the brick back into its crate and replaced the lid, tapping the nails back in with the crowbar.

He stood up, placing the crate back on the hand truck, then slipped his hand into his jacket and withdrew a bulging envelope. He tossed it to Buzzsaw. "Count it, if you—" The sudden squeal stopped him in midsentence. "What the hell was that?"

The sound was repeated, this time higher in pitch, and seemed to splatter off the metal drums. "Son of a bitch..." Sadowski hauled an automatic out of his pocket as Flak Mitchell began to run. "Bastard's wearing a wire." He fired three shots in rapid succession, the first missing Mitchell and glancing off one of the drums with a shower of sparks.

The second shot slammed into Mitchell's left shoulder, spinning him to one side as the third broke his left arm just above the elbow. He sprawled sideways, dead before the echo of the shots had died.

"McNally, grab the shit and let's get out of here." He turned to look behind him, but the others had already gone. McNally grabbed the hand truck and started to run down the aisle toward the door. Sadowski followed, stopping just long enough to kick the dead Mitchell in the side of the head.

CHAPTER TWO

"His name is ... was Adam Mitchell. Flak. Nice guy."

"Where'd they find him?"

"The Hudson River. NYPD got a call about a floater around Canal Street, hung up on the pilings of an abandoned pier."

"And ... ?" Mack Bolan, seated so tentatively he appeared to be in motion, asked the question quietly, then shifted back in his chair to wait patiently for the answer he knew would not be easily extracted.

"What 'and'? That's all there is."

"Hal, that's never all there is. You and I both know that."

Hal Brognola chomped on his cigar. The moist squish of his teeth on the damp tobacco was the only sound in the room. The other man waited patiently, watching Brognola ruminate in front of a huge plate-glass window. The sky beyond was dirty gray. Stray flakes of snow drifted in and out of range of the dim light cast by a green-shaded lamp on the desk that separated the two men.

The big Fed masticated more vigorously, and the seated man fancied he could see the wheels turning in the big Italian's head. The stony features, darkly Mediterranean in cast, seemed to dissolve. The cheeks sagged, dragging the corners of the moving mouth down with them.

Brognola sighed heavily, then dropped like a stone into the padded chair on his side of the desk. In the distance fragments of skyline, etched by the lighted buildings, wavered in and out of focus, no longer obscured by the Fed's broad shoulders.

"What was he doing for you?"

"We don't know."

"What does that mean? Was he out of control?"

"No!" The clipped precision of the response confirmed what Bolan suspected. There was a lot more to this than met the eye. And his friend was not as disinterested as he pretended to be. "No," he said again, this time almost wistfully. His voice sank to a soft whisper. "No, he wasn't out of control. Out of touch, yes, but he would never—"

"Never say never, Hal. You know that. Anybody can be gotten to. All you need is to push the right buttons."

"Anybody? Even you?" Brognola stood up again, the chair hissing as its burden was lifted.

Now the big man was on the spot. He pushed hard, and as expected the other man pushed back with equal force. That was Hal Brognola's style. And you didn't get to where he was without a lot of scrambling. Staying there, as Brognola had done, was more difficult. But as hard as either man might be, and as hard as either of them might push, reality was harder still. In the final analysis reality was the steamroller that would flatten them all. Bolan knew, as perhaps Brognola did not, that there were no exceptions to that rule.

None.

You could pick men carefully, scrutinize their backgrounds, cut down and anatomize their family trees, and you still had nothing certifiable. All you had was a predictive capability. But in the dark world where Hal Brognola and Mack Bolan moved, predictions were about as reliable as those of a gossip rag's psychic, with one difference— people remembered the successes and didn't give a rat's ass for statistics. In their case it was the failures they remembered. You never forgot the taste of bile rising in your throat when you finally, incontrovertibly, learned you had guessed wrong. The pain of betrayal was part of it, and injured pride. Sorrow for the damage inflicted was a major component, and that icy fear that closed on your guts like a frigid vise, fear that this wasn't the only mistake, and maybe not the most serious, that was part of it, too. But eventually you got over those things, pushed them aside and went on, goaded by the speed of events you sought to control and, as often as not, had to settle for containing. But you never forgot, never got over that awful taste.

Never.

They had both been through it more than once. The big guy sympathized with his friend and sometime boss. But friends, because of that understanding, occasionally had to give you a shove, or grab you by the neck and force you to look in the mirror. What you saw wasn't pretty, but you ignored it at your peril, and at considerable risk to others. Bolan sensed instinctively that this was one of those times. He stood and walked around the desk.

Taking Brognola by the shoulders, he guided him back to the chair, pressed him down and took a precarious seat on the windowsill.

"Let's take it from the top, all right?"

Brognola nodded.

"What was he working on, the last time you knew?"

Brognola waved distractedly, as if the question were an angry gnat. "Hell, I don't see what that has to do with this."

"Look, Hal, you can't have it both ways. Either he was bent or he wasn't. Either way, there has to be some connection between what he was doing and what got him killed. And either way, we have to know. Right?"

Brognola nodded again, grateful that someone was willing to push aside the emotional curtain, bring a little logic to bear. "Yeah, you're right, Striker."

"So...what was he working on?"

"Nothing big, not really. At least as far as we knew. Some small-time smuggling stuff."

"What was being smuggled?"

"Military stuff, mostly. Stuff ripped off from arsenals. All in the northeast. It was small-time, really. M-16s, ammo. A few LAWs and TOWs. Some demolitions stuff. C-4 and the like."

"Any leads?"

"Nothing concrete. The stuff was disappearing. The last inventory tipped us. Actually it was a General Services Administration audit. Nobody made much of it at first. We wanted to plug the holes, but that kind of stuff is hard to stop. You know that.''

"But it wasn't all that routine, was it?''

"No, it wasn't.''

"What convinced you?''

"The French pinched a PLO team. They were in a house near Orly with two of the missing TOWs. Probably planning to take out an airliner.''

"That's when Mitchell got involved?''

"A little before that. We were already looking into the missing munitions. Mitchell was working with a guy named Andrews from Army Intelligence.''

"How long?''

"Three months. Then Mitchell dropped out of sight about a month ago. We hadn't heard from him and nobody'd seen him, even Andrews.''

"Okay, now the hard questions.'' The warrior shifted his weight on the windowsill and paused to look out at the swirling snow, tossed in sheets by a restless wind. For a moment, as if a veil had been torn aside, he could see the stark outline of the Empire State Building, its upper floors wreathed in red and green for the approaching Christmas season. Then, as if the giant hand holding the curtain had let go, the snow descended again, its hard flakes scratching against the thick glass with a brittle insistence.

He turned back to Brognola. "What, if anything, did Mitchell tell you the last time you heard from him?''

"He was nervous, kind of antsy. He said he'd been turned on to some hustlers, street types, trying to move some stolen explosives. He also said he'd got somebody interested in making a buy. I wanted him to bust the sellers, but he was thinking bigger than that. He said he thought the buyers were plugged in somewhere, and that he could get inside the network if he let the deal go down.''

"Anything else?''

"No.''

"Did he have backup, other than Andrews?''

"Uh-uh. And even Andrews got cut out. I wanted him to wear a wire and take the sellers down, even gave him the wire, but he nixed it. The last I heard from him was a phone message. I wasn't even here when he called in."

"You still have the message?"

Brognola leaned forward and opened his desk drawer. He came out with a small pink phone sheet and tossed it on the table. "There it is. I can't make anything of it."

Bolan leaned forward to snare the paper. He held it toward the lamp. In a crabbed hand, the marginally legible style in which three-quarters of all phone messages are transcribed, were the words "Mitchell. Arlington Metal. Urgent."

Brognola didn't wait to be asked. "I can't figure it out."

"There's no date. When did this come in?"

"Last night. I checked, and there is an Arlington Metal on the waterfront south of Chelsea. I didn't tell NYPD. I thought it was best you handle it."

The big man nodded. "This one's special, isn't it? It matters the way a lot of them don't."

"Yeah, it matters. Flak was a goofy kid, but I liked him. And we go back a ways. His father was a good friend. I'm almost like his godfather, especially since Dicky, his father, died."

"Okay. Give me anything else you have. Mitchell's address, Andrews's address. The files, the whole works."

"I already got all that stuff together." Brognola leaned down and yanked the bottom drawer of the desk open. The drawer stuck and Brognola cursed. "God, I hate borrowing somebody's office. Nothing ever works like it's supposed to."

The big man knew Brognola was talking about a lot more than lend-lease furniture.

Brognola tugged again, and this time the drawer came all the way open. He reached down and grabbed a sheaf of manila folders, bound with a thick rubber band that curled the folders into a semicircle. He slammed the drawer shut with a bang then tossed the folders on the desk. "It's all there. It isn't much, I admit, but it's all I've got."

The warrior didn't say anything. Brognola wasn't finished, and he knew it.

"I want these bastards, Striker. I don't care what it takes, I want them. Flak was..." He choked off and turned away.

Mack Bolan picked up the folders and placed a hand on his friend's shoulder. Wordlessly he walked across the office and opened the door. Brognola had turned off the lamp and pulled his chair around to stare out into the storm. Etched against the gray, his bulk quivered softly in the darkness.

Bolan closed the door silently. Some things were better left unsaid.

CHAPTER THREE

Mason Harlow did his best to ignore the alarm clock. He rolled over, pulling the cover over his head, and tried to drown out the sound. When he failed, he groped in the pre-dawn darkness until he found the edge of the nightstand, then grabbed for the clock. He missed, knocking it to the floor. Cursing, he sat up.

The clock, still buzzing insistently, stared back at him from the floor, its dim green face a rectangular eye on the carpet. He threw his legs over the edge of the bed and noticed the green pallor cast over them from the clock. For a second it reminded him of the gray-green patina of the bronze sculptures in his garden. It made him feel good.

Harlow bent over to retrieve the clock, clicking the alarm off in the same motion. Replacing the clock on the nightstand, he lay back, drawing the sheets up to his waist. It was six o'clock and the full-length window was outlined in sharp gray as the sun struggled to come up.

Absently he reached for the woman beside him, envying her ability to sleep through the uproar. Stroking her bare shoulder, he sighed. Life was good. Better than he had ever imagined it could be. How often, he wondered, had a poor boy from rural Washington realized a dream like this? Instead of getting up at the crack of dawn to slop hogs and milk cows, he could sleep as late as he wanted and let others worry about the menial chores. Every day but today, he reminded himself.

He clicked on the small lamp on the nightstand and rolled to his side. The woman stirred briefly, then settled back into sleep. Harlow tugged the sheet free and pulled it down to her waist. She lay on her stomach, both arms wrapped around her pillow. The curves were every bit as impressive this morning. And, despite the booze, he remembered them clearly. Her left breast, flattened by her weight, swelled softly and he smiled, remembering the slightly bitter taste of her nipple, the gritty feel of it between his lips.

Harlow sighed again.

It was a shame to have to leave a woman like this, especially so soon after meeting her. Idly he took a handful of her long hair, letting it sift through his fingers. So smooth and so cool, like the finest silk, it whispered softly. The contours of her back were so starkly etched. He had never seen a woman with so small a waist.

For a minute he thought about waking her. His rough workman's hands hovered over her bare back like uncertain birds. He could bring her along for the trip, but that would almost certainly raise more eyebrows than even he was willing to do. Instead he decided to leave her a note and a key, giving her the run of the place for three days. Harlow sat up again and stretched before standing on the deep-piled, blue Chinese carpet.

He crossed to an antique secretary and turned on a small light. Taking a piece of embossed stationery and a mechanical pencil, he scribbled the hurried invitation and folded it in two. From a large Mesa Verde bowl, delicately etched in a thousand intersecting black lines, he grabbed a spare key to the house. He walked to the woman's side of the bed and tucked the note and key into her handbag, which was lying on a high-backed Chippendale chair with her jumbled clothes. He thought too much of what he owned, and too much of himself, to consider the possibility that she might refuse. How could she? A two-thousand-acre farm in the heart of Virginia horse country wasn't something you walked away from easily. He walked back to the secretary and turned off the light.

The sun had risen a little higher in the sky and he could make out the massive oak door of the bathroom at the far end of the room. He padded stiffly, his joints creaking a little, still recovering from the strain of an amorous wrestling match the night before.

Pulling the huge door toward him, he stepped through the portal, then closed the door behind him with a soft click. He turned on the light, its mercury switch soundless in the darkness. Harlow turned on the shower, felt the needle spray with an open palm and adjusted the temperature. He lifted the damp hand to his nose and inhaled deeply. The scent of her still lingered. Harlow hummed as he stepped into the hot shower and vanished into the writhing clouds of steam. Today was the big day, and he smiled broadly.

After a vigorous shower he toweled himself off with the short, hard strokes of a carpenter using a plane. Then he shaved quickly, pausing just long enough to ponder a choice of cologne. He opened a second door and stepped into another bedroom, a smaller replica of the first, even to the pattern in the carpet, and turned on the track lighting overhead. He dressed with more speed than taste, opting for a pair of gray slacks and a boldly patterned sport jacket with a healthy dash of yellow and light green.

In a full-length mirror beside the door, he paused to admire the dashing figure he cut. At six-two, his height alone made him noticeable. His tanned skin, reddened by the hot water, contrasted nicely with the closely cropped thatch of steel-gray hair and matching eyebrows. He was a little jowly, he admitted to himself, a roundness echoed by the beginning of a paunch stretching his belt a little tighter than he'd like. But those were minor blemishes, products of the good life, and he was more than happy to endure them. What it cost him in physical attractiveness, he knew, was more than balanced by the magnetic power exercised by the money and influence that made them possible.

He could stand to lose a few pounds but nobody was complaining, at least not the schools of nubiles and voluptuaries who seemed to swarm around him wherever he went these days. And as long as the women weren't complaining, who was he to rock the boat? Leaving the Company was more than an idea whose time had come, it was a stroke of genius. He had connections up the wazoo, the willingness to use them and the genius to maximize their profit potential.

And as a result he was up to his eyebrows in tits and ass. Not bad for a farmboy from the sticks.

Harlow winked at his image in the mirror, then turned off the light, standing still just long enough to watch the after-image of the bulb fade from the glass. Stepping out into the hall, he closed the door softly and walked with the light and graceful step of a one-time athlete into the bright rectangle of orange light tossed onto the gray carpet by the rising sun. He stopped at its center and looked out over the rolling countryside sweeping down and away from the house. Patches of dark green and lingering swatches of red and gold broke the flatness of the morning light. In the middle distance Marlboro Creek, painted orange, marked the valley's lowest point like a bright band of flame. The sun rising over the hills had deepened the shadows across the creek, accenting the fiery band.

Directly beneath him a bed of chrysanthemums, red and white, was still blooming. Clustered around the still-spouting cupid at the center fountain of an elaborately landscaped garden, the flowers reminded him that it was almost Christmas. He'd have a lot of shopping to do when he got back.

Tearing himself away from the view, he hurried the rest of the way down the hall and turned left. An oak railing, waist high, glowed softly in reflected light. Absently he ran his fingers along the smooth wood as he approached the sweeping master staircase. The huge room below, furnished in the lean and clean style favored by modern decorators, yawned up toward the gently canted ceiling forty feet above it. The stairs, recently carpeted because their bare wood was too slippery, brought him in a semicircle against one wall. His briefcase and luggage waited across a flagstone foyer.

Entering the foyer, Harlow spotted his chauffeur, half-asleep over a second cup of coffee.

"You ready, Vincent?" Harlow barked. When the chauffeur snapped his head up, nearly suffering a mild case of whiplash, Harlow laughed. "You bastard. You should go to bed earlier."

"I should sleep later is what I should do, boss."

"Sorry, Vincent, but it couldn't be helped. When I get back you can have a few days off. I'll be hanging around here for a couple of weeks."

"What time's your flight?"

"Ten. We got plenty of time. It's only six-thirty."

"No problem." Vincent downed the last of the coffee and cracked the cup back into its saucer. Seated at the counter he had seemed of an indifferent size, but on his feet he bested Harlow by two inches. A massive man, he looked more like a bouncer than a driver, which was not surprising since that had been his last job.

A Browning automatic, just visible under his tunic, testified that his new job wasn't that different. Vincent bent to grab the baggage, taking a suitcase in one hand and a briefcase and two-suiter in the other. Harlow got the door, and Vincent muscled the heavy bags out onto the patio and down the four broad stairs to the circular drive.

A small cluster of leaves lay against the rear wheel of a Jaguar XJ6, and Harlow scraped them away with the toe of one Italian loafer while the baggage was placed in the trunk. When Vincent closed the lid Harlow walked around the car and opened the front passenger door. He slipped in and tugged the door closed behind him, dimly aware of the solid thunk of the closing. That kind of solidity, which the rich didn't notice and the newly rich never stopped savoring, made him smile again.

Vincent slipped behind the wheel and pumped the accelerator once before turning the ignition. The engine caught with a whisper, its nearly soundless running barely vibrating the floor of the sedan. Harlow craned his neck over the back of his seat as Vincent pulled away.

Resting his chin on one forearm draped over the seat, he admired the view, all the more appealing because it belonged to him.

"You see that woman I brought home last night, Vincent?" Harlow's voice was muffled by his cradled chin.

"Yeah."

"What'd you think?"

"I seen worse, boss."

"Worse, hell. You ever seen better?"

"Not lately."

"Damn right you haven't. That's what makes life worth living, Vincent. Having a woman like that. I'll tell you...when I was a kid, I never thought I'd get within a mile of something like that. You saw them in the movies, maybe, but no place else."

"She an actress?"

Harlow snorted. "Actress? You kidding me, Vincent? She's on the make, sleeps with money, like most of them. If I lost all my money, she wouldn't look at me twice."

"Why do you bother with a woman like that, then?"

"Because it proves I can afford it. Look, most of my life I couldn't afford it. Who knows, the business I'm in, maybe next year I won't be able to afford it again. But right now I can, and I'll be damned if I'm going to walk away from it."

"You planning on going out of business?"

"No, but when they force you to retire from my line of work, you don't get any warning, let alone a gold watch. Want, take. That's the only rule. And I'm perfectly willing to live by it."

"I don't know. Doesn't sound like much fun to me."

"Hell, Vincent, out on the edge, walking barefoot...that's the only real fun there is." The house disappeared behind a tall stand of trees, and Harlow turned to face front. A sudden shadow passed over the car and he glanced up at the sky. Thick clouds were rolling in and the weather didn't look promising. He hoped the storm would hold off long enough for his flight to get off the ground.

After that, he couldn't care less.

CHAPTER FOUR

To say that Flak Mitchell lived simply was to exaggerate the quality of his accommodations. Bolan stared at the rundown building from the street. Chipped paint littered the unswept top step. A set of fresh letters shone on one end of the lintel, the newly bared wood dark, almost looking wet, as if it were just this side of rotten. Two panes of glass were missing from the door itself, but that didn't matter. There was no doorknob, and the door yawned open, dangling from one broken hinge.

Some men got into their cover so easily, it wasn't long before they started to believe their own lies. Flak Mitchell must have been one of them. Bolan felt guilty, judging a man he'd never met, especially since the man was now dead, his chest cut open in an ugly Y and stitched back together with nylon thread. The medical examiner was not particularly concerned with aesthetics.

Bolan climbed the steps, his feet grating on the grit-covered concrete. He didn't know what he was looking for, but there didn't seem to be anywhere else to start, so Mitchell's apartment would have to do. Once he was in the hallway the smell hit him in the face like a wet cloth. The air was sticky and full of the odor of cheap food and heavy spices. Like a thousand other buildings on the edge of the East Village, this one was inhabited by people who did their best to disguise the lousy food with a touch of class.

It didn't work.

But then it never did.

According to the latest information, Mitchell lived on the third floor, in 3C. The floor of the hallway scraped under his shoes as if it were covered with ground glass. In the dim glow of a forty-watt bulb, Bolan noticed the floor was patterned in an intricate mosaic of hexagonal tiles. That kind of work was usually reserved for the classier buildings, and Bolan realized with a shock that this beat-up hull of a place must at one time have been a desirable place to live. But that was a long time ago, long enough that the warrior would have bet a bundle no one within shouting distance had been alive then.

The stairs were slabs of gray marble that once must have been white. Several were cracked, and more than one in the first flight had its lip chipped away. A wrought-iron banister, itself painted at least half a dozen times, judging by the ragged strata that marked each chip and gouge in the finish, creaked as he climbed to the second-floor landing.

He heard a noise back down the stairs, but the light was too dim for him to see anything below the sixth or seventh step. Then, as if he had passed muster for the curious, he heard a door close with a creak, followed by the rattle of a chain latch as he was dismissed as an object of scrutiny.

The next flight was at the other end of a long hall. As if the stairs themselves weren't indignity enough, the residents of the upper floors had to hike back and forth the length of the building to get to each succeeding flight. Bolan looked up at the ceiling and realized there had once been a stairwell at either end of the building. But some long and deservedly unemployed restorational genius had hit on the least efficient configuration, and blocked alternate flights on each staircase. The end result was a constant stream of traffic down each hall, diminishing in inverse proportion to the floor number. The higher your floor, the less traffic trooped past. The device was not unlike the tiered switchbacks carved into a hundred thousand western hills, and Bolan imagined some drunken cowboy leading a team of blind carpenters to get the job done right.

The third floor seemed—if that was possible—even darker than the second. The first door was marked with a peeling vinyl letter *A* about three inches high. The black plastic barely stood out against the dark brown paint of the door, and looked more like a shadow than half the shadows in the gloomy corridor. Bolan made his way down the hall to the third door. A new brass peephole stood at shoulder height dead center in the door panel. In its rectangular name slot, a neatly lettered cardboard insert read A. Mitchell.

Bolan reached into his pocket for the key ring they'd fished out of Mitchell's pocket, and tried the most likely key in the dead bolt. It went in easily, and Bolan felt rather than heard the well-lubricated lock click open. He pushed on the knob, but the door wouldn't budge. He noticed a second cylinder in the door, a few inches above the first, and he tried three more keys before he got one to work. This lock ground roughly, and the key seemed almost too fragile a tool to overcome the resistance. Finally the lock opened and the door swung silently inward.

Bolan instinctively reached for the light switch, but some sixth sense stopped him as he found it. He fished in his coat for a penlight, flicked it on and played the beam in through the open door.

He was glad he had. The slender wire shone like a filament of spiderweb in the moonlight, so thin it seemed barely able to support its own weight. It gleamed in the bright beam, and Bolan swept the light down and to his left, where the wire disappeared into the business end of a detonator. The large brick of plastique would have taken the top three floors off the building if he had thrown the switch. It was a clever, if indiscriminate, booby trap. Bolan stepped in carefully, disconnected the wire and yanked the detonator out of the block of C-4. Crumbs of the dull, putty-colored explosive clung to the pen-sized trigger.

Bolan flipped the switch, and soft light from twin ranks of indirect track lighting flooded the room. It was so different from what he'd expected that Bolan blinked as if to wipe away a hallucination. He closed the door and threw the dead bolt, leaving the heavy police lock disengaged. The floor of the apartment gleamed. Its elaborate parquet design had been stripped and sanded, then coated with several coats of polyurethane. The walls, too, had been redone,

then carefully painted. The apartment was an architect's
dream, as out of place in the run-down building as a dia-
mond in a rhinestone necklace.

A half dozen large canvases, each an abstract of broad
sweeps of a large brush, all done in bold primaries against
white, with black swirls à la Jackson Pollock, hung on the
walls and another leaned unfinished against a tall easel.
Either Mitchell or someone he lived with was a gifted artist. The place was furnished simply, with the leanest Scan-
dinavian designs in plain wood and strictly functional
contours. At the far end of the living room, a wall unit held
an upscale stereo setup and several hundred records.

Bolan walked gingerly to the wall unit. A few record
jackets were stacked alongside a Bang and Olafsen turn-
table that featured more controls than a 747 cockpit. He
shuffled through the empty sleeves, all for Bach Organ
chorales, then noticed a dim green eye staring at him from
the bank of components. A Teac tape deck was on. A fif-
teen-inch take-up reel, one end of the tape dangling freely,
sat motionless, its polished aluminum reflecting the overhead light.

Bolan searched the bedroom, which was as cleanly furnished as the living room. Two drawers were built into the
headboard, but they held nothing more than a few paper-
back books and toilet items. A quick tour of the bathroom
came up empty. A full-length closet seemed like the best bet,
and Bolan opened the door cautiously. The closet had an
overhead light that went on as the door opened. He went
through every pocket methodically but found nothing of
interest. Nothing, that is, except for some women's clothing. Mitchell either had a roommate or a visitor who came
frequently enough to warrant leaving some of her things at
the apartment. But her pockets, too, were empty.

Bolan was about to leave when something against one
wall of the closet caught his eye. A slight color difference,
only noticeable at certain angles, brought him closer. He
now detected a faint seam around a rectangular panel that
had been set into the wall. He felt the edges of the panel with

probing fingers but found no latch, and it was set too snugly to be yanked away with fingertips. He placed his hand against the top of the panel and pressed. The panel swiveled, its top going into the wall and its bottom opening out. It had been built on a center hinge, and was kept in place only by inertia, relying on camouflage rather than strength for its security. A small chamber behind the panel held a single brown letter-size envelope.

The envelope bent as he lifted it, a metal weight in one end too much for the paper. Tearing the envelope, Bolan dumped a thick metal key into his palm. The key was stamped with a number, apparently for a locker. Its top edge was rimmed in bright orange plastic. It looked like a million other locker keys from train and bus stations all over the country.

The pickings were slim, but Flak Mitchell had gone to some trouble to hide the key. If anything in the apartment was significant, the key had to be it. Bolan tucked it in his pocket, left the bedroom and walked back to the door. But something kept nagging at him. Something didn't quite make sense. He caught the glimmering light on the tape recorder again, and walked back to the wall unit.

Mitchell seemed to be something of an electronics buff. It was unlikely he would have forgotten to turn off equipment he obviously had cherished. It was expensive stuff, and well cared for. On a hunch Bolan yanked a couple of loops from the take-up reel, threaded it through the heads and back onto the feed reel.

Punching the Rewind button, he watched the counter tick backward as the tape slipped back onto its reel. When about a quarter had been rewound, he stopped it. Ignoring the amplifier, he slipped a pair of headphones on and jacked them into the deck. Punching the Play button, he listened expectantly. After two minutes he'd still heard nothing but the hiss of empty tape. Rewinding still further, he tried again.

And heard nothing but tape hiss.

Bolan took the headphones off and draped them around his neck. He tilted the deck forward and noticed a small cylinder dangling from one of the input jacks. It was a transceiver. The small red dot on the slide switch showed that it was on.

Bolan snapped his fingers. Brognola had said something about Mitchell having a wire. They had given it to him, but he'd never used it. Or had he? The big guy rewound more of the tape, slipped the phones back on and listened. A few garbled shouts barked into one ear, only one channel of the tape picking up the signal. That was consistent with the transceiver being jacked directly into the recorder. He spooled the tape all the way back, stopping it just before the transparent leader. The tape rolled forward and Bolan heard a hiss, the same hiss as at the end of the tape. Then after a brief burst of static he heard footsteps on the tape.

Bolan listened intently. Wherever the signal had originated, it obviously had been picked up through an open mike without selectivity of any kind. He heard a door close, then harder footsteps as feet slapped on stone, then a dull booming sound as a door closed somewhere. He didn't have to think too hard about that one. It was the same sound he'd heard on his way into the building. Mitchell must have put the wire on and gone to the rendezvous that got him killed.

Bolan shut off the recorder and yanked the reel off the machine. He'd turn it over to Hal and let the techies try to figure it out. He found an empty tape box on the shelf nearby and slipped the tape inside. As he was putting the box into his pocket, a thought hit him. The presence of the booby trap had been bothering him all night. Mitchell certainly wouldn't have set it up—he'd been intending to return home. He also wouldn't have wanted to risk it because the woman probably had a key. Unless maybe she knew?

Or had *she* set the trap?

But why?

Bolan was walking to the door when he saw the latch on the dead bolt swivel silently. He clicked the light off and pressed against the wall. The Beretta 93-R whispered in the darkness as he slipped it out of the shoulder holster.

Some of those questions just might get answered in a hurry.

CHAPTER FIVE

Pete Sadowski rubbed black night cream on his bald scalp, smoothing it on his slippery skin with the patience of a painter finishing a canvas. When his domed head was completely black, he scooped more of the cream from a jar and blackened his neck and forearms. The dull black cream gave his long arms the appearance of twin mat mambas. Idly he flexed the muscles of his forearms, watching their play beneath the skin.

Sitting alongside Sadowski in the jeep, Dave McNally watched the much larger man with a mixture of fear and admiration. Unlike most big men he had known, who usually tried to downplay their superior size, Sadowski seemed to relish flaunting his bulk, using his size to intimidate. It had gotten Sadowski into more than a few fights, and McNally had heard about most of them more than once. In the past six months, he had even been in a few. Now, in the middle of some godforsaken hole in the heart of Africa, he was even less happy about it. He thanked his stars it was a short trip.

For three months, McNally had been cursing his luck, his stars and anything else he could blame for his current predicament. While he waited for Sadowski to finish preening, he thought back, trying to find the wrong turn that had brought him here. Always a sucker for a strong sales pitch, he realized he had been an easy mark for Mason Harlow. It had taken him a week to wise up, but that was already too late. He knew too much, and too many people knew it. He'd thought about running, even turning himself in to the CIA or the FBI, but it was unlikely they would take him seriously, at least not unless he could stick some strong corroboration under their noses. The problem was that Jedwell

was still with the Agency, or at least tied to it. He had
sources inside, friends in high places, as it were. One of
them would be sure to hear about it if McNally tried to roll
over on him.

McNally had even made an anonymous call to the FBI,
but he'd had to fortify himself with a fifth of Wild Turkey
first. The agent had known it just as surely as if he could
smell the booze on Dave's breath. Replaying it over and over
again in his head, McNally realized how crazy his story had
sounded. Put it in the mouth of an on-again, off-again lush,
and you killed it as dead as it could be.

There was no way out, and McNally knew it. He was
along for the ride and in for the duration. In his more sober
moments, which weren't all that frequent to begin with and
were getting less so, he wondered just how long the duration might be. That things would end badly, he didn't doubt.
Whether he would survive in one piece, he hardly dared
hope. Sadowski was a madman and Harlow a cannibal.
Each of them would eat his own young if there was a buck
in it. Multiply that by a few million and you had a fair idea
of just how dire the straits could be.

"You finished, Load?" McNally asked, shaking his head
to free it of the unpleasant breeze of reality.

"What's your hurry, Dave?" Sadowski asked. His lips
moved into what he meant to be a smile. McNally didn't
believe it. He knew better.

"We got fifty miles to cover before we can even start to
work. And we have to be back before sunup. If we don't
move now, we might as well not bother."

"Screw it. We'll haul ass, that's all. That jeep can get
there and back in under three hours. We got seven hours
before sunrise. Just keep your shirt on."

"Look, sport," McNally snapped, "that kind of arrogance can get your butt in a sling pretty quick. We're not
fooling around with some bunch of half-assed soldiers. The
guards at that frog air base are Foreign Legion. They're
hard sons of bitches, and some of them have been through

a lot worse than anything we have planned for tonight. You know anything about the Algerian War?"

"No, why? Bunch of frogs and wogs, wasn't it? Strictly small change."

"Small change, my ass. It made Vietnam look like a Sunday parade, Load."

"So?"

"So, what I'm trying to tell you is if they catch our asses, you'll wish you were dead. But it'll take a long while before you are."

"Come on, the French are our allies. We don't have to sweat it. They're civilized people."

"That's where you're wrong, Pete. Nothing about this goddamned place is civilized. Not a goddamn thing. And the men out here, I don't care where they come from, they get to be just like the desert, man. You spend any time out here and something inside you dies. Civilization dies, man. And there's nothing to take its place. They are coldhearted killers, every last one of them."

"Maybe you should have stayed home. Maybe selling Girl Scout cookies is more your line, Dave. Want me to talk to Mason? Maybe he can get you a paper route, or something...something a little less scary. How 'bout it?"

"Fuck you, Sadowski."

The big man laughed noiselessly, his blackened face a grotesque caricature from the silent screen *Phantom of the Opera*. McNally turned away, squeezing his shoulder blades tightly together to avoid losing it completely.

There was no percentage in arguing with Sadowski, he knew that. He also believed the big man would one day kill him, probably on Harlow's orders. Things had been on a slow downhill slide for the past six weeks. Sadowski barely controlled his contempt, and Harlow had started to ignore McNally altogether.

McNally cursed himself for being a greedy bastard. The money, one hundred thousand dollars, was nothing to sneeze at. He had bills long overdue, a wife and kid, and child support was something he spent on a bottle, as often as not. With the bread Harlow was paying, he could climb out of the hole, maybe even get far enough away from it that he wouldn't have to worry about falling back in.

The one-year contract, which called for the money to be placed in a numbered Swiss account, and all expenses paid, had seemed too good to be true. Add the commissions and finder's fees on top of that, and you had a gold mine. Harlow, whatever else he was up to, knew how to make money. But things had begun to go sour for McNally. An office job had turned into fieldwork, and he'd had enough of that in CIA. He'd been ill-suited to it, despite his father's own successful career in the Agency. For McNally, drifting from job to job and from bottle to bottle had become a way of life.

At the time, Harlow's offer had been like a life raft for a drowning man. When he first started working at Harlow's company, International Advisers, he'd been down so long he had begun to think he'd never get off the bottom of the barrel again. The first few weeks had been a revelation. He'd started to feel good about himself, to get control of his life in a way he never had before. But his initial impression was more accurate than he knew. Now he was all but convinced of it. It was apparent the life raft was sinking beneath him.

The things he'd done for money had been ethically gray at best. Now he'd crossed the line entirely, and there was no going back. Not ever. Not alive, and probably not even dead. More than likely he would end up a desiccated husk lying on the downwind side of some dune, the sun baking his skin to crisp leather after the deliquescent sands had sucked him dry.

Maybe he'd be better off that way, he thought.

"You say something, Dave?" Sadowski asked.

"No, just talking to myself, I guess."

"Some audience."

"Yeah...you got that right." McNally cranked up the jeep. The roar of its engine seemed to vanish almost immediately. He was certain that he wouldn't be able to hear it fifteen feet away. The desert had come to seem to him like a fathomless maw that swallowed everything—men and their machines and the noise they both made—with colossal indifference. Never long on self-confidence, McNally felt positively insignificant in the sub-Saharan wilderness.

The jeep lurched out of the small encampment, its tires hissing over the dry soil. Sadowski hummed in a saw-toothed baritone. He couldn't carry a tune, and the racket irritated McNally's already frayed nerves. But the volatile big man was proud of his extensive repertoire of fifties rock and roll tunes, all of which sounded alike when filtered through his profoundly unmusical sensibility. McNally didn't dare ask him to be quiet.

To take the edge off the trip, McNally tried to get Sadowski talking. The man was an idiot, but mindless babble was infinitely preferable to tuneless cacophony. "You think we can take out the Mirages?"

Sadowski didn't respond immediately. He continued to hum, shifting slightly to what McNally guessed must be another song. After a minute or two, Sadowski said, "No problem. I got all we need right here." He patted two large canvas bags on the rear seat. "Thirty charges. According to Jedwell, that gives us plenty of extras. All we got to do is set the timers and toss them up the afterburners. When these babies blow, they'll take those planes apart. The jet fuel should take care of the pieces."

"You sound like you're looking forward to it."

"Hell, why not? I'm good at what I do, and Jedwell is paying me a bundle."

"I guess..."

"Guess, nothin', Dave. How the hell else could I make six figures a year, guaranteed?"

"Doesn't Jedwell seem a little odd to you?"

"Shit, all them spooks is odd. When I was in Nam, I knew a guy, Air America pilot, I think, who was CIA, too. Those bastards were everywhere. Anyway, he collected ears—Charlie ears...had a bag with what must've been thirty-five or forty. They looked like them dried fruits they sell in health-food places, you know...apricots and figs.

He'd sit around the base, playing with them like they was toys or something. Every once in a while he'd pop one in his mouth and kind of roll it around for a while. Said he wanted to keep them moist. I seen a lot of weird things over there, but that was too much, even for me. Anyhow, after that, Jedwell seems like a little old lady."

"You think he's still on the Company payroll?"

"That's what he says."

"You believe him?"

"Don't matter whether I do or not. Long as he pays me, the son of a bitch can work for Uncle Gorby, for all I care. Why, don't you believe him?"

"I don't know. It just seems kind of funny. Him being so tight with the Libyans and all. It doesn't make any sense."

"Spooks ain't supposed to make sense. All they supposed to do is make things happen. And that's where we come in, ain't it?"

Sadowski started to hum again, a signal that he was no longer interested in conversation. McNally listened, hoping that for once he would recognize the tune, but he drew a blank.

He turned to look at the bags bouncing on the back seat. "That stuff okay back there? It won't blow, will it?"

"Not unless you get too nervous, Dave. That plastic shit is powerful stuff, but unless you rig it, you could kick the stuff around the block and not worry about it."

"Even with detonators already in place?"

"Quit bellyachin', for Christ's sake. I swear to God, I don't know why I have to get stuck with you. What have you got on old Mason, anyhow?"

"What do you mean?"

"The day he puts up with you by choice is the day the world ends. He's everything you're not. He's as cool as a cucumber and could talk his way out of anything. Hell, he's a natural salesman. I think if he had the chance, he could talk the Pope out of St. Peter's. Man must be worth twenty million bucks. You ever see that farm he's got in Virginia?

Man, horses up the wazoo. House must have thirty rooms. I counted eight bathrooms.''

"Doesn't that make you wonder?"

"Like I said, if the checks keep coming I don't give a shit about anything else. When the money dries up I move on. What could be simpler?"

McNally lapsed into silence. He chewed on his lip for a few minutes. The wind whipping past the jeep made his skin feel hot, as if he were dehydrating. He thought about jumping out of the jeep, but it was crazy. If Sadowski didn't kill him, he'd die in the desert. He was nearly bottomed out, but suicide wasn't for him.

The jeep lurched to a halt, snapping him back to reality. "Time for a hike, sport," Sadowski grunted. "The airfield's about a mile from here."

"You sure we can find our way back to the jeep?"

"I can." Sadowski laughed. "Don't know about you. Grab a bag."

CHAPTER SIX

Captain Lucien Picard stood on the edge of the tarmac, twenty yards from the end of the runway. Behind him twelve Mirage fighters were little more than dull shadows, their clean lines all but obliterated by the darkness. He hated the desolation of this armpit of Africa. Everything he had been told had proved to be true...in spades. Born in Algeria, he should have expected the worst. Even there Chad was spoken of with the kind of reverence usually reserved for those places where the worst sinners were asked to spend a little time. But the reverence had been understated, hadn't done justice to a place where even the nighttime sky seemed parched, the deep blue somehow bleached just a bit, as if the daytime sun exercised more than a little influence.

He lit a cigarette, removed the filter with a snap of his fingers and tossed the small cylinder over his shoulder. As Picard walked away from the parked fighters, he felt the tarmac give way to a crisp, raspy grit, soil that hadn't seen water in months. When he first arrived in Chad two weeks ago, he had been certain he wouldn't mind. Now he couldn't wait to leave.

Working for SDECE, the French intelligence service, had seemed like an exciting adventure when he first joined up. Two tours in the army, consistent with family tradition, had been a tune-up. His father had been at Dien Bien Phu in the final days, before that with the Maquis. And his father's father had been in the trenches for that all too brief time of resistance against the *Boches*, in the early days of that war. But a little mustard gas had prematurely ended that brief chapter in the Picard military heritage.

The military history of France in the twentieth century was spotty. It had as many downs as ups, and the downs were deeper and left more lasting impressions, but the military was the family tradition and Picard had nothing better to do. Kicking around the Sorbonne during the height of student protest had engaged his political instincts for a brief interval, but the upheaval and the unruly confrontations among supposed allies had gotten old rather quickly. He'd tried taking political science seriously, but the more he looked at it, the more political and the less scientific it seemed. Bored, and feeling just a little betrayed, he'd joined the army, the family DNA finally overcoming his naive determination to defy it.

And now he was in Chad.

The air base might as well have been in Antarctica. He couldn't have been more cut off from the only world in which he felt truly comfortable. His political convictions, still rebellious, still somewhat leftist, had been unable to ease the discomfort he felt whenever exposed to the harsh realities of the Third World. It had been so easy to sympathize, to be enthusiastic about the stirring of nationalist pride, cheering on the underdog as it struggled to its feet. But there was something brutal, almost dehumanizing, about the physical environment in which such movements took root. Picard had toyed with the notion of writing a lengthy article on the determining role of environment in the brutality of nationalist movements. Even now, ten years after the idea had first occurred to him, he wasn't quite ready to abandon it.

And little that he had seen had contradicted the theory. The grinding poverty and backbreaking labor required to make a living in Indochina must surely have somehow shaped the will of the NLF, and just as surely the arid desolation of Algeria had played a role in the relentless insistence of the FLA. He had missed that one, but he knew men who had been there, on both sides, and even now their faces were as parched and barren as the Algerian landscape.

Now, standing in the desert night, he wondered what Chad would do to him. He pulled viciously on the cigarette, as if the smoke could somehow cauterize the discontent he felt in his chest. He scraped his feet across the dusty soil and walked farther away from the end of the airstrip. He turned to look back in the direction of the barracks, the low, blocky buildings rectangular lumps backlit by the security floods. One light burned in a window, and Picard wondered whether it belonged to someone as disenchanted as he.

Ostensibly he was here to scrutinize the entire complement of two hundred officers and men. Rumors had been floating around for weeks that something was about to blow. Details were sketchy and, as usual in such cases, often contradictory. But there were a couple of common threads unifying all the stories, and they were taken seriously enough to warrant an on-site investigation. The kernel of all the stories was that a small band of terrorists had somehow managed to penetrate the base, and that sabotage was imminent.

Picard had come willingly, curious to see a part of the world about which he had never heard anything good. Now he knew why, and after two weeks he was about to mark the rumors down as nothing more than the speculations of bored men too long isolated in conditions far from ideal. The nearest town was twenty miles away, and it was hardly deserving of the name. The sun, day in and day out, was hot enough to fry your brains. And worst of all, there was absolutely no relief from the tedium of the daily routine.

Picard had the feeling that if the stories weren't true, the men themselves would start sabotaging things just to break the monotony of their lives. You could amuse yourself just so long with jokes about Khaddafi. And yet Libya was still probing at the border, from time to time sending armored columns across the desert, poking tentatively, almost reluctantly, like an internist using a new instrument.

War hysteria would build and fade, its rhythm as relentless and unpredictable as the waves pounding away at a beach before a coming storm. That Libya had designs on Chad was indisputable. How serious those designs were, though, seemed to change with the seasons, or perhaps with the flow of Soviet weapons into Tripoli. Khaddafi seemed more adventurous than skilled as a military leader, and he distributed matériel as spontaneously and lavishly as he did the oil billions that kept him afloat.

But knowing all that did not make Chad any easier to take. Or any easier to like. Picard had quickly come to loathe the place. Standing in the desert night, he felt as alone as a man abandoned on the moon.

As he ground his cigarette into the dust and started back to the edge of the airstrip, a flash of light just over the horizon caught his eye. The sun was still well below the edge of the world, but there was no doubt that what he had seen was a reflection.

A second later the sky split open with a tremendous howl. Klaxons blared, and the sound of slamming doors seemed to rush from one end of the base to the other. Almost at once, huge orange flowers burst open along the airstrip as one by one the Mirages were torn apart, then consumed in their own fuel. So much for the possibility that the old Italian had been mistaken.

Picard dived to the ground as a high-pitched whine screamed up out of the darkness, as if sprung from the ground itself. A moment later the roar was overhead. Outlined against the roaring flames as it streaked by barely a hundred feet off the ground, Picard recognized the unmistakable profile of a MiG-25.

It was too dark to see the markings, but it almost certainly was a Libyan fighter. Picard scrambled toward the command post as two more MiGs flashed by. This pair flew higher, and Picard watched mesmerized as brilliant cylinders tumbled end over end toward the barracks area. The cylinders vanished in the pall of thick oily smoke billowing over the base, and then the earth shook. Picard nearly lost his balance with the trembling beneath him, and he reached out like a wire walker, using his arms for balance.

The whine of the MiGs disappeared into the sky, and high above Picard could see the short bursts of flame as the jets climbed almost straight up. He was certain they'd be back for another pass. He raced toward the barracks and gasped as he burst through the gate into the living compound. Two of the buildings were totally destroyed. The incendiary bombs dropped by the MiGs had torn the flimsy structures to pieces and drenched them in flaming jelly.

More than a hundred men had been sleeping in each of the buildings. Picard ran to the nearer barracks, hoping to God and whatever else was holy that no one was trapped alive in the holocaust. The roaring flames were sucking up oxygen at such a rate, and the superheated air rushed skyward at such a pace that a wind of hurricane force swept dust and scraps of wood and paper into the blaze. The air rushing past sounded like thunder or a gargantuan waterfall.

Picard saw black shadows, silhouetted against the bright orange flames, scurrying in every direction. They reminded him of ants attacked by a child with boiling water. They raced back and forth, not knowing what had happened, and even less what to do. Searing heat washed over him in waves. Timbers split with cracks and snaps, as if the building had been full of fireworks. Thankfully he heard not a single human voice.

The captain raced in a broad circle, skirting the flames, and joined several men standing helplessly on the other side. Three fire trucks screeched across the runway tarmac, and crews began spraying the wreckage of the fighters with chemical foam. Another pair of pumpers screamed to a halt as close as they could get to the burning barracks. Several men ran toward the wellhead, trailing hoses behind them. The heavy diesels of the pumpers chugged in anticipation.

When the lines had been connected, the throb subsided as water rushed through the lines. Three men took a hose from each of the trucks and trained a pulsing stream of water on the ruins. The flames cracked and sputtered as the first water hit and instantly boiled away. Waving the huge nozzles in broad figure eights, the men tried to cover as much as possible of each building, knowing, as did everyone else, that it was too late to save anyone inside, too late to save the building, too late, in fact, to do anything but go through the motions. They had been trained to fight fires, and that was all they could do. Picard envied them. At least they could do something to keep their minds alive. He felt numb, standing in front of the blazing junk like a dumb animal.

Small knots of men stood around as if shell-shocked. This wasn't supposed to happen, not out here in the middle of nowhere, and certainly not to them. They weren't even at war. They were supposed to be making sure that nothing happened, and instead something had happened, and it had happened to them.

Picard walked back toward the gate. He was puzzled but couldn't put his finger on the reason. The MiGs had vanished almost as quickly as they had come. And that seemed odd somehow. Trying to piece together the sequence of events, it struck him. The planes had bombed the barracks, true enough. But what had happened to the Mirages?

He had been out there on the edge of the strip when the raid started. He had seen a glint of light in the distance, he remembered. All hell broke loose and the barracks went up. But the planes had been blown up before the MiGs made their first pass. There had been no rockets, no strafing, no nothing on the airstrip. Yet a dozen fighters were now little more than smoldering mounds of foam-drenched wreckage. Why?

His first impulse was to find Colonel Marnier, but what would he tell him? He couldn't very well convince the base commander there had been sabotage, not without something to substantiate such a wild claim. Everyone had seen and heard the MiGs. He had seen them himself. And yet the Mirages, a dozen of the best fighter planes in the world, had exploded almost simultaneously before the first MiG made a pass.

Picard sprinted through the gate toward the airstrip. If there was any evidence of what had happened, he'd have to find it before the cleanup began. Once daylight came everything would be swept into a mound—clues, evidence, wreckage, foam—then removed.

Picard reached the first jet, which was no longer recognizable as anything at all. Covered in foam that popped and shifted like something alive, it hissed and vented small puffs of smoke through bubbles that grew on the surface of the licorice-smelling foam and then burst with the thick, wet popping sound of a partially filled balloon. As the foam dried, it grew more viscous, and the bursting bubbles left rings behind, like craters on the moon.

Picard didn't know what he was looking for—he wasn't even sure there was anything to find. But he knew this was his one chance. He walked swiftly along the strip, wanting to get a quick look at the whole area before too much traffic disturbed it.

He glanced once at the sky, but it was a black void now, the stars gone, drowned by the harsher light below. It was hopeless; there was no way in hell he could find anything here. Stepping off the tarmac, he backed away from the runway a bit and walked along idly, scraping at the sand with the toe of one boot. Ten yards away, small oval shadows in the orange glare caught his eye. He moved closer, noting how they were arranged in pairs. Footprints!

Picard ran to the nearest fire truck and grabbed a flashlight. He sprinted back to the tracks and followed them for several yards. Sure enough, it was a trail. It might not mean anything, but it was all he had. He ran back onto the tarmac and grabbed a mechanic he knew.

"Get a jeep and meet me here in five minutes."

"Where are we going?"

"I don't know. I'm going to tell Colonel Marnier we'll be gone for a while."

The mechanic was back with the jeep in less time than it took Picard to tell the base commander he had something he wanted to check out. As the jeep pulled away, Picard told the driver to keep the lights off. He didn't want to call attention to himself.

Slowly, following the tracks with only an occasional burst from the flashlight, they had gone little more than a mile when a pair of beams lanced out at them, passing just over their heads. He told the mechanic to kill the engine. In the sudden quiet, they could hear the cough of another engine two or three hundred yards ahead. The engine roared, and the light beams lurched violently.

"Follow them," Picard snapped. "But don't let them know we're here."

CHAPTER SEVEN

Bolan pressed himself closer to the wall as a crack of dim light broke around the door. It grew to a width of two inches, so slowly that Bolan wasn't certain the door was moving at all. The whisper, when it came, seemed louder than a shout in the tense darkness.

"Flak? You in there? Flak?"

The voice was low, husky and definitely frightened. Bolan shifted the Beretta in his hand, his palms feeling somewhat slippery. The door opened wider. "Flak?" Outlined against the pale light from the hall, Bolan saw a slender hand grope toward the light switch. At least he knew something about the caller now. Whoever it was hadn't rigged the explosives.

The warrior slid back along the wall as the hand finally found the toggle. The overhead lights went on with a click, and Bolan blinked to adjust to the glare.

The hand moved slowly, delicately, seeming to exude a shape from the thin wrist as it moved forward, exploding suddenly into the full figure of a young woman, bulky under layered sweaters and a down jacket. She seemed to sense something as she reached to close the door behind her. She paused, then, as if deciding it was too late to do anything else, she turned to confront the big man. His black clothes, against the rich white behind him, gave him the appearance of a three-dimensional shadow.

Bolan moved swiftly as her jaw fell open. She was about to scream when he slapped an open palm over her mouth and his gun hand behind her head. When she was securely in his grasp, he kicked the door shut with his left foot.

"Don't scream. I won't hurt you." This was the last thing he had expected. "I'm going to let go. Just don't scream, and don't worry."

The woman's eyes were huge, and he noticed they were an odd pale green. He had never seen eyes that color before. "If you promise not to scream, nod your head."

He realized she couldn't nod if she wanted to, so he relaxed his grip a little, and felt the pressure of her head against his open palm. He let go slowly, prepared to resume his grip at the first sign of a scream.

When he brought his hands back toward him, she turned slightly and caught sight of the automatic pistol. Her eyes grew wider still, but Bolan dropped his hands to his sides, the Beretta dangling loosely. She seemed to understand he meant her no harm, and she sighed her relief.

"Who are you?" Bolan asked, slipping the Beretta back into its holster.

"Isn't that my line?" the woman asked. She made a weak attempt at a smile. "Where's Flak?"

"Answer my question first." Bolan turned the dead bolt, relocking the door. He walked over to a low sofa, more an oak frame covered with huge pillows than anything else, and sat down gingerly.

"Don't worry, it'll hold you." This time the smile was genuine. "My name is Alison Brewer."

"Flak's girlfriend?"

"That term's a little old-fashioned, isn't it? But then, judging by your clothes, you're not exactly Mr. With-it, are you? I live here...with Flak. I guess we're roommates. The contemporary kind."

"Sit down."

Alison walked to a tall director's chair and perched on the front edge of the canvas. She sighed again. "Look, if something's happened to Flak, just tell me. I don't need all these theatrics."

Bolan shrugged. "Flak's dead."

Alison didn't seem surprised. She closed her eyes, as if finally accepting something she had known forever. "When?"

"They found him this morning. I'd say it happened two days ago. That's the medical examiner's best guess."

"You're not a cop, I can tell that. So what are you? Who are you?"

"You don't need to know that."

"But I *want* to know. I have that right. You broke in here, waved a pistol in my face then tell me a man I've lived with for three years, off and on, is dead. I think I'm entitled to know what happened."

"I guess you're right. But before I tell you anything, I want you to answer a few questions for me."

"How do I know I can trust you?"

"You don't. But then if you lived with Flak Mitchell for three years, you must have learned how to trust people, and how to know who deserves it and who doesn't."

"Okay...ask your questions. Then tell me what happened. Then go away and don't ever come back."

"How long have you known Flak?"

"About eight years, I guess. Why?"

Bolan ignored her question. "What about his friends, other than you? Do you know any of them?"

"You really aren't going to answer my questions, are you?"

"No."

"All right. He had a few, not too many, though."

"Did you ever meet any of them?"

"No, not really. I mean, whenever we socialized, we went out with my friends. I used to tease him about having two separate lives. He didn't like that, but what else could I do? I tried to press, but he'd get mad. After a while, I gave up."

"Do you know what he did for a living?"

"Yes. At least I used to think so. Now, I'm not so sure."

"Why do you say that?"

"Because he had been acting a little weird lately. He was jumpy, always on edge. I don't know. It wasn't anything he said, or anything like that. Just a feeling I got."

"So what did you think he did for a living?"

"Some kind of security work. Insurance, I think. He had funny hours. Sometimes I wouldn't see him for a few days. When he'd get back, he never said where he'd been."

"And you never asked?"

"No."

"Why not?"

"You said it yourself...trust. I mean, we weren't married, and I had my own life. I didn't think I had any right to pry into his. He'd tell me what he wanted me to know, that's all."

"He ever mention any names, names connected to his work?"

"No."

"What about papers, a diary, notebooks, something like that."

"Not that I ever saw."

Bolan reached into his pocket and pulled out the key he'd found in the bedroom. Holding it up, he asked, "You ever see this before?"

Alison reached for it, and Bolan dropped the key into her palm. "Yeah, it's a locker key. From the gym at the Y, on Twenty-third Street."

"Yours or his?"

"His. We used to go there a couple times a week. He had a locker. He rented it by the year. I used one of the coin-op lockers."

Bolan stood up.

"I guess the interview's over."

"For now."

"You going to tell me what happened?"

"I'll tell you on the way."

"On the way where?"

"You can't stay here."

"Why not?"

Bolan nodded toward the plastique block. "That's why."

Alison looked puzzled. "What the hell is that?"

"Plastic explosive. It was wired into the light switch. If I hadn't got here first, well . . ."

Alison sighed, then her head collapsed forward on her chest. She started to cry, small choking sobs at first, then just a silent shuddering. Bolan walked to the chair and put his hand on her shoulder, but she shrank away. "Don't you touch me. Just don't."

Bolan dropped to one knee. Prying her hands away from her face, he looked into those pale green eyes, still large, now made opalescent by the tears. "Come on. Get your things. Anything you can't afford to be without. Pack it and I'll take you someplace where you'll be safe."

"My whole life is here. Look at this place. The music, the paintings. I can't leave here. This is where I work and—"

Bolan cut her off. "Look, Alison, you can't stay. It's too dangerous right now. Whoever killed Flak came here and rigged that bomb. If they don't read in the paper that a bomb went off in this apartment, they'll be back. They might even be waiting outside right now, to catch the show in person. Maybe they think you know something, or maybe there's something here they don't want anybody to find. Either way, your life is in danger. Do you understand?"

Alison shook her head. "Yes. But who, why did they...?"

"I don't know, yet. But I'll find out. Come on, get your things."

Bolan waited patiently while Alison Brewer scurried around the apartment. Having something to do seemed to calm her. The activity helped her forget, at least for the moment. When she had finished, she lugged a bulging canvas suitcase into the living room. Unable to zip it shut, she had settled for holding it closed with the pair of vinyl straps that buckled on either side of the handle. Wisps of cloth stuck out around the perimeter.

"I guess I'm ready. How long do I have to stay away?"

"I don't know. I'll make arrangements for the place to be watched. But we'll want to stay out of sight. Whoever shows up might lead us to others who are involved."

Bolan grabbed the suitcase as Alison took a final look around the apartment. The bag was heavy, but he chose not to remark on it. When Alison was satisfied she hadn't forgotten anything of immediate importance, they walked to the door, Bolan motioning to her to open it. He shifted the bag to his left hand and fisted the Beretta. "Put the light out before you open the door." She looked at him quizzically but did as she'd been told.

"If that peephole works, check the hall first."

With the interior light off, Alison could sweep aside the plate covering the peephole without betraying her presence at the door. "Are all these dramatics necessary?" she whispered pettishly.

"I don't know, but if they are and we don't bother, we won't get a second chance."

"Better safe than sorry, huh?"

"That's about right."

"Where's your car?"

"Around the corner, about a block down."

"Should I follow you in my own car?"

"How stupid do you think I am?" Bolan asked. "Never mind. Let's go."

Alison let the peephole fall and turned the crank on the dead bolt. It slid back noiselessly, and she turned the doorknob. The dull glow of the hall light appeared around the edge of the door. She pulled it open farther, then it suddenly slammed back wide, knocking her to the floor. A bulky figure filled the open doorway, leaving little room for light to seep in around it.

Bolan heard the telltale spit of a machine pistol, and the sound of glass breaking against the back wall. He aimed high and pulled the trigger, the Beretta hissing once, then again. A dull splat, like that of a rotting tomato striking stone, had barely died away when the colossal shadow toppled into the room facedown.

Bolan waited, but nothing happened. "Alison, are you all right?" he whispered.

"I think so. And I think maybe we better just take your car."

Bolan smiled for the first time since entering the apartment.

He crept to the dead man, rolled him on his side and stripped his wallet and weapon. The gunner looked vaguely familiar, but Bolan wasn't sure whether it was the man himself or the type of which he was a classic specimen.

He dragged the body all the way into the room and listened intently. The hallway was quiet. Bolan got to his feet and pressed against the wall, inching toward the open doorway. A slight hiss, too shallow to be steam in the hall radiator, echoed sibilantly down the hall. Someone was waiting, probably wedged into a doorway on the same side of the corridor as Mitchell's flat.

There was only one safe way to find out. Hauling the bulky corpse to its feet, gritting his teeth against the weight, Bolan poised himself just inside the doorway. Counting under his breath, he allowed the dead man to sag backward then, on ten, shoved him face forward into the hall. A burst of gunfire slammed into the corpse, the bullets striking dead meat and lifeless bone with a ferocity even the warrior hadn't expected. Behind him, Alison cried out in terror and he was sorry he hadn't warned her.

The sound of gunfire died away, but Bolan had learned what he needed to know—one man was in the hall, armed with a machine pistol. Bolan steeled himself for what he knew was a risky maneuver. Hefting the big man's gun, he aimed carefully, and without warning emptied the magazine in a tight semicircle around the lock of the door across the hall. Before the thunder stopped reverberating, Bolan leaped across the hall, slamming shoulder first into the door and shattering what was left of the lock.

Spinning to a halt, he immediately stepped back to the door, Big Thunder in his fist. The gunner, frozen by the unexpected assault, tried desperately to slip deeper into the doorway, but he had run out of room. Bolan aimed carefully, firing three quick shots. The .44-caliber AutoMag sounded like artillery in the hard-walled hallway.

The first slug shattered a length of molding from the doorframe and ripped through the assassin's shoulder. As the wounded man staggered forward, Bolan nailed him twice more, the third and last shot blowing a hole in the shooter's temple as he fell. The gray-and-red debris of the headshot splattered down along the wall and oozed slowly to the floor.

Bolan dashed back across the hall and grabbed Alison, who was still screaming, and dragged her to the door. In her terror she had clenched her fists around the handle of her suitcase, and it slammed the doorway as the warrior hauled her through. She stared at the dead man in the hall, turning her head as Bolan pulled her past. She seemed fixated on the gruesome sight, her eyes locking on and swiveling the way a compass needle follows a magnet.

CHAPTER EIGHT

The Cairo Hilton was more luxurious than Mason Harlow remembered. Before starting Worldwide Specialty, Inc., he hadn't been to the Egyptian capital in several years, and the only thing in the Middle East that rivaled violence, both for frequency and effect, was change. He stared out an eleventh-floor window at the traffic below. From 150 feet in the air, Harlow decided, cars were cars. Judging by the tangle below, he could have been almost anywhere on the face of the globe.

Letting the curtain fall back in place, he turned up the air conditioner and walked back to the bed. He kicked off his shoes and lay down on top of the neatly stretched spread. Years of military service had left their mark on him, and neatness was a compulsion.

Closing his eyes, he started to drift. The air conditioner hummed quietly, its compressor fan occasionally rattling the least little bit to break the monotony. Harlow was feeling rather good about himself and liked, when time permitted, to recite the litany of reasons he should.

He had three thousand acres in prime horse country. He had nine million dollars already deposited in Switzerland, a like amount in operating accounts in the United States, three successful businesses and unlimited prospects. It had been a long time coming, but he felt safe in judging himself a success. Harlow wasn't overly introspective—at least on the ethics of his accomplishments—but then he had never met a man he admired who was noted for his compunction.

And now, on the verge of his greatest triumph yet, he had every reason to feel satisfied with himself. And he did. But the feeling troubled him. He kept thinking back over the years of struggle, the 5:00 a.m. rising to milk cows and pitch hay, the grueling strain of football practice squeezed in between school and night work at the Mobil station, the two part-time jobs he juggled while carrying a full load of course work at Washington State and, most of all, the hustling that characterized six years in the Marine Corps.

Through it all, the motto of his mentors, the men he looked up to—most of whom barely knew he existed—was "stay hungry." And he didn't feel hungry. He worried that he was getting sloppy, that he was slowing down, so he pushed himself.

Harlow stood up and unbuttoned his shirt, twirling it like a toreador as he took it off and draped it over the back of a chair. He walked to the bathroom, where he turned sideways to stare at himself in a full-length mirror beside the sink. The T-shirt, stark white and as taut as an albino drumhead, stretched unwrinkled over his expanding paunch. He stood well over six feet tall and no one would have taken him for fat, but he *felt* fat, fat and out of shape. The paunch weighed more heavily on his mind than on his scale. Harlow backed away from the mirror cautiously, as if he expected the image in the glass to attack him the moment his back was turned.

In the middle of the room, he slapped his gut twice, sucking it in for a moment, then did a quick two dozen jumping jacks. He found himself short of breath, and realized that he was no longer able to go both ways in a football game for sixty minutes, and, more to the point, that he was no longer young.

Still panting, Harlow slipped the shirt back on, struggled with the buttons and, smoothing the cloth carefully, snagged a tie from the closet door. He did a passable Windsor, snugged the tie up under his florid chin, then smoothed the collar into place.

Grabbing a silk blazer from the closet, he shrugged it on, then adjusted his tie. He stepped back into the bathroom and examined the image in the mirror. He was satisfied. He looked every inch the successful businessman. "And why not?" he asked himself. "Why the hell not?"

Harlow crossed to the door and flicked off the light as he stepped into the hall. He walked with a slight limp, a memento of a claymore outside of Bien Hoa. The skin grafts weren't pretty, but the leg had been saved. The two guys on his left hadn't been so lucky. One of them had deserved it, being the asshole who triggered the mine in the first place, but life wasn't always precise in the justice it exacted.

In the elevator Harlow stared at his fellow riders with a kind of childlike fascination. Still high on playing hardball with the big boys, Harlow sometimes had to pinch himself to snap out of the admiring coma into which he frequently fell. A nonstop talker and an even more zealous self-promoter, he had built himself a reputation as that rarest of all American curiosities—the bullshit artist who delivered.

Many, including those who did business with him, kept a generous supply of salt on hand whenever they had to sit down face-to-face. Most of them thought his fantasies harmless, and most had long since decided that Harlow himself had no idea what was true and what was fabrication in those elaborate monologues he delivered over blue-plate specials in the best restaurants on four continents. But since he invariably picked up the tab, they were more than willing to let him blab on.

Harlow's real gift—if it could be fairly said he had one—was a fetching guile that knew no shame. Caught in a lie, he would justify it by telling a still bigger one. A greedy man, he knew the secret of his success was that unacknowledged kinship he had with other greedy men. Old school ties were denied him; Washington State was about as far from Ivy League as you could get. But Company men stuck together, and they were every bit as capable of greed as the next man.

Working most of your adult lives in a shadowy world where truth and fiction were often deliberately indistinguishable, and where the only reward was the admiration of your peers, it got tempting, when retirement time approached, to wonder what had been in it for you. When you realized the answer was nothing, not even a gold watch, bitterness was not an uncommon reaction.

Harlow had always danced one step ahead of the sheriff, two ahead of the hangman. A master at turning liabilities into assets, he knew the surest way to a bitter spook's heart was through his wallet. Cultivating such men with all the care of a master horticulturalist mothering orchids, he had built a hothouse out of flattery and largess. It had bought him some priceless examples of the species, and now he could already feel the smooth silk of the blue ribbon. All he needed was patience—patience and a little luck.

In the lobby, he nodded at some men he had never met, smiled at another for no reason other than that he looked prosperous, a virtue sufficient to gain a place in Mason Harlow's hall of fame. It was eleven-thirty, and Harlow quickened his pace. The lunch meeting was scheduled for noon on the button.

He hadn't seen Brice Harkness in more than five years. They had very little time and a great deal to discuss. Out on the street Harlow caught a cab. He gave his destination then sat on the edge of the seat as the driver zipped in and out of heavy traffic.

Harkness was at the American Embassy, under diplomatic cover. It was a fiction common to both sides in the continuing struggle, a struggle that no longer meant anything to Harlow except for what profit he could extract from it.

When the cab pulled up in front of the embassy, Harlow paid the fare and slipped out of the vehicle. He stood on the sidewalk for a moment, admiring the building. Its clean lines and blocky shape seemed out of place in a city whose streets were lined with buildings of such variety they recapitulated the history of architecture.

Stepping to the gate, he nodded benevolently to the Marine guards on duty, like a fond uncle greeting favorite nephews. Inside the building the brisk businesslike atmosphere made him feel more comfortable. Here was a place he understood, a place where efficiency was sought and standard procedures made certain it would never be found. Harlow knew his way around red tape, negotiating his way among its tangled strands with all the confidence of a spider in its own web.

The receptionist directed him to Brice Harkness, and Harlow smiled at her, admiring the half-moons of freckled flesh peeking at him from her blouse. By the time he reached the door to Harkness's office, the uncertainty that always lingered after a few moments of introspection was all but gone.

The door was open and Harlow stepped through it with a high-voltage smile already in place. Two women busily bent over typewriters, the click of the keys drowning out the sound of his feet on the tiled floor. He cleared his throat with exaggerated intensity, and one of the women looked up without stopping her work.

"Can I help you, sir?"

"The name's Harlow. I have a lunch appointment with Mr. Harkness."

"Oh, yes, sir, he's expecting you. I'll tell him you're here." She picked up the phone and pressed the intercom buzzer, which Harlow could hear rasping in an inner office. "Please go in, Mr. Harlow," she said after replacing the receiver.

He smiled and stepped around her desk, rapping it with his knuckles in thanks. Harkness was seated at his desk as Harlow entered.

"Mason, long time no see." Harkness stood and extended his hand. Harlow clasped it firmly and turned up the voltage on his smile.

Harkness was everything he had learned to hate. Choate and Dartmouth educated, slim to the point of patrician emaciation, he spoke in that clipped, affected style that did not require movement of lip or lower jaw, as if even that was too much work for the privileged.

"You're looking good, Brice," Harlow said, pulling up a chair. "You ready for lunch?"

"I'm always ready. Have to watch the calories, though. I'm afraid I've put on a few pounds lately."

Harlow laughed. "You could have fooled me. I've seen guys in refugee camps who weigh more than you do."

"Maybe they eat better," Harkness responded. "You want to talk here, before we eat, or do you want to wait and do it over coffee?"

"It can wait."

"Fine, let's go, then." Harkness stood and adjusted the three sheets of paper on his desk before stepping around it. He ran his fingers through an unruly shock of silver hair and adjusted the knot of his tie.

Harlow led the way into the outer office, and waited in the doorway while his companion advised his secretary where he'd be. Out in the hallway, Harkness said, "I know a little French place a couple of blocks from here. We can walk, if you don't mind the heat."

"If I did, I'd have to get out of the kitchen, Brice, and I'm not ready to do that."

The men walked the two blocks to the restaurant in silence. Once inside, they ordered drinks, and Harkness leaned back in his chair. "What can I do for you?"

Harlow leaned in, like a conspirator divulging a master plan. "I'm working on a little op with the Libs."

"Oh?" Harkness seemed intrigued.

"Yeah. Can't tell you much, but the last time I was in Langley, Phil Marshall suggested I stop by. He said you might be able to help."

"How is Phil, anyway?"

"Fine, fine. Being DDO seems to agree with him."

"Always the politician, wasn't he? Well," Harkness sighed, "I guess it paid off for him."

"Sure looks like it. Anyhow, I need a little slack on some shipments of electronic equipment. To Tripoli."

"What can I do? Libya's outside my sphere of operations."

"Operations, maybe. But not influence. Just spread the word, wherever you think it'll do good. Worldwide is doing a little Company business. That's all anybody has to know."

Harkness smiled. "I see."

"How about it?"

"Why not? Couldn't hurt to smooth out a few wrinkles between me and Phil. Ops people are so fucking touchy...." The expletive sounded more shocking coming from the genteel Harkness. "What are you working on, anyway?"

"All I can tell you is that I've opened a pipeline into the colonel's inner circle. And I'm not talkin' Colonel Sanders."

"That *is* interesting. I assume this is deep cover?"

"You've heard of the Marianas trench?" Harlow smiled.

"That deep, eh?"

A waiter appeared at Harkness's elbow, and he turned his attention to the menu. Harlow opened his own bill of fare. "This one's on the Company cuff, Brice."

Harkness didn't ask what company. Some things didn't need saying.

CHAPTER NINE

Alison Brewer walked to the window and pulled back the curtain. Instead of the neon glare she'd expected, she found herself staring into a steel plate. She turned to Bolan with a look of puzzlement.

"What is this place? I thought you were taking me someplace where I'd be safe. It looks more like a prison."

"Look, Alison. I don't want to keep you here against your will, but I don't know what's going on out there." Bolan gestured vaguely toward the window. "Somebody killed your boyfriend, and somebody planted a bomb that would have killed you, too. I don't know who killed Flak, and I don't know if the people who did it are responsible for the bomb."

"You don't seem to know a hell of a lot."

Bolan said nothing. Her words were all too accurate. "If you want to take your chances out there, okay. I can't make you stay. But I think you're better off here. At least you can be protected. Flak was a trained agent, and he couldn't take care of himself. I don't think you'd have any better luck."

"What was he really doing?" Alison asked. She dropped the curtain and walked to the nondescript sofa in one corner of the room. Sitting carefully, almost primly, she leaned back on the sofa and crossed her legs, her purse hugged in her lap with crossed arms. She looked like a child hanging on to a teddy bear for dear life.

In a way, that was exactly what she was.

"That's part of the problem. We don't know."

"Who is this 'we' you talk about? Who do you work for?"

"You don't need to know."

"I don't need to know anything, do I?" She sat up abruptly. "For all I know, *you* killed Flak. Maybe you'll kill me, too."

"Then why would I have disconnected the bomb? Why not just let it blow you up, get rid of you that way?"

"I don't know. Maybe you think I know something. Maybe you want me to trust you so I'll tell you what you need to know. Maybe *then* you'll kill me."

"Maybe."

"Well?" Alison edged forward on the sofa, staring at him expectantly.

"Well what?"

"Am I right?"

Bolan ignored the question, turned his back and walked into another room.

Alison stared at the doorway. Sitting motionless, she debated a hundred possibilities, but none of them made any sense. Nothing made sense at all. She opened her purse and slipped her hand inside. Keeping her eyes riveted on the doorway through which the big man had disappeared, she pulled her hand out of the bag, her knuckles white around the butt of a Smith & Wesson .22 automatic.

Setting the bag aside, she stood up quietly and tiptoed to the doorway. Bolan, his back to her, was leaning over a small counter in a kitchenette. She held the gun in front of her, turned her head slightly to the side and closed her eyes.

"I want you to tell me what's going on," she whispered.

Bolan turned to see the gun wavering unsteadily. With her eyes closed, she couldn't see him except as a dark mass through the redness of her eyelids, but the white knuckles were a dead giveaway. She was close to pulling the trigger, probably a lot closer than even she realized.

Moving almost imperceptibly, Bolan slid his hand under his jacket and pulled the Beretta 93-R from its holster. He placed it gently on the counter and stepped to one side.

"Alison, open your eyes. Please."

"Why should I?" She screwed the lids even more tightly closed.

"Alison, please put the gun away. I've put my own gun on the counter. Open your eyes and look at me."

"No! You'll just try to confuse me."

"Look, we're on the same side. We both want to know what happened to Flak. You can't do it yourself, and neither can I. We have to work together."

"You're lying."

"I—" He stopped when he saw her fingers shift uncertainly on the gun. Alison was getting edgy. Bolan moved slightly farther to her right, but the kitchenette was too tight to allow him to get away from the muzzle of the small but deadly automatic. If Alison pulled the trigger, she would probably hit him in spite of herself.

"Alison, listen to me. . . ."

He took a small step toward her, but she was still too far away for him to reach her gun hand. He was about to shift gears when he saw movement behind her. Backlit by the small lamp in the living room of the safehouse, a man was moving stealthily toward the unsuspecting woman. Bolan could not make out his features, but there was no mistaking the gun in his hand. And the silencer threaded into the muzzle meant he was a pro. That he hadn't already fired meant he posed no immediate threat to either Alison or himself. More than likely, he was someone from Justice.

Bolan raised a finger to his lips, then waved his hands to signal he should not use the weapon. The man nodded that he understood. Alison opened her eyes just as Bolan dropped his hands. The movement puzzled her momentarily, then, her eyes widening still farther, she began to turn. The man in the living room moved quickly, charging forward and slamming into her with his shoulder.

Knocked off balance, Alison let go of the gun, which flew onto the counter and went off. At the same time, she careered into Bolan, who had begun to move forward. He caught her to keep her from falling, and she turned in his grasp and began to beat at him with clenched fists.

Bolan pinned her arms until she realized she was not going to be hurt, then she stopped struggling. She sighed once, then began to cry. Bolan continued to hold her, patting her shoulders until the sobbing, too, subsided. The newcomer, baffled by the scene in which he had just played so crucial a part, watched as if dumbstruck, his hands at his sides, the gun still dangling from his fist.

Alison looked up at Bolan again, her eyes red-rimmed, still wet, but more striking than ever. She laughed uncertainly.

"I'm . . . sorry, I—"

Bolan cut her off. "Don't worry about it. I understand." For a moment, they had both forgotten the newcomer. Bolan looked over her shoulder and snapped back to reality. As if on cue, the new arrival holstered his gun.

"Got here in the nick of time, it looks like," he said. The smile seemed genuine, if a bit uncertain. "You're Mack Bolan."

Bolan nodded at the man's statement.

"Who's she? Mitchell's girlfriend?"

"Yeah. And you're . . . ?"

The man smiled again, this time more easily. His dark complexion and dark, curly hair gave him the appearance that Bolan thought of as "all-purpose ethnic." He could have been anything from Lebanese to Jewish, Puerto Rican to Italian.

"Leon Alvarez."

"What brings you here?" Bolan asked.

"I think I better wait until Miss . . ."

"Brewer. Alison Brewer."

"Sorry if I gave you a scare, but I didn't know what the hell else to do."

Alison looked at the floor, embarrassed by her actions. "That's okay," she whispered. "I guess I had it coming."

"How did you get in here?" Bolan asked.

"I might ask you the same thing, if I wanted to be a smartass. But since I don't, and since we have some important business to discuss, how about we tuck Miss Brewer in for the night, and go someplace we can talk privately?"

"It's Ms," Alison snapped.

Alvarez looked at her as if he hadn't understood. "What?"

"I said 'It's Ms.' You called me 'Miss.' I don't like that."

"I don't give a flying..." Alvarez caught himself. "Sorry, *Ms* Brewer." He looked at Bolan. "Shall we go?"

"Let me have a word with Alison first."

Alvarez nodded. "All right. I'll wait in the other room."

When he was out of sight, Alison looked at Bolan. "You're not going to leave me here alone, are you? I mean, if he got in here, other people can, too."

"I won't be long. But the sooner we get him out of here, the better off you'll be. I don't know who he is or why he's here, but I intend to find out.

"If you know how to use that gun, keep it handy. The door can be locked securely from the inside. As soon as we step outside, lock it up tight. I'll call you before I come back. If anybody else comes to the door, don't let him in. I don't care what he tells you. Just stay put."

Alison didn't seem reassured.

"You ready?" Bolan asked as he stepped into the living room.

Alvarez stood up without answering. He walked to the door and turned to wait for Bolan. Looking past the big guy, he said, "You keep this door locked, *Ms* Brewer." He smiled broadly.

"Don't waste the high-voltage charm on me, pal," she advised. "You're no Ramon Navarro."

"Who's he?" Alvarez looked puzzled.

"Never mind," Alison said. She looked doubly pleased for having baffled him.

Alvarez glanced at Bolan, then shrugged. He turned to open the door and stepped into the hall, Bolan right behind him.

"Remember what I said." The warrior closed the door and waited for the staccato snapping of locks being secured, then followed Alvarez down the hall.

When they were outside the Executioner grabbed Alvarez by the arm. "You know who I am, but I want to know who you are, and what you're doing here."

Alvarez sat on the second step, tugging his coat around him to cut off the wind. "It's a long story, Bolan."

"I got time."

Alvarez looked up the block, facing away from his companion. He seemed to be deciding whether—and how much—to tell his inquisitor. Hiking his feet onto the first step, he nestled his chin between his knees and patted the step with a gloved hand. "Have a seat. It's pretty complicated."

Bolan sat down reluctantly.

"You're interested in what happened to Flak Mitchell, right? Well, so am I." He shivered a moment. "Geez, I'm not used to this cold weather."

"If I want a weather report, I'll buy a TV."

"Surly bastard, aren't you?"

"You don't know the half of it," Bolan growled.

"All right, all right. I'm CIA. I followed you from Mitchell's place. Just got back from North Africa. There's shit going on over there you wouldn't believe."

"Tell me about Mitchell."

"I told you. It's complicated. Mitchell was onto something, the same thing I was looking at from the other end. He got sloppy and got himself wasted. I have the feeling the same thing could happen to me."

"What are you talking about?" Bolan made no effort to conceal his mounting exasperation.

"The Libyans have got a supplier, somebody here, in the U.S. Weapons, explosives, hell, even missiles. I don't think I have to tell you what that means. The good colonel has been giving these toys to everybody from the IRA to Baader-Meinhof. It wouldn't surprise me if he was trying to come up with a nuke or two, as well."

"That's hardly news."

"Maybe not, but something's shaking, and we've got to get a handle on it before it blows up in our faces. Trouble is, everyplace I turn, I keep running into stone walls. Whatever's going on has a sponsor, and a well-connected one at that.''

"You telling me somebody in our government is supplying Libya with weapons?"

"Looks like it. But every time I get close, something happens. Somebody gets dead.''

"Where does Mitchell tie in? Or what makes you think he does?" Bolan was intrigued, and the edge of hostility in his voice had vanished.

"Some of the shit I turned up in Libya was papered over, dummy invoices, shipping labels, that kind of stuff. The alleged shipper was the same metal outfit Mitchell mentioned in his message to your boss.''

"Arlington Metal?"

"Yeah. My guess is they're covering the shipments. So Mitchell tumbled to it somehow, but when he got close he screwed up. They blew him away.''

"What do you know about Arlington Metal?"

"Not a hell of a lot. I can't find who owns it—it's changed hands a dozen times in the past fifteen years. It was a proprietary at one time. Now, I don't know.... ''

"You mean it was a CIA operation?"

"Not sanctioned, but you know how things are. Could be. Anyhow, that's why the director of Central Intelligence wants me to look into it.''

"So where do you fit in?"

Alvarez laughed nervously. He shifted his feet on the steps. "Like I said, Mitchell got close and they whacked him. I'm getting close, too—I'm supposed to. But then so was Mitchell, and it didn't help him very much.''

"You talked to Mitchell's partner? Andrews?"

"Never even heard of him. I just got wise to the Mitchell connection. Haven't had time to do much but explore the Arlington Metal thing. That, as you can imagine, is on top of the director's triage list. Why, what do you know about Andrews?''

"Nothing. I'm going to talk to him tonight, if I can find him. Want to come along?"

"No, I have a few other bits of business to take care of. I'd appreciate it if you let me know. I'm staying at the Chelsea Hotel. You can reach me there tomorrow—if I make it through the night."

Alvarez stood up suddenly and walked away without a word. Bolan watched him go, still not knowing whether to believe him. There were so many pieces and so few of them fit neatly together.

It was time to talk to Andrews.

CHAPTER TEN

The tape reel and the key lying on Hal Brognola's desk seemed small. He looked at them for a long, silent moment. His thick fingers rose and fell, soundlessly tapping the wood on either side of the tape reel.

"And you say this is all you came up with?"

"Yeah. That and the woman, Alison Brewer."

Brognola shook his head from side to side. The motion was slow, almost dreamlike, as if he were underwater or lying in bed with a high fever. "You'd think a man's life would amount to more, wouldn't you? I mean, when you die everybody grabs their piece, and the bones just lie there, unburied. Nobody really cares enough to bother." He spun the tape reel in place, the polished aluminum looking frail under the thick fingers. "And this...is *our* piece."

"What's wrong, Hal?"

"Nothing." He sat back in the chair, rocking gently back and forth for a few moments until inertia brought him to a halt. He shifted his weight and the chair creaked. For a moment it was the only sound in the office. "Where's the woman now?"

"A safehouse on the West Side, you know the place, in the middle forties. She'll be all right there for a few hours, as long as she listens to what I told her."

"Will she?"

"I don't know. She's scared, so she might. For a while. Once she gets over the initial fright, probably not."

"I can't spare anybody to stay with her. Not for a couple days."

"I got a bigger problem than that, Hal."

"What problem?"

"A guy came into the safehouse just after I got there with Alison Brewer. Says his name's Alvarez. CIA."

"So what? That house has been there for a long time. Several agencies have used it from time to time, but it's only old-timers who remember it's there. Chances are Alvarez has been around a while."

"He also knew my name."

"I'll check on Alvarez as soon as I can."

Bolan nodded. "First name's Leon."

"What else can you tell me about him?"

"Not a heck of a lot. Says he's working on something special for the DCI. He claims Mitchell's assignment and his overlapped somehow, something to do with Libya. He wasn't exactly talkative."

"But I gather you don't believe him. At least not completely. Am I right?"

"I don't know. I was getting strange vibes. Something's going on that's very different than you believed. This is a lot more complicated than some little smuggling deal that happened to involve government property."

"What makes you think so? What Alvarez told you?"

"That just reinforces it. I was already leaning that way before I met him. No, it's the whole pattern of things. Killing Mitchell, that could be anybody, any kind of deal gone sour. But rigging a bomb in a dead man's apartment, that's something else again."

"You think the woman knows something she's not telling?"

"No, I think she knows something she doesn't know she knows. But her biggest problem is that somebody else out there thinks so too."

"You going to check out this key?"

"Yeah. How long before you get anything on the tape?"

"Twelve hours, minimum. The reel could take at least that long to listen to, depending on the recording speed. Then tests, you know how it goes."

"Yeah, I know how it goes." Bolan stood. "I'll check back when I can, Hal. Get somebody on the Brewer woman as soon as you can, okay?"

"Will do. And Striker, listen. Until we know different, Alvarez is just like anybody else out there."

"Understood. Anybody hear from Andrews yet?"

"No."

"All right. I'll stop by his place as soon as I check out the locker."

Bolan left the office feeling vaguely dissatisfied. It wasn't exactly irritation with Brognola, and it wasn't the first time he had felt that way. Waiting for the elevator, he dissected the feeling, trying to identify the source of his uneasiness. It wasn't until the door opened that he could put his finger on the trouble.

He had agreed to help Brognola with missions of mutual interest, but when he got involved with the government, his whole life became hurry up and wait. As frustrating as it was, he could usually rationalize it, or at least push it aside so it couldn't interfere with his performance. But there was a bureaucratic absurdity to it all, and every once in a while it intruded in a way that couldn't be ignored. The idea that lives could be saved or lost, depending on which lab was available and who had priority in the pecking order, was about as antithetical as it could be to Bolan's own ideas about how the world should work. He was realist enough to know that any system broke down at its weakest point, and the more people involved, the more likely it would run imperfectly—if at all. He was a man of action who worked best alone.

He stepped into the elevator, turning the key over in his hand during the ride down. It was such an ordinary-looking key, its metal slightly discolored by time, its embossed lettering starting to disappear under the pressure of thousands of fingers. A galaxy of scratches had scarred the rim of the key, taken a chunk or two out of its plastic cap. It was a key like any other. And then Bolan understood what had been bothering him . . . it was how ordinary death had become.

That the continued existence of one or more human beings might depend on who possessed the small hunk of plastic and metal now so anonymous in his hand seemed, in fact was, ridiculous. But there was always the other side of the coin. The key might mean absolutely nothing, all its significance might be self-generated, the product of a mind whipped to a frenzy by wishful thinking.

But right now the key was about all there was. Whether or not Alison knew anything was anybody's guess. Whether the tape from Mitchell's elaborate wire scheme would yield anything more was just as questionable. So, for the moment, it came down to the key.

And the missing Harry Andrews.

Bolan was in the parking garage almost before he realized it. He slipped into his rented car, trying to push the vague sense of futility from his mind; he didn't like acknowledging uphill battles.

The car rumbled through the underground concrete maze as he worked his way to the surface and pulled out into traffic still fairly heavy for a cold night. He cruised crosstown, hanging a left at Ninth Avenue. It would be easier to leave his car in midtown and hop a cab to the gym. He swerved up the ramp to the Port Authority bus terminal garage.

Climbing the ramp, he swung the Olds in a tight circle, parking on top against a low brick wall fifty feet from the ramp. He walked back down and caught a cab as it pulled away from the curb at the back of the bus station.

During the ride downtown he stared out the window and resisted the cabbie's attempt to engage him in a discussion of the relative merits of the Jets and Giants, preferring to concentrate on the problem at hand. To atone, he paid the fare with a five, telling the driver to keep the change.

The gym, too, was open all night. Bolan climbed the steps two at a time and, inside, followed the green arrows to the locker room. The place seemed deserted, almost too quiet.

In a city like New York, even 2:00 a.m. was a good time to work on your jump shot for somebody. But as he passed the gym, it, too, was empty.

Alarms started to go off in his head. Where was everybody? Bolan made the last turn and drew his Beretta, the short hairs on the back of his neck beginning to rise. He moved cautiously now, arm cocked, gun ready. He stepped softly, like a stalking panther conscious of its own body, not only of its grace and power'but also of its limits. Every nerve was screaming.

The entrance to the men's locker room was thirty feet ahead. The twin doors were open, thrown back against the hallway wall on either side, but the locker room itself was pitch-black. The inside of the room, he knew, would be a maze. In a facility of this size, there might be a dozen or more rows of lockers, back to back, side to side. Walls of steel boxes with narrow aisles, some perhaps a little wider to allow for wooden benches bolted to the floor. But no matter what the layout, it was a potential nightmare for a man alone.

Hallways intersected directly in front of the entrance, long, dim corridors extending left and right, their institutional green walls shading into pools of darkness in the long gaps between ceiling lights. Holding the Beretta in his right hand, Bolan reached through and felt along the wall for a light. His fingers encountered a raised box, then the gritty, dirty feel of a toggle many times painted over, and greasy from frequent use. He clicked it up, and the unpleasant white of overhead fluorescents flashed once, then stayed lit.

Bolan stepped cautiously into the room, the only noise the tinkle of the fluorescent tubes as they heated up. In a moment, that too was gone, replaced by the distant hum of a bulb on the way out. Bolan looked left and right, the gun leading his eyes just a bit as he scanned the corners of the room.

Seeing no one, he stepped in and sprinted into the center of the aisle opposite the doorway. "Anyone here?" His words echoed in the room and then, at a great distance, came back to him from the ends of the corridor outside. When his voice died away, nothing took its place. The basement of the gym was deserted. Relaxing just a bit, he reached into his pocket for the key. He read the number, committed it to memory.

Judging by the locker next to him, his goal was nearly eight hundred numbers—and two or three aisles—away.

At the end of the aisle, Bolan slipped sideways two, then three rows, and ducked back in among the lockers. This was it, the aisle where he'd find Mitchell's locker. He moved forward with eyes on the small metal plates bearing the numbers, taking in the end of the aisle with his peripheral vision.

Finally Bolan stood in front of the right locker—and knew immediately that something was wrong. Something smelled odd. Under sweat and liniment, he smelled something vaguely like mothballs...and something more unpleasant. He inserted the key in the lock, the scratch of metal on metal irritating him. The key slid in and he turned it almost reluctantly.

The door creaked open, and Bolan finally knew what had been screaming at him all along. He had killed two birds with one stone. Harry Andrews stared out at him from the locker, his eyes wide open. But they didn't smile at him. They didn't move at all. The rope around his neck took care of that.

CHAPTER ELEVEN

Marielle Trebec tugged gingerly at the beaded chain to the left of the heavy drapery. With a solemn grinding, more appropriate to a cathedral vault than a bedroom, the shrouds of thick damask began to part. A brilliant scarlet light poured through the widening crack, staining her thighs and shoulders redder than blood.

The play of muscles in the sanguinary light made her rib cage a bloodstained pool, rippling under a strong wind. Lying back on the bed, Mason Harlow smiled. He felt proud of himself, and Marielle knew it. It was part of the senseless charade they had been playing for several weeks. The pride had shown itself before, always for reasons that made no sense, but which Marielle nevertheless understood. The ability to understand Harlow was her trump card, one he knew she held, but which he kept daring her to play. And every time she played it, he cashed in his chips and smiled benevolently, proudly, as if he had given her the skill to defeat him.

Conscious now of Harlow's eyes on her, she flaunted her body, at once teasing him and rewarding him. There was in Harlow something of the passive participant, of the voyeur. He was capable of as much pleasure in looking at her as in touching her. But that was a weapon he didn't know she had. Playing it to the hilt, Marielle dropped the beaded chain and drifted languorously toward the center of the undraped window. The sun was setting, and she interposed her body between it and Harlow, simultaneously reducing herself to little more than a seductive silhouette and overshadowing the reclining man who watched her.

Feeling less than honest, she mimicked poses long overdone in girlie magazines, jutting first a hip, then a breast, always on the edge of losing her balance, as if emphasizing her body gave it added mass. She felt awkward, but knew Harlow wouldn't notice or, if he did, would neither know why nor care.

Turning to offer him a profile, she pouted. "When's your wife coming home?"

"Who knows? Who cares?" Harlow grunted, slapping the mattress alongside him. "Come over here and sit down. I feel a little horny."

"When don't you, Mason?"

"You love it. You women are all alike. You burn your bras and march around ranting and raving, but it's all bull. You eat that crap up. Don't tell me any different."

"You're hopelessly out of touch, Mason. No woman this side of a mental hospital has burned a bra in fifteen years."

"Who gives a damn? It was just a figure of speech. You know what I mean."

Marielle walked to an elaborate dressing table running the full length of the wall opposite the window. She sat down stiffly and grabbed a hairbrush. She worked at the long red tresses with short, sharp strokes, almost vicious in their insistent tearing at her sweat-tangled hair. Suddenly aware of the pungency of their mingled perspiration, she felt vulnerable and exposed. She wanted to get dressed more than anything she could remember. The hiss of the hairbrush was almost hypnotic, and she lost track of time and her thoughts. Staring into the glass, she cast a cold eye on her own flesh, not with that hypercritical detachment of a beautiful woman who wished she were more beautiful still, but with the hard, resentful stare of a woman who begrudged such beauty in another. It was as if she had become two separate people.

In a way she had. That was a facet of her reality she preferred not to examine too closely. Half closing her eyes, she watched the sun set behind her, its color spilling over her shoulders, heightening the red in her hair until the two of them merged into a single crimson shadow, as flat and featureless as an emblem on a flag.

It took her several moments to realize Harlow was talking to her, and then she had to ask him to repeat himself.

"I asked you how you'd like to spend a little time on the Riviera."

Harlow stroked his stomach with an animal grunt. The gesture repulsed her, and Marielle swallowed hard before answering, "I've been there before."

"You don't understand. I don't mean staying in some cheesy hotel, with those snotty frog waiters looking down their noses at us. I mean stay at my place. You won't believe it."

"You seem to forget that I, too, am a 'frog,' as you so graciously put it."

"Yeah, but you're different. You're more like me. You got street smarts, and you don't look down on people just because they got a lousy accent."

"What about your wife? What will she have to say about this little vacation?"

"I told you, forget about Lois. She doesn't tell me what to do. And besides, she won't know anything. As far as she's concerned I'm on business. Anyway, I'll be working. I got the big one on the line, kid. And I'll be damned if I let this one get away."

"Oh?"

"You don't need to know any more than that. What do you say? You want to go, or not?"

"What if I say no?"

Marielle slapped the hairbrush down on the dressing table. She stood slowly, stretched her arms over her head for full effect, then sidled toward the bed. Crossing her arms over her breasts, she stood staring down at Harlow. He laughed, then lay back on the pillow with a satisfied smile.

"You won't. Like I said, you're just like me. Nobody appreciates money like a poor kid. If I make this deal, I'll be rolling in dough. If you don't want to roll with me, it won't be hard to find somebody who does."

"You're such a romantic, Mason. How can a girl possibly refuse an offer like that?"

"I knew you'd go. Why don't you cut out all that hard-to-get bullshit?"

"You already answered that for yourself. It's not just money a poor kid knows how to appreciate. It's anything he doesn't have and can't get easily. If you have to work for it, you appreciate it a little more. You respect it."

"Fuck that. Respect is like any other commodity, kid. If you have the money, you can buy anything you want."

Marielle knelt beside him, stretched one long leg across his ample stomach, then settled down like an accomplished equestrienne on a favorite mount. "Why don't you tell me more about this great deal of yours?"

Harlow slid a palm over each of her hips, rubbing gently against the bones, as if mapping their contours in his memory. Slowly he widened the compass of his circles, then slid his hands up along her sides, stopping briefly at each rib.

Marielle thought how clinical and premeditated the maneuver was, executed with an awkward precision as if he had read it in some manual. She smiled through half-closed eyes, her observation of the man beneath her as detached and unemotional as his own stilted lovemaking. With a smug chuckle, probably borrowed from a third-rate skin flick, he closed his hands over her breasts. "Later," he said. "Right now I got more important business to attend to."

Marielle leaned back and caught a glimpse of the two of them in the mirror, like some bizarre beast from Greek mythology, smeared in red by the setting sun. She could make out neither of their faces and exhaled slowly, trying to keep a tight rein on her loathing.

In his pride, Mason Harlow mistook it for a sigh of pleasure.

AT MIDNIGHT, Marielle slipped from the bed and tiptoed into the bathroom. Without turning on the light, she grabbed a robe from behind the door. Still barefoot, she crossed to the door, muffled the sound of the turning knob with a cupped palm and opened it. A pale oblong of light from the hall splashed on the thick carpet, its deep pile slightly darker from the pressure of her feet. She slipped into the hall and shut the door gently behind her, but not far enough for the latch to engage.

Still walking on tiptoe, she hurried the length of the hall to the head of the staircase, the polished wood cold under her bare feet. Down on the first floor, the dim glow of permanent lighting gave the high-ceilinged room a cavernous appearance. Shadows clustered up near the ceiling and filled the corners of the room.

At the foot of the staircase, a narrow hall led away to the left. Marielle entered the hall cautiously. Harlow was extremely security conscious and had boasted of the elaborate and sophisticated electronic devices he had installed to assure his privacy and safety. At the far end of the hall, Marielle found herself in a small, high-ceilinged alcove. A tall, narrow door led into the chamber, and three more—identical to the first and centered in each of the three remaining walls—stared her in the face. None was open. Bright brass doorknobs—each keyed—gleamed in the indirect light from sconces high on the walls.

Marielle had no idea what she was looking for, and even less of where to find it. She crossed the small alcove, shivering as her feet met the thick slabs of slate comprising the floor. The door directly opposite the one by which she had entered was locked, and the knob refused to turn at all. She tried the door on the left, and it swung open easily. From the darkness beyond she caught a slight whiff of cedar and a sharp, pungent chemical odor. Striking a match, she found herself peering into a walk-in closet.

She backed out slowly, closing the door as softly as possible and damping the sound of the latch as she pulled it home. The door to the right was also unlocked. She lit another match, this time finding herself looking into a pool of darkness. A hallway led off into the recesses of the house, and gray lumps, probably some of Harlow's antique furniture, hugged the walls on either side. Harlow was proud of his French Provincial collection, which he had acquired with zeal and displayed with neither taste nor feel for the genuine beauty of each piece.

Marielle was resentful of the furniture, since it represented the more rapacious side of American new money, and more particularly since that money had pirated away from her homeland countless unique and priceless pieces, all that was left of French glory. She tiptoed into the hall, shaking the match out as it burned to the end. She paused long enough to light another, then moved on down the hall.

She had gone twenty or twenty-five feet when yet another door materialized at the outer edge of the light cast by her match. She extinguished the flame, then moved slowly toward the door with extended palms. When her fingers encountered the cold, hard wood of the door, she stopped. She leaned forward, pressed her ear to the door and listened.

Hearing nothing, she reached for the knob and turned it just enough to discover that it was unlocked. She turned it all the way and pulled back. The door resisted her tug for a moment, then gave with a hiss. She stepped across the threshold into near darkness that was broken only by a pale blue flicker. Her eyes adjusted slowly to the light, and she turned to the left, toward its source.

A broad mahogany table stood crosswise at the left end of the room. The light came from a pair of television monitors mounted high on the wall. The screen on the right flicked periodically from scene to scene. In the other, she saw the doorway through which she had just come. Her back and shoulders were visible in the upper half. The lower half of the screen was obscured by the head and cap of a man in camouflage fatigues who watched the screen intently.

A second man, similarly dressed, smiled at her. "Next time use a flashlight. It's easier on the fingers."

The first man turned away from the screen and smiled. "You lost, or ain't ol' Mason enough for you, darlin'?"

"If he's not," she snapped, "this is the last place I'd come looking to do better. Where's the kitchen?"

"You took a wrong turn back a ways, honey. Go back the way you came and make the first left."

"Thanks." Marielle smiled like a big sister, trying to make sure they didn't get the wrong idea. The last thing she needed was one of them to get the idea she was hitting on him.

She turned around and walked through the door, closed it softly and leaned back. In the darkness, she could hear only her own breathing. Her hands trembled and she squeezed them together as if trying to change their shape.

When she had regained control of herself, she lit another match and walked back the way she had come. Her nerves were getting frayed. She felt stupid and lucky at the same time. Stupid enough to make a huge mistake, and lucky enough to get away with it. But that was once. Good luck had a way of leaving behind those who came to count on it too readily.

Next time . . . she thought. But she couldn't afford a next time.

And she knew it.

CHAPTER TWELVE

Bolan stepped out of the cab at the southeast corner of Thirty-seventh and Eighth, crossing Eighth Avenue against the light, dodging through the traffic like a halfback in a busted play. He stopped in the middle of the street to let a bus go by, then ducked through the noxious black cloud spewed out by the chugging behemoth. On the far sidewalk he headed north, walking briskly and keeping close to the buildings.

Most of the dilapidated structures were garishly painted on the first floor only, landlords satisfied to disguise the rot to a height only a little above eye level. The thick paint on rotten wood was gouged and chipped, the ugly scars bright under harsh yellow and white lights twirling like a game-show set. As he neared the bus station he quickened his pace, as if trying to outrun the stink of garbage from the alleys, only thinly veneered under onion- and pizza-filled smoke.

Two figures huddled in a darkened doorway just ahead. The shadowy stone arch seemed out of place along the circus-lit strip. Small groups of young women were clustered here and there, legs bare in the frigid air, hemlines just visible at the edge of synthetic fur jackets. They talked in whispers, stopping just long enough to challenge passersby to try the thrill of a lifetime. Each refusal was met with a storm of insult, most impugning the virility of the uninterested. Bolan spotted a tall man in Army fatigues loitering against the wall, apparently chatting with a leggy blonde in black net stockings a mile long. As Bolan passed, the tall man glanced at him with flat, expressionless eyes and whispered something to the blonde.

Stepping into Bolan's path, she spread her legs wide, anchored on impossibly spiked heels. "Hi, handsome." She smiled. *"Parlez-vous français?"*

"Excuse me," Bolan said, stepping around her.

Not easily discouraged, she latched on to his arm and teetered after him, her heels rapping on the pavement. "What's your hurry, baby? The little woman expecting you?"

"There is no little woman. Goodbye."

Giving Bolan her best pout, she whined, "Can't a girl make an honest buck?"

"If you want to make an honest buck, get a nine to five."

Bolan stared at her, and she stopped in the middle of the sidewalk, reassuming the spread-legged stance. She yelled something incomprehensible, but Bolan didn't bother to try to understand her. Just ahead, the Port Authority bus terminal loomed over the avenue, its blocky glass-and-brick facade as impersonal and desolate as the people who slept on its benches.

Bolan sprinted into the crowded terminal, his feet sucking at the sticky marble floor. He dashed onto the escalator at the center of the main lobby, taking its sluggish stairs two at a time. On the second floor he ducked into the elevator bank and waited impatiently for the car. When it arrived he stepped in quickly, turning to watch the scattered crowd in the hall behind him. The car hummed in its shaft, creaking like an arthritic old man after a long nap. At the top floor, Bolan stepped into a dimly lit hallway. A graffiti-laden sign pointed to the right, its barely legible arrow spelling PARKING in block letters.

The terminal parking garage in midtown was open all night. Like most of them, it had an open-air lot up on the roof, an acre and a half of asphalt under a hazy glare so pervasive not a single star was visible.

The lot was half-empty, most of the cars parked close to the doors. Clotted shadow—thrown by the few working overhead lights—filled the aisles between cars. Bolan's car was at the far end of the roof, just off the exit ramp. He sprinted across the roof, his feet crunching on the graveled tar. Yanking the key ring from his pocket, he inserted the key into the door lock and slipped behind the wheel. He was about to turn the ignition, when something caught his eye through the fogged windshield. He swiped at the condensation with a gloved hand, wiping a small circle just over the steering wheel.

A blurry outline smeared the frozen dew on the driver's side of the hood. Roughly in the shape of a hand, it had to have been recently made. Leaving the key in the ignition, Bolan snapped the hood release and stepped out of the vehicle.

Walking to the front of the car, his back against the low stone wall overlooking the down ramp, he felt under the lip of the hood. When he found the secondary latch, he opened the hood all the way. With a cigarette lighter in hand, he leaned into the shadows. A gust of wind blew out the small flame, but not before he spotted a wire that shouldn't have been there. Cupping the lighter, he thumbed it into life a second time, then leaned forward, curling his body around the fragile flame to block the wind.

A pair of yellow wires was fastened to the starter terminals with alligator clips. Straining to see into the tangled shadows, he traced the wires carefully with his free hand. A small dark metal box had been attached to the fire wall just below the steering column. It looked fairly straightforward—a simple bomb with no timer and no sophistication. But what it lacked in complexity it more than made up in efficiency. Had he turned the key, an electrical current would have shot through the device, more than enough voltage to set it off.

Bolan carefully detached the alligator clips to avoid accidentally triggering the blast with a static charge. He peeled away the tape securing it, working now in darkness since he needed both hands. The small, compact package was heavy, and he realized it had been packed with nuts and bolts. On detonation, they would have torn through the fire wall like a hail of gunfire, shredding flesh and bone already rent by the blast itself.

The bomb was clean and elegant in its death-dealing efficiency. A fairly common design, it was a favorite of terrorists the world over. He had seen more than one like it before, and not coincidentally, realized they had been rather common in Vietnam. The NLF, which had raised the booby trap to a high art, had been forced by matériel shortages to improvise. What better improvisation than to take random junk, and in disposing of your enemy get rid of waste at the same time? It was the ultimate in recycling efficiency.

Bolan jerked the detonator out of the puttylike plastique and slipped it into his pocket. He closed the hood and stepped to the driver's door, opened it and tossed the now harmless explosive into the passenger seat. A squeaky hinge caught his attention, and he turned toward the door from the stairwell to the roof just as it swung closed.

The warrior dropped to one knee and peered into the shadows massed against the building. No one had been on the roof, so someone had to have come out that door. He was suspicious. Someone coming to pick up a car wouldn't have taken such pains to avoid being seen. Keeping to a crouch, Bolan backed along the front of the car, slipping between the bumper and the brick wall.

He worked his way across the front of the vehicle, but still saw no one. Dropping to his stomach, he slid under the car, creeping toward the rear wheels. He lay motionless, holding his breath, and listened. The sounds of traffic drifted up from below, an occasional horn and the heavy rumble of a bus punctuating the monotony.

Bolan didn't like the isolation of his position. The car was his only cover, but he was pinned down. If more than one man had come onto the roof, he could be in serious trouble. The waiting was nerve-racking. The big guy was not used to passive anticipation, but he had to wait for his visitor, or visitors, to make the first move.

Or did he?

Swiveling to the side, he measured the distance between the Olds and the mouth of the down ramp. The gap was at least fifty feet, without a shred of cover. It was time to do something. Bolan slipped out from under the car, staying close to the rear wheels. As he got to his knees he heard a crunch, a careless foot too hastily placed on the gravel. It came from somewhere to the left, among the scattered cars.

Bolan strained to see into the shadows, but couldn't pierce the darkness. He waited for the sound to be repeated, breathing in quick, shallow drafts, but the silence had returned. He rolled to the wall and scrambled to his feet. The sharp spit of a suppressed weapon was followed immediately by the dull splat of breaking safety glass. He glanced at the Olds for a second, just long enough to catch the glint of spidery cracks on the windshield. A quick calculation of the angles confirmed that the shot couldn't have come from the same place as the careless footstep.

There had to be at least two.

Bolan sprinted toward the ramp, keeping low to minimize the target. He stutter-stepped to throw off the shooter's timing, then hit the tar in a quick shoulder roll and came up at the corner of the low wall. Two shots slammed into the brick, just to the right of his head, and he ducked down into the ramp. Its gentle curvature offered little cover, and the distance was too great to make a run for it. He'd be a sitting duck to a gunman at the head of the ramp. Three shots had already been fired, and he still didn't have a clue as to how many shooters there might be, or where they were.

A narrow ledge ran the length of the building, and beneath it latticed girders dropped straight to the street, four stories below. If he could reach the ironwork, he could work his way down, but the overhang was more than six feet, and once he grabbed the iron, he would be defenseless. That left one possibility. It was risky, but seemed the least unacceptable option.

Retreating down the ramp a dozen yards, below the sight line of anyone on the roof, he slipped over the ramp wall, then started creeping back along the six-inch ledge. The small outcropping was smooth and slippery, and small patches of ice from the recent snow made the going even more treacherous. As he approached the small V-shaped opening where the ramp and retaining wall met, he heard a rush of footsteps on the gravel roof.

Crouching, Bolan ducked into the V and reached for his Beretta. The gray haze over the wall was broken by three shadows, but Bolan's angle was too sharp for an effective shot. Once they located him, he would be pinned, and the three shooters could fan out and take turns popping shots at him.

"He must have gone down the ramp," one of the gunners said. "You two check it out. I'll wait here."

Bolan pressed closer against the stone, until he could feel every ripple in the wall, hugging it as closely as a coat of paint. The men moved less cautiously now, and Bolan heard their shoes scrape on the concrete of the ramp. A minute later, one of the men yelled up from the first turn, "Don't see him."

The voice on the roof yelled back. "Go on down to the next level. I'll meet you there."

Bolan counted to ten, then peeked over the retaining wall. The guy on the roof was about fifteen feet away, bent over at the waist and looking straight at him. Thin as a rail, he looked like the shadow of a bullwhip, coiled and ready to snap. He hesitated; then, with the jerky motion of a Japanese animated cartoon, he swung his arm forward, a Browning automatic glinting under the pale overhead light. Bolan shifted his weight, swinging the Beretta over the wall and firing in a single motion. The gunner gurgled, reaching for his throat as the Browning clattered to the tar. Bolan fired a second time, aiming dead center on the collapsing shadow.

He swung his leg up and over the wall and reached forward to grab the slippery brick with his left hand. A heartbeat later, a slug slammed into the concrete ledge, spraying his ankle with slivers of mortar.

Bolan tumbled to the roof and swung around just as the first man roared out of the ramp. Squeezing off a quick burst, he sent three 9 mm rounds into the guy's midsection. The warrior watched the guy sprawl forward, dark red seeping out of his crisply starched fatigues. The last man, a bushy-haired hard case in a pea jacket, stopped dead in his tracks, stared at his fallen companion, then at Bolan. Slowly, he started to back down the ramp, his hands raised just above his shoulders. Bolan leaped to his feet as the man broke into a run. A moment later he was gone, swallowed by the shadows of the garage level below.

CHAPTER THIRTEEN

Bolan raced down the ramp. Ahead of him, he could hear the heavy steps of the fleeing gunman. The Executioner moved cautiously, but knew that he was in no danger as long as he could hear the man running. The ramp curved out into Tenth Avenue, where a jumble of old brick buildings stood bleak and silent.

At the bottom of the ramp, Bolan spotted the gunman running toward the next corner. A second later, the fleeing gunner disappeared around the corner of a ramshackle three-story building. Bolan ran to the corner, but the gunman was no longer in sight. Ducking into an alley just past the corner, he waited a few minutes on the off chance that the gunman might poke his head out of a hole. A police car appeared up the block, and Bolan shrank into the darkness. The last thing he needed was to try to explain his presence—and his weapons—to a suspicious cop.

When the blue-and-white drifted past, the officers were absorbed in conversation, and neither glanced into the darkened alley. You didn't have to deal with something you didn't see. Overworked cops had no intention of looking for trouble.

As the cruiser vanished up the block, Bolan stepped out of the alley and ran back to the ramp. Sprinting upward, he noticed flashing lights on the roof. Someone must have found the dead gunners and called the cops. The spiraling red flashers stabbed repeatedly at the brick, painting it an off red. The crackle of the police radio, punctuated by bursts of static, slashed through the cold air.

Bolan had a choice. He could leave the car and make his own way back to the safehouse, or he could try to tough it out with the cops. Remembering the shattered windshield, he chose the less sticky route. He turned around.

At the bottom of the ramp, Bolan doubled back toward the bus terminal, grabbing a cab in front of the Eighth Avenue entrance. A second cab, idling at the curb across the street, slipped in behind. It was off duty, and after a brief glance at it Bolan turned his attention elsewhere. As his taxi threaded its way through the neon jumble, Bolan found himself watching out the back window.

Bolan wrapped on the Plexiglas shield between front and back seats to get the cabbie's attention. The driver looked at Bolan in the rearview mirror, his face anything but friendly.

"What's the problem, buddy? Realize you lost your wallet?"

"Somebody's following us. Run the next light, and turn down a side street."

"You been watching too many spy movies, pally."

"Indulge me." Something in Bolan's tone made the driver glance uneasily into the mirror. He'd had too many close calls with the loose cannons of late-night New York to argue too hard.

They were heading downtown now on Broadway. At Thirty-Fifth Street the traffic signal was already turning from amber to red when the cab shot forward and swung into Thirty-fifth. Bolan looked through the back window. The tail was playing it cool—the nose of the second cab just peeking out at the corner.

"Pull over to the first open curb you get to," Bolan barked at the driver.

"Look, pal, I already logged your destination. You gonna screw up my paperwork?"

"Just do it."

The cabbie shrugged with a resignation that spoke volumes. He'd seen it all, and some days there was just no point in going to work. This, apparently, was one of them. They were in the garment district, and the side streets were cluttered with delivery vans. The cab swerved suddenly, screeching to a halt in front of a corrugated garage door. It wasn't a legal parking place, but Bolan didn't need one. He crammed a ten into the small tilting pocket in the Plexiglas and opened the door. "Keep the change," he said, rapping the glass with his knuckles.

"Yeah, yeah." The driver yawned.

The warrior slipped out the curb-side door and ducked behind a huge truck parked with its right side up on the curb. The cab squealed out into the street and roared away, trailing a swirl of exhaust in the cold night air.

Bolan peered up the block, waiting for the light to change. The crosstown signal was already blinking and a moment later it changed to red. The second cab took the corner slowly, the driver apparently suspicious. It shot forward suddenly when the driver realized the street was empty. He gunned the engine and peeled a little rubber as he roared up the block to the next corner. Bolan watched for a moment as the cab stopped, ignoring the green light.

He raced back toward Broadway and turned the corner, the long line of trucks massed at the curb shielding him from the driver's vision. Back on the more heavily traveled avenue, he hailed another cab, instructing the driver to turn into Thirty-fifth Street. They pulled up behind the tail, now idling at the red light.

As the light changed, Bolan's driver leaned on the horn, prompting the lead driver to move out. Bolan had his driver fall back and follow at a discreet distance. They followed the cab for nearly twenty blocks, until it pulled into a parking lot just north of Union Square. Bolan watched as the driver left the cab and slipped into a Buick. The man continued on down Broadway, detouring around the Square and picking up Broadway again at Fourteenth Street.

At Astor Place, the Buick hung a right and cruised slowly for a couple of blocks, finally pulling over to the curb. Bolan watched as the driver got out of the car and locked it. He paid his own cabbie, who drove away, then he waited in a doorway until the unsuspecting driver he'd been following started to walk through Washington Square Park and turned left on West Fourth. Bolan took up the pursuit. Back on Broadway, the man quickened his pace, glancing at his watch every half block or so.

The streets were deserted, and Bolan could hear his own soft steps falling on the pavement. The sound seemed louder than it was, the cold air heightening the effect of each slap of leather on concrete. The man ahead was careless, never looking once over his shoulder. He seemed nervous, possibly about having lost his quarry or about missing an appointment.

The man was moving rapidly, nearly running now, and suddenly veered to the left, heading toward the Bowery. Crossing the broad sweep of Lafayette, he dashed in front of an onrushing cab. Still a block behind, Bolan could hear the cabbie cursing through his open window. The sprinter ignored him, raising one arm over his shoulder without looking back. Bolan didn't need to see the gesture clearly to know what it was. And in the sudden illumination of onrushing headlights, Bolan realized the driver was the third gunman from the garage roof.

The streets were dirty and the wind was picking up, starting to swirl paper and dust in the air. Small patches of ice gleamed dully in the gutter, their surfaces gray with ground-in dirt. Overhead the sky seemed to be drawing closer, and Bolan looked up instinctively at the lowering clouds just as the first flakes of snow materialized.

As if the sky had suddenly split open, the snow doubled and redoubled in intensity. The swirling flakes obscured his quarry, and Bolan started to run. In a block, he'd lost his man. The snow had begun to accumulate, and faint smears on the light dusting of snow turned east at the following corner. Uncertain whether the tracks had been made by his man—but having no other option—Bolan followed the small clots of compressed snow for another two blocks.

Halfway up the next block the footprints vanished down a flight of stairs and into an alley. Bolan walked silently down the stairs, but there was no sign of which way the man had gone. What little snow had fallen in the narrow passage had melted immediately. Bolan moved cautiously, conscious of the possibility that he had been seen.

The building to the right presented him with a ragged brick face, unbroken by window or door from foundation to eaves. The building on his left featured several windows, but not a glimmer of light shone from any of them. Halfway to the rear a doorway was set back in the cinder-block wall, and Bolan approached it carefully, pressing his ear to its sheet-metal sheathing before trying the knob. He heard nothing but a low mechanical hum from beyond the door, which probably came from the furnace.

He moved past the door without trying it, saving it as a last recourse in case he drew a blank farther down the alley. At the rear of the building, the wall juked to the left, creating a small alcove in which a half dozen garbage cans sat collecting snow. The sweetish aroma of rotting food swirled around him. A second door at right angles to the alley was set into a stone wall nearly eight feet high. Beyond the wall, an open garden stretched through to the next street.

Bolan moved into a narrower passage where the alley continued down along the garden. Here the stone wall had been replaced by chain-link fence. He looked back to the building and noticed a sliver of light along one side of a second-story window.

It was a slim chance, but beggars couldn't be choosers.

The warrior moved back along the fence and reentered the alley. Making his way to the metal door, he listened briefly, then tried the knob. It resisted for a moment, then squealed as it started to give. He twisted harder and caught a break. The doorknob came away in his hand. He pushed, and heard the lip of the dead bolt scrape against the seat, then slip free. Somebody—either the superintendent or a tenant—had been careless. On such small hubs did worlds revolve. Bolan stepped inside and closed the door behind him.

The basement was pitch-black. Bolan used a small flashlight as he inched his way forward. The overhead clearance was low and tangled with pipe and cable. The usual jumble of long-unused junk and maintenance equipment lined one wall, and a furnace and water heater stood together at the center of the oblong room. Against the far wall a rickety flight of wooden stairs was partially hidden by the bulk of the furnace. As Bolan moved past the obstruction he spotted a thin sliver of light at the top of the stairs. He climbed tentatively, checking the placement of each foot to avoid squeaking boards.

At the head of the stairs he placed his ear to the lower panel of the door but heard nothing. An old-fashioned keyhole made a bright spot of light halfway up the door. Placing his eye to the keyhole, he found himself peering down a tiled hallway toward a flight of stairs. The door was unlocked, and Bolan eased it open and stepped into the hall. He made his way to the front of the building and peered through the thick wavy glass of the door leading into an outer hallway. He scanned the names on the mailboxes, but not all were marked, and none of the names was familiar.

The light he had seen was on the third floor, and wet footprints on the hall tiles suggested someone had recently entered. He climbed two flights of stairs, then paused to get his bearings. The light had been to the rear, and he stood looking at three doors, each of which led to an apartment with one or more rooms at the rear of the third floor. Eliminating the least likely possibilities, he made for the leftmost door. The question was, now that he was here, what the hell could he do? Breaking down the door was an option, but it would accomplish nothing. Sitting and waiting might take all night, and more to the point, might find the jaws beginning to close. Neither was an attractive prospect.

That left the keyhole approach again, but this time there was none to peek through. On a chance he cupped his hands around the peephole mounted in the center of the upper door panel. The inside cover was off center, and a cloudy half-moon of light, distorted by the fish-eye lens, floated before him. At one end of an oval table, three men were drinking coffee. Only the hands of a fourth man were visible.

One was the man he had followed; the second was Leon Alvarez. It was the third man who made him wonder what the hell was going on. Why was Stanley Mills, former Deputy Director of Covert Operations of the CIA, having coffee with Leon Alvarez—allegedly still on the Company payroll—and with the man who had just tried to kill him?

Bolan backed away from the door, holding his breath as a floorboard squealed. With many new questions and no answers to old ones, he walked down the stairs to the basement door. He slipped out the way he had come in. It would be much more useful to wait and see what happened.

It was still snowing, and Bolan hugged his coat tighter to his body. It could be a long night.

CHAPTER FOURTEEN

Mack Bolan stood in the darkness, shivering against the unrelenting wind. The building across the street was all but obscured by the snow swirling in tight clouds. The flakes stung his cheeks like a thousand needle points. A single streetlight up the block waxed and waned with the wind-blown flakes. He was waiting for Leon Alvarez.

The meeting in progress on the third floor across the street was more than a little troubling. Mills was the biggest unknown in the equation. Bolan had known of his work, and had even met him once when Mills was still with the CIA. But Mills had been out of the Company for nearly three years. The cloud under which he had departed had still not dissipated.

It was ironic that the presence of Mills simultaneously supported Alvarez in his claim that he was with the Agency and called his integrity into question. As so often in the shadowy world of intelligence, appearances were less helpful than confusing, and speculation less helpful still. Rather than barging in and confronting Alvarez and the others, Bolan decided the most prudent course was to watch...and wait.

After what seemed like an eternity, he looked impatiently at his watch. He had been watching the place for more than an hour. The conversation had seemed to be on the verge of winding down when he'd slipped out of the building. The apartment didn't appear to be large enough to accommodate all four men on an overnight stay, so some of them had to be leaving.

Bolan stamped his feet in the accumulated snow, trying to force the blood to circulate. He was getting stiff and numb from the inactivity. The street was fully covered now by snow, two to three inches deep. If anything, the weather was getting heavier. Bolan pressed deeper into the alley, trying to get away from the wind.

He stared so hard at the tall glass doors across the way that they had started to move. He knew the motion was illusory and fought against it with some success. More than once some shift of light and shadow through the murky glass deceived him, teased him into heightened expectation. So well did he control the nervous impulse that when the left-hand door suddenly swung open, he almost missed it.

Two men walked out, and the door was closed with such force that the loose glass rattled in its frame. They clomped down the steps and stood talking at the foot of the brownstone staircase. One of them kept checking the sky, as if waiting for a change in the weather, while the other gesticulated vigorously, his hands waving spastically. The speaker was agitated. Scraps of his hoarse, angry whisper drifted across the street, but they were muted by the snow and mutilated by the wind. Bolan could tell only that the man was lecturing. The recipient of the tongue-lashing seemed indifferent, and impatient for the scolding to end. Bolan couldn't see their faces.

The angry speaker finally stopped, his posture suddenly receptive, as if he were waiting for a response. The second man, however, said nothing. He fished in the deep pockets of a dark blue parka, finally removing a pad. He scribbled a few words with a pen, shaking the paper several times to keep the snow from dampening it. He tore the top sheet from the pad and handed it to the lecturer, then stuffed pad and pen back into his jacket. He reached into the other pocket for something, and a moment later a small halo surrounded his upper body as he lit a cigarette. It was Leon Alvarez. The light was too feeble to illuminate the other man.

Alvarez sucked greedily at the cigarette, then when it was lit, shook his hand and tossed away the match. Without a word he turned sharply and walked away. He muttered something over his shoulder, but the wind ripped it to pieces before scattering the fragments over Bolan.

"Fuck you, Leon," the other man shouted. "You hear me?"

Alvarez didn't alter his pace or call back a reply. The other man stood staring after him, but said nothing more. Finally he stomped back up the steps, nearly losing his balance when he slipped on the packed snow, then kicked his foot angrily at the doorjamb to dislodge snow before stepping in and closing the door.

His shadow on the glass vanished almost immediately, and Bolan watched Alvarez, now half a block away. He was barely visible in the clouds of whirling snow. The warrior waited another twenty seconds, then started after him.

By the time he reached the corner, Alvarez was a block north, walking swiftly. Both men found the going heavy. The cold snow packed under their feet, quickly turning to smooth, slippery white ice. Bolan watched the agent appear and vanish repeatedly as he drifted past lighted store windows. Each time the man disappeared, Bolan held his breath, fearful Alvarez might not reappear.

They had walked nearly ten blocks, slipping and sliding on the snowy pavement. Bolan hoped Alvarez didn't have a car parked somewhere. He hadn't seen a single cab, and if Alvarez got away from him, there'd be no way to track him. At Cooper Square, Alvarez ducked down the steps leading to the subway, and Bolan followed. He waited a minute to allow Alvarez time to get a token, and then took the second flight into the underground station.

When Bolan reached the platform, Alvarez was at the far end, near where the front of the train would be. The warrior leaned against the cold tile and stared at his feet, keeping his face averted. In the poorly lit station there was little chance Alvarez would recognize him. He was, for all the world, just another late-night commuter watching the unexpected snow melt from his cuffs and shoes.

A rumble began to echo through the station, its volume focused and magnified by the tunnel as an uptown train approached. Bolan tensed himself and waited, keeping an eye on Alvarez, who stopped his ears against the train's thunderous arrival, punctuated by the high-pitched hiss of air brakes. The agent stepped onto the train after a quick glance down the platform.

Bolan waited to make sure it wasn't a feint and ducked onto the train just as the pneumatic doors began to close. The train jerked, a jolting chain reaction that ran from car to car as each began to move. The filthy car rocked from side to side, and Bolan worked his way forward to peer through the grubby glass into the next car, which was virtually empty. He pulled the door open and stepped onto the platform across the gnashing gap to the next car.

Bolan had trouble entering the next car when the door refused to budge. He yanked sharply, and it slipped halfway open and stopped. He turned sideways to squeeze through the narrow opening, and cursed when the door stayed open. It refused to move, and the loud echo of the clattering wheels was deafening.

Bolan lurched forward as the train pulled into the next station, and stood in the doorway to see whether Alvarez got off. Late-night trains were short, and Alvarez was in the next car. Bolan took a seat two-thirds of the way along, where he could see Alvarez through the doors.

Alvarez seemed intent only on his journey, and dangled distractedly from a center pole, his body jerking back and forth as the train lurched through the tunnel. Once he turned to the rear and seemed to be staring straight at Bolan, but his face betrayed no sign of recognition, and Bolan had, in best New York style, instantaneously averted his gaze. What might have been taken as cause for alarm in any other mass transit system was no more than expected on the IRT.

The train screeched to a halt in the next station, and Alvarez got out. He sprinted up the steps to the street, and Bolan followed him into the nightmare that was Forty-second Street.

Alvarez walked quickly through the snowy streets, soon crossing Sixth Avenue and entering the zone of skin flicks and hookers, pimps and pushers. The thousands of lights on the peep shows and movie marquees painted everything—including the snow—a jaundiced yellow. Big-legged women in miniskirts and makeup, fake fur and leather thrown over pinched shoulders to keep off the cold, loitered in doorways. Alvarez barged straight on with his head down, ignoring the propositions and taunts. Bolan crossed to the south side of the street and tailed him from a half block behind.

Alvarez turned north at Ninth Avenue, and Bolan suddenly realized where he was going. Fishing in his pocket for a quarter, he stepped into a phone booth, dropped the coin and punched the touch-tone buttons impatiently.

The voice on the other end, when it finally came, was sleepy. "Hello?"

"Don't open the door to anybody, until I get there. Understand?"

"Bolan?"

"Do you understand?"

"Yes. I . . . what's going on?"

He didn't answer. Alison Brewer would have to wait for her explanation. He slammed the phone back into its cradle and sprinted after Alvarez. Three blocks north, Alvarez turned down Forty-fifth Street, moving even more quickly, his feet skidding on the snow. He fell once and didn't bother to brush off the snow as he got to his feet.

Bolan was narrowing the gap, but not quickly enough. He stepped off the curb into the street. What little traffic there had been had churned through the snow, leaving slush and bare pavement behind. The footing was better, and Bolan began to run. Alvarez was less than a block ahead of him now, and the gap was closing rapidly.

When he reached the steps of the safehouse Alvarez paused briefly to look up at the sky before beginning his climb. The first shot took him by surprise. Alvarez stumbled and fell, then struggled to crawl behind a parked car. Four men stepped out of the shadows across the street, and Bolan instinctively drew his AutoMag, its grip cold and clammy in the winter air. He raced up the block, but with the line of parked cars between them, he could no longer see Alvarez.

One of the four gunmen spotted Bolan and dropped to one knee. The warrior dived into the slush, spinning to his right and snapping off a shot as he came to rest against a mound of muddy snow. He felt like an animal scrambling into a burrow as he squeezed in between an old Volkswagen and a battered Ford van. All three gunners, their attention diverted from Alvarez, now focused on him.

Bolan fired again, and this time the bullet found its mark—the kneeling gunner groaned and fell forward in the snow. One of his compatriots grabbed the wounded man by the heels and dragged him unceremoniously behind a station wagon. Bolan fired again, taking out the windshield of the wagon, and the three uninjured gunmen split up. One, the burly man who had been driving the taxi, crossed to Bolan's side of the street. Another crouched and scooted forward to get abreast of the prostrate Bolan. Both men kept up a steady alternating fire, keeping him pinned to the ground. The third man was nowhere to be seen.

And Leon Alvarez hadn't moved.

CHAPTER FIFTEEN

The heat woke Mason Harlow early. Despite the curtains on his window, the room was as bright as midday. He glanced at the clock and cursed when he saw the time. Seven o'clock was just too damn early. Up half the night drinking flash, the local bootleg, he felt as if he'd been drunk for a week. He groaned and sat up on the edge of the cot.

He walked to the window and pulled the curtain aside, squinting from the burst of light and heat coming through the window. It felt like a slap in the face. His head ached, and he cursed himself and the Libyans for a project that seemed rapidly falling to pieces.

Lamenting the difficulty of finding good help, he dropped the curtain and staggered unsteadily to the small bathroom. Gritty sand scraped under his bare feet, and despite the unbearable heat, the bare wooden floor felt as cold as the thin ice on which he had suddenly found himself skating. Al-Hassan, the bastard, had reamed his ass for nearly three hours the day before. Harlow had been tempted to tell the creep to go fuck himself, but that was not the best way to handle the assistant director of any intelligence agency. When the agency in question had you by the balls, discretion was the only advisable course.

Waw al-Kabir was a hick town, not that different from the kind of dusty, backward armpit of civilization he'd been born into and spent the rest of his life running away from. Now, forty-odd years later, he was right back in it, and the smell was getting to him. Al-Hassan had insisted on secrecy, and the small camp at Waw al-Kabir was his idea of a secure site.

Harlow made a mental note to ream Sadowski out, and knew, without raising the question, that McNally was rapidly becoming a liability. The weak sister was also a lush, and precariously close to the edge of expendability. On the other hand, McNally was his ace in the hole.

The cramped bathroom reminded Harlow of every backwater motel he'd stayed in, out-of-the-way places where indoor plumbing was the latest novelty, and dental work was the province of the wealthy. He turned on the tap and knew without even testing it that the cold water was tepid. It dribbled into the basin, vaguely yellow, and looked about as inviting as camel piss. Harlow scooped up handfuls of the lukewarm water and splashed his face repeatedly. He shook his head, trying to wake up, but the splitting headache seemed to resent the activity.

Grabbing a towel, Harlow dried himself rapidly, rubbing a little life into the waxen face staring at him from the crazed mirror over the sink. He tossed the towel into a corner and went back to the bedroom. He was just slipping into his shirt when a belligerent knock rattled the door. Before he could answer, the lockless door swung open, slapping the bare wall behind it, driving the knob into the plaster.

Framed in the door, starkly outlined against the harsh light outside, stood Colonel Fadi al-Hassan. Harlow groaned.

"Mr. Harlow, we have a great deal to discuss."

"Come in, Colonel. Don't stand on ceremony."

Al-Hassan ignored the sarcasm and walked across the wooden floor, dropping into the only decent chair in the room.

"We are running out of patience with you, Mr. Harlow."

"What is it now, Colonel?"

"You have been working for us for more than a year, yes?"

"You know I have. I thought we went over all this yesterday."

"So we did. But we have just received some disturbing new information. We must move faster now, much faster."

"Look, Colonel, I already told you. You send me people who can't even read and expect me to teach them complicated techniques in six weeks. It can't be done."

"And what of the devices you were to construct for us? Can't that be done, either?"

"I told you, I'm working on it."

"You must work faster."

"Dammit, Hassan, you know what happened the last time we pushed too hard. Five of the village idiots you sent me blew themselves into hamburger. Two of my own men were injured. And they took nearly half our supplies with them to kingdom come."

"You are well connected, are you not?"

"Of course..."

"Then you can get replacements. We pay generously. We expect a fair return on our investment."

"Demolitions is not like a mutual fund, Colonel. You want a fair return, you have to be patient."

"There is no more time for patience."

"Why not?"

"Because a delegation from your State Department is in N'Djamena at this very moment."

"So?"

"The subject under discussion is military assistance to the government of Chad. As you are well aware, Chad has one of the largest deposits of yellow cake in the world. That would be... useful, not to say valuable, for us. Military assistance from the United States could be a substantial obstacle. We are not happy about that possibility."

"Look, I'm plugged in, true. But I'm not the Secretary of State. What the hell do you want me to do about it?"

"Quite simple, really." Al-Hassan stood and adjusted his mirrored sunglasses. He reminded Harlow of the redneck sheriff in the old Dodge commercials.

Harlow, still barefoot and pantless, felt foolish and vulnerable. Al-Hassan, as if to reinforce those feelings, looked pointedly at Harlow's lower extremities. He smiled a tight, sardonic smile, then said, "If there is no one for your State

Department to talk to, then there is no problem. You see
what I mean?''

"You want me to arrange for that?''

"I do.''

"That was never part of our bargain.''

"It is now, Mr. Harlow.''

Harlow slipped his pants on and snugged the belt in place.
He walked to the window and pulled the curtain back.
Staring out the window, he seemed to be studying something in the dusty street outside. Finally he sighed. "It'll
cost.''

"You have already been very well paid, and we have precious little to show for it. We think it would be a token of
your good faith if you were to take care of this yourself.''

"Out of my own pocket?''

"However.''

"You drive a hard bargain, Colonel.''

"That is what I am paid to do, Mr. Harlow. Just as you
are paid to train our people, and to produce.''

"And if I say no?''

"I remind you, your passport—and those of your people—are in the safe in my office. I think it would behoove
you to think quite seriously about that.''

"That's blackmail, extortion.''

"Mr. Harlow, we have long since come to an understanding, have we not? Money is what concerns you. Performance is what concerns us. To date, you have our money
and we have yet to see your performance.''

Harlow sighed. He thought he could hear the ice cracking beneath him. He walked to the small table in one corner of his room and picked up the unmarked bottle and a
glass. Holding the glass and the bottle in one hand, he unscrewed the cap then poured a half glass of the clear liquid
and slapped the bottle back onto the table without recovering it. He downed the flash in one gulp.

"Colonel, I'm a businessman. And I know when I'm in
a bind.''

"I never underestimated your ability to see how things stand, Mr. Harlow."

Harlow laughed. "You put things with such delicacy, Colonel."

"And why not? We are not all barbarians here, Mr. Harlow. I have spent time in Europe. I know how the West thinks, how it moves. I know how things are done."

"I see that."

"And we have very little time, Mr. Harlow."

"How little?"

"Perhaps two weeks, perhaps less."

Harlow whistled through clenched teeth. "I'll see what I can do."

"I knew you would."

"But I'll need my passport. I'll have to attend to this personally, and there is no one here I can use. The men here are explosives experts, not marksmen."

"Of course. But let me remind you that Libya has a long memory...and longer arms."

Harlow nodded. "I understand. I'll leave tonight. And I'll need Mr. Sadowski to go with me."

"Why?"

"Like I said, I'm a businessman. The secret of success in business is not in knowing everything. It is in knowing who knows what. Mr. Sadowski has contacts I don't have."

"Very well, but the others must stay. The training must continue. We are already well behind schedule."

"Mr. McNally can handle that. He knows what he's doing."

"Does he really?"

"Of course. He'll be in charge while I'm away."

"You have three days, Mr. Harlow. A plane will be ready to take you and Mr. Sadowski to Tripoli in one hour. If you are not back in Tripoli by Friday, I'm afraid I'll have to send for you."

"Don't worry about it. I'll be there."

Al-Hassan smiled. He walked to the door, still wide open, and took the knob in his hand. He started to pull it closed, then stopped and turned back to Harlow. "Virginia is not so very far away, Mr. Harlow." He closed the door softly.

Harlow went back to the bathroom and ran a comb through his hair. He looked as if he'd been shot at and hit. Things weren't supposed to go this badly. He had had the world on a string forty-eight hours ago, now it felt like the string was wrapped around his neck. He was breathing rapidly, the short, sharp gasps of a man about to be hanged hissing through his taut lips.

Sadowski's room was at the other end of the compound. Harlow shuffled along, kicking at the dust. Al-Hassan's threat was not something to be taken lightly. He'd been painted into a corner, and there was no other option. He had to deliver and he had three days to find the right men.

He barged into Sadowski's room. The big man was still in bed, and he sat bolt upright as the door banged open, grabbing an automatic from under his pillow. Harlow didn't comment on it. He understood Sadowski's reflexes. "Load, get dressed. We got a problem."

"What now? McNally fuck up again?"

"No. It's worse than that. We have to get to the airport. I'll tell you about it on the way."

"Damn. I just got here. You know, Harlow, I'm beginning to get a little tired of being jerked around. And I sure as hell am sick of membership in the mileage club of half the fucking airlines on the planet. This little deal was supposed to be a cakewalk. No sweat and free ice cream for everybody. You remember telling me that?"

"Just shut up and do what I tell you. My nuts are in a vise here. And so are yours."

He watched Sadowski dress, shuffling his feet impatiently. He hadn't expected to be home again so soon. But there were silver linings in every cloud. He'd see Marielle a lot sooner than he expected. His wife was still in London. It might not be so bad, after all. Before they left, he'd call Randall in D.C., have him make all the arrangements. Marielle could meet him in New York.

"Harlow, I'm not so sure I want to know what you're up to, and I got a feeling that vise you're talking about can only handle one set of nuts at a time. I also got a feeling whose they are."

Harlow didn't answer the big man. He was too busy listening to the sound of wheels turning in his own head.

CHAPTER SIXTEEN

The Executioner watched a new figure materialize out of the snow at the other end of the block. The three remaining gunners maneuvered along the rows of parked cars, oblivious of the new arrival. Bolan wormed toward the curb on the south side of the street, concentrating on the man skipping from car to car, slipping and sliding in the snow and slush.

The guy was being careful, staying in tight, and Bolan couldn't get a clear shot without exposing himself. There was only one way to get out of the bind. A head-high brick wall set in the row of buildings just behind him would provide some security, if he could reach it. The odds were little better than even, but staying in the slush-filled gutter gave him no chance at all. He'd have to risk it.

Bolan got to his knees, pressing flat against the curved door of a parked car. A dark lump fifty yards up the block was the approaching gunner, who seemed to have sensed that something was about to happen. He stayed motionless, every bit as conscious of his minimal cover as Bolan was.

The warrior scanned the opposite side of the street, but the gunman's cronies were nowhere to be seen. They might be anywhere along the far curb, behind any of the cars. It was nearly impossible to protect himself if he stayed where he was.

Bolan glanced to the west end of the block, but the newcomer had vanished. He wondered whether it had been some streetwise resident who knew when to get lost, or if he should add one more to his already full complement of worries.

The warrior stood quickly and dived across the sidewalk, sliding into the alcove through its open gate and slamming into the base of a brick wall. The impact momentarily knocked the wind from his lungs. He shook himself and skittered backward, like a giant black crab, into the recesses of the alcove, which was full of shadows and smelled of garbage. He banged against a stray garbage-can lid, and the clatter was deafening. A dog barked somewhere deep in the building behind him.

Bolan felt along the rear wall of the small enclosure but found no outlet. He didn't like being trapped in a corner, but at least he wouldn't have to worry about his back. He walked cautiously back to the entrance. The wrought-iron gate was nearly invisible in the darkness, and he pushed it flush against the wall to keep it out of his way.

Peering out into the street, he spotted the first gunman, now twenty yards nearer. The opposite side of the street still seemed deserted. He watched as the wary gunner slipped behind a van and moved to the street side of the line of cars. Bolan cradled Big Thunder carefully in his hand, training the big .44 dead center on the van.

Pinned as he was in the alcove, Bolan had limited visibility. Taking out one man had helped, but not much, and any attempt to broaden his visibility might expose him to one of the three remaining gunners. By the light of a single streetlight, Bolan was able to follow the hidden gunner's progress. His bulk cast a slight reflected shadow as he passed along the street side of the parked cars.

He had slipped past the van now and was nearly abreast of the opening in the wall. Bolan waited patiently. The hidden man was crouched, his long legs draped in the ample folds of an open trench coat. Bolan watched his blurry outline in the canted window of a passenger car directly across the street. When the hardman gathered himself, coiling his legs like a cartoon kangaroo, Bolan was ready.

His leap brought the gunner up over the hood of an '81 Buick Riviera. He curled like a breaching whale, half coiling himself into the shape of a croissant. Bolan squeezed once, then again. The .44-caliber slugs slammed into the arcing hit man just off center. The guy's gun dropped from his hand as he fell toward the hood of the Buick, clattering on the hood for an instant until the shooter landed on top of it.

Curled into the fetal position, the gunner clasped at his midsection, struggling to pull aside the flaps of his trench coat. He spun once, and his kicking legs slammed into the windshield, launching him off the car's hood. He landed in the slush and lay still.

Bolan leaped from one side of the gateway to the other, hoping the activity would draw fire. Unless and until the other two gunmen revealed themselves again, he would have to sit tight. Leaving the safety of the alcove would almost certainly get him killed, unless he knew where they were. It was hard enough to watch your back with two men hunting you in concert. When you had no idea where either of them was, the odds were about as long as they could get.

And Bolan wouldn't want to bet on the outcome. He knew, as did everyone who walked the fine line between giving death and receiving it, that long odds were every bit as long every time out. Just because you managed to walk away from a tight box one time, you had no right to assume the next time was any easier. Eventually the laws of statistical probability became your worst enemy. You were haunted by them, always wondering when they would be invoked, and by whom.

A soldier on the front line knew the feeling. He joked about the bullet with his name on it, not to tempt fate, as some thought, but in the belief that there is no terror like the terror with no name. If you could call it, categorize it, identify it, you had some control over it. Some took the extreme position, the defiance of looking for it, proclaiming to anyone who would listen and even to those who wouldn't that you shouldn't be afraid of death at all. It could only find you if and when you stopped looking for it.

Bolan was not without superstition, but that was one he didn't share. He knew death was something that found you whether you ran to it or from it. Your time was just that. It was yours and no one else's. But Bolan also knew, as one would expect an executioner to know, that cocky was careless . . . and careless was dead.

Plain and simple.

A light was still visible in the building where Alison Brewer waited. He had told her to sit tight, but the longer it took him to get to her, the more likely she would panic. Bolan had to find a way to smoke out the remaining gunmen, or to get behind them and cut the odds a little.

He scanned the glass on the other side of the street. The snow was swirling even harder now, and visibility was marginal. Most of the windows on the building across the street were elevated, up above the street level, and the angle was bad. Skipping his gaze from car to car, he hoped to catch a glimpse of movement, anything that would betray the presence of one of the gunmen. He bounced his glance from one end of the block to the other.

Not a thing was moving.

Taking the bull by the horns, the Executioner dropped to a crouch and inched toward the opening in the wall. He felt boxed in, as if the walls of the alcove were closing in on him. He had to get out, but the footing was treacherous. The accumulated snow, now nearly six inches deep in spots, would make a decent cushion if he fell, but he didn't want to run on it unless he had no other choice.

He leaned forward, bracing himself on one hand like a lineman waiting for the snap. As if in response to a count only he could hear, the big man in black charged forward, hitting the gate in full stride. He dived headlong, skidding to a halt between two cars. His chest and shoulders had plowed a considerable mound of snow ahead of him, forcing some of the cold slush down his collar. He ignored the discomfort as he maneuvered himself into a crouch.

Total silence had greeted his charge. If the gunmen were still there, they were either blind or very patient. Nothing else could explain the complete lack of response. From up the block a burst of light splashed on the thick snow in the street. Unmarked, the thick carpet reflected the glare of a pair of headlights.

Bolan caught sight of a blocky vehicle, moving slowly on the slippery pavement. Whatever else New York drivers might be, they were anything but confident in harsh winter weather. Unlike their counterparts in Chicago, for whom snow was a way of life, New Yorkers greeted snow with one of two responses: either a reckless indifference, or a timidity that was itself reckless.

The truck coasted, its driver kicking the clutch in and out of first, the gears grinding a little and moaning with the intermittent strain. As the vehicle drew closer, Bolan watched it out of the corner of his eye, still searching the nooks and crannies of the far side with a restless attention. Dark blue or gray, the van was little more than a backlit mass, like a cinder block on wheels as it droned up the block. Bolan could hear the crunch of its tires on the virgin snow.

The van stopped about thirty yards away. The driver killed his headlights, leaving on only the harsh yellow parking lights. A swirl of condensed exhaust spiraled up and disappeared in the snow. Bolan could hear the wind now, the high-pitched whistling as it slipped through the gaps between cars, and the soft, bassoonlike moan as it echoed on its passage between buildings.

A door slammed in the direction of the van, but Bolan could see no one. Suddenly the clutch popped and the van spurted forward. A figure sprinted out from behind it and ducked between two cars on Bolan's side of the street. Now he knew why he hadn't seen anyone. A second later and the van was right in front of him. Bolan, off balance and reluctant to shoot first, waited as the van drifted past, again coasting.

The vehicle's rear doors swung open and a staccato popping, dampened by a suppressor, took out the rear window of the car to his right. Bolan hunched down as the shattered glass rained over his back and shoulders. He fired two quick shots into the dark interior of the van, both shots glancing harmlessly off the metal walls, the ping of their impact echoing and dying away quickly in the swirling snow.

Heavy steps to Bolan's left signaled the approach of the other gunner—the guy was coming up the street side. Bolan crabbed back and spun to look up the curb side of the parked cars, but saw no one. The warrior was jammed now—he couldn't poke his head into the street without exposing his position to the hardman in the back of the van.

Getting to his feet, he sprinted along the curb, stopping two cars up, and ducked in behind a battered Ford station wagon. Its high roof would give him a little cover from the van man. The footsteps stopped suddenly, and Bolan could hear heavy panting—the gunner had stopped to catch his breath. Dropping to his knees, Bolan crawled along to the next gap, moving carefully to avoid warning his target. He could hear the rasp of his coat on the crisp snow.

The breathing had become inaudible, and Bolan listened intently under the wind. He counted slowly to ten, and when he still heard nothing, began to inch forward. A loud thump overhead caused him to roll and he looked up into the face of the gunner, who was standing on the roof of the car, an Uzi gripped firmly in both hands. The black hole of the suppressor was pointed straight at Bolan's head. Bolan brought up Big Thunder, knowing even as he moved the heavy automatic that it was already too late.

A sharp crack, then a second, split the wind and the gunner screamed in pain, swinging the Uzi in a tight arc. Its familiar spit danced on the pavement beside Bolan's head, spattering his face with snow. The gun rode high, then slipped away in a broad arc, hitting the roof of the car as the gunman pitched forward. He landed with a thud on the clotted snow, his booted feet draped over Bolan's legs.

The warrior heaved backwards, hauling himself out from under the dead man. His pants felt soggy where the slush had soaked through. He sighed and got to his knees, wondering where the shots had come from.

He ducked between two cars and watched the van. A brief burst of light flashed as the hidden gunman scrambled into the front seat. Bolan brought Big Thunder around and squeezed off two rapid shots. The heavy thud of the slugs tearing through the back of the driver's seat was followed by a continuous blare of the horn. The Executioner sprinted to the van and leaned in through the driver's open window. The man lay draped over the steering wheel, two ugly large holes just below and to the right of his left shoulder blade oozing blood.

"Good evening, *monsieur*. You and I have a few things to discuss."

Bolan whirled at the sound of the voice. "Who the hell are you?"

"Captain Lucien Picard, SDECE."

Bolan shook his head. "Not now."

CHAPTER SEVENTEEN

Bolan raced to the fallen Alvarez, Picard plodding along behind him. The wounded man lay facedown in the snow. A bright red patch around his right shoulder was evidence of serious bleeding. As Bolan knelt beside him, Alvarez groaned. "Give me a hand, Picard," Bolan snapped.

The latter reached down and grabbed Alvarez under the uninjured shoulder as Bolan tried to turn him over. Alvarez swiped one mittened hand halfheartedly at Bolan's hand, then groaned again. He tried on his own to sit up, but the pain was too intense.

Bolan succeeded this time in getting Alvarez on his back. Leaning over to open the coat, he noticed that one side of the wounded man's face was deathly white, possibly frost-bitten, where it had lain against the slush and snow. There was no point to fooling around outside. Alvarez needed medical attention, the sooner the better.

"Help me get him inside," Bolan said, grunting as he struggled to haul the man out of the snow. Alvarez struggled, as if trying to break free. "I'm all right," he mumbled. "Let me go."

The captain looked to Bolan for guidance, and the big guy shrugged. Picard let go, and Alvarez pitched forward. The Frenchman caught him, nearly losing his footing on the slippery pavement. Walking unsteadily, Picard half pushed and half dragged Alvarez toward the stone steps leading to the front door of the safehouse.

Picard stood to one side of the landing, supporting the semiconscious Alvarez, while Bolan opened the door with his key. The heavy glass was bulletproof and shatter resistant, and looked innocuous enough to the untrained eye. The reinforced frame—heavy steel under a wood veneer—

seemed ordinary, although better maintained than most on the block.

Picard stopped for a moment to catch his breath, then guided Alvarez through the doorway as Bolan held the door for him. When the heavy barrier was back in place, the case-hardened dead bolt snapped shut with a finality that was not unfamiliar to many New Yorkers of less exotic vocation. Bolan punched the numerical pad on the electronic lock of the inner door.

"Pretty fancy," Picard observed.

Bolan motioned him through to the inner hallway. Picard hoisted Alvarez again and stepped inside.

"Where to?"

"Third floor."

Bolan leaned against the glass at an angle, trying to see up the block where the van still stood, its engine still vainly signaling the heavens with meaningless scrawls of vapor.

"That won't attract any unnecessary attention, will it?" Picard asked.

"Not for a while, and especially not on a night like this. Eventually it might, but by then it will have been taken care of. I'll make the call as soon as I get upstairs. We have to get somebody here to look at him."

"Lead the way," Picard said. "I could use a cup of coffee."

Alvarez suddenly slipped to the floor, and Picard grabbed him by the uninjured shoulder. He hauled him upright, then bent quickly, tilting the man over one shoulder. When he straightened up, he had the now unconscious agent dangling like a sack of potatoes. Picard grunted, looked pointedly at Bolan's gun, but said nothing. He began to struggle up the steps, resting his weight as best he could on the smooth polished wood of the handrail.

On the third-floor landing, Bolan slipped past him. "This way." Picard grunted again, but followed without protest. Bolan quickly unlocked the door and stepped back for Picard to enter.

The Frenchman slipped the doll-like form of Alvarez forward through the door. Alison Brewer stood wordlessly in the foyer, one hand clenched to her mouth. She stared past Picard at Bolan, whose impassive features betrayed nothing of what he was feeling. He stepped in after Picard and handed the gun to Alison. "Watch him. I'll be right back."

Bolan disappeared through the inner door, and Alison stood trembling, the gun feeling heavier by the second. Only the distant drone of Bolan's voice kept her from screaming. When he returned, she took a deep breath. She was certain she hadn't drawn one the whole time he was in the other room.

"Alison, go in the back bedroom and stay there until I call you."

He took the gun from her and gestured to Picard. "I've put a call in for a doctor. Let's get him in the front bedroom."

The Frenchman placed his burden heavily but not ungently on the bed, then bent over to loosen Alvarez's collar. "He's lost a lot of blood, but I think he'll make it, if the doctor gets here quickly." He glanced at Bolan, but the big man said nothing. "I could use that coffee now."

"I have a few questions first," Bolan said. "To begin with, why were you outside tonight?"

"Can't we get something hot to drink before we talk? I'm nearly frozen. This is not exactly the most congenial climate to visit after spending a few weeks in the desert."

"First some answers, then we'll talk about coffee."

Picard seemed to mull over the proposition. After a moment's hesitation he nodded once. "Of course. I suppose I'd be just as careful, in your shoes."

"So?"

"I was following someone. I certainly had no idea this was going to happen."

"Who were you following?"

"One of the dead men. The driver, actually."

"Who was he?"

"I don't know."

Picard took a deep breath and held it. When it was obvious Bolan would say nothing until he received an answer, however unsatisfactory, Picard expelled the breath in a small explosion. "I don't know his name. I don't know any of their names."

"Then why follow them?"

"I started trailing the driver at Bardai, a small town in Chad. There was some sabotage at our air base there. I followed the saboteurs to Pic Bette, just over the border in Libya. There they met with the driver and several other men. I listened to their conversation, trying to decide what to do. It wasn't possible to follow them all, and I decided to follow the driver because he was coming here to the United States. That seemed like the most promising lead. I had a man with me, and he stayed with the others. The driver was the only man who left Libya, at least at that time."

"But . . . ?"

"But when I got here, I followed the driver for a day and a half. And I found one of the saboteurs had also come here to New York. I wanted to stay out of sight, gather as much information as I could. I was convinced the sabotage was part of a much larger operation. I didn't want to make a move until I knew more. I guess that's out of the question now."

"Anybody know you're here? Anybody on our side?"

"If you are asking whether your government was officially notified, the answer is no. But you can check it out through channels. Paris will confirm my identity and my assignment. There was not time to acquaint them with the recent particulars, however."

"What about the man with you? Wouldn't he have filed a report?"

"No. He was not SDECE. He was just an air-force sergeant. He had no idea who I was or what was going on. He simply joined in the chase after the saboteurs."

Bolan was beginning to relax. The guy's answers sounded square, and he could certainly sympathize with the need to act without consultation. Hell, half his professional life had been conducted in more or less the same fashion. And there was no denying the guy had done him a favor, saved his life. But it still had to be checked out. Plausibility cut both ways when a man had to decide who was who and what was what. The better the opposition, the better their cover.

The Frenchman eyed Bolan's AutoMag curiously, more like an appraiser than a man afraid it might be used on him at any moment. Bolan remained silent for a long minute, watching Picard, waiting for signs of nervousness, some shift in the eye or twitch of a muscle. The subject of his scrutiny, however, was almost placid. So often it came down to instincts, and Bolan's were finely honed. He'd learned to trust them, learned that you lived longer that way. Everything about Picard seemed genuine. It was time for a gamble.

The Executioner put his gun away.

The Frenchman turned and walked toward an overstuffed armchair against one wall, tossing a question over his shoulder. "Why were they after you?"

"They weren't. They were after Alvarez. When I saw him go down, I tried to help, and they turned their guns on me."

"And I suppose you just happened to be out for a walk on a night like this?"

Bolan glared at the impertinence, but Picard didn't seem to notice. He started to hum and steepled his fingers before asking, "When will the doctor get here?"

"Soon. Were you at the house in the East Village tonight?"

"The East Village? I don't know what that is."

"The old apartment building, down past Cooper Square."

Picard looked stunned for a moment. "You were following Alvarez, weren't you? That's why you happened to be there in the street when he got hit...." He stared expectantly at Bolan, but the big man showed no sign of surprise. Picard pressed on. "Do you know any of the men in that meeting? Were you part of it?" He paused, then said,

"No, you couldn't have been. You must have been outside, just as I was."

"What do you know about Stanley Mills?" Bolan asked.

"Never heard of him. Was he at the meeting?"

"You wouldn't happen to know anything about some stolen plastic explosives by any chance, would you?"

Picard took an unopened cigarette pack from his coat. He stared at the cellophane as he undid the band. Tearing it open, he tapped the pack smartly against the heel of one palm, extracted a cigarette and lit it with a match. Only then did he look back at Bolan. "I might," he said, smiling. "Why?"

When Bolan said nothing, Picard puffed on the cigarette a few moments. "At the risk of sounding the least bit naughty, let me make you a proposition."

Bolan waited.

Picard smiled again. "As you Americans say, I'll show you mine, if you'll show me yours."

Getting somewhere at last, Bolan relaxed for the first time since the shooting began. "You first."

CHAPTER EIGHTEEN

The Hungry Hessian was not going to threaten Twenty-One or, for that matter, McDonald's. Its decor had all the class of an aging camp follower, and needed twice the paint. It was so dark inside, some regular patrons were known to bring flashlights. It was not the sort of place Bolan would have chosen to hang out, but choice had little to do with his presence.

The seedy bar on the Lower East Side was, according to word on the street, the single best place to hook on as a merc. Those in the market, whether to hire or be hired, spent long hours at one of the dark tables, shuffling their feet in the rancid sawdust on the floor. He and Picard were going to try to get inside the mysterious organization the Frenchman swore was responsible for the bombing of the base at Bardai. Word was they were looking for marksmanship instructors and demolitions experts, in a hurry. Letting them foot the bill for transportation appealed to the sardonic Frenchman's sense of humor, and it made practical sense.

The smell hit Bolan as soon as he pushed the door open, reminding him of a barracks after a three-day leave. Soldiers were not known for their ability to control their drinking. An all-nighter or two, combined with large quantities of unfamiliar food, usually brought more than one bunkmate to his knees on any given Saturday. The consequent miasma was for neither the faint of heart nor the weak of stomach. Judging by the ripe air in the bar, at least a few of its patrons didn't bother to wait until they got home.

As the door creaked closed behind him, he stopped just inside the doorway, blinking to adjust to the gloom. If he didn't know better, he might have thought he'd been blinded by some light he'd never seen. After twenty or thirty seconds spent squeezing his eyes shut tight, outlines began to emerge. A handful of green-shaded overhead lamps, outfitted with bulbs unlikely to be found anywhere outside of a refrigerator, dangled over an occasional table, but the denizens of the bar avoided those tables with a kind of scrupulousness not seen in their choice of career.

Bolan moved into the room, careful to avoid stray feet and elbows as he threaded his way among the tables. As his eyes grew more accustomed to the darkness, he could see that half of the unlighted tables were occupied. A thin bluish-gray haze hung in the small halos surrounding the suspended lamps; the sweet aroma of grass formed an undercurrent beneath the stale, beery smell. It reminded Bolan of more than one Saigon dive, and he'd bet a year's pay most of those in the room had seen more than one Vietnamese back alley.

The Vietnam War, perhaps because it was unpopular, maybe because it had been lost, or maybe for both reasons and a dozen others, as well, seemed to have bred more than its share of lifetime soldiers. The bitterness and disillusionment of that conflict seemed to have scarred more than bodies, searing themselves into souls with all the permanence of a branding iron. War junkies, men who missed the smell of cordite and the stench of day-old blood, kept crawling into holes to wait like lizards for some twisted calling. When it came, they would crawl out again, change their colors to suitably mottled jungle rags and go off in search of thunder.

Bolan had known more than one such emotional cripple.

He walked through the sweet-smelling dark to a vacant table and sat down, facing the door, and realized almost at once that he was a virtual copy of a half dozen other men in the murky bar, each leaning on an elbow, chin propped on heel of hand, eyes boring through the subterranean twilight.

Looking from table to table, carefully, trying not to stare, Bolan surveyed his fellows one by one. The nearest man, who looked pasty even under the passive illumination, appeared to be nearly fifty. Under iron-gray hair, thin on top, cropped closely on the sides, he sipped distractedly at a draft. The head was almost gone, reduced to small flecks of foam scattered on the inside of the glass. The man was slender, almost painfully so, and weak eyes glittered dully behind thick rimless lenses. Bolan noticed they were bifocals and wondered why a man who needed such assistance was sitting in the Hessian. A stiffly starched blue oxford shirt with a button-down collar billowed out behind the man, nearly filling the space between his spine and the back of the chair. The fit was so nearly perfect, Bolan thought of the safety air bags in automobiles. With such a cushion carried right inside your shirt, you would need neither seat belt nor air bag to survive a high-speed collision.

Two more typical specimens of the breed sat whispering beyond the scholarly-looking man. The smaller of the two, vaguely Mediterranean of face and cast, chewed vigorously on an unlit cigar. As if he felt someone staring at him, he began to fidget, then suddenly locked his gaze on Bolan. He leaned forward and said something to his companion, then buried his face in a beer mug.

Bolan stood up and walked to the bar, where he ordered a beer. On the way back he passed close to the men's table and got a good look at the guy's companion. The latter glanced up, his eyes holding Bolan's for a long second, then turned away. The man's expression altered slightly, but the warrior wasn't sure whether the man had recognized him or was disappointed not to have done so.

Resuming his seat, Bolan turned his attention to the door, but something kept bringing his mind back to the two men at the table. There was something familiar about the second man. Bolan had either seen him someplace before, or was reminded of someone who closely resembled him.

Before he could decide which, a flurry of activity captured all eyes in the bar. Loud laughter just outside the door echoed in the stairwell, seemingly reinforced by the concrete walls just below street level. The door creaked open and three men entered, including one of the biggest men Bolan had seen in a long time. The man's bald pate shone dully under the dim overhead lights, as if his scalp had been lightly oiled. He said something to the others, who smiled as he cracked his knuckles. He laughed louder than the other two, a sound that seemed louder still in the claustrophobic bar.

Bolan checked his watch and glanced around the darkness one more time. Picard was already overdue. The Frenchman had some things to attend to, but the open call was slated for nine o'clock and he'd sworn he'd make it on time. It was now nine-fifteen.

The newcomers moved through the room, conscious of all eyes turned their way, and seeming to relish the attention. The bald guy swaggered a bit more broadly, and widened the sneer that seemed to be his normal expression. One of the others waved to the bartender, who came out from behind the bar.

Drying his hands on a damp apron, the man joined the three new arrivals and led the way toward a back room. He opened the door and leaned in to flick on the light. A dull green glow, brighter than that at the tables, spilled out of the back room. The bartender stepped in for a moment and waited for the others to follow. The big bald guy went first, and Bolan heard the scrape and thud of furniture being rearranged.

A moment later the bartender reappeared and slipped back behind the bar. He rattled around on a low shelf, then grabbed an upended pitcher and filled it with draft beer from a Coors tap. He slapped the jug onto a tray, added three glasses, then hoisted the tray and marched back to the small room. A low hum of voices stopped abruptly; the man reappeared and stood in the doorway.

He cleared his throat and looked around the front room. "Soup's on," he called, then made his way back to the bar.

Bolan watched the sudden scurry with amazement. The thin guy in the blue oxford danced gracefully through the throng and found himself first in line. Bolan kept his seat, not wanting to appear too anxious. Immediately behind the slender accountant type, the big man who'd given Bolan the once-over mumbled under his breath.

The front door opened, and someone slipped inside. He was halfway into the room before Bolan recognized Lucien Picard. By agreement, they were not going to apply together, knowing that the contract agents usually preferred to hire men who were strangers to one another. It gave the boss the upper hand if nobody on a crew was too comfortable with anyone else.

Picard sat down two tables away from Bolan, with his back to the big guy, and watched the developing scuffle at the head of the line. The smaller man, who would have seemed mousy even at an accounting convention, lurched forward, obviously propelled by the moose behind him. Somebody in the dark room laughed, but the accountant ignored it. He resumed his place as if nothing had happened.

The moose gave him another shove, this time harder, and he slammed into the doorframe with a bone-wrenching crash. The big man mumbled something Bolan couldn't hear. Whatever it was offended the accountant, and he lashed out so quickly, Bolan wasn't sure he'd seen it. The behemoth fell backward, holding both hands to his throat, and the accountant stepped forward to lean down. This time he moved more deliberately, but there was no mistaking the crack as he broke the moose's nose.

The big man's companion reached for his hip, but the accountant caught the hand in midair. "Don't," he whispered, and glared at the larger man with such contempt it seemed to freeze everyone and everything in the bar. The room was suddenly, utterly silent.

A moment later, the bald guy leaned through the door, all but blocking the sickly green light. "You assholes can't keep it together, get the hell out. We got serious business to do here."

He glanced at the man on the floor. "What the hell happened to you?"

The fallen man mumbled something through his hands, but it was unintelligible. "Looks like you better move on, buddy. You can't handle yourself in here, you sure as hell ain't no good to us."

Looking at the injured man's companion, he said, "Take him home. And when you get him there, tuck him in."

The behemoth spoke more clearly, and this time everyone in the bar understood him. The bald guy leaned down and hoisted him easily from the floor, a healthy portion of shirt crumpled in one huge fist. He tossed the man in the general direction of the door and watched him scatter tables and chairs as he tried to keep his balance.

The man with the paunch stepped out of the back room. "What the hell's holding things up, Load? We got a tight schedule. Let's haul it."

The bald guy nodded and stepped back into the room. A moment later the line started moving as, one by one, the eager applicants filed in, discussed their qualifications with the straw boss and tried like hell to sell themselves. Bolan stood in line, Picard two men behind him. The monotonous shuffle was soporific, and Bolan felt as if he were going to fall asleep.

As the line shortened Bolan could hear the questioning, and it was obvious what the contractors were looking for. Half the men in front of him couldn't pass a physical in an old-age home, and most of the others were out of touch with reality, and had little more than a hitch in the Army to recommend them.

As reluctant as he was to go through the process, he knew it would make his job much easier. If they trusted him, picked him themselves, they would be much less suspicious.

When his turn came, they had already chosen three men, including the oxford shirt. The three selectees sat in one corner of the room, each staring straight ahead, either afraid or unwilling to talk among themselves, or perhaps both.

The ruddy man with a bulge over his belt, the buttons of his shirt gaping a little and showing half-moons of T-shirt, had been doing most of the talking. He took a long look at Bolan, and smiled.

"You look like just what the doctor ordered. What's your name?"

"Belasko, Mike Belasko."

"Right. Any combat experience?"

"Some."

"Nam?"

Bolan nodded.

"What weapons you comfortable with?"

"What have you got?"

"Cocky son of a bitch, ain't he?" The questioner turned to the big bald man. "Load, what do you think?"

"What do I think? I think if he smartmouths me, I'll send him home in little pieces."

Bolan ignored the taunt. He looked impassively at the big man, who smiled broadly, content with himself and satisfied he'd intimidated the applicant.

"You know anything about demolitions?"

"A little."

"Plastique?"

"Yeah."

He turned to the paunchy man. "Okay." Pointing to the bench where the other three sat, he said, "Wait over there. We'll be done in a half hour."

"That's it?" Bolan asked.

"What'd you expect, an IQ test?" The bald giant laughed.

"I guess not," Bolan replied. "Nobody around to grade it."

CHAPTER NINETEEN

Mason Harlow watched Marielle brush her hair. She was sitting on the edge of the bed in her underwear. Harlow lay beside her, one hand resting on her hip. He squeezed it with disinterest, more a mechanical motion than an expression of affection.

"How'd you like to see New Orleans?" he asked. "It should appeal to you, being French and all. I mean, there's lots of French history down there. Besides, it's a hell of a lot warmer than New York."

"What's the matter, is your wife coming home?"

"No, she's still in London. Why?"

"What's wrong with the farm, then?"

"I won't be at the farm for a while."

"You don't mean to say you'd miss me, do you?" She put the brush down on the bed and turned to face him. She studied his features, but there was nothing there to tell her what he was thinking.

After a long pause Harlow heaved himself up onto one elbow and reached for her hand. "Yeah, I guess I would miss you."

"You guess?"

"Now, honey, don't go getting possessive on me. You know I hate that."

"I'm not getting possessive. But I do want to know where I stand. Is this a long-term thing we're having, or are you going to get tired of me? I'm over thirty, and I have to plan for my future, you know."

"Honey, you stay with me, and your future is set."

"Suppose I say no?"

"Why would you want to do that?"

"I hardly ever see you. You leave in the middle of the night and I don't hear from you for days, sometimes weeks."

"Then come with me to New Orleans."

"For how long?"

"I don't know, two, three days."

"Then what?"

"Then I have a business trip."

"Where to?"

"You don't need to know that."

Marielle stood and walked to the dressing table in a corner of the room. She grabbed a pair of jeans draped over the back of a chair and struggled into them, her back to Harlow. Without saying anything, she slipped a Nike sweatshirt over her head, taking care not to undo the work she'd just done on her hair. Harlow never took his eyes off her.

When she had finished dressing, she sat down and pulled on a pair of high-tops, tying them loosely and wrapping the ends of long green laces around the pure white leather of the sneakers. The entire performance took more than four minutes, but Harlow felt as if he hadn't drawn a breath the entire time.

Finally, as if she had made a point the best way she knew how, Marielle looked at him. "I'll go on one condition."

"You name it."

"I go on your business trip, too. I am tired of hanging around waiting for you. I want to see the world while I'm still young enough to enjoy it. And I don't mean a grand tour of the world's hotels. I want to see places, things. Meet interesting people."

Harlow sat up. He wasn't enamored of the idea. Marielle was a sharp trophy and a great piece, but the last thing he needed was another millstone, no matter how good in bed. He already had one woman's claws in him, right through to his wallet. But then, Tripoli was pretty boring, and Marielle would add a little spice to his stay, which threatened to be a long one. He sighed.

"All right, you can come, but I have a condition of my own."

"What is it?"

"If you get bored and want to come home, I'll send you home, but you have to promise you won't bug me again about going along. Fair enough?"

Marielle considered the offer for a moment. "Fair enough," she said. She grinned enigmatically for a moment, then in one fluid motion stood up and removed the sweatshirt. Walking toward the bed, she said, "Seal it with a kiss...?"

Mason Harlow smiled and lay back on the bed. He congratulated himself on another good idea.

THE BASE WAS EVERYTHING Bolan expected, and more. He'd seen a hundred like it, and never got used to it. The primitive conditions seemed to be a hallmark, as if training, of whatever kind, required early Stone Age facilities. It struck him that the universal trait of advisers—from football coaches to drill instructors—was an appreciation of the caveman mentality. It was as if you couldn't learn unless the Neolithic Age were replicated and force-fed to you...and as if mankind had learned nothing since.

He, Picard and four others had been met at the airport by two Neanderthals in jeeps. The three-hour drive since then had taken them through a Cook's tour of rural poverty. The run-down farms and battered barns and silos looked like something out of the Depression. Paint seemed to be scarce in rural Louisiana, or at least the will to apply it.

Heading into the marshland on the southern edge of Lake Pontchartrain, Bolan had flashed back to basic training, to Southeast Asia and a dozen other places, each of which had been the scene of training or combat. It struck him that much of the world's violence took place in its lushest vegetation, as if death and destruction could somehow be balanced by the fertility in which it occurred.

Now the warrior found himself staring at four barracks, their naked wood walls gleaming like old bone amid the greenery. The place had a hundred clones in various places around the world, from the Contra bases in Honduras to the old CIA camps in Guatemala. Bolan stared at the camp with a mixture of resignation and contempt.

The hardguy who had been his driver grabbed his arm. "You didn't expect nothing better, did you, buddy?"

Bolan turned to look at him, but said nothing.

"Grab your gear and get moving. You want a bunk, you'd best haul ass." He laughed, and brushed past Bolan to lead his half of the new contingent toward the nearest barracks.

The second group arrived as Bolan stepped onto the low wooden porch running the length of the barracks. He stood in the doorway, looking over his shoulder until he spotted Picard climbing down the second jeep. The second Neanderthal made a similar speech, then headed toward the barracks, his three new charges trailing along behind him.

When all the men were inside, the two goons stood aside and watched as they chose bunks and arranged their meager possessions. One or the other barked a command to hurry up every few minutes, but other than that there was no conversation.

When the men were finished, one of the goons stepped to the center of the long narrow room. "All right, listen up. The boss is going to be here later on, but we ain't gonna wait for him. We got exactly two days to get you guys in shape, and then we move out. All we want to do here is make sure you're as good as you claim. You make the team, you move on. You don't, we cut you loose right here."

One of the other new arrivals, the skinny accountant type—still wearing his blue shirt—asked, "How are we supposed to get home?"

"What's the trouble, Specs, throwing in the towel already? Look, you're all big boys, and this ain't no charity operation we're running here. You can get yourself home. If you can't cut it, you might as well leave now."

"Don't worry about me," Specs replied. "I can cut it. I just wanted to know as a point of information."

"What are you, some kind of college man? Point of information, shit. Listen up. We gonna get right to it. Tony will give you your weapons. First thing we want to do is get some idea of your shooting skills."

The man identified as Tony stepped outside and returned lugging a wooden crate. He slammed it down on a rough-hewn table, then took a survival knife from his belt and pried the lid loose. The men crowded forward, Bolan lagging a little behind, not wanting to seem too eager. Tony grabbed a rifle from the case and unwound the thin, oily rag in which it was wrapped.

Bolan recognized the weapon immediately. He heard Picard whistle softly, a sign that he, too, knew what it was—a Sauer S90. The rifle was scoped, and at more than a grand, Bolan knew he was looking at no ordinary weapon.

The warrior stood back with his arms folded, watching as Tony unwrapped a half dozen of the Sauers. When all the weapons were free, Tony grabbed one and handed it to Specs.

"Carter, get the ammo in the storage room, will you?" The other merc nodded, and disappeared. He was back in a couple of minutes with a large crate made of the same rough wood as the one that held the rifles, but which was more cubical in shape.

Carter dropped the ammo crate on the table and borrowed Tony's knife to pop the lid. The nails gave with a squeal, and the lid opened like a clamshell. Carter pushed it all the way back, not bothering to remove it, and hauled out a box of ammo. He dumped the shells on the table and started separating them into six groups. The hundred didn't divide evenly, so he opened a second box and extracted a few more, until each cluster of shells numbered eighteen.

Tony glared at Specs, who was mumbling something to the man next to him. "Something bothering you, pal?"

"That's not an assault rifle."

Tony glared at him. "So what?"

"I thought we were going to be training guerrillas? They can't use that kind of rifle. It's not a combat weapon."

"What're you, a wise guy, or what? Just shut up and listen. If I want any guff from you, I'll ask for it."

Specs clamped his jaw shut with an audible snap. He said nothing further, but it was obvious he wasn't happy. Bolan made a mental note. It might come in handy.

"All right," Tony bellowed. "Anybody here familiar with this weapon? How about you, Four Eyes?"

Specs didn't respond, and Tony smiled. "Owlface over there is right. This is not an assault weapon. But it is an ideal weapon to demonstrate your abilities as a marksman. No way in hell we're trucking you assholes halfway around the world to train people if you can't hit the broad side of a barn. Sooo...we're gonna go out to the range, and you'll show us what you can do. Grab a gun and some ammo to get started, and we'll bring some more in a little while. Carter will show you where the range is. Any questions?"

When none was forthcoming, Tony smiled again. The expression was getting on Bolan's nerves.

Bolan grabbed one of the Sauers and pocketed the dozen and a half shells. Carter led the way through the door, and Bolan brought up the rear. They resembled a bunch of Boy Scout rejects on a weekend hike, and Bolan felt vaguely ridiculous. There was something about this whole setup that didn't ring true. He was beginning to wonder whether Picard's information was accurate, and if so, whether they might have picked up with the wrong bunch. It was almost laughable, trying to picture these guys training terrorists.

On the other hand, when six-year-olds could be trained to kill for the Ayatollah, anything was possible in this worst of all possible worlds.

CHAPTER TWENTY

The sun was rising higher in the sky, its light bleaching the green from the surrounding woods and turning it a dark gray. Despite the lateness of the year, it was humid, even sticky. Bugs swarmed in the air, their angry buzz a constant undercurrent like white noise. The forest itself was silent, as if everything were watching the six men arrayed in a ragged line on their stomachs.

Tony and Carter strutted back and forth like parodies of British officers in a B-movie. Tony did most of the talking, swaggering from end to end, the cardboard silhouettes of the targets jutting out of the woods behind him. His hands were clasped behind his back, and the sleeves of his shirt were rolled above the biceps, as if he had been studying the style of punks from the fifties. Even his closely cropped hair threatened to break out into a flamboyant pompadour. From time to time he paused, flexing the muscles of his arms self-consciously. Bolan kept waiting for him to start snapping his fingers, while some hidden orchestra broke into something from *West Side Story*.

Bolan glanced once at Picard, who seemed absorbed, even fascinated, by the histrionics.

"Now listen up," Tony barked, planting himself at the center of the line. "We got lots of ammo, so don't worry about it. When I get out of the way, I want you to bang away. Make sure you aim at your own target. When you finish the first batch of ammo, we'll tally your scores and set up for a second go-round. We're going to grade you on accuracy and speed, so don't lay there with your thumbs up your asses."

Satisfied with his performance, Tony permitted himself another swagger up and down the line. When he returned to the center point, he asked, "Any questions?"

The diminutive blue oxford shirt responded. "You got any preference on killzones, or do we just go for the bull's-eye?"

Tony snorted. "If you think you're that good, take your pick. For the rest of you, the bull's-eye is good enough. At this range, I'll be surprised you don't all get a few Maggie's drawers."

That seemed to satisfy Specs, and when he said nothing further, Tony concluded, "All right, then, load up and get to it. Carter, start the watch."

The other man, who had said nothing to the marksmen, clicked a stopwatch and backed away from the shooters. Tony stepped between Bolan and Specs, rather than walking the width of the range and risking a shot from an over-eager applicant.

Bolan took his time, working with a practiced fluidity rather than haste. After slipping five shells into the magazine of the Sauer, he checked the action and drew a bead on the bull's-eye of his target. He fired one round, gauged the hit, then adjusted the scope to compensate for the slightly high strike.

He emptied the magazine quickly, placing his next four shots in a precise row from left to right across the target figure's chest. The noise of the firing was incessant as each of the shooters ran through his allotment of ammunition. Bolan finished firing third, and was conscious of someone standing behind him.

Still prostrate, he turned to find Tony looking down-range, squinting at the target. "Not bad, buddy, not bad. You do much shooting with a scope?"

Bolan shook his head.

"You could have been a little faster, but I like your concentration. Let's check the scores." The roar of gunfire ended while he was speaking, and the last few words were shouted against a sound that wasn't there. The other shooters swiveled their heads to see why he was yelling.

"Carter, check the targets, mark them, then put new ones up."

Carter worked his way along the row of silhouettes, marking each score on a clipboard, marking the target itself with the number of the shooter's position, and slipping new silhouettes in place on the wooden frames supporting them. Bolan noted that the new targets, rather than consisting of rough concentrics approximating the human form, similar to the array of isobars on a weather map, were more like those used at police qualifying ranges, with killzones clearly marked.

While Carter set up the new targets, Tony distributed more ammunition, dropping twenty shells—enough for four full loads—in the damp earth next to each of the shooters. When he had finished, he called for attention.

"All right, this time we're going to go for something a little different. You'll notice four killzones marked on the silhouettes. I want you to distribute your shots equally. Time, as you might expect, is now a factor. This test will be in four parts. When we've completed this round of the testing, there'll be one more. This time, we won't start the clock until your weapons are loaded. And for each round the clock stops as soon as the first man empties his weapon. And so do you. Anybody fires after the clock stops, he's automatically disqualified. Hop to it."

Tony paced back and forth again, this time restlessly. He stayed behind the men, and Bolan wondered whether it was supposed to make them more nervous. He checked the line out the corners of his eyes, but no one seemed unduly apprehensive.

"Everybody ready?"

The question itself cracked like a gunshot. When no one objected, Tony started the count. "Five...four...three...two...one...fire!"

This time, Bolan didn't waste any time. With mechanical precision, he blew out the small oval superimposed on the target figure's head. Through the scope, he could see a few tatters of black paper waving in the wind.

He finished first, and Tony knelt beside him to clap him on the back. "Nice work, Belasko. I like your style." Bolan heard the creak of Tony's knees and the squeak of boot leather as he straightened up. The instructor's voice, when he spoke again, came from high above his head. Bolan half turned, and felt the toe of Tony's boot on his hip. "Don't turn around. The target's what's important, buddy."

Tony walked away, his feet squishing on the soft, damp earth. Without looking, Bolan knew there would be small, footprint-shaped pools of water where the big man had stepped.

"All right. Belasko, here, makes the rest of you guys look like pussies. You want to hang in here, you better take care of business. Next round, ready? Five...four... three...two...one...fire!"

Bolan quickly reloaded the Sauer's magazine, his fingers getting into the precise sequence of motions of their own accord. He was aware of a slight distance between himself and his actions, as if he were watching himself from a considerable height. He was not unfamiliar with the peculiar, almost dizzying sensation, but he had never gotten used to it. Something in him resented the loss of conscious control, even though he knew that his life frequently depended on it. In the field, there was often no substitute for the disembodied response of a finely honed sensibility on autopilot.

Bolan fired the first shot, this time aiming for the left shoulder of the target. This area was larger than the first, but only a few inches from top to bottom. For a moment he forgot about the circumstances, getting into the process, relishing every placement. He was an artisan relishing his own skill at an esoteric craft.

The smell of cordite tickled his nostrils, and the buck of the Sauer felt good, solid against his shoulder. Once again he finished first, this time opting for a tight row laterally across the shoulder of the target. He smiled slightly in satisfaction, then realized he ought not to be too perfect. He could not afford that loss of control that placed achievement above reason. There was some hidden purpose to this trial, and it would behoove him to lie back a little, not let them see just how good he was.

He watched Carter move across the row of targets, his clipboard held at an angle in an almost girlish pose. The delicacy of Carter's movements contrasted with his bulk as he scribbled on the score sheets.

Tony's bellow startled Bolan, and he turned to look over his shoulder at the swaggering instructor. "You guys better get it in gear now. Belasko is beating the pants off you. You got to remember, only the top three make the team."

Bolan held back for the rest of the test. When the fourth round was completed, Tony announced the scores. Bolan had placed second behind Specs. Picard was a distant third.

The three top qualifiers were led away, while Carter stayed behind with the losers. Tony seemed in unusually good spirits, whistling scraps of pop tunes through his teeth. The rasping and decidedly unmusical sound grated on the nerves, and it was all Bolan could do to keep himself from tapping the instructor on the shoulder and asking him to be quiet.

Back at the barracks Tony led the three men past their own quarters to another of the low wooden buildings. He clomped onto the wooden porch and rapped at a rickety-looking screen door. The merc turned to look at the three men behind him, standing just off the porch in a tight semicircle.

Rapping again, this time a little louder, Tony turned back and leaned forward with his nose to the screen. "Wait here a minute," he said, yanking the door open and stepping into the shadows.

Bolan heard Tony's heavy boots on the wooden planking, then a muffled conversation. He looked at Picard, who smiled quietly, as if proud of himself.

"I guess we did all right, no?" he asked.

"Yeah, I guess. But what the hell is this all about?" Specs answered.

"Doesn't matter to me as long as the money's there on Fridays."

"I don't like it," Specs whispered. "Something ain't kosher about this. I thought we were supposed to train people. Looks more like we're being tested for some kind of hit squad, or something." He laughed uneasily.

"So what?" Picard shrugged. "You wouldn't have come this far if you had scruples."

"Yeah? Maybe you don't give a damn what you do for money, but I have my principles."

"What bank you keep them in?" Picard said. He smiled disarmingly, but Specs glared at him before turning away.

Tony was back to the door before Specs could respond. He held the door wide and invited them in. "Follow me."

They walked through the dark room, Tony leading the way into a small office at the far end. He stood in one corner. "You all met Mr. Harlow, I believe."

Harlow was seated behind a scarred wooden desk. He wore a khaki shirt half-unbuttoned, its sleeves rolled up past his elbows. He shuffled a set of manila folders into a neat pile and tapped the top one with a thick finger.

"You guys don't leave many footprints, do you?" He stared at the trio, then indicated some folding chairs with a wave of his hand. "Sit down. Which one of you is Martin?"

Specs cleared his throat. "That's me."

"You were the best shot, I understand. That right?"

Specs nodded. "Guess so."

"How is it I can't find out too much about any of the three of you?" He waited expectantly, but no one said a word. "I'm not complaining, mind you. In fact, I kind of like it. But I also like to know what I'm getting for my money. Understand? That's why I did some checking."

"Yes, sir," Specs said.

"Langley doesn't have anything at all on two of you. And nothing much on Belasko."

Bolan shrugged. "Maybe there's nothing to know."

"Maybe...maybe." Harlow stretched, then covered his mouth to suppress a yawn. "Right now, you don't have any idea why I hired you. I know what I told you in New York, and that's true, as far as it goes. But there's more to it. It'll all become clear in due course. The Company always operates on a need-to-know basis. I imagine you understand what that means."

"Sure," Picard said. "It means you'll tell us what you want to tell us, and we can believe it or not. The truth, insofar as it is knowable, isn't something that matters."

"If I didn't know better, Mr. Picard, I'd say you were a cynical little bastard. Would I be right?"

"I also operate on a need-to-know basis, Mr. Harlow. And you don't need to know that."

Harlow laughed, shaking his head. "Fucking wise guys. They're everyplace you go. Anyhow, you're right. Just watch your step and do what you're told. The rest will take care of itself. So if you have no questions, we have a deal."

Harlow smiled broadly.

CHAPTER TWENTY-ONE

Mack Bolan and Lucien Picard sidestepped their way through a tangled throng of people. The streets of the French Quarter were crowded on a Saturday night. The evening on the town was supposed to be their "reward" for making the team, all expenses paid and no questions asked. But working his way down Bourbon Street, the warrior had a head full of unasked questions. So far, two men were dead, and he didn't seem any closer to explaining that fact than he had been before they died.

Picard had some information, and a larger supply of speculation. It all made sense, but it was too sketchy and the holes in the explanation would accommodate a Mack truck. That Mason Harlow was into something was certain. That it was tricked out in enough cheap finery to please a whore and enough glitter to make a third-rate magician smile was certain. But Harlow played his cards close to his vest. His explanations were full of innuendo, like the sales pitch of a used-car salesman, full of partial truths and used-to-be-sos.

The attempted hit on Alvarez troubled him more than most of the glitches. It was far from clear that Alvarez himself was clean. He showed up at a Company safehouse right behind Bolan and Alison Brewer. That could be explained easily enough. He was, or used to be, a Company man. Brognola had been able to determine that much, but little more. The big boys at the spook house were not noted for volubility. They protected their own, once and future. And there was one big collective ass to be covered. That was the specialty of the house.

But then somebody tried to take Bolan out, and Alvarez wasn't in the clear on that. A few hours later Andrews showed up dead, as dead as Flak Mitchell and with about as much information. Then Alvarez sat down with a couple of Harlow's men, and Stanley Mills, once one of the Company's own. It was possible the whole thing was a spook show, and Alvarez had been thrown to the wolves: he had outlived his usefulness, so it was okay to take him out. It covered tracks, even laid a false trail, and cost nobody a thing.

But whose trail was being covered? And more to the point, why?

Picard swore he could tie Harlow to the bombing of a French air base in Chad. Harlow dropped hints that he was plugged in, working on something deeper than deep. Those facts could be reconciled, but not easily.

Bolan and Picard moved past a dozen restaurants advertising creole delights and good-time jazz, and at the corner of Bourbon and St. Philip, the Frenchman grabbed Bolan's sleeve. "That's it, no?" He indicated a small sign reading Maison Dominique.

"That's it," Bolan agreed.

They ducked through the crowd and stepped off the curb, waiting for the traffic to grind to yet another halt as the light changed. Picard led the way, choking just a little as the noxious fumes of a hundred cars swirled around him.

The restaurant was down two steps from the street, its front windows laced in delicate scrolls of wrought iron painted a glossy black. The woodwork around the door and windows was ornate, and covered in a muted red, flat enough not to reflect any of the neon or passing headlights. They stepped through a small door, Bolan ducking to keep from hitting his head on the lintel.

Inside, a beautiful young brunette, dressed like something out of a Napoleonic epic, waited behind an elaborately carved podium that was lighted by a slim brass lamp.

"Gentlemen, may I help you?"

"Three for dinner, *s'il vous plaît*," Picard cooed.

"You have reservations?" she asked, picking up the red leather register.

"No, we don't."

She dropped the book back on the podium. "Very good, sir. This way, please."

She led the way down another pair of steps and through open French doors. The room beyond was larger than it appeared from the street, and must have been carved out of the basement of several adjacent buildings. With a swish of taffeta the hostess led the way across the large, dimly lit room. When the two men were seated, she asked, "Do you want to leave a message for the third party?"

Picard gave her his best Continental smile. "No, thank you, *mademoiselle*, he'll find us."

She nodded curtly, as if to say she'd heard it all before, and he should quit wasting his pseudocharm on someone who knew better. "Very well."

Picard watched her walk back toward the entrance. "Nice shoulders," he observed.

Bolan ignored him.

"So Alvarez is recovering nicely, eh?" Picard asked, changing the subject abruptly.

"So I'm told."

"What do you make of Harlow?"

"I'm not sure. The guy is full of hot air, but I don't know whether he's conning us or himself."

"Maybe both," Picard suggested. "But I got a feeling we're on the right track."

"Why?"

"It all fits. This training thing, I can't figure what it's about, but I've been listening to Tony and Carter. The plane leaves tomorrow for England, and we pick up another flight, a charter, and it isn't going to Malta. That's just a cover for the real destination."

"Which is?"

"Tripoli."

"I can't buy it," Bolan said. "It's too sloppy, too many loose ends."

"What do you mean?"

"Think about it, Lucien. If you were running some kind of undercover operation, would you let those three guys walk away, the guys who didn't make the cut? This looks more like a hit than guerrilla training. If you were running a school for assassins, would you let some flunk-outs walk around loose?''

Picard mulled it over, fiddling with a bread stick. He was about to answer when a busboy appeared with a silver pitcher. He righted three water glasses and filled two of them with a tinkle of ice. He left the third empty and carried off the fourth. When the busboy had gone, Picard said, "No. That's not very smart. But then Harlow doesn't seem that smart.''

"Don't bet on it. I've seen guys like him before. Half the time there's more under the surface than you'd expect. They want people to think they're dumber than they are. It gives them an edge. You get lazy, you underestimate them, and when you're least expecting it, they take your head off. Sometimes literally.''

"Have your sources put anything together on him?''

"Bits and pieces so far, nothing much. There's more, but he's got a network that would boggle your mind. So many threads, and you follow one only to get caught in three more. You pick one of those, and you run out of string.''

"Is he still connected, like he says?''

"Nobody seems to know. Or at least nobody's talking.''

Bolan looked up in time to see Alvarez in the doorway, nodding to the hostess. The agent watched her leave, then turned and walked toward their table. He sat down without ceremony. "Sorry I'm late.''

"No problem. Glad you could make it," Bolan said. He looked at the man carefully, with the thoughtful expression of a carnival man trying to guess his weight. He noticed the sling under Alvarez's jacket, one empty sleeve dangling like a limp flag. "How's the arm?''

"It's been better. I guess this is Picard?''

"That's right," the Frenchman said. "Nice to meet you.''

"Nice to meet you," Alvarez responded. "Nice to be *able* to meet you. I guess I owe you one.''

"You can pick up the check." Picard was smiling, but Alvarez looked at him sharply, as if for some hidden meaning.

"What have you got on Harlow?" Bolan asked.

"Why don't we order? Then I'll fill you in, when we can talk without interruption."

He signaled for the waiter, who took their order for a round of drinks. They placed their food order at the same time, waving aside the obligatory recitation of the daily specials. When the waiter had gone, Alvarez drummed his fingers on the table thoughtfully.

"Harlow has quite a history, and quite an operation. Six years in the Marines, followed by six more in CIA then four in Navy Intelligence. The funny thing is, half the people I talk to never heard of him, the other half say he's still an agent. But nobody knows for whom. I checked in with a couple of old friends at Langley, and all they'll say is that they know him."

"What's he doing now?" Bolan leaned forward.

"He's running something called Worldwide Specialty, Inc. They have three or four offices, one in D.C., one in New York, one in London and a couple or three floating offices in Europe and the Middle East. Half his payroll is former intelligence people. Maybe not even former."

"What do you mean?"

"Well, I'm not sure. Seems Harlow has been recruiting men left and right, everything from regular Army to mercs. Sends them off to do this and that, and the RA guys pick up where they left off with their old units as soon as they get home. They get official leave. Harlow's got a fistful of strings he can pull."

Alvarez picked up Picard's water glass. "You drinking this?"

When Picard shook his head, the agent took a long pull and smacked his lips. "Damn medication makes me thirsty. Thanks."

He seemed to be planning his next chapter, idly drawing a circle on the thick linen tablecloth, then smoothing it out with his palm. Finally he resumed. "Worldwide is even more interesting. It's an old CIA proprietary. Harlow leveraged a buyout when he left NI. The only thing is, nobody knows where he got the money."

"Family?" Bolan asked.

"Uh-uh. His folks were dirt-poor. Farmers, or something, in the Northeast. Nope, if he got the money from them, IRS will be more than curious."

"Then maybe it's still a Company company," Bolan offered. "Could be the buyout was a dummy."

"Maybe," Alvarez agreed.

"What are they into?"

"You name it. Electronics, security, mining technology, oil drilling equipment, weapons. The whole nine yards. And his letterhead looks like a spook's *Who's Who*. Guys from CIA, DIA, NSA, State and a couple of admirals and generals. I don't know what he's up to, but if it's genuine, it's pretty impressive."

"Look," Bolan said, "we have to know everything there is to know about Harlow. And I don't think we have very much time to get our act together."

"I did manage to find somebody who knew him, a former boss, and he doesn't like Harlow one bit. I know an enemy is a tainted source, but we shouldn't worry about it. I'd rather err on the side of excess. I have an appointment with the guy tomorrow," Alvarez said. "If I get what I expect to, we'll have the info we need by tomorrow night. When are you flying out?"

"Four in the morning."

"Shit! All right, don't worry about it. I'll find you as soon as I can."

CHAPTER TWENTY-TWO

Mack Bolan looked out the window of the chartered 707. He could see very little of the night through the small oval glass. Off in the distance a low line of lights glittered through a haze like a mirage on the edge of the horizon, winking in and out of view. He felt like an immigrant arriving in a strange new country, knowing little of where he was and even less of what might happen to him.

The plane had parked on a tarmac apron way off at one end of the unidentified airfield. He could see puddles of water on the ground beneath the wings, and a dim reflection of the sleek outline of part of the big jet. The boarding had been accompanied by more mumbo jumbo than a boys' club initiation ceremony. They had been blindfolded and led out of the black-windowed bus, and once on board they had been instructed to leave the blindfolds in place until told to remove them.

Unused to feeling helpless, resenting the forced dependence and more than a little aware of unaccustomed vulnerability, Bolan had been helped into a seat and buckled in. He didn't like it at all.

When the plane had finally taken off, an unfamiliar voice, probably that of the pilot, had told them they could remove their blindfolds, and Bolan had whipped his off in a hurry. The shade was down on the window, and he snapped it up, still blinking against the compression of the cloth, his eyes blurry, shot through with small phosphene flashes.

He had tried to figure out where he was, but they were already high in the air and the runway lights of the airfield below had winked off before he could get a fix on them. The surrounding countryside was bleak and virtually unlit. In the middle of the night, only an occasional lamp or shaded window in an isolated farmhouse or two could be seen.

The runway had been rough, suggesting the base was either small or poorly maintained. There had been no noise to speak of in the brief passage from bus to plane, and except for an occasional warning to watch his step, no one had said a word. He wanted to know where the airfield was, because he didn't like *not* knowing, and because something told him that all the rules by which he played had suddenly been canceled. This was alien territory, the kind of place where medieval cartographers had drawn vast blanknesses and warned of the danger with the simple advisory, "Here be dragons."

But what dragons?

And where was here?

A sudden burst of light brought him back to the moment, and a large vehicle rolled up. He could just see past its brilliant head- and worklights, and by its contours recognized it as a fuel truck. Four men scurried around, but their costumes told him nothing. Dressed in nondescript blue coveralls, they could have been anyone, working anywhere. Paying out the lines to refuel the plane, they worked with all the feverish activity of cartoon dwarfs. One man climbed into the cab, and the big diesel engine roared as they started to pump aviation fuel into the bowels of the Boeing.

The same man jumped down from the vehicle, and Bolan caught a glimpse of a vaguely familiar color as the half-zipped coveralls yawned for a second then closed. A sudden roar erupted overhead, and the all too familiar whine of a high-performance fighter peaked and died. Bolan crammed his face against the glass to get a look at the plane, but it was gone before he could get a fix on its location.

Peering over the back of the seat in front of him, he spotted Picard, also glued to the window. The hoses fell away, and with a final flurry of activity the dwarfs withdrew, their truck backing away and vanishing in the swirling fog. The plane rumbled beneath Bolan's feet and shuddered as it began to taxi. Nosing around, it began to roll faster, and with the suddenness of a paparazzo's flash, twin lines of fire exploded off into the distance. The runway lights bathed the plane and the puddled tarmac, erasing all other light, and for a moment Bolan found himself in a finite universe of tar and rainwater.

The big plane picked up speed and Bolan watched the flaps in wonder. It still amazed him, as many times as he had seen it and from whatever angle, that something so large and so heavy could move with such deliberate grace. The runway began to fall away, and the lights grew smaller. They passed over the red and blue line at the end of the runway, then the fog swirled in and swallowed the plane completely. Even the tar was gone now, and the world was nothing more than gray suspension.

The plane continued to climb, and burst through the top of the storm. The stars were back, brighter for their absence, and Bolan caught a glimpse of familiar constellations. The seat belt warning bonged, and the light went out. He stood to stretch. They had been in the air for nearly eight hours now, and his legs felt stiff and cramped. He walked to the rear of the plane to the men's room, bracing himself on the backs of seats as the plane dipped and rose, buffeted by the turbulent air.

Standing at the rear of the cabin, he snapped a plastic cup from the dispenser and filled it with water. He stood facing front, drinking the water with a thoughtful inattention. He counted heads quickly, making it eighteen, including himself, only four of whom he recognized. Picard and Specs, like himself survivors of the entrance exam, and Tony and Carter, the apelike instructors, were the only familiar figures.

The other thirteen could have been anyone, but probably included analogs both of himself and of Tony and Carter. Blindfolded, he had been unable to tell how many men were similarly kept in the dark.

He noticed that Picard and Specs had seats to themselves, as did a handful of the others. Tony and Carter sat together, and he wondered whether the other pairs were also instructors. It made sense, and in the absence of more concrete information he accepted the assumption. Having a working hypothesis made him feel more secure, less vulnerable.

As he made his way back to his seat, the warrior carefully scrutinized the seating arrangements, with the same nervous care a first-time flier gives to the flight attendant's discussion of exits and oxygen masks. Bolan always worked on the theory that a little knowledge was a dangerous thing, but not nearly as dangerous as none at all.

In his line of work, what you didn't know could get you killed.

Bolan dropped into his seat and stared out the window. He was exhausted and closed his eyes. Conscious that his scrutiny might be noticed and call undue attention to him, he slept.

MARIELLE TREBEC GLANCED nervously around her. The hotel was well kept, but seemed bizarre, alien. Unlike most European hotels, this one did not swarm with camera-toting tourists. The brazen blare of American English was absent, as was the distant monotony of Muzak in the lobby.

Tripoli was not what she had expected. She fiddled with her handbag as she sat, crossing and uncrossing her legs nervously. The air, although conditioned, seemed full of heat and sand. She saw no other women, and the men who drifted through the lobby seemed unduly conscious of her.

She felt naked, and it was not a comfortable sensation. She tugged at her short skirt, but it refused to cover her knees. The light blouse, almost transparent, seemed a magnet to passing eyes, and she understood now why Mason Harlow had insisted she wear a bra.

"Trust me, Marielle, I know what I'm talking about." And apparently he did.

She was exhausted from the circuitous trip. The New Orleans flight to London had taken forever, the flight from London to Malta seemed longer still, although it wasn't. But worst of all had been the flight on a small jet from Malta to

Tripoli. Now that she was here, she wanted only to go to their room and sleep.

She watched Harlow at the check-in desk, his jacket slung over a shoulder, half-moons of perspiration under his arms reminding her of the oppressive heat outdoors. It seemed to be taking him forever, and she wondered whether she was losing her grip. She had always been proud of her iron nerves, but they seemed to be failing her now. Being alone in America or Berlin or Paris was one thing. Being alone in a culture that was so alien to her it might as well have come from the moon or Venus was entirely another.

Finally Harlow finished at the desk. He waited for a bell-hop to take the key and spoke to him in rusty French, indicating the luggage. When he had finished, he crossed the lobby with a huge smile on his face. Marielle noticed the stubbled whiskers and realized the trip had taken its toll on Harlow, as well. Although he was doing his best to seem buoyant and good-humored, something was eating at him. She could see it in his eyes. The irrepressible confidence was beginning to erode.

He dropped onto the smooth leather beside her and patted her knee. "Tired, huh?"

"Yes," she said. "Very."

"See, I told you it was no picnic. But business is business, and I got to hustle to make a buck. I guarantee, you'll never ask to go on another business trip with me when this one is over."

Marielle said nothing. She inhaled deeply, held it for a long moment, then let it out in a long silent whistle. She stood up and tugged at her skirt again, wishing she had worn pants, although Harlow had warned her against it. At least she wouldn't have felt so defenseless.

"You ready?" Harlow asked, getting to his feet.

"Yes."

"Let's go, then."

He led the way across the lobby, heading toward the elaborate bronze doors of the elevators. One swished open as soon as he pressed the button, and they stepped in quickly, turning to face the lobby.

On the ride up Marielle leaned against the wall of the car. Harlow looked at her with a puzzled expression on his face. "Are you okay?"

"Yes."

"You sure you're not sick or anything?"

"I am just tired, that's all. I'll be fine after a little rest."

"Well, you can rest up tonight. I have a meeting in a couple of hours, so you can get a good night's sleep."

Marielle glanced at her watch. Harlow noticed the gesture.

"I know, but time, tide and business wait for no man. My father used to say that."

"Was he a businessman?"

Harlow snorted. "Hell no, he was a farmer. And not a very good one, either. Why the hell do you think I work so hard? I told myself once I left that farm I would never go back. I'll be damned if I'll end up like him."

"You don't sound very fond of him."

"Fond? No, I guess not. Why should I be?"

"He was your father, after all. Family is important."

"Maybe in France, honey." He patted her hip with one rough hand. "But not in the good old U.S. of A. Dog eat dog. Get what you can, and step on anybody who tries to get in your way. Making money is all that counts. Any way you can."

"That isn't the most moral approach to doing business, is it?"

"Fuck it. I like what money can buy, honey. And I'll do whatever I have to, to get it. You know that saying, you can never be too rich or too thin? Well, I don't give a shit about thin. But I swear I'll never be too rich."

The elevator bounced to a halt, and Harlow stepped out before Marielle could respond. Following him down the hall, she realized she didn't even have a response. How could you argue with a man with so single-minded a purpose?

The door to their room was already open, and the bell-hop stood to one side, the bags already neatly arrayed on the luggage rack. Harlow thanked him, fished a five-dollar bill out of his pocket and stuffed it into the extended palm.

The bellhop looked at the bill for a second, as if he weren't sure what it was.

"That's the only real money in the world, kid. U.S. dollars. Take it."

The young man folded the bill carefully and tucked it with great ceremony into his hip pocket. He bowed with what Marielle took to be deliberate sarcasm and closed the door behind him as he left. Harlow seemed to notice nothing amiss. When the door closed, he threw the latch and turned to Marielle.

"You too tired for a quickie before I go?"

CHAPTER TWENTY-THREE

No one noticed the Peugeot parked across from the Saudi Arabian ambassador's residence. It wasn't new, it wasn't old. Its color was unremarkable and it needed to be washed, but just a little.

Packed in the trunk was one hundred pounds of plastique. The small electronic device planted in the center of the massive block of explosive was smaller than a pack of cigarettes, and just as deadly.

Barouk Ali Yassan, the Saudi ambassador to France, was tall and slender. Unlike most of his counterparts in the Arab world, he preferred Western dress. His black hair waved back off a high forehead, calling attention away from his expensive suit, custom-made in Rome by a tailor who earned less in a month than Yassan had paid for it. The Arab's car was a Cadillac Seville. Too large to navigate the Paris traffic with reasonable dexterity, it suited Yassan's image of his station, and more to the point, of himself. The slight reddish tint of his cheeks wasn't evidence of embarrassment at his social advantages.

As the Cadillac nosed through the wrought-iron gates embedded in the ivy-drenched fieldstone wall—behind which the ambassador conducted those social obligations incumbent on a representative of one of the world's richest countries—a second Peugeot cranked its engine. While its driver shifted into gear, the passenger craned his neck over the rear seat. "Ready," he said.

He counted slowly as the Cadillac crossed the pavement and edged into the street. "Three...two...one..."

"Bingo!"

The second syllable was lost in a roar as the first dusty, undistinguished Peugeot mushroomed toward the early sky, just losing its morning haze. A ball of fire ballooned outward, enveloping the Seville, shrouding it momentarily in black smoke. Then the heavy American car, as if its driver had forgotten something, backed awkwardly toward the stone wall, this time not bothering with the gate. It squashed against the wall, and as if in slow motion, collapsed in on itself until its fuel tank ruptured. Kindled by the fiery scrape of metal on stone, the gasoline ignited, flickered, then blew.

The ambassador and his chauffeur were killed instantly. Not so lucky was the back-seat passenger. The ambassador's eleven-year-old son was still conscious as the car caught fire.

No one noticed the second unremarkable Peugeot as it left the curb—and the scene—as slowly as it had arrived. The driver was more relaxed now, his passenger smiling.

"Bingo!" he said.

HARROD'S WAS BUSY. It was nearly Christmas, although the seasonal rush was still to come. Across Brompton Road, a young man stared out a window on the sixth floor, watching the heavy traffic. So many people bustling around, it was hard to know where they were all going, and how they managed to get there.

The small room in which he sat was cluttered with mops and pails, stacks of paper goods and rolls of hand towels for the dispensers in the Ladies and Gents. The janitor, whose room it was, slumped in a corner, bleeding onto the discolored tile floor. Cleaning up would be a problem for someone else, this time.

The young man reached down for his gym bag, unzipping it with a tug. He worked quickly, without so much as a glance at his busy fingers. The room was quiet except for the occasional muffled click of well-oiled metal on metal, the rasp of thread on thread.

Gently, almost lovingly, he placed five flat black metal containers on the radiator housing just below the windowsill. He took the first and slid it into place. It was time to begin. The initial burst of fire caught the milling crowd by surprise. The second clip was in place and nearly empty before anyone could place the source of fire. Sixty rounds of 9 mm ammunition into a crowded London street. Twenty-seven victims, eleven dead and sixteen wounded.

The third clip was quickly exhausted. By this time the street was nearly deserted. The dead and wounded, all but four, had been dragged to safety. The gunman fired with the abandon of a child with a new toy. Chips of paving stone spattered, smears of metal marked the points of impact.

With human targets all but gone, he turned his attention to the windows, any windows. The shattering glass rained down into the street and poured into the buildings. It was a silent rain, or nearly so, drowned by the hammer of his weapon and the howling sirens drawing nearer.

With one clip to go, the gunman hefted his weapon, admiring its design, the compact economy of modern death. The first truck carrying tactical police screeched to a halt at the near corner. He greeted them with a burst of fire, then sat back to wait. They would be here soon, and he would be ready. Dying was nothing to fear. It was why he was here. It would make him a martyr, assure him the favor of Allah.

The antiterrorist team wasted no time, and the door to the janitor's room was flimsy. As they entered he emptied his remaining clip, raising himself to stand before the open window. Their fire drove him backward into the air, and he smiled as he spun into space. Whether at a job well done, or at the supreme irony of his weapon's place of manufacture, no one would ever know. The Uzi, now empty, cartwheeled in a glittering black arc into the bloody street below.

His dying fingers released a small red button on the diminutive black plastic box clutched loosely in his hand. The basement of the building blew first, folding outward like a cardboard accordion. The massive weight of the hotel's twenty stories crushed straight down, the rumble sounding like the end of the world to those in the lobby. On the other floors it was simply the sensation of sudden movement that alerted them.

Outside, in the cloud of boiling dust, the tactical police stood motionless, London's finest rendered by Madame Tussaud.

THE BANDSHELL in Central Park was nearly lost in the sea of people. The mayor of New York was scheduled to dedicate a portion of the park recently set aside and redesigned. Never one to miss an opportunity to gather a little free attention, the mayor planned to announce there his campaign for a second term. Warm weather and the free concert scheduled to follow the ceremony assured him of a large audience.

The mayor's controversial personality had garnered more than a few detractors, but he reveled in the combative style controversy had made necessary. And he never allowed barriers to come between him and his admirers. As always, he refused to permit elaborate security. Most American politicians had learned well the lesson of Dallas in 1963. But not all. If there was a way to drive his bodyguards crazy, the mayor had tried it at least once. Today was no exception.

Where most public figures would have been firmly ensconced behind a bulletproof podium, the mayor mounted the bandshell stage shielded from the throng only by a hand mike. His voice echoed through the trees in the grove behind the bandshell, and reechoed in the stand of pines at the rear of the crowd.

"How'm I doing?" he asked. The roar that greeted his question must have been reassuring. It was the last thing he heard. The second shot hit him before he staggered. No one heard it, either. When the mayor fell to the hardwood floor, there was a subdued mooing sound from the crowd. A young woman close to the stage was the first to see the blood, and the first to scream. Two policemen rushed up and sprang onto the stage. The crowd surged forward.

Too little, and too late, one cop reached for the mike and asked for a doctor. At that, the crowd began to expand away from the stage. Others began to scream, a piercing wail that passed through the fluttering leaves. The mayor's aide-de-camp grabbed a telephone backstage to call for an ambulance.

Concealed by dense underbrush in the stand of pines, a young man stashed his weapon in a crevice among the boulders. He stripped off his thin calfskin gloves, threw them in after the gun, then joined the throng milling aimlessly about. His left hand worried nervously at a small black box in his pocket.

He stopped a young woman. "What's going on?" he asked.

"Someone just shot the mayor," she replied, clearly upset.

She passed on before he nodded his satisfaction. Later, she wouldn't remember seeing him. He watched her walk into the trees, away from the bandshell. He was glad she wouldn't be there.

When he pressed the button on the small black box the bandshell mushroomed outward, splintering into thousands of whirling wooden knives. Those closest to the blast were killed outright by the concussion. Hundreds of others weren't so lucky. They lay blinded by wooden spears, impaled on splintered floorboards. Fractured skulls and broken arms by the dozens taxed the city's emergency medical services to the limit.

By then, the slim young man, no longer carrying the small black box, was gone.

THE ROUND MAN REACHED for his napkin, dabbed at the corner of his mouth more daintily than his size would have suggested likely and pushed back from the table.

"Colonel, I can't tell you how happy I am you like Continental cuisine."

"There are limits to my tolerance for puritanism, whether rooted in Islamic fundamentalism or not, Mr. Harlow." Al-Hassan smiled.

Harlow laughed. "That's something better kept secret, Colonel. It wouldn't do us any good if your image were to undergo significant alteration."

"I can keep a secret, Mr. Harlow."

"I wouldn't be here if you couldn't. And I'm not a stranger to secrecy myself, eh?"

"Let's hope neither of us loses the knack." Al-Hassan's jaw tightened, and his smile was forced.

"That sounds dangerously like a threat, Colonel." Harlow got to his feet and began pacing back and forth behind the table. "You wanted action, I gave you action. You wanted technique, it was given to your men. I have supplied weapons, explosives, know-how and training. I have delivered everything you wanted, in spite of difficult circumstances and being burdened with less than sophisticated personnel."

"I am a restless man, Mr. Harlow. I like to keep myself...occupied. There is nothing to worry about. As long as you continue to give me the things I want, and I give you the money to do them, we will both prosper."

"There's one thing I wanted to talk to you about, Colonel. I think it's about time for another payment. Your demands have placed rather serious demands on my resources. Doing things your way is more expensive than I am used to. I can't continue to do business like this. You have to be more flexible. Either give me better people, or give me the money to hire them myself. There has been one near miss already, and we can't be lucky indefinitely."

"Now who's threatening whom? Why don't you sit down, Mr. Harlow? The Mitchell business was unfortunate, but it was your mistake, not mine. I am confident of that. By the way, I think you should look a little more closely at your Mr. Martin." Al-Hassan opened a small silver box on the table and removed a slender American cigarette. He lit it, puffed thoughtfully for a moment, then smiled.

Harlow seemed baffled. "Why? What are you talking about? What's wrong with Martin? Or is this another one of your mind games?"

"Perhaps nothing. But who knows? You have your sources, and I have mine. Whatever. It is merely a suggestion. Do with it what you please. I just want to make sure the Mitchell business won't happen again. But we have more important matters to discuss. Please, sit down. I have completed planning for our new campaign. Your role in that campaign is vital, as you know. I don't need the details, but I must know whether we are still on schedule, and have your assurances that it will be done. I think we should discuss the general outline before you leave."

"I think we should discuss money, Colonel. That's what I think."

"Mr. Harlow, don't worry about it. You think too much about commerce. There are higher considerations."

"That's what you think."

"You worry too much about it. Frankly I am not comfortable working so closely on such ... significant matters with a man who has his mind on other things. It disturbs me, for personal as well as strategic reasons."

"And I'm telling you, the last thing you want to do is allow this to become a personal matter. If you lose control, you start acting illogically. And if you make one mistake, you won't get the chance to make another."

Al-Hassan smiled broadly before responding. "You did."

Harlow grunted, then turned to the map on the wall behind him. He didn't need to be reminded. His pride was mortally wounded and he had a bad feeling in the pit of his stomach. He wasn't sleeping well, and that was always a bad sign. And al-Hassan was being kind. He had made not one mistake, but two. And despite the old saw, the third time was no charm.

"All right, Colonel, let's take a look at the campaign, shall we?"

The two men pored over an elaborate map of Chad, sprinkled liberally with red, black and green map pins. Each red flag represented a bombing. The black pins, of which there were few, represented hijackings. The six green flags were, as their scarcity suggested, special. They were assassinations. And every single event would take place within the span of a single week, beginning with the single most important act—the assassination of the president of the country.

Mason Harlow had always found al-Hassan tiresome. The man's ego was monumental, and he had no idea how complicated it was to arrange things in a democracy. It took money, and more money. In the colonel's kind of police state, you could force people to do what you wanted. But in the wide-open world beneath the surface, a world Mason Harlow knew better than any other, things were far more complex. And expensive.

Al-Hassan had tens of millions of dollars at his disposal, and the bastard continued to argue over nickels and dimes. Maybe it was time to cut his losses, time to retire. Once this mess was over he'd pack it in. Let the al-Hassans of the world haggle with somebody else. And even as the thought passed through his mind, Mason Harlow knew he couldn't do it. He knew himself well enough to know that as long as there was a buck up for grabs he'd be right there grab-bing...with both hands.

The only thing his father had ever told him that made any sense at all was still with him. All the money in the world ain't enough.

CHAPTER TWENTY-FOUR

The 707 squealed as it hit the airstrip, its big tires throwing off small puffs of black smoke until they began to spin on the hot tar. Mack Bolan eyed the bleached buildings curiously, their studied architecture a deliberate echo of a civilization as old as any extant. There was pride in the buildings, and an obstinate insistence on the integrity of a design rooted in thirteen centuries of defiance.

He didn't need the sign on the terminal to tell him where he was. The big Boeing drifted past the airline gates, many of them no longer used by the Western airlines who had paid for their construction. Tripoli was paying the price of Western ostracism. Once a city that appealed to the dreamer and the tourist with a taste for the exotic, it was now anathema to most of them, and had been reduced to the destination of fools more hardy than wise.

As the plane taxied up to a seedy-looking gate, boasting of an efficiency that didn't quite compensate for its lack of style, the passengers began to shuffle restlessly in their seats. Tony and Carter stood before the plane had come to a halt, getting their gear down from the overhead racks. Most of the others did the same, but Bolan stayed in his seat. He was more interested in what was going on outside.

The plane finally lurched to a halt, shuddering as the pilot gave the engines a final goose before braking in a right-angled nook at the rear of the airport. On the apron below, several yellow baggage trucks parked in a row spoke of a more innocent time in the airport's past.

The seat belt warning bonged, and the light went out, but Bolan was the only one still seated. Lucien Picard looked over his shoulder, his face an expressionless mask, but Bolan ignored him. Picard already had a duffel bag slung over one shoulder, and stood in the aisle near the forward exit. A moment later the door swung out and sunlight poured in through the gaping hole in the fuselage. Bolan still sat glued to his window, watching a gangway, its yellow paint half chipped away, the metal bright and unrusted in the arid air.

The Mediterranean Sea was just a few miles away, but the great void of the Sahara laid first claim on what errant moisture drifted south, soaking up the humidity with a greed matched only by that of Libya's ruler.

A portly man in short-sleeved white shirt and khaki trousers shuffled onto the apron, rushing forward as if trying to recover a balance perpetually undermined by the effect of gravity on the soft roll of stomach sagging over his belt. His features were all but washed away by the bright sun, and it wasn't until he reached the foot of the gangway that they took on enough definition for Bolan to recognize him.

Mason Harlow had come to welcome his recruits. Bolan watched the first few men descend the gangway, then stood and yanked his own belongings out of the overhead rack. He took his time, conscious of Tony's eyes boring into his back. When he was ready he turned, his face as composed as ancient stone. Tony glared at him but said nothing.

He walked slowly down the aisle, his duffel bag slapping at the seats, the rough canvas rasping off the vinyl upholstery with the sound of new corduroy trousers. When he reached the exit Tony stood aside. As Bolan stepped past him Tony reached out and grabbed the bag by one strap.

"You better watch your step, Belasko. You're in the big leagues now, bud."

Bolan looked over his shoulder for an instant, shrugged and turned away. This was neither the time nor the place to show Tony he was no rookie. That time would come soon enough.

Bolan could hardly wait.

As he walked down the metal stairs, his feet tolling like a distant bell on the heavy steel, Bolan watched Harlow, glad-handing each of the new arrivals in turn, like a man running for office. But the confidence was artificial. Bolan couldn't help but notice the nervous darting of Harlow's eyes, their flat expression. His good cheer was all in his pumping hand and phony smile.

As the last new man off the plane, Bolan received a perfunctory repetition of the routine, as if Harlow couldn't wait for it all to be over. The jolly con man was anything but happy, and Bolan wondered at the change. Still in the dark about the true nature of their mission, he found himself considering whether even those rules still applied. Harlow looked like a man on a runaway carpet. But either it had magic he hadn't suspected or it had been pulled out from under him; Bolan couldn't tell which.

Beyond the small knot of men a group of Libyan soldiers talked among themselves. Their commander, affecting the sunglasses of a third-rate dictator, eyed the newcomers with undisguised contempt. He spoke to a noncom out of the corner of his mouth, but never took his eyes off Harlow. Bolan thought he had the look of a warden rather than a colleague.

Harlow talked with Carter and two other men, then walked to the foot of the gangway and called for Tony to hurry up. Tony poked his head out of the doorway and waved, then disappeared again.

The Libyan lieutenant walked over to join Harlow. The two men exchanged words too low for Bolan to hear, but there was no mistaking the lieutenant's impatience. Finally raising his voice, Harlow held his palms up, as if to ward off the smaller man.

"All right, all right. Just hold your horses, will you?" Then turning back to the plane, he called again, "Come on, Tony, move your ass. You're holding things up here."

This time there was no immediate answer from the plane. After two minutes Harlow started to climb the steps, but the lieutenant grabbed his arm, tugging him back to the apron. The lieutenant brushed past and double-timed it up the steps, the soles of his boots slapping the metal stairs. The clangs echoed back from the high glass wall of the terminal, their initial slaps ringing with the sharp snap of pistol shots.

The Libyan disappeared into the plane, and angry shouting, muffled by the walls of the fuselage, issued from the open doorway. A moment later Tony stepped onto the gangway landing, followed by the Libyan with his side arm drawn. Tony stumbled and nearly lost his balance, reaching out to grab the handrail until he recovered his equilibrium. He continued down the steps, glancing back over his shoulder now and then. If looks could kill, Bolan thought, the Libyan detachment would have been leaderless.

When the head merc reached the apron, the lieutenant flattened his pistol against the middle of the man's back and gave him a shove. Tony stumbled and nearly fell again. He dropped his luggage and spun around, fists clenched at his sides. Harlow grabbed him by the arm, pulling him close to whisper something in his ear.

"I don't give a shit," Tony hissed. "That bastard better cool it."

"I'll talk to him, but not now. You understand, I don't want him to look bad in front of his men."

"Screw that. You tell him if he shoves me again, I'll rip his lungs out. Go on, tell him."

Tony watched Harlow pull the lieutenant aside The two men whispered angrily, the Libyan gesturing with the pistol. Harlow grabbed the wrist of the man's gun hand and patted him on the shoulder. Finally, with a last angry look in Tony's direction, the lieutenant reholstered the weapon and marched off to rejoin his men.

Harlow ambled back and draped one arm over Tony's shoulders.

"You tell him?" Tony demanded.

"He put the gun away, didn't he?"

"Yeah, but did you tell him?"

"I told him, I told him. Don't worry about it, Tony."

"I'm *not* worried. That bastard's the one who should be worried."

"Forget about it, I said. Just forget about it. You want to get even, wait till we're out in the desert. He can always have an accident, you know? Nobody will miss the son of a bitch, believe me. His own people can't stand him. He's only here because his uncle is some muckamuck or other. These Libs are crazy, I'm telling you, they're just nuts. I dunno, must be the sun or something. Fried their brains."

Tony seemed mollified, and Harlow told him to join the others. Bolan had watched it all with keen interest. Tony had shown him something. He still didn't like the man, but you had to give credit where it was due. And the significance of that fact was not lost on Mack Bolan.

If the entire operation had seemed like a clown show, it wasn't safe to conclude that all its participants were clowns. And if Tony was more than Bolan had thought, the same might be true of some of the others, some of whom he had seen for the first time the night before, on the plane.

Harlow walked back to the gangway and climbed up to the third step. "All right, you guys, gather round." He waited for the men to cluster around the foot of the gangway. "There's gonna be a bus here in five minutes. It'll take you to the hotel. After we check in you'll have the rest of the night to yourselves. But we're leaving early tomorrow, so you better make it an early night."

"What time?" one of the men asked.

"Five a.m. sharp."

Several of the men groaned. "Why so early?" Carter demanded.

Harlow looked at him for a long moment, as if deciding what tack to take. Finally he shrugged. "Because this is not a Club Med vacation. We have a job to do here, and we're on a short leash. You're all getting paid well. You want the money, do the work. If not, well . . ."

"What happens if we miss the bus?"

"Don't. That's all I'm gonna tell you."

"But what happens?"

Harlow sighed. "All right, you want to know, I'll tell you. You miss the bus, you're on your own. We ain't running a commuter service, so there's one bus and one bus only. You'll have to surrender your passports for the duration, so it don't take a genius to figure how deep the shit'll be."

Harlow squinted over their heads, then pointed. "Here comes the bus."

HARLOW WATCHED Tony Masseria carefully. The big Italian had been with him, off and on, for two years, and he was fond of the kid. Unused to confiding in anyone, he had tended to keep himself closed off from his employees, using Sadowski and McNally as buffers. But McNally was hitting the bottle too much. It was time to cut him loose, but not until he could get some value in exchange. McNally was a marker, a poker chip he'd cash in to buy himself something he needed.

Sadowski was another story. His mean streak was the initial attraction. A ramrod had to be mean enough to break a few bones. Pete Sadowski had that quality in spades. But lately he didn't seem to mind butting heads with the boss. He had a smart mouth, and he wasn't frightened of anything. The combination wasn't yet a liability, but Harlow could see the day when it would be.

Maybe Masseria was the answer. Maybe it was time to draw a new circle of wagons. Tony had balls, and he did what he was told. What the hell? Harlow shrugged, as if in response to a question.

He signaled the waiter and hollered as he approached, "Another round." He looked at Tony without saying anything.

"Something the matter, Mr. Harlow?"

"I don't know. Maybe." Harlow swirled the remains of a J&B on the rocks in the bottom of his glass, watching the watery liquor, almost colorless now, ride partway up the side of the tumbler.

"I want you to do me a favor."

"Sure thing. What is it?"

"Can you keep a secret?"

"I guess so, yeah."

"I mean really keep it?"

"Sure I can."

"Okay, nobody, and I mean *nobody* is to know about this. Not Sadowski and especially not McNally. Understand?"

Tony nodded. "Whatever you say, Mr. Harlow."

"All right." Harlow leaned toward the younger man and lowered his voice. "I want you to keep an eye on the new guys, especially Martin, the guy with the glasses. Can you do that for me?"

"Sure. What am I looking for?"

"I don't know. Maybe nothing. You'll know if you see it. Okay? Can you do that?"

"Yes, sir."

"You see anything, Tony, you tell me. Nobody else. There's a few bucks in it for you, too."

"Thanks, Mr. Harlow. I appreciate it."

The waiter brought a second beer for Tony and a J&B double for Harlow. He walked away slowly, and Harlow stared after him suspiciously. "Bastard," he muttered.

"You say something, Mr. Harlow?" Tony asked.

"Nothing, no. You're all right, Tony, you know that? You remind me of me, once. A long time ago." He downed the Scotch in a single swallow and stood up, slapping the glass on the table at the same time. "Don't miss the bus, Tony," he said. "I mean it, now."

CHAPTER TWENTY-FIVE

Mack Bolan had trouble sleeping. The oppressive heat and the monotony had been chipping away at him for five hours. He felt as if half the bones in his body had been jarred loose by the tightly sprung bus. Measured solely by the yardstick of physical demands, and not counting combat, the demands of which could not be measured by any yardstick at all, the previous day had been one of the worst since the very early days of basic training. The human body, by some measurements a masterpiece of functional design, had the disadvantage of being intended for less rigorous pursuits than warfare. The incessant demands made by conditioning and training went far beyond anything he had ever been called upon to do in the field. A more jaundiced man than Bolan might presume the purpose of such training to be elimination by overkill. But he knew the reasoning behind such deliberate punishment, and he agreed with it. You had to be ready for anything and have a little something in reserve. No one, especially not the enemy, should be able to anticipate the limits of your endurance.

Lying there on the thin pallet of his barracks cot, he counted the aches, each one a bright beacon of pain. Like any other program of training he'd endured, this one seemed to bear no relation to anything he had been told he would be doing. The streak of sadism in his instructors was familiar, but it still hurt.

He had thought he would breeze through, relying on his superior conditioning to get by without difficulty. He even feared his acting ability might not be adequate to the task of fooling the instructors. After all, he was supposed to be down on his luck, one more piece of human flotsam carried by a tide he neither felt nor understood to a place he'd never been, all to do a job he didn't understand.

So much for that.

The campaign of brutalizing pressure had begun almost immediately. Sadowski was the worst, pushing men half his size and twice his age, stretching joints and pushing the limits of endurance beyond their normal tolerance. Bolan had taken an instant dislike to the man, and nothing he'd seen since had convinced him he was wrong. Sadowski seemed to sense the dislike in some primitive, even animal way. He didn't understand it, but it had kept him off Bolan's back.

Picard seemed to be holding his own, but the haggard look on his face was all the proof Bolan needed that Picard, too, was at the end of his rope. It was too early, and the incessant badgering too impersonal and too pervasive, to conclude Sadowski suspected them. On the other hand, the big man was just mean enough to bust everybody's chops in an effort to disguise any suspicions he might have.

Bolan sat up on the cot, the predawn light throwing pale blocks of illumination on the floor. Slapping at one of the bugs on his neck, he got up, then walked barefoot to the nearest window. He stared out at the desert, a pale flatness stretching as far as the eye could see. Under the light of a full moon, the endless dunes, their undulations flattened by the minimal light, had turned the color of old pewter.

The barracks was on the edge of the camp, and nothing obstructed his view. He watched for several minutes, wondering why, wondering what he could expect to see in such a dead and silent place. A small spark appeared high in the sky, slashing to the southwest like a yellow laser beam. Against the dark blue of the sky, Bolan detected a faint trail of smoke as the meteor winked out. A moment later it was gone. Not even a trace of its passage lingered on his retina. His memory struggled to keep the brilliant flash alive, but soon it, too, was gone.

Then, lower in the sky, almost invisible against the moonlit panorama, another light appeared, its unwinking red small and pale. The harder he tried to focus on it, the more illusory it seemed to be. It looked like a plane's running lights, but they were nowhere near an established air lane. The light was far enough away that it seemed stationary, more like a beacon than something moving through the night.

After ten minutes, the red was only slightly brighter, but there was no mistaking it…an airplane was heading straight for the base. Bolan tiptoed back to his bunk and slipped on a pair of pants and a shirt. The clothes smelled of hard work and were stiff with dust and sweat. Water was a luxury here, and laundry was far down the list of priorities.

Bolan sat down and pulled on a pair of socks and cat-footed to the door, a pair of combat boots in his left hand. A right angle of dim light marked the door to Sadowski's room, which served as both office and sleeping quarters. The light, Bolan knew, meant nothing. The big man slept with his light on, and was probably fast asleep.

Bolan crept to the door and placed an ear to the panel. The room beyond was quiet. Sadowski was either asleep or out of his room. Either way, there was nothing to be gained by worrying about it.

The screen door, equipped with an elementary alarm, was held closed with a simple hook and eye. Setting his boots quietly on the floor, then slipping the hook free, Bolan slid his knife under the doorframe, pinning the alarm button closed. It was no more complicated than a refrigerator light switch, and about as secure. Before easing the door open, he tore a match from the book in his shirt pocket. The cardboard was too thick, and he peeled one layer free with a thumbnail. The match resisted for a moment as he tried to slide it into the gap between the button and its seat. The match bent, and he pulled it back and peeled the other end. Trying again, this time he managed to get the paper match a quarter inch into the switch. He tamped it home with his thumb, then carefully pulled the knife blade away.

Bolan stepped through the doorway onto the dry earth, reaching back for his boots. He eased the door closed and crept across the silver soil, feeling the dry grit rasping under his socks. He moved laterally, sliding half the length of the barracks, then knelt down to pull on his boots.

The red light on the horizon had drawn closer, and Bolan circled behind the barracks and drifted out into the desert a couple of hundred yards. Away from the buildings, he dropped to his stomach to watch. There were sentries, but guard duty wasn't taken all that seriously. The beautiful part of being a terrorist is that you have little to fear from those unwilling to use your methods against you.

The base itself was not that large, its principal feature being a small airstrip, capable of handling helicopters, small planes and transports with short takeoff and landing requirements, but little else. The largest structure in the encampment was an L-shaped warehouse, slashed with blotchy paint in an imitation of camouflage. All that succeeded in doing was calling attention to the building, outlining it against the unrelieved beige tedium of the parched earth.

The mix of professionalism and pathetic ineptitude constantly kept Bolan off balance. It was hard to figure out whether Harlow was a clown or an assassin. That he was dangerous was an independent matter, and Bolan suspected that a dangerous clown could be more trouble than an assassin. Measure and countermeasure relied in no small degree on logic and predictability. An opponent who was liable to do the unlikely, let alone the unthinkable, was the most dangerous of all.

The warrior got to his feet and walked among the dunes, his feet tracing a broad, rough circle in the dry soil as he moved to the other side of the base. Checking the sky from time to time, he watched the red light draw closer. The distant hammering of the plane's engines rose and fell, like a remote radio station, its signal too weak for inexperienced fingers on the tuning knob.

As it approached the light rose higher in the sky, and Bolan watched in fascination. Coming from the general direction of Tripoli, far to the north, the plane began to drift off to the west. Bolan could see its outline now, smeared a dull silver by the moon. The unblinking red light sparkled like a ruby in a cheap setting.

The sound of the engines was almost constant now, still oscillating somewhat, perhaps interrupted by air currents. The plane swooped in a wide arc, drawing abreast of him then passing two or three miles to his left. The pilot banked and the plane was immediately recognizable as a C-47, the venerable workhorse of U.S. military transports.

The C-47 had done invaluable service since before the Korean War, and hundreds of the planes were still in service around the world, some in National Guard units and hundreds in private hands, the backbone of dozens of local air freight companies. And Bolan was only too well aware that the CIA also owned a couple of dozen, using them for all sorts of clandestine operations from Air America flights during the Vietnam War to Contra resupply missions in Central America.

As the plane finished its arc and started to double back, it was five miles downfield. The plane began to descend, and Bolan could see the shifting play of light as the pilot manipulated the elevators, flaps and ailerons. The red light vanished, leaving a silver sliver in the sky, swooping down like a gigantic sickle in the hands of an invisible harvester.

The engines coughed once, sputtered briefly and then died. The pilot was trying for a dead stick landing, more dangerous than intelligent. Bolan watched in amazement as the big plane dropped steadily, its feathered props turning idly in the slipstream. He had seen it done once before, with disastrous consequences. A plane the size of a C-47 made the proverbial lead balloon graceful in comparison.

The plane fell steadily, now less than half a mile away. Bolan thought he could hear the air whistling under the C-47's wings. The airstrip was only hard-packed earth, but its texture set it off from the surrounding desert. Its smooth surface must have been clearly visible from the air, slightly shiny under the full moon.

The tires touched down, throwing small clouds of dry soil into the air. Instead of the familiar squeal of hard rubber on tarmac, Bolan heard the rough scrape of sandpaper for a moment, then nothing but the squeak of the big plane as it bounced along the airstrip. The pilot was good, and he handled the cumbersome plane with a fluidity that was almost graceful.

The plane taxied up to within thirty yards of the warehouse, the pilot gently pumping the brakes. A series of short, high-pitched squeals, like the cries of a frightened rodent, were now the only sounds made by the transport. Without engines, the pilot was unable to maneuver with any assistance other than momentum. He knew he was only going to get one shot, and he made the best of it, parking the big plane in the heart of the L like a baby in the crook of its mother's elbow.

The landing was a masterpiece, and accomplished with virtually no sound at all. It was doubtful anyone in the barracks would have heard the plane arrive. Bolan maneuvered closer in, painfully aware of how little cover the flat earth afforded, and of the brightness of the moonlight flooding around him.

The cargo bay doors of the C-47 swung open, and the ramp yawned down with a dull thud. Bolan edged in closer, hugging the earth behind a low dune, feeling the sand slip under his collar and through the buttons of his shirt. A handful of men scurried down the ramp, each lugging a wooden crate. Like hungry ants, they made several trips, stacking two dozen identical boxes five high on the bed of a cargo hauler. A tall figure stood in the crook of the L, arms crossed on its chest, watching the unloading. Bolan recognized Sadowski by his height.

When the flatbed was piled high, Sadowski stepped out of the L and walked to the tractor. He conversed briefly with one of the men from the plane, who then climbed into the tractor seat and cranked up the engine. The tractor stuttered, jerking the trailer along behind it until it picked up enough momentum to keep slack out of the hitch.

Sadowski huddled with the others, and three of them hopped into a jeep parked against one wing of the L, two in

front and one in back. Bolan wished he had field glasses. He
was too far away to hear what was being said, and in the
silver glare from the moon, facial features were blurred, the
dull shadows of cheeks and noses further obscuring the
men's faces.

Sadowski bent over the rear seat of the second jeep, removing an AK-47, which Bolan recognized by its unforget-
table contours. He jumped into the back seat, cradling the
Kalashnikov. The sharp report of a backfire drifted across
the flat compound as the jeep cranked up. It backed uncertainly away from the warehouse, then spun its tires in the
soft earth for a moment before regaining traction.

The familiar whine of a jeep transmission in first gear cut
through the night and the vehicle swerved toward him,
picking up speed. The engine rose and fell as the driver
worked his way through the gears. The jeep would pass
about one hundred feet to Bolan's left. The driver had not
bothered with headlights, and the warrior hoped no one was
interested in anything but conversation.

At close range, the passengers were no longer unrecognizable. All three men had been at the camp in Louisiana.
Bolan felt the sudden sharp jerk of surprise as he realized
that he had been lied to. Told that he, Picard and Specs had
made the cut and the others had not, he now found himself
staring after incontrovertible evidence to the contrary.

A moment later, the jeep roared past. Before Bolan could
turn to watch where it went, a flurry of movement back near
the warehouse caught his eye. Two men had jumped in the
second jeep, which lurched away from the wall and spun
around to come in his general direction. It sped into the
night hard on the tail of the first jeep. Carter sat on the
passenger's side, two rifles in his lap. Unable to tell what
they were, Bolan assumed they were Kalashnikovs, like the
one on Sadowski's lap. The man at the wheel was Tony.

When the second jeep was out of sight, Bolan got to his
feet to stare after it. Unwilling to return to the barracks, he
stood, hands on hips, staring into the desert night.

The dim silver veneer of the moonlight was strangely beautiful in the barren silence. Bolan took a few tentative steps forward, his hands still on his hips, then he stopped, as if hypnotized. There was a sudden burst of light. It vanished in the dry air when he heard the first shot.

Several more sharp reports cracked somewhere out over the sand, dying quickly as if the air were reluctant to transport the sound. He knew now why the men had been brought to the base. As he had told Picard, they were loose ends.

Mason Harlow had just cut them off.

CHAPTER TWENTY-SIX

He had been watching the brownstone for more than three hours, and Leon Alvarez was getting tired. The temperature was in the middle twenties, and the gusty wind brought it several degrees lower. Unwilling to call attention to himself by running the engine, he had decided to endure the cold as best he could. His breath kept fogging the windshield, and he leaned forward to rub the frozen condensation into a small ridge of ice. His gloves were damp from the melting ice, and he shivered in his heavy parka.

His arm was still in a sling and the occasional ache kept him awake. Glancing at his watch, Alvarez decided it was time for another coffee. He nestled the three cups lining the dash one into another and opened the door.

The wind whistled through the open door, triggering another bout of the shivers. He slipped out of the car, grabbed the three empty cups with his one good hand and closed the door. Walking in the street, Alvarez headed for an all-night deli up the block, slipping on patchy ice. Ridges of frozen slush and shoveled snow lined the curbs. When he reached the deli he stepped between two cars and climbed over the mound of ice, keeping his balance with one hand on the hood of a Chevy until his feet were firmly on the sidewalk.

Inside, the sleepy-eyed counterman stared at him flatly, as if expecting trouble. Alvarez ordered two more coffees and a Danish, and browsed through the front pages of left-over newspapers on an iron rack beside the front door. The counterman filled the coffee cups, asking over his shoulder, "Cream or sugar?"

"Black," Alvarez answered, still reading the small print on the day's *Post*. The counterman snapped plastic lids on both cups and tucked them into a brown bag, tossing the plastic-wrapped Danish on top. He patted the counter with nervous fingertips. "Three-eighteen," he said.

Alvarez pulled four ones from his parka and smoothed them on the counter. Holding his hand out for the change, he said, "Cold as hell out there."

The counterman looked at him with those flat, black eyes as if Alvarez had just declared he was from Venus. Skipping a beat, then another, he finally said, "Yeah."

Bracing himself for the wind, Alvarez opened the glass door with his shoulder and stepped out into the cold again. A small curl of steam swirled out of the bag, and he wondered whether the second cup would be cold before he got to drink it. He walked to the corner and stepped off the curb, then scurried down along the street side of the parked cars.

Alvarez balanced the paper bag on the roof, then yanked open the car door just in time to catch the bag as it slid toward the windshield propelled by a gust of wind. Leaning into the car to drop the bag in the passenger seat, he slid in behind the wheel, slammed the door and rapped the lock into place with a gloved hand.

The apartment building across the street was almost dark, only three lights still on on the upper floors. One of them, Alvarez knew, belonged to Stanley Mills. This was the second night of what promised to be a long, uninteresting surveillance. He almost envied Bolan and Picard their exotic mission. Almost, but not quite. He'd been there, and he knew just how desiccating the desert could be, leaching juice out of mind and body alike. It could turn most Westerners into whispering husks fit for little else but blowing away to crumble like old corn leaves in the desert, bleached of color by the pitiless and constant sun.

But when the hawk was out, New York was no place to be, if it ever was. It couldn't be more different from East Los Angeles, or more hostile to one raised there. But this was Stanley Mills country, and the Upper East Side was where you had to start if you wanted to find out what the hell he was up to.

Alvarez was still angry at the near miss that had put his arm in a sling, but he didn't know whether he was angry at Mills, on the possibility the old man had known about the hit, or at himself for not having guessed. Either way, there was plenty of rage to keep him warm, even on a night like this.

He ducked down in the seat to get a better look at the upper floors of the building, and to lower his own profile. A posh neighborhood like this was the toughest place to conduct long-term surveillance at the street level. Lurking strangers sooner or later caught the attention of some old lady who lived behind a third-floor window. Having nothing better to do, she'd indulge her favorite hobby, dialing 911.

Mills lived on the fifth floor, and the light had burned steadily since sundown. The timing had been so perfect, Alvarez had wondered whether Mills might have one of those photosensitive timers used for illusory security by those who had something to protect but not enough to pay someone to do it. An occasional shadow passing behind the drawn shades had laid that fear to rest.

Alvarez pulled the Danish from the bag, balancing the sack in his lap while he pulled out one of the two coffees. He bunched the stiff brown paper closed and tucked the second cup into the console of his Grand Prix, where it joined some loose change, a half-empty pack of Camels and three partial books of matches.

He unwrapped the Danish and took a bite before uncapping the coffee. He stared up at the fifth-floor window and gulped down two quick mouthfuls of the coffee, ignoring the heat. A shadow grew dark against the window for a moment and flung its arms out, one at a time, then resumed its former shape, a little bulkier than before. Somebody had put on a coat. Alvarez took another bite of the Danish, then rewrapped it as the light went out.

He started the car, taking a long pull on the coffee while the engine settled down from a rough idle to a smooth rumble. Leaning forward, he clicked the defroster on, the sudden surge of coolish air blowing dust back into his face. He rubbed the glaze from the windshield and driver's window, polishing the latter with the sleeve of his parka. A moment later, a shadow appeared in the lobby, just visible through the pebbled glass of the front door.

The shadowy figure pushed the door open, accompanied by a doorman, who stepped through first, the brass buttons of his coat catching rays from the streetlight just to the left of the entrance awning. Stanley Mills stepped through, tugging a camel-hair topcoat tightly around his neck. His carefully styled white hair was immediately blown into a wild shock by the wind, and he reached up with a gloved hand to smooth it back into place.

A moment later the nose of a large sedan appeared in the exit of the building's underground garage, and the man at the wheel spun out into the street and slammed it smoothly into reverse. The tires screamed for an instant then caught, and the car rocketed backward ten yards, and stopped cold. The driver hopped out, held the door for Mills, then sprinted back to the warmth of the garage.

The vehicle, a Lincoln Town Car, rolled forward a few feet, then shot ahead in an attempt to make the light at the next corner. Alvarez fought the steering wheel of his own car, and muscled the Grand Prix out away from the curb just as the Lincoln squealed to a halt as the light turned red.

Alvarez hung back a few yards, watching as Mills nervously checked the rearview mirror a couple of times. The reflection off his glasses was picked up by the mirror. When the light changed, the Lincoln sped away, and Alvarez took his time, letting Mills get a half block ahead of him. The old man might have retired from the Agency, but old was only a matter of degree. Mills couldn't have been more than fifty or so, and he knew more than his share of tradecraft. It behooved Alvarez to let the nervousness seep out of his quarry. If he hung too close, Mills was almost certain to make him. If that happened Alvarez would have wasted two frigid nights drilling himself a dry hole.

The Lincoln made a turn to head west at Seventy-ninth Street. It zipped through the park on the transverse, and Alvarez dropped even farther back. At Eighty-first and Central Park West, where the transverse came out on the west side of Central Park, the light was red, and Alvarez coasted slowly forward, waiting for it to change. He watched the tight swirl of exhaust from the tailpipe of the Lincoln, and stepped on the gas only when the cloud grew suddenly larger.

The luxury car drifted past the Museum of Natural History, hung a left on Columbus, then a right to get back on Seventy-ninth. Alvarez caught the light and cursed.

The Lincoln rolled steadily downtown, hitting its stride on Tenth Avenue and clipping off twenty blocks at a time. In the Tribeca area, Mills slowed up, hung a left and pulled into the parking lot of an all-night skating rink. Alvarez watched him come back out to the street and enter the rink, before he pulled his own car into the down ramp.

Forking over the five-dollar admission, he was conscious of loud music thumping up through the soles of his feet. He could feel the heavy bass as he climbed the ramp. He didn't hear it until he pushed through the black swinging doors into a nightmare of flashing lights and glowing smears of paint on the huge canvas panels covering the walls.

Alvarez stopped to rent a pair of skates, keeping one eye on the crowd as he waited for the counter girl to hunt down a pair in the right size. Under blinding strobes, he spotted Mills, his white shirt a phosphorescent blaze under black light, sitting at a table in the snack bar. The agent waited patiently, watching from a bench across the rink.

The choice confronting him was not an easy one to make. Stanley Mills had seemed like the key, ever since the meeting on the Lower East Side. When someone had tried to hit Alvarez, it grew more logical still. Mills's presence at the meeting had taken him by surprise. It was only prudent to assume a connection between that surprise and the attempted hit following so hard on its heels.

The connections between Mills and Mason Harlow were the most intriguing aspect of the puzzle. Like filaments of ether, ghostly fingers that could be felt but not seen, the ties binding the two men seemed too numerous to explain away as the simple coincidence you would expect when two men had served long, overlapping tenures in the netherworld of the intelligence community. It was a world where nothing was what it appeared to be, and where appearance was everything.

Since his meeting with Bolan and Picard, Alvarez had done some digging. So far he had uncovered nothing, but the probing spade had struck something hard enough to throw off sparks in the darkness. The shadowy glimpses of figures distorted beyond recognition, like the phantoms cavorting under the pulsating strobes of the skating rink, flitted back and forth across the landscape of his imagination like banshees in a drunken Irish nightmare.

The two men sitting with Mills were ciphers. The older man was himself so out of place in the Dantesque purgatory that it seemed deliberately provocative. It was impossible to imagine that no one would find him remarkable, the white-haired dandy sitting so composed and serene in this wild place. Was that the point? Alvarez wondered. Was Mills making sure that someone could place him on this scene, and if so, why?

There were a hundred answers for every question, but the main one was what to do when Mills rose to go, as he surely must. Following him might be fruitful, but he might then lose the other men forever. He could always find Mills again. And then, before he had made up his mind, the choice was presented to him. Mills reached across the flat black round table and shook hands with both men, then stood to go. He looked out at the rink for a long moment, as if admiring the long legs of a buxom redhead, her pirouette a dazzling whirl of hips and elbows, frozen a hundred times a minute under the flashing strobes.

Alvarez himself stood mesmerized by the performance, again and again as each flash of the strobe etched the woman in frozen time for a millisecond or two. He was reminded of those dog-eared comic books whose pages, when flashed rapidly in succession, showed a stiffly animated Bluto doing the unspeakable with Olive Oyl, while a smiling Popeye cheered them on.

And then Stanley Mills was walking, a foppish stick figure in dandified strut, his forward progress a hundred still frames each etched with perfection worthy of a Disney film. As he neared the door, Alvarez stood petrified by uncertainty. And then Mills was through the Day-Glo doors, leaving them swinging back and forth, the arc rendered in fractured increments.

The two men at the table had not yet moved, and Alvarez counted under his breath. On the third one thousand, the two men stood in unison, as if they, too, had been waiting for Mills to vanish before making up their minds. And Alvarez knew he could not turn his back on this new link in the chain. He waited as the men neared the swinging doors, each with a pair of scuffed black roller skates draped over their black-shirted shoulders.

Alvarez, more comfortable now that Mills had gone, less frightened that he might be recognized, watched as the two men stopped at the desk and turned in their skates. They crossed to the checkroom and recovered their coats, each donning a pea jacket and dark blue knit watch cap. Every inch navy men, Alvarez wondered whether they, too, were bound to Mason Harlow by some nebulous strands.

He followed the two men, now as alike as two peas, their differences erased by the clothing they wore against the frigid air. As he reached the top of the ramp leading down to the double glass doors of the entrance, the two men pushed out into the street and a blast of cold air roared up the ramp, swirling scraps of paper and glittering tinfoil on the black mat floor.

He hurried down the ramp, pulling his coat around him, struggling with the sling. Halfway down the ramp a metal door opened on the left, and a woman in a leotard stepped onto the ramp. She noticed the sling and smiled.

"Roller derby, or what?" she asked.

"Something like that," Alvarez mumbled. He glanced at her sideways as he ran past.

At the glass doors he paused for a second, not wishing to burst out into the night without knowing where his prey might be. Right now he had the advantage of anonymity. Calling attention to himself by too rushed a departure would jeopardize the only edge he had at the moment.

Pausing to count under his breath, his one good hand on the thick, cold glass, he heard the woman call after him, "I'm still here, if that's what you're wondering." There was no mistaking the teasing invitation in her voice.

"Too bad," Alvarez muttered. "I'm never there when I catch a break."

He completed the arbitrary count and shoved the glass outward, turning sideways to let the blast of air slide by him on either side. It whistled through the gap until the door was halfway open, then howled past the edge of the door as he stepped through. As the door slowly closed, drawn by the pneumatic piston hinge, he heard the whistle return, rising in pitch until it died with a strangle as the rubber edges of the doors met.

He walked casually to the left, reaching the corner of the building and turning it just as the two men reached the rear parking lot. Alvarez stopped and pulled a pack of Camels from his parka, tapping one butt free and struggling to light it one-handed. The first match died in the stiff wind, and he took two at a time, striking them together and catching the larger flame before it, too, could be ripped away.

He puffed vigorously, buying time, and giving his presence some rationale in case the men might glance over their shoulders. When the cigarette was securely alight he walked down the gentle incline toward the parking lot, tripping over the first of three asphalt speed bumps in the driveway.

He reached the rear corner just as a car door slammed.

CHAPTER TWENTY-SEVEN

The roar of a returning jeep bounced off the vertex of the warehouse and echoed back at Bolan, magnified until it sounded like thunder. The powerful engine alternately strained and whined as it struggled through the heavy sand then soared over the crest of a dune, only to dig in deeply at the bottom of the next. Headlights suddenly speared out of the darkness, and he dived to the ground, pressing himself flat as the bouncing jeep cast its high beams just over his head, then sent them soaring up at an acute angle. The path of the jeep and the swerving lights was too unpredictable for him to risk standing.

He began a crablike crawl to the side, moving as quickly as the awkward posture permitted. There was the danger that the bright lights might highlight the path he left in the sand, but the risk of staying where he was was even greater. The jeep settled into a steady roar as the ground flattened out and its traction grew steady.

Bolan worried about the second jeep, wondering whether it might take a separate path, which he might unknowingly crawl directly into. Reaching the relative safety of a low mound, he scrambled to his knees and craned to see over the barrier. The lights were more stable now, and the driver seemed to have settled into a rhythm. The lights angled away from him, dancing up and down the warehouse wall as the vehicle approached. Less than a hundred yards away now, he was able to make out the shadow of Sadowski in the passenger seat. It was too dark to tell who was driving.

The jeep passed him and even the refracted light died, leaving only the harsh blades scratching at the weathered wooden walls of the building. The driver killed his engine, and the jeep rolled the last fifty yards in virtual silence, only the crunch of its thickly treaded tires on the sand breaking the quiet.

Sadowski jumped down from the jeep and passed in front of the headlights. A shadow of colossal proportions splashed across the warehouse doors, gradually shrinking as he approached them. He hauled one of the huge doors to the side, and the gaping blackness inside swallowed the headlights. He walked back to the jeep and climbed in, just as it lurched ahead and disappeared through the opening.

Bolan edged forward, keeping low to the ground. His curiosity was more than piqued. There was no doubt in his mind that three men had just been shot to death out in the desert. The reasons for that wanton slaughter were far more murky. A passion for a swift justice of biblical simplicity kept tugging at his conscience, telling him to do something and to do it immediately. But Mack Bolan was no hothead. The Executioner had no room for mindless action, not when so much might be at stake. As yet, he was baffled by Harlow and his schemes. To fly off the handle, no matter how crude the provocation, was unacceptable.

Bolan lay still for several minutes, but the huge black rectangle of the open warehouse door remained undisturbed. He crept forward, angling away from the door, still conscious that the second jeep might appear at any time. When he had drifted far enough to the right that only someone standing in the doorway would be able to see him, he rushed forward, his boots crunching the sand in short, sharp jabs.

As he reached one end of the L, he flattened himself against it and paused to listen. One tall, narrow window was centered in the wall a foot above his head. If there had been any movement inside he would have heard it, but the interior was deathly still. If he hadn't seen the two men enter, he would have thought it was deserted. He eased closer to the edge of the short wall and paused before turning the corner.

Still hearing nothing, he slipped along the unopened door. With his back pressed flat against the rough wood, he heard nothing but the scratch of splinters against the cloth of his shirt.

The silence and the open door made him uneasy. The whole sequence of events was too pat. The yawning darkness seemed like a deliberate invitation, but for whom? And to what? It wasn't possible Sadowski knew he had been out in the desert. He had been too careful for that.

Unanswered questions bothered him, and there were far too many already. Bolan took a chance. He ducked through the door, hitting the concrete floor in a flat roll, spinning back to a tight crouch against the inside of the door. He held his breath, but nothing suggested he had been heard. The uninterrupted quiet hummed louder in the enclosed space.

Stepping cautiously, he backed away from the opening. A dim bulb deep in the interior filled one end of the warehouse with patches of soft light and shade. Bolan felt resistance against his back, and groped behind him with one hand until he felt the rough wood of a tall crate. He eased around the obstacle, ducking in behind it and flattening himself in a narrow gap between it and a stack of wooden boxes.

He was about to step across a narrow passage into a tight aisle when he heard footsteps on the sand outside. Someone who had no reason to conceal his presence was walking along the wall, just before the open door. The steps were steady, almost mechanical in their regularity, those of a man running through a routine. Bolan pressed back into the cranny, reached inside his shirt and drew his Beretta. Quietly, holding his breath, he slid off the safety and braced his gun hand against the side of the crate. He could feel ragged splinters poking into his skin as the steps drew near.

The newcomer grunted, almost as if talking to himself. An oval smear of light crept through the open door, moving like a living thing across the sand and creeping up over the lip of the concrete pad. It retreated slightly, as if the man behind the light were frightened of something, then stopped about halfway in, a bright parabola unnaturally cropped at its open end.

The man shifted his weight uneasily, and the sand crunched under his feet. He whispered, "Who's there?" The words barely made it through the door, then died. As if encouraged by the silence, he repeated the call, this time in a stronger voice. "Who's there?"

The question bounced around the narrow aisles just inside the door. Still no answer. The light moved tentatively, darting from side to side, still not completely through the open door. The man mumbled something Bolan couldn't catch, stepped heavily once, then again. The flat oval of the flashlight was now all the way through the door, the head of the light itself wavering in a nervous hand. A blade of light, distorted by the cheap lens, slashed out from its side and flashed on some bright nail heads on the crate Bolan leaned against.

A hand and arm appeared behind the slowly moving torch, as if drawn in against their owner's will. "Who's there?" The silence had made the man uneasy again. He stepped into the doorway, but his face was shadowed and Bolan couldn't recognize him.

Something clattered in the recesses of the warehouse, as if some loose slats had been knocked to the concrete. The loud slap of the falling wood echoed sharply, then died away. The man in the doorway froze for an instant, then ducked all the way in, flattening himself against the bottom end of a tall stack of boxes. The sentry seemed reluctant to proceed deeper into the warehouse, but unwilling to walk away from his responsibility. Bolan had been there more than once.

Drawing a revolver from a holster on his hip, the guard played his light up along the stack to get his bearings. It splashed on the corrugated-metal ceiling, then went out with an audible click.

Bolan watched the man creep forward, staying close to the packing crates. As the guard moved deeper into the aisle, his head and shoulders were outlined by the dim light in the far corner. A second clatter of loose boards, this time quickly muffled, bounced off the metal ceiling and the guard stopped in his tracks. He crouched and hollered, "What's going on in there?" His voice quavered, its uncertainty magnified by the emptiness, and bounced back as if mocking him.

Bolan was pinned where he was. Any attempt to leave now would lead to discovery at best, and at worst might get him shot. He waited for the guard to regain his confidence, hoping the man would move farther into the building so he could leave.

A crash echoed from the guard's position, and the man cursed. His outline disappeared as he bent to retrieve something, and the repeated click of the flashlight switch was followed by another angry mutter. The flashlight landed with a crash just to Bolan's left, where it rolled to the door, fragments of its lens tinkling to the concrete.

The guard vanished, his outline swallowed by the shadows as he moved deeper into the aisle. In another minute he'd be far enough inside for Bolan to risk creeping to the door. He held his breath, listening to the tentative progress of the guard. Underneath the rasp of hard leather soles on sandy concrete, Bolan heard another sound: the whisper of rubber soles. He strained his eyes into the shadows but saw nothing. The warrior dropped to a crouch, hoping to get a better angle against the light, but still saw only shadows.

The rubber soles whispered again, somewhere to the guard's left, and in the back of Bolan's brain the same question kept circling: Where the hell was Sadowski? The big man had come in with someone, and both seemed to have disappeared.

Suddenly the guard was thrown into bright relief by a brilliant beam of light. His shadow spilled on the floor, unnaturally elongated, and lost its definition against a wall of cartons. The guard turned toward the light, lifting a forearm to shield his eyes. "Who the fuck is that?"

A rush of footsteps answered him, and the burly form of Pete Sadowski careered out of an intersecting aisle, catching the guard with a shoulder and knocking him to the floor. Sadowski straddled the prostrate guard, his hands around the man's throat. Both men were starkly etched by the bright beam, which began to waver as if the hand holding it were suddenly nervous.

"Load, what the fuck are you doing? Leave him alone." It was Tony Masseria.

Sadowski's massive forearms rippled as he continued to throttle the fallen guard. The big man rocked back and forth as he used his weight to increase the pressure. The guard's legs kicked, his heels rattling on the concrete. Sadowski grunted each time he rocked forward. The thrashing legs gradually stopped kicking, reduced first to the simple scratch of cloth on the sandy floor, then lay altogether still.

Sadowski grunted once more and released his grip. His right hand moved to his chest for an instant then rose in a bright arc. Bolan saw the knife, its serrated edge glittering brightly in the wavering beam, and as it began to descend the light went out. The thud of body on body echoed down the dark aisle, and Sadowski cursed at the impact. His breath left him with a deep sigh.

The silent struggle in the darkness was brief. And then the light returned. Sadowski stood over the prostrate guard, aiming the torch at a sinister black handle projecting from his chest. In a heap to the left, partially out of sight, lay Tony Masseria. Sadowski bent down, the light diminishing as the beam drew closer to the floor, and grabbed the handle of the knife. He withdrew it with a sharp tug, and Bolan could hear the sickening sucking sound as the chest reluctantly surrendered the blade.

Sadowski turned the light full on the motionless Masseria, who groaned and struggled to sit up. He managed an uneasy balance, his head cradled in his hands. "What the hell's wrong with you? What'd you do that for? You didn't have to do that...."

"Quit bellyaching. We got work to do. It looks like your man Martin just killed a guard."

"What are you talking about? *You* did that. Are you out of your mind?"

"Look, if Harlow wants you to watch Martin, then Martin shouldn't be here. I never did like that little four-eyed fuck anyhow."

"You're crazy, you know that? I never should have told you. Harlow told me not to tell you, and I didn't listen. Jesus Christ..." In the harsh light, Bolan could see the icy glaze in Masseria's eyes turn to water. Thin bands of shimmering silver lined his cheeks.

"If you wanted Martin out of here, why not just take him out? Why kill an innocent man, too?"

"You don't know nothing, you know that? The other three were different, see. Nobody knows they were here. But with Martin, we got to have a reason, so the rest of them don't get upset."

"Upset? Is that all? Upset? Jesus..."

"Come on, we got more work to do. Get the hell up and earn your pay for a change."

The light went out.

CHAPTER TWENTY-EIGHT

Alvarez glanced in the direction of the sound in time to see the headlights of a dark blue Chevrolet flash on. The car's starter whined, the drain on the battery dimming the lights a little until the engine caught and the alternator took over.

He walked slowly across the asphalt, careful not to slip on the patches of ice missed by the plow. His own car was in a row nearer to the building, and he walked briskly toward it, for all the world nothing more than a man anxious to get out of the cold. He slipped into the front seat of his Grand Prix and watched the Chevy back out of line as he cranked his own engine.

He caught a glimpse of the Chevy's front plate before it leaped forward and slipped out of sight. He turned on the heater and backed slowly out of his parking place, falling in line behind the Chevy, now stopped at the top of the ramp. Its left-turn signal was on, but Alvarez remembered the traffic was one-way. He put his own right blinker on and watched helplessly as the Chevy slipped out, heading the wrong way.

He waited for the Chevy to hang a right into West Broadway, another one-way street, but this time it observed the traffic regulations. When the car had gone, he sped into the street, ran a red light and gunned it, speeding two blocks to the next legal left. The detour had taken him a block south, the peculiar angles of Tribeca streets had cost him another. He was a block south when he saw the Chevy go by. Alvarez ran a second red and just squeaked through an amber on Canal as he hung a left and fell in behind the Chevy.

The Chevy hit a groove, clipping off more than a dozen blocks before catching a red with Alvarez a block behind.

When the light changed, he laid a patch and was forced to brake at the next corner. In the rearview, Alvarez spotted a blue-and-white, and hoped the other driver had also seen it.

The light changed and the driver eased out slowly, drifting over into the left lane on the broad one-way uptown avenue. The dark waters of the Hudson were on the left. Alvarez realized he was just a few blocks south of the waterfront piers, and dropped back a little farther as the driver braked at Twelfth Avenue. Alvarez coasted down the long block and could hear the Chevy engine being gunned as the driver waited impatiently for the light to change.

On the green, they were off and running, this time on a wide uptown stretch with the lights spaced much farther apart. To the left, along the river, cyclone fences separated the two-way traffic from broad parking lots in front of warehouses and abandoned buildings. They passed Fourteenth Street, and Alvarez was able to stay two blocks behind.

A brick warehouse loomed up on the left, and the Chevy's left-turn signal started to blink. Alvarez watched the car drift through the southbound lane and nose into a driveway, then duck down along the northern side of the brick building. He coasted by, keeping his eye on the Chevy's taillights, until he caught a light one block north. In his side-view mirror, he watched the car's lights go out, then ducked around a corner, ignoring the red signal.

The first open space on the crowded side street was a garage driveway. Alvarez spun the Grand Prix in, its right side halfway up the sidewalk, and got out. Sprinting back along the street, he reached the corner just as the Chevy's dome light went on, then off. He heard the slam, then the echo, of a car door closing, followed quickly by a second.

Alvarez panted as he darted across Twelfth Avenue, the cold air sending shivers through him as he sucked it into his lungs. At the edge of the parking lot a section of fence had been peeled back away from its post, and he slid through the gap, his parka catching on the sharp ends of the severed wire.

A small yellow sign over the side door of the brick building caught his eye, but he couldn't make out the lettering in the dark. He ducked low and shuffled toward the building, keeping the Chevy between himself and the darkened doorway.

He bent down behind the rear of the Chevy. Closer in, he could now read the sign; the paint of its lettering had half peeled off, but there was no misreading it. He had followed two of Stanley Mills's contacts to Arlington Metal.

Working his way to the front of the car, he stepped to the brick wall, pressing himself flat and easing toward the rear of the building. He stopped beneath a window, blocked with painted plywood, and listened. He could hear a low murmur, but it was machinery, not voices. Continuing on, he stopped beneath a second window to listen again. Still nothing but the low sibilance of heavy machinery, possibly a conveyor of some sort. The hiss and clank was too regular and too free of accent to be molding or stamping equipment.

At the corner he noticed an iron stairway leading to a platform two flights above. He climbed the stairs slowly, taking care not to let his feet clang on the metal steps. Grasping a rickety rail with his good hand, he could feel the cold iron even through his glove.

At the landing above him he paused to survey the length of the catwalk. It was little more than two feet wide and seemed to connect to a series of double doors along the upper reaches of the building. In front of each doorway a break in the catwalk railing suggested they had been intended for access from outside, perhaps by crane.

He moved along the catwalk and stopped at the first set of doors. He tried the handle, but it refused to turn. The second was open, but the hinges protested with such a squawk he decided to pass. The third was golden. The handle turned easily, and the door swung noiselessly out. Alvarez slipped inside to find himself on an interior replica of the catwalk outside. It was as if he had stepped right through the surface of a mirror.

In the vast recesses of the building he could see huge idle machines arrayed seemingly at random on the concrete floor thirty feet below. A broad, deserted conveyor clanked away in the gloom, carrying nothing and attended by no one he could see. The light was minimal, most of it streaming through a half-raised corrugated wall running the length of the building front to back, along the side he had just skirted.

A block of light marked the spot where the catwalk pierced the sheet metal, and he tiptoed along the corridor. Stooping just short of the opening, he drew his gun from the holster under his arm. He felt a little better with the gun in his hand, but not much.

Creeping the last ten feet to the block of light, he slid his feet along the slick metal, trying to avoid the impact of shoe on steel, knowing the vibration might echo elsewhere in the building.

At the opening he flattened himself against the corrugated wall and pressed his cheek forward just far enough to see around the rusty metal edge. On the floor below, under flickering fluorescents, four men were busily stuffing and patting a sticky-looking, puttylike substance into five-gallon cans. Both of the men he had followed were there, their peacoats off and piled on a folding chair behind the area where they were working. A fifth man was tamping the gray matter tightly into the cans and pouring a darker material on top. The sixth and last man fixed plastic lids in place, then banded the rims with metal rings crimped by a huge pincerlike tool.

Alvarez didn't know what the dark stuff was. Or why it was being packed into the cans. But he had recognized the other substance. He had tugged on Stanley Mills's coat and found the C-4.

The continuous racket was giving Alvarez a headache. The building was poorly heated, and huddled up near the roof, he was freezing. His hands were getting numb and his ankles ached. He tried to estimate the number of canisters, but the pace was nonstop and he had no idea how long they had been at it before he arrived. He watched the glowing face of his watch, checking every five or ten minutes as the phosphorescent hands wound interminably through one circuit then another. After three hours, there was still no sign of a letup.

Alvarez shifted his weight, stretching his legs in front of him, and leaned against the cold wall behind him. The metal of the catwalk was freezing, but his legs needed the relief. He put his gun in his lap, then took off his glove to massage the stiffness out of his knees.

His left arm ached constantly, and he had no painkillers left, having exhausted the supply he had brought in his pocket for a night he had expected to be much shorter. The wound began to throb and the entire shoulder felt as if it were going to burst from some pressure deep inside his body.

At three-thirty the six men knocked off. They had been working continually for more than two hours, and now they sat on barrels and packing crates. One man disappeared through a doorway and reappeared a moment later dangling a six-pack by its plastic wrapping. He plunked the beer down on the end of the still-clinking conveyor and pulled one beer after another from the webbing, tossing each in turn to one of the other men. Yanking the final can free, he popped the lid and took a long draft. He said something Alvarez couldn't hear, but it made the others laugh. They lounged around, joking and sipping slowly on the beers. Alvarez was thirsty, and he felt envious, like a wino with his nose against a restaurant window.

A tall thin man, built more like a delicate wading bird then a human being, seemed to be in charge. His long hair, still dark but noticeably thinning, suggested an age somewhere in the area of fifty. He was dressed in jeans and a work shirt with sleeves rolled nearly to his elbows, a thick sweatshirt with cutoff sleeves covering it like a vest and flapping loosely across his midsection. Alvarez guessed his height at six-three or -four, and he couldn't have weighed more than 150 pounds. Broad bands of muscle lined his forearms, and the backs of his hands were thickly veined.

They were the hands of someone's grandfather, still strong after a lifetime of manual labor.

The thin man finally stood up, reassembling his long limbs like the articulated pieces of a construction crane. He said something to the others, and the collective groan reached Alvarez in his perch up near the ceiling. Four of the men disappeared off to the right, and the thin man and one other who stayed behind—a short dark man in a checkered flannel shirt drawn tight across massive shoulders—started loading the canisters onto the conveyor.

They worked steadily, gradually reducing the huge mound behind them, taking two at a time and slapping them with an audible thump onto the thick rubber of the belt. Alvarez got to his knees, bumping his wounded shoulder once and sending a flash of pain to the pit of his stomach. For a moment he thought he might vomit and was grateful he'd eaten nothing but the piece of Danish. The nausea subsided while he held his breath, and he tried again to maneuver out of the tight squeeze.

Doubling back along the catwalk, he stayed low to keep it between him and anyone below. He maneuvered past pieces of tall machinery that reached up to the ceiling, in some places no more than an arm's length away from the low railing on the inner edge of the walkway. Just ahead, a tangle of cables afforded him some cover and smeared its shadows over the wall behind him. When he reached the cables he was able to look down to the far corner.

The corner was lighted more brightly than the rest of the building, and he could see clearly. The other four men were busy retrieving canisters at the end of the conveyor, stacking them on wooden skids. One skid was already full, piled high with the twenty-gallon minidrums in five layers of eight by eight.

The bottom of each canister fit snugly into a recess in the lid of the canister beneath it, locking the columns together like a Lego set and giving each skid stability. The second skid was quickly filled, and one of the men picked up a large tool something like a chain saw. A wavering band of black metal shimmered behind it, like the tail of a dark comet, and the man quickly banded each layer, crimping the band in place with a turn of his wrist. When he was finished with that procedure he quickly threaded two more bands around the skid, feeding them between the two tiers of the skid, then crimping them in place. He rotated ninety degrees and repeated the process. When he was finished, skid and canisters were one tightly wrapped package.

He covered the entire skid with a thick canvas bearing the stenciled legend:

ARLINGTON METAL NYC
Epoxy and Fixative

When the canvas was secure he moved on to the second skid.

Alvarez was awed by the volume of matériel, possibly several tons, and its explosive power was incalculable. Should it detonate, it would take out several square blocks and rain debris across the Hudson and from the Battery to midtown. He knew C-4 was inert by itself, but the sheer potential of that much of the plastic explosive took his breath away.

The crew had hit its stride now, and several more skids were finished in short order. When the eighth and last had been banded and wrapped, the thin man walked into the far corner of the warehouse. He was out of sight, but Alvarez could tell by the sound that he was opening a freight bay door. It rattled on its rollers and its electric motor sent vibrations throughout the huge room. A moment later the roar of a diesel thundered into the warehouse, and the agent saw a red glare in the far corner, which grew suddenly brighter as a truck backed in and braked.

The truck door slammed, and the bay door shuddered back down, rattling on its metal tracks, closing with a final slam as the metal banged into the concrete floor. Before the echo died, the thin man reappeared at the rear of the truck.

He turned the handle on the vehicle's rear door and shoved upward.

A second rumble joined that of the truck, and an awkward looking forklift dashed out of the shadows, its forked tongue licking at the slats of the nearest skid. With a groan it began to hoist the heavy pallet, backed to maneuver, then darted forward, depositing the pallet on the rear of the truck bed.

The forklift operator seemed to know what he was doing, backing away then moving forward again, this time using the fork to push the pallet deeper into the truck. The heavy skid moved reluctantly on the truck bed, but the operator refused to give in. He gunned the engine and its powerful sound swelled to thunder in the enclosed space.

When he was satisfied he had moved the skid as far in as it would go, he took a second pallet and dumped it behind the first. It overhung the tailgate by a foot or so, and he struggled to shove both pallets a little deeper. He repeated the process for the right side of the truck and soon had half of the skids loaded.

When the truck was loaded, the thin man, who had been sitting on a folding chair off to one side, got to his feet and closed the tailgate. Alvarez had difficulty seeing whether or not the truck had been locked. He watched, scarcely breathing, as a second truck was backed in next to the first and loaded with the same dispatch as the first.

When the sound of the forklift had died, and he had hauled the second door down and latched it, the leader of the six-man team said, "That's it for now. Be back here in an hour. We have to get this load to the airport by six sharp."

"What's the hurry?" one of the others asked.

"How the hell do I know? I just take orders like the rest of you. Harlow wants this stuff in the air by six-fifteen. That's all I know. Go get some breakfast and we'll meet here in an hour."

"That's cutting it awful close."

"You rather work on an empty stomach, fine by me."

"Screw that."

"So I'll see you at five." He waved them away, then as an afterthought added in a loud voice, "Oh, by the way, you ain't here at five, you don't get paid. *Capisce?*"

An audible click drifted through the warehouse as the lights died. Alvarez held his breath for a long count. The ticking of the cooling engines was the only noise he heard for several minutes. He glanced at his watch—four-fifteen. That gave him less than an hour. He inched along the catwalk in the dark, slipping once and nearly pitching over the low safety rail to the concrete floor below. He took a deep breath and could hear the thumping of his heart. He flattened his one good hand over his chest and felt the pounding with his fingers, then pressed, as if he could still the heart by force of will.

He resumed his tentative crawl and reached the exit door after another minute. Backing out into the frigid night, he sighed long and hard. His nerves were starting to come unwound. He backed down the ladder, stopping twice, thinking he'd heard something. Each time he told himself it was just nerves, but each time he lost precious minutes listening and waiting.

When he finally reached the ground his hand was shaking in a nervous tremor. His shoulder ached, but the medicine was in his car. It would have to wait.

For one giddy instant the germ of an idea blossomed, and he thought about hiding in the back of one of the trucks, but it was just short of suicide and he knew it. On aching legs, the knees still stiff and sore, he sprinted back to the fence, slipped through the ragged hole and dashed across Twelfth Avenue.

He got into his car with his heart still pounding, sat quietly, his hands on the wheel, listening to the noise and its echo in his throbbing temples. He had a bitch of a headache. Opening the glove compartment, Alvarez tilted a couple of painkillers into his palm, then washed them down with the cold coffee.

What the hell am I going to do now, he wondered.

CHAPTER TWENTY-NINE

Mack Bolan slipped back into the barracks and removed the match from the alarm switch. He crept back to his bunk, careful not to make any noise. Sitting down on the cot, he slipped his boots under it and lay back, his arms folded behind his head. He stared at the dark ceiling, his eyes darting from corner to corner as if he expected to find some explanation of what he had just witnessed.

Fifteen minutes later the door banged open and the alarm failed to go off. Sadowski clomped over to his office and opened the door. The soft light of a small bulb outlined the big man for a moment as he ducked under the low door-frame and closed the door behind him. The alarm didn't sound, and Bolan realized Sadowski must have shut it off before he went out.

An hour later the warrior was still awake. The sun was beginning to rise, and the windows of the barracks glowed redly. Small scarlet parallelograms were splashed on the floor, some distorted where they spilled over the sleeping men. Every instinct screamed for Bolan to charge into the office and confront Sadowski, but he struggled to control the urges. It was more important to get to the bottom of this bizarre operation.

Bolan realized that his anger was personal as well as objective. Very little but luck separated him from the three dead men lying out in the desert or the hapless guard on the warehouse floor. They had been victimized by circumstances one final time. Unable, for whatever reason, to fit into things as they were, those men had tried to hang on by doing the only thing they knew how to do. They were expendable in the ultimate sense, men who had outlived their usefulness even to men like Mason Harlow. He had taken them in as dead letters, and now they were simply dead.

The sun began its daily climb just opposite the window through which Bolan stared. Its red rim was barely visible above the sill, floating just out of sight like some malevolent bubble, full of red poison. The face of his watch no longer glowed in the rising light. He glanced at its hands. In an hour Carter would be stomping around like a caricature of a drill instructor, banging an iron triangle to get them up. He closed his eyes.

But he did not sleep.

Loose pieces floated through his mind's eye, changing shapes as he watched, like jagged amoebas. They fit one way, then grew apart as their outlines changed. No matter how he tried to force them to coalesce, the pieces would not hang together.

At six o'clock the alarm bell sounded. The earsplitting clatter sent the men stumbling for their weapons. The overhead lights flashed on, and Bolan, rifle in hand, found himself staring into the amused face of Mason Harlow.

"Rise and shine, you assholes." Harlow himself carried an AK-47. He fired a short burst into the ceiling, splintering the wooden slats of the roof, and sending a few men diving for cover.

"I told Load to get a better system here. Sadowski, where the hell are you?"

The screen door opened and a rifle poked through, its muzzle stopping just inches behind Harlow's head.

"Right here, fucker...."

Harlow, his eyes big as saucers, turned as Sadowski stepped into the barracks. He kept the gun leveled at Harlow's face, the muzzle wavering just a bit as he maneuvered through the opening.

Harlow reached for the gun, but Sadowski froze him with a hiss. "Don't...don't do it. How many times I got to tell you, Harlow, don't screw around with guns. They ain't toys."

"Come on, Load, put it away. We got a problem here."

McNally joined the chorus. "You out of your mind? You could have got somebody killed. What the hell's wrong with you?"

"Forget it, will you? We have more important things to discuss."

Tony Masseria appeared in the doorway, his face blurred by the screen. He stepped through, letting the door squeak closed and bang into his back before stepping past Harlow.

Harlow made placating gestures with his hands, then put a finger to his lips. "Look, we got a serious problem here. Where's Specs Martin?"

"Over here. Why?" Martin stepped forward, wearing only fatigue pants and a T-shirt. His bare feet rasped on the sandy floor. "What do you want?"

Harlow stepped back toward the screen door. He glanced at Sadowski for an instant before answering. "Show him, Tony."

Masseria looked at the floor and shuffled his feet. Then Bolan noticed the folded towel in Tony's hand. Masseria took a step forward then stopped, as if he weren't sure what he was supposed to do. He looked at his hands with detachment, then held the towel out. Slowly, almost tenderly, he unfolded the top layer of terry cloth, and Bolan saw the dark stain underneath. Masseria then peeled the second layer away and Bolan saw the ugly knife for the second time that morning.

"Look familiar?" Harlow asked.

"Yeah," Martin answered. "I have one just like it."

"Get it," Harlow barked.

"What for?"

"Just get the knife, all right?" Harlow seemed to be gaining confidence as he spoke.

Martin turned to walk through the crowd of men, who were whispering among themselves. As he reached out to push them aside, they moved of their own accord, as if repelled by some magnetic force, backing away instinctively before his hands made contact. As he passed through, the men stayed where they were, in a pair of curving lines, one on either side of the barracks. Martin opened a footlocker in front of his bunk and pulled a tray out. He tossed the tray onto the unmade bunk and removed a small leather bag from the trunk.

He rooted around in the bag, his hands moving more and more quickly. Suddenly he stopped and looked at Harlow through the double arc of men. His face seemed frozen in a state of complete bewilderment. "It's not here."

"Where is it?" Harlow demanded.

"I don't know. It was here yesterday. I saw it." He looked toward Sadowski. "You saw it, didn't you?"

"Yeah, I did. Yesterday." Sadowski turned to Harlow. "Where'd you get that one?"

"Found it," Harlow said. "In the warehouse."

"What the hell was it doing there?" Martin asked, his voice tight and half an octave higher than usual.

"That's what I want you to tell me." Harlow grinned ghoulishly, then brought the Kalashnikov around to aim it at Martin's midsection. "Now!"

"I don't know. I told you, it was here yesterday."

"What's going on here?" Bolan demanded. The men turned to look at him, as if to thank him for voicing the same question they'd been asking themselves.

"Butt out," Sadowski snapped. "Let Mr. Harlow finish."

"Finish what?" Bolan asked.

"Shut the fuck up, and maybe you'll find out." Sadowski balled his fists and took a tentative step forward. Bolan didn't flinch.

"Matt Milovich is dead. This knife is what killed him," Harlow announced. He allowed the significance of the statement to sink in before continuing. The barracks was perfectly still. A single angry fly, crashing repeatedly into the ceiling and buzzing his frustration, made the only sound. "Since it's Martin's knife, I want to hear what he has to say about all that."

"I don't have anything to say. I didn't kill him. Why would I?"

"If I knew who the hell you were, I might be able to answer that."

"You know who I am. What the hell are you talking about?"

"I know who you *say* you are. That's all I know. I checked on you, and I couldn't find anything. That makes me wonder why."

Martin looked helplessly at the others. He held his palms upward, as if begging them to vouch for him. "What can I say?"

"Nothing," Sadowski barked. He stepped forward, raising his rifle.

"Wait a minute," Bolan hollered. "The knife doesn't prove anything."

"I told you to butt out," Sadowski warned. Bolan saw the muzzle of the Kalashnikov waver an instant, then slowly drift in his direction.

Harlow raised a hand. "I think we ought to investigate this matter a little further. Until then, it would be prudent to make sure Mr. Martin stays put." He looked at Sadowski, then at Martin. "Would you mind going with us? I want to ask you a few questions."

"I told you, I don't know anything."

"Then it shouldn't take very long, should it?"

Sadowski took Martin by the upper arm and shoved him toward the screen door. The smaller man stumbled and fell, striking his head on the doorframe. The wall of the barracks rattled at the impact. Sadowski bent down and hauled Martin up by the belt. He shoved the captive through the screen door, and Martin's elbow struck the wire, leaving an odd bubble in the mesh.

"I think everyone should just go on about his business until we get to the bottom of this," Harlow announced. He turned to go. The men stood motionless, too stunned even to mumble. As Harlow's hand pressed the open door, a shot, quickly followed by two more, cracked outside.

Bolan rushed to the door, pushing Harlow aside. Specs Martin lay facedown in the sand, three dark red stains, each the size of a silver dollar, slowly spreading across the back of his T-shirt.

"Son of a bitch tried to run," Sadowski drawled. "What a stupid thing to do, huh?"

Bolan stared at the big man, who seemed to be daring him to disagree. Dave McNally stood in the doorway. "What are we going to tell the Libs?"

"The hell with the Libs," Sadowski replied. "Don't worry about it."

"But I do worry about it," McNally snapped. "Somebody has to."

"For Christ's sake, you're always worrying about something. You even worry the sun might come up in the desert every damn day."

Harlow seemed to have regained his composure. "Look, what's done is done. Let's just forget about it. We have too much to do as it is. You know how hard it is to get things done here."

"You got that right, Harlow. Seems like you better get your act together soon." Sadowski seemed to have switched sides, agreeing now with McNally. Bolan watched the delicate chemistry among the three men with interest.

"You take care of last night's shipment?" Harlow asked with a broad wink.

"Old business, Chief. Dead and buried." Sadowski laughed.

"What shipment? What are you talking about?" McNally asked.

"Shit, man, you spend too much time with your nose in the bottle. I didn't bother to try to wake you up. You were too far gone." Sadowski seemed to be deliberately baiting him.

McNally whirled to face the taller man. "That's a goddamned lie. I wasn't drinking last night."

"Whatever." Sadowski shrugged.

"Look, I think we should go over to my office and discuss this," Harlow said, his voice taking on a slight conspiratorial tone.

Bolan realized he and Picard were the only men still paying attention to the conversation. The others had gone back inside to their bunks or to busy themselves getting dressed. No one said a word.

Harlow stepped outside and started toward the other barracks, McNally right on his heels. Sadowski followed, but not before he stepped to the door and gave the room a quick scan. He grunted with satisfaction. His eyes seemed to linger on Bolan, who averted his gaze. The door banged shut, and Bolan turned to watch the departing trio. Something didn't seem quite right, and he realized that Sadowski was staring back at him through the screen.

The sun shone off the big man's bald head, giving him a halo of fire. He yanked the screen door open again and stepped back inside. Everyone in the barracks stared at him expectantly.

"You clowns can have the morning off," he said. The announcement was greeted with a chorus of halfhearted cheers.

As Bolan finished dressing he noticed Tony Masseria sitting on Martin's bunk. He still held the open towel, the dark blood crusting the knife beginning to flake. He stared at his hands as if they belonged to a stranger. Sensing someone watching him, he turned toward Bolan. Sighing once, he shook his head and folded the towel carefully over the knife.

Tony stood and placed the knife, still wrapped in the towel, in Martin's leather bag. He put the bag in the trunk, replaced the tray, closed the lid and slipped the padlock in place. Everyone in the barracks was watching him. He snapped the padlock closed.

The click sounded like a gunshot in the sudden quiet.

CHAPTER THIRTY

The painkillers had quieted the throbbing in his arm, and Leon Alvarez shrugged out of his heavy parka. The heater whooshed constantly, bathing him in a steady stream of warm air. He eased the sling off his arm and slipped out of his shirt, twirling the sling into a narrow band, then wrapping it around his upper arm. It slid out of his grasp once, and he cursed aloud. Rewinding the slippery cloth, he crimped one end of the rolled sling between his upper arm and rib cage, then maneuvered through two loops, the pressure of the cloth making him wince.

With the cloth now in position, he grabbed one end in his teeth, twisting the second around it in a clumsy knot. He tugged the cloth tight with a jerk of his head, then worked a second loop, using the tips of his fingers. When the makeshift reinforcement was as snug as he could get it, he tugged the knot one more time with his teeth, then cut the loose ends with a pocketknife.

He slipped his shirt back on and fumbled with the buttons. The fingers of his left hand were a little clumsy, but that should improve as he got accustomed to using them again. The shirt was a bit snug over his wounded arm, but nothing that couldn't be lived with for a few hours. He shrugged back into the parka and zipped it carefully. He slipped an automatic revolver into his coat pocket and patted it with the tentative pleasure of a man coaxing a little extra good luck from a favored talisman.

Alvarez watched as the freight bay door rose into the air. With his engine running and the windows of the car closed, he heard nothing, and it looked like a scene from an old movie. The gray night and smears of shadow along Twelfth

Avenue gave the entire scene the appearance of the product of an exaggerated imagination working overtime.

The first truck rolled out of the warehouse before its lights went on, the vehicle seeming to move stiffly, as if the weight it carried were beyond its capacity. The freight bed seemed to twist independently of the frame. Alvarez was sure the entire operation was accompanied by the incessant squealing of metal distorted to the very limit of its tolerance.

It lumbered to the unopened gate, and Alvarez watched the driver jump down and unlock the heavy chain, then push the gate to one side, walking it back on rollers until the opening was wide enough to let the truck pass through. Exhaust in small, unsteady puffs rose up behind the vehicle and disappeared against the thick haze boiling over the river.

Lights suddenly exploded in the mouth of the warehouse. Twin beams stabbed out and the second truck rolled forward as soundlessly as the first. Alvarez held his breath. The freight bay door closed, seemingly of its own accord, while the second truck nosed up behind the first.

He wondered what they were waiting for, and almost instantly, as if in response to his unspoken question, the thin man appeared at the far end of the warehouse. He angled across the tarred parking area, then climbed up onto the running board of the first truck. He leaned forward, as if trying to hear the driver over the truck's engine, then jumped down and ran to the second truck, where he repeated the process.

Finally he dropped off the running board and stood back, hands on hips, his breath puffing in round clouds, nearly perfect globes of condensation ripped almost immediately by the wind off the river. He waved the first truck on, and it twisted on its frame once again as it rolled over potholes in the parking lot, then down the driveway into Twelfth Avenue.

The second truck seemed to have less difficulty, as if its load were less of a strain. When it nosed out into Twelfth, the thin man rolled the gate closed and resecured it with the heavy chain, snapping the thick padlock closed with a jerk of his wrist so familiar Alvarez could almost hear it.

Alvarez watched the vehicles coast to the light at the corner, resisting the urge to roll into position at the light. Traffic was still extremely sparse, and any car would naturally attract the attention of the drivers. They had to be skittish. They were rolling along with enough high explosives behind them to take out much of the West Side. Only an idiot wouldn't pay attention to his surroundings in such circumstances.

The light changed and Alvarez watched the trucks disappear past the corner of a tall brick building on his right. He counted ten before putting his lights on, then rolled slowly to the corner. He could see the tail of the second truck now nearly a block away. Checking for traffic, he spun through a ninety-degree turn, taking a chance on running the light. He drifted slowly uptown behind the trucks.

The agent kept a nervous eye on the rearview mirror, but the avenue behind him was empty. It was nearly five-fifteen now, and the early-morning rush would gradually build. Alvarez knew the trucks were headed for an airport, but there were three to choose from, and it was too early to eliminate Newark. Both it and Kennedy were at the outer edge of the time constraints, which made La Guardia the most logical choice, but he could assume nothing. And if he lost the shipment, it would be gone for good.

Thinking about that much power in the hands of Mason Harlow—or anyone he would work for—made Alvarez shudder. He goosed the engine while he waited for his own light to change. Way off in the distance, at the far edge of the fog, he watched the sequenced lights flash to green, and a chain of green spots advanced toward the trucks. He was so intent on the lights he failed to notice a panel truck slip into position on his right rear fender.

The advancing green lights reached, then passed the trucks, and he stepped on the accelerator, feeling the Grand Prix straining as he started to ease up on the clutch. The powerful V-8 rumbled, and the vibration of the floorboard was an agreeable throwback to his youth, hot-rodding up and down the California coast. Unconsciously he started to hum a jumbled medley of Beach Boys and Jan and Dean hot-rod hits as he popped the clutch and hit the gas just right, getting maximum rpms without a loss of traction. It was a good takeoff, and he smiled for the first time that night. Some kinds of joy never lost their thrill. First and foremost on his own list was the kick of a competition-tuned muscle car responding to his every move.

The quick start caught the driver of the panel truck by surprise, and Alvarez was nearly a half block ahead of him before he could recover. He goosed his own engine, and the tires spun on the slick pavement. Alvarez glanced in the rearview mirror and frowned. He hadn't seen the truck, and its sudden desire to keep up with him was disturbing.

The trucks were cruising under the Westside Highway, and Alvarez tried to hang in, but the panel truck was gaining rapidly. It roared by on the right, then cut sharply in front of him. Alvarez spun the wheel and skidded broadside, narrowly missing one of the huge steel columns supporting the roadway overhead. He wrestled the Grand Prix back under control, shooting between two columns and zigzagging like a skier through several more pairs. The panel truck drifted to the left and roared ahead, moving uptown in the downtown lane. Alvarez slid to the right and drew abreast of the truck. He kept one eye on the overloaded vans, which continued to move north as if nothing were happening behind them.

At Thirtieth street the trucks turned right, heading across town. Alvarez dropped into third gear and floored it. The Grand Prix fishtailed on the slippery concrete until the oversize tires caught and the car flashed forward. The panel truck roared up behind him as he ran a red light at Thirty-second Street. The huge glass monstrosity of the Javits Convention Center towered over him, and just ahead, the avenue become one-way only, for downtown traffic.

Alvarez drifted over toward the curb, as if intending to make the turn, easing up on the gas as the panel truck crept up behind him. He swung right and hit the wheel hard, flashing in a tight 180 as the panel truck flew by. He could smell the burning rubber of his tires as he slammed the transmission into first and roared back out of Thirty-second Street. Behind him he could hear a squeal as the panel truck braked.

Running through the gears, Alvarez highballed it down to Thirtieth and hung a left. The two trucks were almost wrapped in fog three or four blocks ahead of him. He sprinted to the next light, slowing just in time to avoid a newspaper delivery van as it accelerated through an amber light.

Glancing at the rearview, he saw the panel truck swing in behind him. Alvarez knew he'd never make it to the airport with the continual harassment of the panel truck, and if he let them stop him, they'd win anyway. The only avenue open to him was to take the panel truck out of the picture. He swung into a deserted parking lot just before Tenth Avenue. Leaving the car running, he jumped out and slipped down between two cars parked at one edge of the lot.

He drew his gun and waited for the panel truck to follow him into the lot, his hands clammy on the cold steel of the Browning Hi-Power automatic. He kept shifting his grip on the gun, flexing his fingers like an arthritic getting up in the morning. Ignoring the driveway, the panel truck bounced high over the curb, slamming back on all four wheels with a squeal of rubber. A shower of sparks blossomed underneath as its muffler and tailpipe scraped the pavement. The vehicle braked in a controlled spin, as its driver wheeled it around to face the Grand Prix.

From where he was hiding Alvarez could see nothing behind the windshield, which reflected the brightening gray as the sun tried to come up behind the fog. Through the glare, the two men in the cab of the panel truck were nothing more than watery shadows. He hunkered down, getting a little more cover for himself from the cars on either side.

Alvarez moved back, then eased himself up over the rear deck of a battered old Buick. He drew a bead on the center of the windshield of the panel truck and waited for its occupants to make a move. The windshield wipers flapped on as the driver tried to improve his view of the deserted lot. Then, cautiously, like a fledgling trying its wings, the truck doors opened simultaneously. Alvarez could hear the squeaking of their hinges.

The passenger stepped down gingerly, one foot at a time. Alvarez watched the sneaker-clad feet shift, and ducked instinctively when the man peeked out around the open door and fired a short burst of suppressed fire from a submachine gun. The windshield of the Grand Prix dissolved with a shattering crash. Alvarez waited, holding his breath and his fire. A second pair of feet hit the asphalt on the driver's side.

Alvarez shifted his aim, waited for the driver to plant himself, then squeezed. The Browning bucked in his hand, and he was rewarded with a yelp of pain. The driver pitched forward onto the pavement, grasping his ankle. Alvarez fired again, this time planting a 9 mm slug dead center. The driver uncoiled like a dying snake, squirming around for a moment, then lying still.

Shifting his attention back to the passenger, he watched the feet, saw the man shuffle, then saw one foot disappear. Squeezing off two quick shots, he saw sparks fly as both slugs glanced off the front fender and slipped through the crack of the open door. He heard a groan, and waited. The second foot stayed planted on the tar. The passenger turned and Alvarez fired again, this time driving his shot straight through the door. The passenger dropped his weapon with a clatter and crumpled to the pavement.

Alvarez stood up cautiously, then slid out from behind the old Buick. He walked toward the panel truck, ready to hit the deck at the first sign of movement. Neither of the men uttered a sound. He checked the passenger first, rolling him onto his back. Two neat holes, one just above the other, had been drilled through his leather jacket. Blood seeped out around both holes, and a glistening stream oozed out under the leather at the belt line, soaking the front of the man's acid-washed jeans.

Alvarez pulled him to one side and closed the door. Picking up the Uzi, he walked around to the driver's side. He glanced at the driver, who was sprawled on his back. There was no need to look any closer. He, too, was dead.

He bent to retrieve the driver's weapon, a stainless-steel Coonan .357 Magnum. He tossed both weapons into the passenger's bucket seat and climbed up into the truck. The Grand Prix was a hot number, but he couldn't afford to drive it around with no windshield. It was a Company car, and sanitized. No one could connect it to him.

He slammed the driver's door and popped the clutch. The panel truck veered around and lurched back over the curb and out into Thirtieth Street. The trucks were long gone, but there was still a chance. Alvarez gunned the engine and sped across town to Third Avenue, hung a left and headed toward the Triborough Bridge. If the trucks were going to La Guardia, and that was his best bet, he could still catch them.

If not, tomorrow might not be another day.

CHAPTER THIRTY-ONE

An hour later, Sadowski swaggered into the barracks with more than his customary arrogance. It was before noon, but the sun was already high in the sky, and he was sweating heavily. The smell of him seemed to balloon out and fill the room, as if it had been a vacuum before he entered. Bolan was lying on his bunk.

Sadowski sat down on the next bunk, which was vacant. The spring groaned wearily under his weight, and Bolan guessed the man must weigh somewhere in the neighborhood of 270. For several minutes he just sat, staring at Bolan with interest but saying nothing. The warrior watched the play of Sadowski's fingers, which wriggled stiffly, restlessly, as if he were nervous about something.

Bolan resisted the urge to speak first. If Sadowski was uncomfortable, he might learn something useful. The large man ran his hand over his tanned scalp, a nervous gesture Bolan thought must hark back to the time when he had hair, or perhaps it was a phantom, like the pain an amputee feels long after the limb has been removed.

Finally Sadowski sighed. "Look, Belasko, we got off to a bad start, I know that. And some of it was my fault. But we've got a job to do here, and you're gonna have to play a crucial part in it."

Bolan raised himself on one elbow and rolled onto his side. "I'm listening."

"What I mean is, I'm not apologizing or anything, but I think we both ought to forget about what happened before. It ain't going to help either one of us. And it might fuck things up here. This is a delicate operation, high priority and all that."

"I'd like to believe that, Sadowski, but nobody has told me a damn thing about what I'm doing here. All I know is I was told one thing in New York, hauled halfway across the country to shoot holes in paper, which as far as I can tell has nothing to do with instructing guerrillas, and then dragged around the world in the dead of night."

"Yeah, yeah, I know. But there's a reason for it."

"I remain skeptical about that."

Sadowski bristled. "You calling me a liar?"

"Not at all. But you have to admit, we're pretty well in the dark. I have my suspicions, but I think I'll just keep them to myself. At least until I get a little more information."

"That's why I'm here. We have a meeting in a little while. You're invited."

"Why me?"

"Because Carter tells me you scored the best on the marksmanship tests."

"Such as they were. But actually, Martin—you remember him, don't you?—came in first. We didn't have much competition. And the other guys weren't that bad. They should have been here, too. That was the deal we made."

"Deals are made to be broken."

Bolan paused an extra beat, letting Sadowski shift uncertainly. Sadowski's eyes darted around the room as if looking for cue cards or some prepared text that might help him get through a difficult moment.

"What happened to the others, anyway?"

"Oh, we just sent them back to the holes they crawled out of in the first place." Sadowski was not an accomplished liar. Diplomacy was not something that came easily to him, and dissembling was an alien art form to this huge man, who no doubt had lived his life by a much more direct code of behavior. Smash what you don't like, and let somebody else pick up the pieces.

Bolan smiled at him, daring Sadowski to lie to him again. The big man's gaze danced here and there, never lighting for long, and never on Bolan's face. "I see," Bolan said. "Like baseball camp, right? You bust your hump for three weeks, blow a few grounders in front of the boss or look like a jerk when you can't hit the curveball and the team gives you a train ticket back home."

"Yeah. Listen, about this meeting."

"I'm kind of beat, actually. This is supposed to be a day off."

"You can relax later. You want to know why you're here, you're about to find out."

"Who else?"

"A few other people. You don't need to know now. You'll see when you get there."

"But I want to know." The edge in Bolan's voice made Sadowski lean back a bit, like a child suddenly afraid he might be punished. There was more than a little bully in the big man, and like most bullies, he found the going easiest when there was no opposition.

"Harlow, McNally, me, Picard, Rogers, Masseria and Carter. Oh yeah, and Harlow's woman. You must've seen her. Red hair and big tits."

"Why her?"

"You seen her? She's quite a piece. And Harlow is pussy-whipped for sure."

"What time is the meeting?"

"Half an hour." On safer ground now, Sadowski seemed to have regained his composure. "Make sure you're there."

"Where?"

"Harlow's office, in the warehouse. You seen Rogers around anywhere?"

"Not lately."

"I'll find him." Sadowski heaved himself up off the bunk, the springs sighing with relief.

Bolan stayed on one elbow and watched the big man go. He wondered what was going on. Some faint tingle, like an alarm going off at a great distance in the middle of the night, kept ringing. He lay back down, puzzling over the change in Sadowski. That he had lied was obvious. Why was not so readily apparent.

Before he could devise some credible explanation, Picard came in. He took Sadowski's place on the adjacent bunk. "You heard?"

Bolan nodded. "Yeah, what do you make of it?"

"Damned if I know. But I got a feeling we're about to take a giant step closer to the heart of things."

"Maybe. Maybe not."

"Sadowski seem different to you?"

"Yeah. But I can't figure why."

"Neither can I."

"You remember those guys who were with us in Louisiana?"

"Yeah, why?"

"They're here."

"But I thought they didn't make it."

"They didn't."

"Then what are they doing here?"

"Nothing."

"You're talking in riddles."

"They came in last night." Bolan sat up, dropping his feet to the floor. "About four in the morning."

"Where are they? I haven't seen any of them."

"You won't, either. They came in on a C-47, unloaded some stuff, then went out into the desert with Sadowski, Tony and Carter. They didn't come back."

Picard whistled. "You sure?"

Bolan shrugged. "And it was Sadowski who killed Milovich, not Martin."

"Are you kidding? How do you know?"

"I saw it."

"Holy Jesus!" Picard whispered. "But why?"

"I don't know. I think it was just a way to get Martin, but what I can't figure out is why they wanted to do that. And I don't believe Martin tried to get away. He had no reason. He knew he was innocent."

"This is getting more bizarre all the time. I don't like it. Remember what you said about loose ends? Well, that's what we all are. We do what we're supposed to and we're expendable. If we don't, we're useless. Either way—" he drew a finger across his throat "—we're loose ends. Damn!"

"We're along for the ride, Lucien. There's nothing we can do but play out the string as far as we can. And watch our backs. We have to go along with the program until we figure a way out."

Picard glanced at his watch. He shook it, then held it to his ear. "Damn thing stopped." He took it off and wound the stem rapidly, then looked at Bolan. "What time you got?"

"Ten-twenty."

Picard set his watch, then strapped it back on. "We might as well go see what this is all about."

"I don't think we have any choice. Do you?"

Picard said nothing. It was obvious he didn't like the threat to them both implicit in the question. He stood up and stretched. "I always hated this part of the world. I don't know why, but I think it has something to do with how vulnerable it is, how susceptible to manipulation by men like Mason Harlow."

"That's why we're here, isn't it?" Bolan asked softly. "To make sure it doesn't happen this time?"

Picard snorted. "And who will be here next week? Or next month? You think we can make a difference?"

"If I didn't, I wouldn't be here. I'd be someplace nice and quiet, sitting there with a book and a fishing pole, watching the sun set. If I can't make a difference, I have no reason to do anything at all."

Picard grinned. "Quite the optimist, aren't you, Mr. Belasko."

Bolan stood up. "Let's go."

They left the barracks, walking across the dusty compound in tandem. They covered the hundred yards in short order, but both men were sweating when they reached the modest shade of the warehouse wall. Keeping out of the sun, they walked into the heart of the L and stepped in through the open door of the warehouse. It was dark inside, but no cooler.

Harlow's office was against the far wall, a ramshackle cube of plywood and Plexiglas tucked into the vertex of the L. It was brightly lit, and its door was open. Three men were seated inside, facing away from the window. One of them was Sadowski, the others were unrecognizable.

Bolan stepped into the office first, Picard hanging back and shuffling in a moment later. Mason Harlow was the picture of the comfortable executive, tilted back in a worn leather chair, his feet propped carelessly on the desk, one heel crumpling a few stray sheets of paper.

"Gentlemen..." He greeted them expansively. "I guess we're all here."

Bolan looked around the room. He recognized Rogers, Sadowski, Tony and Carter. On a chair to Harlow's left sat a striking redhead. The rumpled fatigues she wore did little to disguise a spectacular figure. The shirt was partway open, offering a generous view of a freckled chest and more than a little cleavage. Bolan was already sitting down when Picard walked in. The Frenchman seemed to start when he saw the redhead, then spun to look for a chair. No one but Bolan seemed to notice the struggle on his features.

"I guess we can begin," Harlow said, tilting forward in the chair and dropping his feet to the floor. "You've all been told what this is about. But I want you to forget everything you've been told up to now. It was all smoke, a necessary subterfuge, as I'm sure you'll agree once you are apprised of the true nature of our business here."

Sadowski shifted in his chair, its wooden joints creaking as he adjusted his purchase on the uncomfortable seat. The others sat motionless. Bolan kept one eye on the redhead and one on Picard, but she showed no sign of recognition, and Picard had regained his composure.

"As you know," Harlow began, "we have not exactly been friendly with Libya for some time. I'm here to do something about that. All of us are. That's what this is all about. It means, though, that we're going to have to demonstrate our goodwill. It won't be easy, and it might mean we have to do a few things we don't totally agree with.'' He paused to examine each man in turn, trying to gauge the effect of his opening remarks.

"If you have any reservations, all I can ask is that you trust me. I have been in touch with the chief of staff in Cairo, and he's prepared to smooth the way for us. That's all I can tell you about that. And I don't have to remind you what plausible deniability is all about. If we fuck up, we're on our own.

"I'm leaving right after this meeting for an appointment in Chad. I'll sketch in the details when I get back. But I want you to understand right now that you don't know the big picture. And you won't for a long time, if ever. Now, here's what we're going to do."

CHAPTER THIRTY-TWO

N'Djamena is the quintessential Third World capital. A disordered mixture of the ancient and the imperial, the colonial and the modern. In a way, it is Chad in a nutshell. That, of course, is not so surprising. As the country's largest city, its population of a half million nearly ten percent of the entire Chadian populace, it tries to be all things to all people. And, like most such attempts, it falls more than a little short.

The architecture seemed to reflect the divided mentality of the population. A broad mix of Muslim, Christian and tribal religions made for an unstable stew, constantly on the edge of a low boil. The Muslim fundamentalists had so far made only the shallowest of inroads, but the uneasy balance was ripe for destabilization. The sub-Saharan drought of the late seventies and early eighties had done nothing to reassure the have-nots that the haves knew what they were doing, but a great deal to convince them that what little was being done had very little to do with them.

And yet, despite a thousand pressures from a hundred different directions, Chad had remained fairly tranquil. A cynic could easily have constructed a compelling argument that destabilization wasn't worth anyone's bother. A dedicated Marxist would have explained things by falling back on Marx's old chestnuts concerning the proletariat's need to understand itself before change was possible. A capitalist ideologue would say Chad was the Third World in microcosm, coming along at its own slow pace, not expecting too much too soon. The reality was probably a complicated blend of all those points of view and a dozen more. But the upshot of all the theorizing was indisputable: Chad's stability endured as much out of ignorance as out of any inherent sense of social justice.

But the tranquillity was only skin-deep. There were wolves at the door. And they were hungry. Libya had long coveted Chad and had been trying for more than a decade to take it by main force. Theories on why were few, and relatively simple. They all took into account the one indisputable fact about which there could be no argument: Chad was rich in uranium ore, perhaps as rich as any place on Earth. And Libya wanted it all.

Having tried to beg, borrow, steal and, when all else had failed, even to buy a nuclear weapon or two, the inscrutable powers that seemed to be—in Libya—had decided that if you could buy the technology, the rest would take care of itself, provided you had the natural resources. The rub was that Chad had what Libya didn't: yellow cake, by the ton.

Not to worry. If you had enough money and bought enough guns, you could take by force what no one was willing to give you freely. The result was a war that surpassed that between Iran and Iraq in longevity but not in fierceness. The tentative probing of Libyan fingers for the Chadian jugular had been a sometime thing. But, as in all wars, people had died, most of them innocent and all of them unnecessarily.

But that was a permanent condition on the planet, one tailor-made for men of vision, men who could see opportunity long before it got close enough to knock on the door. Sure, people died but that was a part of life. Or so Mason Harlow was fond of telling anyone who would listen.

From the window of a fifteenth-floor suite in N'Djamena's flagship hotel, the streets were paved with gold. Or so it seemed. A master at playing all ends against the middle, Harlow had a busy morning ahead of him. He watched the sun come up like a king surveying his domain.

Far below and to the east, the early-morning sun glinted on a minaret and a cross-bedecked steeple. Each spire took the sunlight and shattered it into a hundred slivers, then splashed them around the city with indifferent largess, like two rich men spewing pennies to a crowd of beggars. As he watched, the sun changed from red to bronze, then to yellow and finally to white. Twice its usual size, more aggressive than he was used to, it stabbed repeatedly at his eyes. The gradual change of color seemed incremental as he blinked and wiped away an occasional tear. Each time he closed his eyes, the white-hot ball glowed on his retinas, slowly fading like molten steel left to cool in a rolling mill.

Already dressed, he paced back and forth in front of the window. Things were getting hairy, and the king wasn't so sure he was in charge anymore. He thought back over the long, tortured route that had taken him so far in such a short time. It all seemed orderly, logical, well thought out. But too many people wanted a piece of him. He cursed those who worked for him, forgetting it was he who had chosen them, and he who had given them their marching orders. Harlow looked at the floor, where the sun smeared through the window and painted everything with gold, everything but the small space in which he marched. He wondered whether a careless painter felt the same way looking at the infinite expanse of wet paint between himself and the only door.

Now he was digging deeper, and the sides of the hole seemed to tower above him. He felt more than a little claustrophobic, and swore to himself that, once he climbed out, he'd hire somebody else to dig from now on. He was too important for that kind of shit work. He was an idea man, a mover and shaker. Hell, buying a few hardguys to waste the jerk running a two-bit armpit like Chad was easy, and it was a small enough price to pay to save his own skin.

The struggle of keeping up appearances had begun to take its toll. For that, he blamed everyone but himself. If the others had more guts, they wouldn't have to be coddled. It seemed like he had to be brave for them all. And when he was alone, he trembled.

Three days and it would all be over. He'd cut and run, and even the Libyans wouldn't find him. Ticking off his bank accounts on mental fingers, he smiled for the first time that morning. Twenty million dollars ought to be enough to keep him in booze and broads for a while. Hell, he might even marry Marielle, if Lois was out of the picture. And if he could arrange a hit on a head of state, getting rid of one pain in the ass of a wife ought to be a cinch.

But he was getting ahead of himself. He had three days to get through. They would be tricky, but he was sure he could do it. If only...

And he scowled. That was the story of his life. If only this and if only that. It was about time to stop worrying about what might go wrong and make sure nothing did. He could satisfy al-Hassan and pay off his debt. Talk was cheap and big talk was cheaper still. But the bastard had been pushing him. Imagine the balls of the bastard, trying to hold on to his passport. Who the hell did he think he was?

Harlow felt giddy, the way he did when standing on a tall building and looking down. Like the old joke said, it wasn't the fall that killed you; it was the sudden stop. For an instant he imagined a swan dive, falling through space with arms extended. He could see himself struggling to keep his balance as if he could veer away from the pavement at the last minute, coast a block or two and touch down like a chubby Peter Pan. That was how it was supposed to be. That was, in fact, how it had to be, if he was going to get out of this mess with no broken bones. Al-Hassan had given him a shove. The rest was up to him.

For a second he clenched his fists, an impotent rage freezing them in place. He wanted to lash out, to strike someone, anyone. All he had to do was find a scapegoat, a lightning rod, someone to siphon off all the anxiety of the past few weeks. He stepped into the pool of light and walked to a table in the corner of the room. He ripped the paper seal on a bottle of J&B, unscrewed the cap and poured himself a stiff shot in a water tumbler. He downed the smoky liquor with a shudder, poured another shot and walked back to the window.

That bastard Mitchell was to blame for all of his troubles. The son of a bitch had had the nerve to spy on him, to set him up to take a fall. That hadn't worked, and Mitchell had gotten his, but things hadn't been quite right since. Closing his eyes again, the sun slamming at the lids insistently, he watched it all unraveling as he knew it could. He had one last chance to haul his butt out of the fire.

Harlow rubbed his chin, felt a small clump of whiskers he'd missed and walked to the bathroom. He couldn't afford to let himself come unglued, and he knew it. He had appearances to keep up and people to see. It wouldn't do to look like anything less than the successful businessman he was supposed to be, and the master intelligence man everyone knew him to be. He grabbed his razor from the sink and drew it twice over the stubble. He heard the rasp of the blade on his dry skin and felt the sting. He splashed cold water on his face, shook his hands free of loose drops before reaching for the towel.

When he was dry he leaned in toward the mirror. His eyes were red rimmed, almost bleary. Harlow tossed the towel over the edge of the shower stall, then opened his shaving kit for some Visine. He dropped a little of the fluid in each eye and blinked it away. Leaning in again, he fancied the redness was already receding.

Harlow downed the rest of the Scotch, slapping the tumbler hard onto the enamel. The glass shattered in his hand, sending a small sliver into his right thumb. He threw the broken remnants into the tub, ducking as more slivers flew out of the tub and splattered over his legs. He looked down at the shiny fragments sparkling on his shoes, like the first few flakes of snow on a cold day. He gathered his pant legs at their creases and shook each leg in turn, then stamped his feet to get rid of the slivers.

As he shifted his weight the glass ground underfoot, crunching and scraping on the small white tiles and grinding into the grouting. He went to brush the slivers from the backs of his hands, then thought better of it. Turning on the tap, Harlow let cold water carry the small shards away. When he shut off the water, the larger pieces, too heavy for the water to carry down the drain, glittered in the bottom of the sink.

He couldn't get a handle on things. Everything he tried did damage to something he'd already accomplished. The world was a dangerous place for a nervous man. He knew that, had known it most of his life. And he had never been nervous before, not this nervous, anyway. Harlow shook his head, then stared at himself in the mirror as he would someone who suddenly materialized in front of him. The reflection was that of a stranger. Everything he had believed about himself was called into question in that one instant. He shook his head slowly from side to side, half hoping the image would remain motionless. But as he moved it followed suit, as he knew it would.

Loose ends. There were too many loose ends. Mitchell was one, and he had been cut off. Martin was another, and he was gone, too. Alvarez was threatening to become one. Mills had warned him Alvarez was nosing around, but that was a problem solved. Wasted in New York, thousands of miles away, and there was no way they could connect him to that, any more than they could connect him to what happened to Mitchell. Loose ends. A simple matter. Anyone with a pair of scissors could take care of something like that. All he had to do was turn him loose.

So, that left the difficult matter of keeping Colonel al-Hassan happy. He had bought time with a few bombs well placed and efficiently utilized. The colonel was still grumbling, but not nearly as much, and the new shipment of plastique would take care of that, that and the little matter of a hit on the president of Chad. Both projects were well on the way to completion. The plastique would make it into Tripoli within twenty-four hours. Forty-eight hours after that, Chad would need a new leader. Small things, these were, loose ends. But they could be fixed and who better to fix them?

For a moment, he wished Marielle was with him. But she was a different kind of problem. She was a distraction, the last thing he could afford until it was all under control again. Then they could go to the villa on the Riviera. He was working too hard. He needed a rest.

He wondered whether he could trust her with Sadowski. And whether it made any difference. What he didn't know couldn't hurt him. Or could it? Suppose she was unfaithful to him with that beast? Or with one of the other men. Suppose, suppose...

Too many loose ends.

CHAPTER THIRTY-THREE

Alvarez laughed out loud when he caught the trucks on the approach ramp of the Triborough Bridge. It was one of those rare confluences of luck, instinct and common sense that seemed so logical when they panned out, and so silly when they didn't. The heavily loaded vans paused at the tollbooth. He drove way to the left and handed three singles to the toll taker as the second truck slipped back into the traffic. The panel truck was anonymous enough that it might not be noticed by the truck crews, but he didn't want to run any unnecessary risks.

To buy time he rolled his window halfway down and asked directions to La Guardia, listening with half an ear as he watched the trucks start on the long haul across the bridge. He thanked the attendant absently, kicked the panel truck in gear and stuttered out into the early traffic.

It was too early for most commuters, but delivery vans of every size and shape were already beginning to clog the bridge. One of the problems with Manhattan was the limited access to the island. Every bridge and tunnel became a bottleneck shortly after dawn and stayed that way until well into the evening. This was the first, and as far as he could remember, the only time he had been grateful for the herd of horn-honking, exhaust-belching cowboys who were responsible for keeping the city open and well provisioned. Much of the traffic was inbound, but the outward-bound lanes were cluttered with deliverymen on the way to load up for a second run.

The nondescript, unlettered trucks stood out in the crowd, and Alvarez dropped into the slow lane, ducking in behind a motley assortment of cabs, a stray passenger car or two and half a dozen trucks. He could just see the roof of the trailing truck over the top of a brightly painted bread van. He could hang well back until he left the bridge, and wanted to make certain they didn't throw him a curveball.

It was always seductive, thinking you knew what the other side was going to do. It was a good feeling that all too often made you feel smarter, smarter than the opposition, and smarter than you really were. Alvarez knew only too well that such comfort could get you killed.

Unused to the high, stiff ride of the panel truck, the agent struggled to keep it in line as the cold wind, free of impediment, whipped up the river and hummed through the cables and struts of the bridge. The truck kept bucking him, sliding into the middle lane under the pressure of the wind, then as he tried to compensate, nearly skinning the safety rail.

The sky had grown a little brighter, though it was still heavy and gray. It was well after sunrise and the weather looked ominous. As they neared the far end of the bridge, the first dusty flakes of dry snow fluttered across the windshield, collecting in small mounds around the mud spatters on the glass. The traffic spilled off the bridge into the Grand Central Parkway, and Alvarez smiled when he saw the signs for La Guardia, just a few miles ahead.

He dropped back a little farther, satisfied that the trucks were unaware of his presence and that they could no longer evade him. At the off ramp for the airport he smiled as the two trucks dipped down and to the right, rolling into the tight curve with surprising grace. He zipped into the top of the ramp just as the trucks came halfway around. He could see each driver, and realized they were the two men who had met with Stanley Mills at the roller rink.

On the approach road the traffic thickened, a clutter of early passengers in cars and cabs, and a healthy dose of vans representing every air freight forwarder from Emery to UPS. Halfway in, the cabs and cars splintered off, heading for the airline terminals. The trucks and vans crowded into the freight terminal access, bumping and jouncing like cattle prodded by an unseen cowboy.

Now he was pinned in, propelled along by the press of trucks behind him, unable to change lanes. The surrounding drivers, who seemed to live for moments like this, jockeyed their huge vehicles forward, propelled by equal measures of air brakes and blaring horns. The glut suddenly expanded like a balloon as the narrow access road emptied into a broad asphalt apron. The trucks fanned out, heading for their respective terminals, and Alvarez fell back a little, letting some of the following vehicles stream past him on both sides.

He watched as the two trucks that most concerned him peeled off to the right. The traffic around them quickly thinned out, and was nonexistent by the time they pulled up in front of a low Quonset hut, somewhat removed from the main freight terminal. Approaching it in the panel truck was out of the question.

Alvarez popped the clutch and drifted forward in second. The truck's engine wheezed as it struggled with a speed too low for the gear. When it began lurching and bouncing on its springs, he disengaged the gears and allowed it to coast to a halt at one end of an island. Rags of yellow grass peered through a thin crust of plowed snow as black as coal. He yanked on the emergency brake then slid over to the passenger seat and watched.

Both drivers dropped easily from their big trucks and disappeared into the hut. Behind the jerry-built structure, whose corrugated sides were rusting under an ancient coat of aluminum paint, Alvarez could see the upper quarter and tail fin of a plane. It bore no visible markings other than a registry number.

Alvarez checked his watch. He had heard the thin man say that the shipment was to be airborne by six-fifteen. It was now five-fifty. The chunkier of the two drivers reappeared, climbed back into his truck and swung it around the hut, disappearing behind the building. Alvarez was getting impatient.

Worse yet, Bolan had vanished and he hadn't heard from Specs Martin in days. Having come this far, and gotten this close, he still had nothing he could use. He had no idea where the explosive was being shipped. If it got away from him now, it would vanish into the netherworld of terrorism, because there was no legitimate use to which such a quantity, so disguised, could possibly be put.

If he lost it he would curse himself every time a car bomb went off in Lebanon, or some innocent Irish kid went spiraling over a tenement wall in Belfast. He couldn't let that happen, and there didn't seem to be a thing he could do about it. For one crazy second, he thought about taking the direct approach and calling the police. There must have been a dozen charges to be brought, a dozen reasons to confiscate and impound the plastique. An anonymous tip, a bug in the right ear, would do the trick. But the shipment was only the tip of the iceberg, and Alvarez knew it. The men ultimately responsible for this illegal shipment would no more go down with it than the owners of the White Star Line went down with the *Titanic*. That fate was reserved for the expendable.

When the second driver appeared and moved his truck to the far side of the building, Alvarez knew he had no time left. It was too late for second-guessing, for what-ifs and supposes. He had fifteen minutes in which to do something. He opened the passenger door of the panel truck and stepped down. When his feet hit the dirty snow he still didn't know what he could do. He grabbed a clipboard from the floor of the truck, then slammed the door.

He started walking toward the hut, taking a chipped yellow pencil from the top of the clipboard and tucking it behind his ear. He had heard the expression, taking the bull by the horns, a thousand times, but until this moment he had never truly understood what it meant. Crossing the ice-encrusted asphalt apron, he picked up speed. By the time he reached the far corner of the Quonset hut, he was barreling full-speed ahead.

As Alvarez walked along the side of the building, an uninterrupted string of profanity, scattered by the wind and partially unintelligible, issued from the back of the hut.

Turning the rear corner, he bumped into a short, roly-poly man in dirty brown coveralls, whose thick knit cap was losing a valiant fight to contain a headful of tight, wiry black curls. The chubby man was supervising the transfer of the pallets from the trucks to the bowels of a C-141A Starlifter transport plane.

"Excuse me," Alvarez mumbled. "I didn't see you."

"Yeah, yeah. Look, I got work, all right? Apologize to me later." He turned for a second to look at Alvarez, then turned back to resume hollering at his crew. "You idiots, move your asses. Come on, you lazy bastards, get that forklift moving." As an afterthought, under his breath, he mumbled, "Stupid buggers ain't worth the powder to blow 'em to hell."

He turned away and realized Alvarez was still standing there.

"Customs, right? So what do you want, a guided tour? You know what to do. And don't ask me no questions. You got questions, check the manifests. I just put it on the damn planes. I don't know what it is, I don't know where it goes. I don't want to know. And you want to know why? Because I don't give a shit. *That*'s why I don't know."

Alvarez took a step back, stunned for a moment by the violence of the explosion. The pugnacious little man had just handed him the golden goose. When it dawned on him he stuttered a bit before regaining control. "N-no, no. Look, er, I don't . . . I mean . . ."

"Spit it out, will ya? I'm busy."

"Sorry. I'll, er, I'll just wait till you're done. Don't want to get in the way."

"What, are they sending you guys to finishing school now, or what? Such manners!"

"No, I, er, I'm kind of new. And—"

"New!" The man slapped his forehead with a hamlike palm. "Christ almighty, I don't got enough problems, they got to send a greenhorn to bust my balls."

Glancing down at the smaller man, Alvarez noticed a name embroidered on the coveralls pocket, almost obscured by grease. "Look, Angelo, I don't want to cause you any problems. We both got jobs to do, that's all. Let's make it easy on both of us, all right?"

"Yeah, sure. Why the hell not, am I right? Okay, you wait and I'll get outta your way. How's that?"

"Fine. Thank you."

"And it ain't Angelo. Angelo's dead. These are his." He grabbed the coveralls between a thumb and finger and pulled. "We were the same size. I lucked out, huh?" He laughed.

"Sorry..."

"Forget about it." He turned back to his crew and immediately exploded. "Morris, you asshole, get outta his way. Don't you see the man has a forklift under his butt? Let him use the goddamn thing."

The final skid was lifted off the second truck and disappeared into the belly of the plane. With a belch and a roar the forklift backed down the ramp and the driver killed the engine and hopped off. A moment later three men in coveralls walked down the ramp and stood in a tight circle.

"All right, you animals," the foreman bellowed. "Coffee. Be back in fifteen minutes. We got another plane to load as soon as this one's outta here." He turned to Alvarez, a sarcastic grin sharpening his round features. "It's all yours, kid. The papers are on a clipboard outside the cockpit. Just make sure you're done when we get back."

The crew scurried away like kids after school, and the round man sprinted to the far end of the Quonset. He was gone before Alvarez realized it. He stood there for a moment, the clipboard in his hand, then shrugged.

The freight ramp was slippery under his feet as he climbed into the plane. It was dark inside, the only light coming from the open freight bay doors. He walked along the wooden floorboards, his heels catching in the grooves until he got the hang of placing his feet at an angle to the fuselage. All eight canvas-covered pallets were there, along with several other skids of unidentified merchandise.

He bent close to check an invoice taped to one canvas cover, but it told him nothing he didn't already know. The addressee was Mideast Petro Research, c/o Worldwide Specialty, Inc., 3754 Avenue de Revolutionaire, Tripoli, Libya. The small box reserved for a description of contents contained one word: adhesives. Alvarez smiled at the irony.

Moving deeper into the plane, he found several other skids, consigned to a variety of addressees whose names meant nothing at all to him, either in connection with Mason Harlow or otherwise. At the cockpit he noticed the door had been removed. That could only mean the entire plane, cargo bay and all, was pressurized.

A bundle of loose tarpaulin lay between two skids packed with wooden crates. Alvarez ran awkwardly back to the mouth of the cargo bay. The apron outside was still deserted. Hurrying back to the tarpaulins, he worked one loose and doubled it, tying one edge to the tie bar running the length of the fuselage on both sides. He pushed the others into a flattened mound and sat down, pulling the secured canvas over him.

And he waited.

CHAPTER THIRTY-FOUR

Mack Bolan was on the makeshift firing range when the sound of helicopters erupted on the horizon. He fired the last round in his Sauer and looked over his shoulder to the north. Two blocky specks were rushing toward him, low to the ground and moving fast.

"Don't worry about it," Carter yelled.

Bolan ignored him and climbed to his feet, brushing the dry sandy soil from his fatigues. "What the hell is going on?" he asked.

"Nothing. Just some Libs we have to teach, that's all."

"Teach what?"

"I told you, don't worry about it. You'll find out soon enough."

"What the hell's going on here? Every time I turn around, the rules have changed. I thought I was supposed to be teaching guerrilla techniques. Next thing I know, I'm working on a rifle range."

The other men ignored both the approaching helicopters and the heated exchange. The argument was punctuated by the steady stream of fire from the other marksmen. Bolan wanted to argue further, but bit his tongue.

"All right, everybody, that's it for a while," Carter bellowed. "Finish what's in your weapons, then pack it up. We have to meet the new boys." He glanced pointedly at Bolan, as if to warn him against feeling he was in any way responsible for the sudden change in plans.

The rifles gradually dribbled into silence, one last shot cracking like a whip and echoing off over the sand, drifting back from the low hills in the distance. Bolan slung his rifle over his shoulder and watched the others get to their feet. He looked at Picard, but the Frenchman was impassive. Either he attached no significance to the new development or he was a better actor than Bolan had suspected.

The choppers were heading straight for the encampment. They were no more than fifty feet off the ground, tilted slightly forward as their pilots pushed for maximum velocity. The roar of their engines could be heard as a steady rumble, almost covering the whine characteristic of machinery pushed to its capacity, or a little beyond.

"Listen up, everybody," Carter hollered, struggling to be heard over the roar of the approaching choppers. The men turned to look at him just as they passed overhead. Bolan ducked instinctively, as did Carter and Masseria. The others simply looked bewildered, as if they had no experience with the cumbersome vehicles. When they passed overhead, Carter continued, "Go on back to the barracks. I'll be by in a while to fill you in."

He paused for a moment, then stared at Bolan. "That means everybody."

Bolan recognized the helicopters as Mi-26s, Soviet-made heavy transports doing combat duty in Afghanistan. The ships bore Libyan markings, and no doubt accounted for a piece of oil money no longer in the coffers of Tripoli. They were lightly armed but capable of ferrying forty men at a time over long distances. With their operating range just under five hundred miles, they could have made the flight from Tripoli nonstop, if refueling was possible either here or at a desert base somewhere to the north.

Bolan lagged behind the others as they walked slowly back to the barracks. It was a half mile away, and he had ample time to watch the choppers touch down. A stream of men in combat fatigues poured out of each one. There must have been eighty men, apparently Libyan regulars.

When he reached the barracks, Bolan lingered in the doorway, but the men had vanished, and the desert was as quiet as it had been before the choppers appeared. The vehicles themselves sat quietly, their huge eight-bladed rotors drooping as if wilted by the sun. They looked like gigantic carnivorous insects basking in the heat after a full meal.

Bolan stepped into the barracks and tossed his rifle onto his bunk. It landed with a thud and a creak of springs, then bounced twice before settling. He walked back to the doorway and watched the empty courtyard around the choppers. Except for some whispered small talk behind him, not a sound disturbed the scorching silence. The chatter died down as the men lay on their cots, too tired to do much of anything. In the absolute quiet Bolan felt as if he were the only man awake in the entire camp, a feeling more appropriate to the dead of night than late morning.

The new arrivals had piqued his curiosity. He stepped back into the sun, lifted his cap in one hand and wiped a thin sheen of perspiration from his forehead before slipping the cap back in place. He walked slowly, almost casually, toward another barracks, presumably where the Libyans would be quartered. If they were already inside, they made no sound. But if they weren't, where were they?

Approaching the choppers cautiously, Bolan peered into the cockpit of one, his curiosity getting the better of him. The first thing that caught his attention was the control console. All of the instructions and warning signs were in Russian. That surprised him. Ordinarily matériel was refitted with instructions in the language of the purchasing nation, in this case Arabic. It was a lot easier than forcing pilots to learn a foreign language. That the usual did not apply was something he was coming to expect in this convoluted affair, but that there might be Russian nationals directly involved raised some interesting questions.

Bolan eased down along the wall of the warehouse, and slipped in through the main door. It was dark inside, but at the far end, a large storage room that had been outfitted with several long tables and served as a mess hall was brightly lit. Tall stacks of crates and the miscellaneous machinery of war formed shadowy corridors the length of the L. Bolan slipped into a narrow aisle and walked quietly toward the mess hall.

The room had been fashioned of steel partitions six feet high and topped with Plexiglas panels, which added another six feet. It was open from there to the ceiling, another twenty feet in the air. Smaller crates were stacked on steel shelving screwed together and attached to the concrete floor and steel ceiling struts with heavy bolts.

Halfway down the narrow passage, Bolan climbed up on the shelving. He scrambled from level to level until, twenty-five feet in the air, he wormed his way onto the top level, which sat only a couple of feet below the roof struts. Squirming forward, he was able to squeeze under each beam as he came to it, sharp edges of metal scratching at the back of his shirt and pants. When he had gone about twenty yards, he came to the last beam.

Slipping under it, he found himself just inches from the end of the shelving. He was able to look down into the mess hall over the top of the pebbled Plexiglas. Carter was pacing back and forth in front of the new arrivals, who sat on one side of the long row of tables. He was speaking in a loud, slow voice, his effort at making himself understood filling his speech with odd accents and misplaced emphasis. He sounded like a New Yorker trying to give subway directions to a foreign tourist.

A Libyan officer stood next to him, arms folded across his chest, listening with his head canted to one side. After every two or three sentences he would speak in a quick burst of Arabic. While the officer translated Carter watched with a blank look on his face. After each translation the officer would nod, and Carter would resume his address.

Bolan crept to the very edge of the shelving, pressing himself flat against the dusty metal. The ceiling of the warehouse was drenched in shadow, and Bolan felt fairly secure. He tried to hear what Carter was saying.

"This material is very dangerous, you know, not safe. Unless you understand how to make it work, you can kill yourself and your friends. You must pay close attention to everything we say. If you don't understand something, ask." He stopped and watched the translator, who rapidly explained what had just been said.

Carter took a sip of water, rolled it around in his mouth and spit it onto the floor before continuing. "This explosive is perfect for the kind of operations we will be teaching you here. It can be shaped into almost anything, it is easily hidden and can be disguised as almost anything at all." He paused for the translation and this time swallowed a mouthful of water.

"But you have to respect this material. If you don't, it will get you. It will tear your arms off and put out your eyes. A piece only this big—" he paused to hold two fingers an inch apart "—can destroy an automobile or a small truck. This much—" he indicated a rough block a couple of inches on a side "—can take down a whole house."

He stopped speaking and leaned against the wall behind him, crossing his legs like an indolent cowboy. The translator finished with a staccato burst and smiled at Carter.

Still leaning against the wall, Carter paused dramatically, as if looking each of the eighty new men in the face for a moment, before resuming. "When you leave here, you'll know everything I know about C-4. And I'm here to tell you, that's all there is to know. If I don't know it, it ain't true. The others on the staff are good men, too. They will help you. Listen to them, do what they tell you to do, and never, I repeat, never, disregard an order. We are expecting a new shipment of C-4 in a day or so. Once it gets here, there will be enough explosive energy packed into this warehouse to split Africa in two."

The translator smiled. "English is truly a wonderful language." He turned to the men with the longest statement he made.

The men laughed when he finished, and Carter asked, "What did you tell them? What's so funny?"

"Oh, I just explained what you said about splitting Africa in two. As you know, Libya had for a long time talked only of unifying the continent under Muslim rule. The irony amused them." He smiled broadly.

Carter didn't respond.

Bolan had seen enough. He started to squirm backward along the top of the shelves, taking care not to bang his heavy boots into the bell-like metal. The dust tickled his nose, and he covered a sneeze with one hand. When he was far enough back to risk climbing down, he snaked along the side of the shelving until he found an open area, then clambered down using the shelves like the rungs of a giant ladder.

Once on the concrete he thought it prudent to keep still for a few moments, until he could hear what Carter might be intending for his new recruits. The man's voice droned on, but his words were garbled by the conflicting echoes glancing off the steel ceiling and muffled by the many blind alleys of equipment stacked floor to ceiling.

Bolan heard footsteps in the next aisle, somewhere between his position and the door. He pressed himself into a small opening on a bottom shelf, bending his knees to fit into the cavelike niche. He listened to the shuffling stride of the visitor, who seemed to be searching for something. The man hadn't used a light and was relying on the ambient illumination pouring through the warehouse door.

Bolan twisted around to make himself more comfortable, and the sound of dry leaves thundered in his ear. He jerked his head around and found himself staring at a crumpled invoice stapled to the side of a shipping crate. The shipper was stamped in blurred ink on the top of the invoice, the lettering at an angle and partially obscured by a red customs stamp. He couldn't read the entire name. He didn't have to. The crate had been shipped by "...lington Metal, NYC." He didn't need Kreskin to fill in the missing letters.

Bolan felt along the top edge of the crate. The cover was in place but it gave easily when he tried to raise it. There wasn't much clearance, but he twisted his body around and slipped his arm in the box up to the elbow. His groping fingers encountered a smooth surface. Pressing down, he felt the surface give under his fingers, then part with a tight, dry snap. His fingers sank into a doughy substance up to the first knuckle. Bending his fingers, he pulled them free of the sticky material, tearing a small ball of it loose. His forearm scraped across the rough wood as he pulled back.

Rolling the ball on his fingers in the dark, he shaped it easily into a rod a little thicker than a pencil. It held its new contours easily, like modeling clay, and he lifted the small cylinder to his nose. The scent confirmed what he already suspected—he'd found the missing link. Mason Harlow was sitting on plastic explosive shipped abroad from the very place where Flak Mitchell had been killed.

Bolan reached back into the crate and dug his fingers in deeply enough to tug an entire block of the C-4 loose. He strained to squeeze the plastic-wrapped block out of the crate, then tucked it into his shirt.

The scraping footsteps came closer and were now directly opposite him, just one aisle over. He tried to see who it was, but the narrow openings between supplies and shelving were full of shadows. He listened as the steps moved farther along the aisle, and the sound ceased.

When the silence persisted, Bolan slipped his head out into the aisle. Twenty feet away a gnarled shadow, like that of a Hollywood witch opening a child's coffin, stooped over a long wooden box jutting into the aisle. The figure suddenly straightened and moved cautiously toward him. Bolan ducked back into the crevice, still facing the approaching figure. Just as it drew abreast of the small opening, Bolan recognized Lucien Picard. He reached out and clamped a hand over Picard's knee. "Lucien," he hissed.

Picard stopped in his tracks. "Mack, what are you doing here?"

Bolan crawled out of the opening. As he straightened up he whispered, "We have to talk."

"You're telling me."

CHAPTER THIRTY-FIVE

Alvarez could see a block of gray at the tail of the plane. He kept his eyes glued to the narrow crack between the tarpaulin and the fuselage. His watch read 6:06, less than ten minutes before the scheduled takeoff. In the confined space under the thick canvas the sound of his heart sounded like a drum. His ears felt every thump and he was sure the crew would hear it if they got within fifteen feet of him.

He held the canvas away from the wall of the plane with one hand, staring past the glowing hands of his watch at the open cargo bay. A thud on the wooden ramp echoed in the plane, and he pulled the canvas closer to the fuselage, narrowing the gap to a fraction of an inch.

A moment later a tall thin man appeared at the head of the ramp, the same man he had seen at the warehouse. He hesitated at the ramp head, then yelled back down toward the ground, "All set, Phil?"

A muffled "Righto" echoed in the plane as the thin man stepped to a switch bank on the fuselage just inside the bay door. He reached for one of the toggles and held it down. The vibration of a hidden servo made the floor of the plane shudder, and the block of gray dawn gradually shrank away to nothing.

Alvarez held his breath as footsteps approached him, stopped momentarily and then pushed on past. A succession of squeaks and squeals must have been the pilot taking his seat at the controls. A moment later Alvarez heard a barrage of clicks and snaps, then the sudden high-pitched snarl of the Lockheed's jet engines turning over. The pilot's voice echoed down the cargo bay, but the engines covered it, and Alvarez could only guess he had contacted the tower for flight clearance. The engines rumbled to a fuller-

throated whine and the plane lurched forward before settling into a gentle turn.

The familiar sensation of a taxiing jet boiled in the pit of
his stomach, and the CIA agent swallowed a surge of bile.
Never an easy flyer, he found the present circumstances a
fulfillment of his worst fears. The plane swung in a wide
semicircle, and his head began to spin. For several minutes
the plane stuttered, bouncing roughly over weather strips in
the concrete. Each bounce was echoed by the wings, which
seemed to flap and send a series of diminishing bounces
throughout the plane.

The engines began to scream, and Alvarez could feel the
big plane straining at its brakes. When he thought the pitch
of the jets could rise no higher, it suddenly descended in a
rumbling diminuendo and the plane leaped forward. With
his head pressed against the fuselage Alvarez could feel the
vibration as the plane fought to leave the ground, and the
scream of air past the metal skin was a shriek approaching
the inaudibility of a dog whistle.

Then the ground fell away, and the agent watched it
shrink with his stomach instead of his eyes. He imagined the
small, glistening blue jewels of swimming pools and faded
green diamonds of baseball fields, his mind filling the bleak
canvas of winter with a warmer vision as he struggled to
avoid confronting the paralyzing fear of falling that never
failed to convulse him on takeoff.

He squeezed his eyes closed and listened to the sound of
his grinding teeth for what seemed an eternity. Then, giving
himself totally to the only relief possible, he fell asleep.

THE SCREECH OF TIRES on the runway woke him, and his
head slammed into the wall as the plane veered to one side
before grabbing a secure hold on the ground. By his watch,
they had been airborne for nearly seven hours. He was
thirsty and his shoulder ached. Alvarez poked around in the
capacious pocket of his parka until he found the small
plastic bottle of painkillers nestled between two clips for the
Browning. He gave a start, thinking for a moment he had

lost the pistol, then breathed a sigh of relief when he found it and the Coonan in his other pocket. He removed the Browning and screwed a Company-designed snub-nosed suppressor onto the muzzle, then replaced it. The automatics clacked together as he withdrew his hand, and he felt a little more secure.

He turned the lid on the bottle, popped it loose and dropped a pair of pills into his palm. His throat was dry, and he swirled his tongue around trying to work up some saliva to swallow the pills. They went down hard and he nearly choked.

When the plane stopped moving he waited for the pilot to move back through the plane and open the cargo doors. A low murmur from the cockpit seemed to take forever. After five minutes by his watch, and five years by his beating heart, he heard the scrape of shoes on the wooden floor of the plane. The heavy tread moved past him, stopping at the tail. He braced himself for the throb of the servo, but heard only a wet hiss and splash, followed by a deep sigh. The pilot clomped back to the cockpit and got back on the radio. Alvarez realized they had stopped only for refueling.

Recalling the sound of the trickling hiss, he realized how badly he needed to relieve himself. He squeezed his legs together, waiting for the tanks to be full. The mere thought of taking in fluid increased his agony, and he bit his lip, waiting for the engines to resume their whining.

Twenty minutes later he got his wish as the floorboard began to pulsate. The high-pitched whine began again and the plane staggered back to the runway. The shrill voice of servos came and went, then came again as the pilot worked the flaps. The takeoff was smooth, but his bursting bladder ached and every bounce of the huge tires over the tar strips sent a lance of fire through his insides.

Airborne again, he peered out from under the tarpaulin. The cockpit glowed a soft warm green as if it were lit by the dial of a single huge watch. He pulled the canvas aside and scrambled out, nearly losing his balance from the long period of inactivity. He tiptoed to the tail of the plane and

made an olfactory identification of the appropriate spot.
His delighted bladder seemed unwilling to stop contracting, but he forced himself and hurried back to the safety of
the tarpaulin.

AT THE SECOND TOUCHDOWN, Alvarez was wide-awake.
The constant tension seemed to neutralize the stultifying
effects of the painkillers, and he knew he was really wired.
He slipped the Browning into his palm and cradled it
loosely, one hand up against the edge of the tarp. This time
the pilot clomped back to the switch bank and opened the
cargo bay immediately. It was late afternoon outside, and
the glare of a harsh sun hurt Alvarez's eyes. He watched the
pilot walk down the ramp, stretching his arms behind his
back and shrugging each leg free of kinks before his head
vanished below his line of sight.

Alvarez had no idea where he was. He waited patiently for
the pilot to return, but after an interminable five minutes he
pulled the canvas away from the fuselage and got to his feet.
His bones ached and he felt as if he'd ridden to hell and back
in a refrigerator on square wheels. Keeping one eye on the
yawning bay, he rippled his shoulders, then grabbed one
hand in the other and tugged, trying to loosen up. The effort sent a stab through his shoulder, but the pain felt good,
something real he could focus on.

He walked toward the cargo ramp with the Browning at
his side, half-hidden by the bulky parka. As he drew near
the open doors, a blast of warm air hit him in the face. The
world outside seemed made of white and yellow, all but
bleached by the insistent sun. The air was dry and a small
trickle of sweat starting behind his ear seemed to evaporate
instantaneously.

At the mouth of the bay he realized his parka would attract unwanted attention, but he couldn't leave it on the
plane. Everything that stood between him and annihilation
was in its pockets. He shrugged the heavy coat off and
tucked it under his wounded arm, then reached across his

middle with the other arm and nestled the Browning in its folds.

He stood at the ramp head trying to get a clue as to his whereabouts. Across from the plane, a long low shed, its walls broken by a dozen garage doors, bore several signs in Arabic script. One of the doors was open, and he walked toward it confidently, as if he should have been there an hour ago. The air wavered in filmy sheets over the hot tar, and he could feel the reflected heat on his calves. He plunged through the door and slipped sideways immediately. Once out of the doorway he breathed again, then leaned against the wall. The hot metal of the shed felt good on his back, its warmth baking through his shirt and restoring circulation.

Setting his parka on a nearby barrel, he leaned against the doorframe and watched the plane. A stuttering engine crackled out of his view to the right, and a forklift zipped past like a toy and bounced up the ramp of the aircraft. It disappeared inside, its engine in a rumbling idle for a couple of minutes or so. Then, after an angry snarl of the powerful diesel, it reappeared, backing out under a heavy load. As it tilted over backward onto the incline, Alvarez recognized one of the skids of plastique-filled canisters.

The forklift scuttled off to the right like a primitive model of R2D2, and lingered out of sight for several minutes. It repeated its trip into the plane several times, bringing off all of the plastique skids along with several other pallets before it vanished for the last time. During the entire process he had been unable to see the driver's face. The tall, slender man had never presented more than a near profile, just enough for Alvarez to note his dark complexion and angular nose.

The agent desperately wanted to see where the explosive was, but he couldn't risk leaving the safety of the shed.

The sun started to sink as Alvarez waited, and he was desperately thirsty. Leaving the doorway, he walked to the rear of the large room. The back of the shed was dark, and after staring into the harsh afternoon sun for so long, his eyes had trouble adjusting to the gloom.

In a remote corner his groping hand encountered the edge of a desk or table of some kind. He shut his eyes for a moment, counted to ten, then opened them again. On one edge of the cluttered surface sat an open can of Coke.

He sniffed once to make sure it was the real thing, then downed a mouthful of the overly sweet fluid, which seemed to cling to the inside of his cheeks and only reluctantly slid down his arid throat. He took another swig, swirled it around with his tongue before swallowing and put the empty can back on the desk.

He was halfway back to the door when two men stepped past the edge of the doorframe. They were busy talking, their rapid Arabic sounding like an argument of some sort. One man had his back to the door, while the other, shorter man was facing him. Had it not been for the difference in the debaters' heights and the contrasting light, he might have been spotted.

He ducked behind a half-loaded hand truck, peering between two stacks of cardboard cartons. The argument continued for another minute, now accompanied by waving arms. The shorter man's temper seemed to be rising, and his opponent was backing away from the anger in staggering steps, as if he were being poked in the chest with a stiff finger.

Alvarez looked to left and right, but there was no better cover readily available. Abruptly the tone changed, as if the dispute had been settled, and the men switched to French. Alvarez wondered if men felt capable of dealing with passion only in their native tongues.

The shorter man waved and walked back out of sight, while the taller, thinner opponent turned toward the shed. Alvarez saw his face for the first time, just as he stepped through the doorway and out of the sun. At the same instant the man froze and reached for his belt. Alvarez thought he'd been seen and raised the Browning, but the man spun on his heel and walked toward the plane.

Alvarez watched him ascend the ramp, then reappear almost immediately. He walked purposefully to the shed, clutching a sheaf of papers in his right hand. As he passed through the door he tossed the papers carelessly to one side. Alvarez watched with horror as they landed on his bundled parka, then slipped to the floor. The whispering leaves caught the man's ear and he turned to see what had happened. He spotted the papers on the floor and bent to retrieve them. As he straightened, he noticed the coat. He lifted the sleeve of the coat, more in curiosity than alarm, then let it drop. He turned toward the interior of the shed and took several tentative steps into the gloom. Alvarez started to move, but it was already too late for one of them.

He felt his heart stop. He raised the Browning, all the while hoping he wouldn't have to use it. The man whispered something in Arabic, then repeated it a little louder. He started to back toward the door. As he moved he turned to the left. His hand went again to his belt and came back with a revolver clutched in white knuckles.

He repeated his question, this time angrily. He was staring directly at Alvarez, who fired once, then again. The first shot slammed into the freight handler's arm, breaking the wristbone and passing through his shirt. Alvarez heard the 9 mm slug slam into the wooden surface of the cargo ramp. The second shot ripped through the man's rib cage and found a home.

He collapsed straight down, like a house of cards.

CHAPTER THIRTY-SIX

Sadowski wheeled the jeep in a tight circle, then yanked on the hand brake. He jumped down from the vehicle and stood on the pavement, his hands on his hips. "Would you sweethearts mind getting a move on? We have a tight schedule here. You fuck up, they don't have a sling that can hold your ass."

Lucien Picard was sitting in the passenger seat, Bolan and Carter in the rear. Carter stepped down into the street and narrowly missed getting run over by a cab. Sadowski ground his teeth in irritation, waiting for the other two passengers to join him on the pavement.

"You need a written request, Belasko?"

Bolan took his time climbing out of the rear seat, then turned to look across the broad plaza. He ignored Sadowski with a studied insolence. Getting on the big man's nerves was bound to provoke him, but it could push things off dead center. Angry men sometimes said more than they should, and Bolan knew the string was just about paid out. He needed something he could sink his teeth into, and he needed it soon.

Picard reached under the front seat for a book and crawled out of the jeep before sticking it in his pocket.

"What's that, Picard? What are you hiding there?"

"It's a book, Load. You know, a whole bunch of pages with words on them? Sentences, even."

"You smartasses are really starting to get on my nerves, you know that? Come on." He turned on his heel and led the way into the lobby of a nondescript office building. Crossing the lobby, he and Carter got a little ahead of the lagging Bolan and Picard. They could hear Sadowski muttering angrily, and Carter seemed to be trying to calm him down.

"I don't give a damn," Sadowski exploded. Then, in a stage whisper, he continued, "I'm telling you, something ain't right here. When this is all over, I'm gonna get even. Maybe even a little bit ahead. Then Harlow can kiss my ass goodbye. I'm outta here."

"Forget about it, Load," Carter answered. "You're on edge, that's all. Things'll calm down soon."

Sadowski grunted, stabbing the elevator button with a vicious jab of his index finger. He hit the flat red plastic square so hard, Bolan heard the knuckle crack. He looked at Picard, who nodded.

While they waited for the elevator Sadowski kept sweeping the lobby with a nervous, darting glance, as if he half expected to see someone he didn't want to be seen by. When the elevator finally arrived he ducked in quickly and didn't turn around until the door sighed closed.

Bolan watched the dial click through more than a dozen numbers, stopping finally at the fifteenth floor. Sadowski led the way down the tiled hall to an unmarked door. He looked both ways before trying the knob, then stepped in quickly, gesturing for the others to follow. He closed the door softly, then turned the simple latch with a click.

They were in a small vacant office. It was unfurnished except for a metal desk pushed all the way into one corner. A standard desk chair, its four coasters clotted with tangled hair and dust, was upended on one edge. A brown metal wastebasket sat in the leg well.

Sadowski stepped toward the front wall of the empty room. His feet slapped the naked tile with a strangely hollow sound. It echoed from one corner of the high-ceilinged room. Planting his feet in a wide stance, he cleared his throat. "Okay, this is the first position." He crooked the finger of one hand in the rapid style of a traffic cop. "Come here, but don't get too close to the window. Stand over there. Take a peek one at a time. Pay particular attention to the statue in the fountain at the middle of the plaza."

He watched them as one by one they peered from the window, bending close to see through the dirt-filmed glass. Bolan went last. When he straightened up, Sadowski said, "Okay, now you got to pay close attention. We don't get another look until tomorrow. If you don't get it right the first time, that's all she wrote."

"So what's the big deal about the statue?" Picard asked.

"I'm coming to that. Hold your water. We got four firing positions. Everything is coordinated around that statue. As soon as the limo passes that statue, the team up here takes him out. Belasko, that's you. There'll be three other shooters around the plaza, and they'll all fire at the same time. It's got to be tight, and it's got to be visual. No radio, understand? Not until it's done. And Carter will handle that."

"Why no radio?" Bolan asked.

"Because I said so," Sadowski snapped.

"But who *told* you to say so, and what reason did he give you?"

Sadowski snorted, expelling all his breath in a single explosive burst of frustration. "Because we can't risk it. Too many monitors in the capital. Anybody picks up the signal, it could blow the whole operation sky-high." He glared at Bolan, his features twisted by rage into a ball of writhing snakes. "That enough for you?"

"Just asking."

"All right, the stuff will be here for you. All you have to do is get here. On time."

"How many loads?"

"What's the matter, hotshot scared he'll miss?"

Bolan didn't take the bait. He repeated the question, this time more softly. "How many loads?"

"Five rounds. If you need any more than that, it'll be too late."

"Where are the other shooters positioned?"

Sadowski looked up sharply. Bolan saw the tail end of a cloud drift past, and then Sadowski smiled. "You ask a lot of questions for a hired gun."

Bolan shrugged. "It can make a difference."

"Yeah, it can. But not the kind of difference I want made. Just worry about yourself. Carter knows where they are. You don't have to."

Bolan backed off. It was one thing to anger Sadowski, get him to drop his guard a little. But it was something else again to make him suspicious. "What about self-defense?"

"That's covered. We got some inside help here. But you can bring along some lightweight stuff. Handguns only. Don't show up here like a one-man battalion. Security in this toilet is less than perfect. But there's no point calling any unnecessary attention to yourself." He straightened up, flexing his shoulders as if to bolster his confidence, and moved toward the door. "Let's go. We got the rest of the tour to cover."

Back in the hall Sadowski started rushing them, taking the stairs instead of waiting for the elevator. Once in the street he jumped into the driver's seat and cranked the engine, gunning it impatiently while the other three climbed in. Picard nearly fell out of the jeep as Sadowski jammed it into gear and jumped away from the curb.

They crossed the plaza, the heart of N'Djamena, which gave the capital the feel of a medieval village grown out of control. Bolan stared at the jungle of buildings surrounding the broad open space on three sides. On the fourth, the presidential palace, a Woolworth version of Versailles, with tall arching windows and a wilderness of balconies, stood at the center of the governmental complex. The parliament met in one wing of the ornate structure, and a welter of anonymously modern office buildings housing the obligatory bureaucracy stood to its right.

The jeep nosed through heavy traffic, and Sadowski handled it well, skipping from lane to lane in the midday snarl. Pedestrians in every conceivable dress, from yuppie pinstripes to a dozen native costumes, stepped indifferently into the flow, either deaf or oblivious to the constant barrage of angry horns.

The plaza spewed its traffic into a series of avenues, each of which narrowed like a funnel to two lanes. Sadowski took the third right, and the jeep slipped into a tangled bazaar. Both sides of the street were lined with open-air shops, their fronts folded back to permit casual strollers access to the merchandise.

The low shops gave way to an array of tents, open on all four sides, sprinkled here and there with wheeled carts under striped umbrellas. Every conceivable odor assaulted the nostrils, from heavy spices to raw fish trucked in from Lake Chad and preserved in wooden boxes full of cracked ice.

Pedestrian traffic was almost impenetrable in the market, and Sadowski leaned on the horn almost constantly, occasionally nudging a particularly sluggish walker with the flat bumper of the jeep. He muttered incessant obscenities under his breath, wrestling the wheel from side to side and riding the clutch. The jeep rocked like a hobby horse, almost leaping ahead a yard at a time. In front and behind, other drivers used their vehicles' horns like cattle prods, stabbing the careless with a sudden blare calculated to induce cardiac arrest.

The traffic slowly thinned, and suddenly they were on the outskirts of the city. The avenue was no wider, but it permitted uninterrupted flow, as if to reward those hardy enough to brave passage through the teeming market.

"Was that really necessary?" Picard asked. "Couldn't we have gone around?"

"Sure we could." Sadowski laughed. "But this way you understand why it's so hard to get things done here. Now you know why an occasional shortcut ain't such a bad idea. Besides which, Belasko and Carter are going to have to go straight through the bazaar when they get off work."

The jeep rolled smoothly over a cobbled road now, and broad, flat farms stretched away on either side. A hundred yards or so off the road, each farm sported a similar cottage, like a meticulous copy of those Bolan had seen in Provence. Far removed from the tacky francophilia of the presidential palace, the cottages were vestiges of a different

France, one more at ease with the land, less concerned with public image and ostentatious display.

A hundred yards ahead, an avenue of trees marched off to the left. Sadowski eased up on the gas and banked into the tree-lined avenue, the jeep's big tires crunching on a thick layer of yellow gravel. Between the trees, dense shrubbery made a solid wall of pale green nearly a dozen feet high. The sound of the engine all but disappeared, swallowed by the heavy leaves.

Two hundred yards off the main road, the trees curved away on both sides and the gravel spread out to form a glittering semicircle like a brilliant slice of lemon. The reflected sun hurt the eyes, and Bolan yanked a pair of mirrored shades from his shirt pocket.

The jeep coasted to a stop at the center of the half circle, and Sadowski gestured toward the columned portico. Clusters of bougainvillea crowded up against the wide flagstone stairs, and three broad windows, heavily grilled in wrought iron, dominated the front of the house.

"This is your gig, Picard."

"What is it?"

"This," he said grandly, swelling his voice to the stentorian tones of a game show announcer, "is the home of number two. The vice president's digs. Nice, huh? The place is quiet, because his semiexcellency is off globe-trotting with the boss man. Security will sweep the place tonight, before he gets home."

"Very impressive place."

"Yeah, I guess. While your buddy Belasko, here, is decapitating the state, you're gonna be fucking up the line of succession. Tony will be here with you. He knows the layout, and I suggest you spend a little time with him when we get back to the hotel."

"What then?"

"Simple. You all meet behind this house. A chopper will be here to take you back to the base. Neat, surgically simple. Very clean."

"And where will you be during the festivities?" Bolan asked.

"Holding down the fort." Sadowski laughed. "Don't sweat the details. Tony will baby-sit Picard. You meet Carter at the foot of the statue in the plaza. Come straight here. You'll all be out of here in an hour. You know the terms. The accounts are already set up in Switzerland. You get back here, you get the papers and the number. Very businesslike. Very professional, like Mr. Harlow explained it. Any questions, ask 'em now."

"Just one," Picard said.

"Shoot . . ."

"My weapon. Where will it be?"

"It's all taken care of. Tony has it. Anything else?"

"What happens then?" Bolan asked. "After the hit? I mean, what happens to the government here?"

"What are you, some kind of political scientist or something? That doesn't concern you. It's covered, that's all you have to know. You do the job, you collect your pay. You're out of it. Like I said, don't sweat the details."

Sadowski threw the jeep into first and spun around the half-moon of gravel. As they headed back toward the main road, Bolan looked over his shoulder at the huge, empty house. Its windows stared back at him like gargantuan, blind eyes.

And in twenty-four hours, he and Picard would have the awesome responsibility of making sure the man who lived there lived to see another sunrise.

He thought about the odds.

They weren't good.

CHAPTER THIRTY-SEVEN

Mason Harlow paced nervously around the office. His knees seemed to find every obstruction and cracked into one after another. Each time he banged a chair or the edge of a desk, he cursed. Each curse was more vehement than the last, and louder. He sat down at his desk and rubbed his left knee absently, yanking the bottom drawer open with his right hand.

He pulled out a half-dead bottle of Scotch, slamming the drawer closed with its bottom, then unscrewed the cap. Harlow let go of his bruised knee just long enough to pull a dusty tumbler close, then resumed his distracted massage. The stream of liquor wavered, some of the dark brown fluid missing the lip of the glass entirely and collecting in a small pool on the desk top. For a moment he watched the pool spread out and start to discolor a short stack of memos. Instead of moving the papers, he smeared the spilled liquor with his hand, then licked his fingers. It wasn't until he took his damp hand away from his lips that he realized how badly he had been trembling.

He downed two fingers neat, in a single swallow, then refilled, this time forcing himself to pour with a steady hand. The second drink had just cleared his lips when the office door opened.

Dave McNally stood in the doorway, a sardonic smile tugging at the corners of his mouth, "And you wonder why I drink. Sauce for the goose, eh, Mason?"

"Shut up."

McNally closed the office door and walked to a folding chair, grabbing it by its metal back and scraping it toward the desk. He sat down slowly, almost primly, the motion unnatural in its formality. Stiffly correct, it lacked grace, and looked to Harlow like bad animation.

"What the hell do you want?"

McNally beamed. "It's all coming undone. You know that, don't you?"

"Fuck you. Everything's under control. In two days we'll all be out of here. It's over and we're out of here."

McNally shook his head. "It'll never be over. Don't you understand that? It took me a long time, but I finally do. We screwed up, Mason, totally and irrevocably."

"Bullshit!"

"You think so? You think a wino is preaching the gospel, is that what you think? Well, let me explain it to you. It's like this: as long as we keep delivering, they won't let us go. As soon as we stop delivering, they *can't* let us go."

Harlow poured another inch of Scotch into the glass. The previous shots had done their work. His hand was steady, almost rocklike in its resolute immobility. The slender stream of Scotch fell straight as a wire into the glass. Harlow set the bottle down and hoisted the glass, raising it above his head in a mock salute. "Cheers."

"Sure, I know. You think everything's all right. You pop a few, and the nerves stop vibrating for a while. But later on, after it wears off, your skin starts to crawl again. I've been there, Mason, as you know very well, and let me tell you, it doesn't work. We're in deep shit and going down."

"Al-Hassan is going to be here in a little bit. If you have things to do, go do them. If you're all set, why don't you go find something to do that looks important? It doesn't have to *be* important, but make it look good. He knows what I'm paying you, and I think he's starting to wonder why." Harlow grinned briefly, without moving his lips. It came and went so quickly, McNally wondered whether it had been there at all. The effect was that of a facial tic rather than a change of expression.

"You won't believe me, will you, Mason? You just won't believe me. You know what I think? I think you've been lying to everybody for so long, you don't know what's true anymore. That's what I think."

"Listen, Dr. Freud, or whoever the hell you think you are, why don't you stuff it? You want to know what's over? I'll *tell* you what's over. Your days of collecting a fat check and giving squat in exchange, that's what's over. Tomorrow morning, you and me are kaput, finished."

"You really believe you can get away with this? Do you?"

"It doesn't matter what I believe."

Mason paused to sip the Scotch. When he resumed, a fine sheen of the whisky coated his lips and reflected the fluorescent light above him. McNally stared intently, as if mesmerized. The whiskeyed lips glittered when Harlow resumed. "What matters is that al-Hassan thinks we can. As long as I give him what he wants, I come out smelling like a rose. He wants a couple of third-rate politicians blown away in the asshole of the earth, I give him what he wants. He wants enough plastic explosive to make gravel out of Jupiter, I give him what he wants."

"And . . . ?"

"And I get what I want. But see, the real secret is what you never understood. Business, it's just business. And nobody really gives a shit. Everybody runs around doing his own thing. Al-Hassan does his thing. I do my thing. You drink. Everybody's happy. QED!"

McNally sighed. "Pour me a drink, will you?"

Harlow snorted. "Truth comes in a bottle, huh? Listen, Dave, you think I like what happened between us? Well, I don't. I don't like it at all. But you know what? It happened. Nothing we can do can change it now. Nothing."

Harlow reached down and opened the desk drawer. He pulled out an unopened bottle of Johnny Walker Black. Again he closed the drawer with the bottle's bottom. He hefted the whisky in his hand, tossing it an inch or two in the air several times. He stared at the label as if McNally weren't even in the room the whole time.

Then his head snapped up and he slapped the bottle on the desk. He gave it a shove and it slid toward McNally, plowing through loose papers and nearly tipping off the edge. McNally caught it with a practiced hand.

"For auld lang syne, Davey boy. My treat."

McNally stood, the bottle in his hand. "You sure you won't need this yourself later on?"

Harlow said nothing. He spun in the desk chair and stared out the window.

McNally shrugged. He closed the door softly on his way out.

HARLOW WAS STARING at the door expectantly. It finally opened and Colonel al-Hassan stepped in without ceremony. Harlow stared at him, but said nothing.

The colonel walked over to the chair McNally had been using and sat down. He removed his sunglasses carefully, unlooping the wire frames from one ear at a time. With the glasses off, his dark eyes seemed to emit their own inner light. His skin was showing the first signs of wrinkling, but other than that he was ageless.

Harlow looked at his own hands, the knotted veins beginning to protrude through the skin. They were the hands of an old man, like his grandfather's hands. But he was too young. There was too much to do yet, for him to think that way.

Al-Hassan watched patiently, a slight smile bowing the corners of his pursed mouth. Finally, with a casualness uncharacteristic of him, he said, "How are things, Mr. Harlow? Everything ready for me?"

"Sure, why not?"

"Oh, no reason. You just seem rather... pensive. I thought perhaps something was troubling you."

"I've never known you to be so solicitous. Worried?"

"Not if you tell me there is nothing to worry about."

"There isn't."

"Good. That's very good. I was wondering, Mr. Harlow, whether the rest of the... supplies, shall I say... have arrived."

"Not yet. Due in this evening. Touched down in Tripoli a while ago. The rest is a piece of cake."

The colonel shook his head slowly. "That's very good. And the other matter?"

"Okay. Everything's okay, I told you. What the fuck do you want from my life?"

Harlow reached for his second bottle of Scotch. He tilted it back and swallowed the final few drops, then tossed it into the corner, where it landed with a crash and spun in a tight circle, the sand on the wooden floor grinding at the label, before slowly rattling to a halt. Al-Hassan never batted an eye, and Harlow laughed.

"Something is funny?"

"No, yeah...nothing. Colonel, you ever hear of spin the bottle?"

"No, I can't say that I have."

"Forget it then. It's nothing. Just a stupid kid's game, anyway."

Al-Hassan stood up and replaced the sunglasses carefully, repeating the process in reverse, then carefully straightening the lenses on his broad nose. "As you might expect, I have to attend to a few matters. I will see you the day after tomorrow, in the evening, then?"

"Sure. I'll be here. I'm not going anywhere. Not that I know of."

"I'll want to talk to you about another project. I would appreciate your input."

Harlow said nothing for a long moment. Then, breaking into a smile, he asked, "How much are we talking about here?"

"You have always been reasonably compensated, haven't you?"

"Sure, yeah, of course. But, you know, I'm getting pretty good at this shit. Better all the time, in fact. You have to consider the experience factor, Colonel."

Al-Hassan smiled. "Tell me, Mr. Harlow, why do you do it? We have paid you what, twenty, twenty-five million dollars in the past few years, more or less? You surely don't need the money."

"That's where you're wrong, Colonel. My old man used to say all the money in the world wasn't enough. I never understood what he meant, not really. For years I used to wonder about it, and every time I thought I knew, something made me change my mind. But I got it now. Now I *really* know."

Harlow stopped abruptly. He seemed to be waiting for al-Hassan to ask him a question. The colonel was more patient. Harlow conceded. "What he meant was, you can't win, see. If you have all the money, then nobody else has any. Then you have to worry about them trying to take it away from you. But if everybody else has all they want, then no matter how much money you have, you ain't shit. You're nothing special, see. And that's the point. Money makes you somebody, but only if you got more than anybody else and they don't have enough."

Al-Hassan nodded as if he understood.

"Tell me something, Colonel. What makes *you* run? And don't hand me any of that glib crap about the will of Allah. You're about as devoted to Islam as I am. You drink, you screw around. Hell, I could figure out all the 'do nots' in the Koran just by watching what you do and turning it inside out. So, what is it? What makes you tick?"

"We are not so very different, you and I, Mr. Harlow. I concede that."

"Mason, call me Mason. Since we're being down-home here, we might as well dispense with the formalities. Here, wait a minute...." Harlow bent down and opened the desk drawer a third time. He pulled a third bottle out, this time leaving the drawer open. He poured a couple of fingers in his own glass, keeping his eyes fastened on al-Hassan's face, then filled a second glass a quarter of the way.

The colonel walked back to the desk. "Mason, it's a simple thing. Really." Staring at Harlow, he picked up the glass and downed it in a single draft. "Money means nothing to me. I have all I want. More, really, than I can ever use. And you're right, of course, about my religious motives. I have made my peace with Allah. If it is sufficient or not I won't know, not, at least, until it is too late."

He rapped the empty glass on the desk, nodding for Harlow to refill it. He watched the Scotch collect in the bottom of the cheap tumbler, then pointed a finger when it was enough. He raised the glass to his lips and smiled.

"No, the real reason I do what I do doesn't even have to do with my desire, such as it is, to serve my political masters. It is simply to prove to myself that no one can stop me. And no matter how many times you do something, there is always the possibility that next time someone will raise a hand and say 'Enough!'" He paused to swallow the whisky.

"You see, Mason, you and I both know that money is nothing. Your father was almost right. But he made one mistake. The real reason we both do what we do is something very, very different. The real reason is that all the *power* in the world isn't enough."

CHAPTER THIRTY-EIGHT

Leon Alvarez closed the shed door, cringing as it clacked and bounced on its rollers. He left it open just a foot or so and went back to the body lying on the floor.

The dead man had dropped a small leather bag, and Alvarez kicked it to one side before pulling the body into the shadows. When he had hidden the corpse between two stacks of crates, then buried it under a pile of flattened cardboard cartons, he went back for the leather bag. It was thin leather and closed with a drawstring at one end. Alvarez pulled the string free and opened the bag.

He smelled garlic and realized how hungry he was. Tilting the bag upside down, he shook it, and three loaves of pita bread fell onto the cluttered table. Lemon joined the scent of garlic in the air. The bread had been sliced open across the top, and the pocket stuffed with a thick, creamy paste of some sort of mashed vegetable and dampened with oil. He felt a bit woozy from the hunger, and his head ached.

Alvarez wolfed down one pita, doing his best to ignore the bitter spices. The food made him thirsty again, and he walked to a small closet in one corner of the shed. He struck a match, and through the half-open door he saw grease-spattered white porcelain gleaming dully behind some greasy coveralls on a hook screwed into the door. The sink featured a single spigot. A paper cup sat on top of the sink, and he filled it from the tap and swirled a mouthful of water around with his tongue before swallowing. The tepid water tasted vaguely of minerals, but he was too thirsty to be picky.

The agent refilled the cup, drank it down, then filled it a third time. Walking back to the messy table, he chewed ravenously at a second pita, washing the dry bread down with mouthfuls of the warm water. He stuffed the third pita back into the bag and finished his water, swallowing another painkiller at the same time.

He went back to the closet and hauled the coveralls off the hook. Holding them up to his shoulders, he decided they would fit him, although perhaps a bit loosely. He stepped into the legs of the coveralls one at a time, tugged the slippery cloth up over his shoulders and fastened the metal buttons halfway up his chest.

Alvarez returned to the table and pushed the leather bag inside the coveralls, then buttoned another button. He tiptoed to the door to peek out at the deserted apron. The Starlifter still yawned open, but no one seemed to be overly concerned about its contents. He yanked his parka from the barrel and slipped the Browning into his open coveralls. With a last look around he stepped through the narrow opening and onto the pavement outside.

Trying to walk naturally, he stayed in close to the long row of garage-style doors. At the end of the shed he turned a corner and nearly tripped over a pair of thick cables. He looked back at the obstacle, then followed the twin lines of black rubber with his eye. Thirty yards away, they disappeared under the wing of an unmarked transport, to which they ascended in a graceful arc. The plane's cargo bay was open to the side, and just inside the door he spotted a familiar canvas. He had found the pallets, at least one of them.

Two men worked busily under the nose of the plane, one holding the nozzle of a refueling line, the other engaged with the double cable and nearly out of sight behind the landing gear. His heart stopped for a second, but neither man paid any attention to him. He glanced over his shoulder, then climbed the narrow stairs built into one edge of the cargo door.

Dim worklights illuminated the interior of the big plane. Alvarez scrambled toward the cockpit down an aisle between pallets strapped to the fuselage with canvas belts double-knotted to security rails. The plane was almost as capacious as the big Lockheed transport, and the pallets of plastique seemed to be the only cargo. As he looked for a place to hide, his glance fell on a short row of lockerlike metal cabinets toward the tail of the plane. He worked his way back past the open door, crouching to lower his profile.

Two voices grew louder on the apron as he reached the first of the cabinets. He yanked the door open, but the cabinet was crammed with emergency equipment. The next one was half-full, but there was still not enough room for him to squeeze in. Trying to close its door while opening the third cabinet, he lost his grip on the door handle and the door swung back out.

The third cabinet was empty and he ducked inside, jamming his parka behind his knees. He shoved the door of the second cabinet shut again, and he heard the catch rasp but fail to take hold as he tugged his own door inward. By grabbing the lock bar angled across it waist high, he managed to snug the door closed. Working the bar manually, he would still be able to reopen it from inside.

The voices had grown louder, and he could hear heavy steps climbing the wooden surface of the ramp. As they drew near, both men laughing over something Alvarez hadn't heard, a loud bang on his door made him jump. His hand leaped into the coverall and felt for the Browning as he held his breath.

"Fucking doors never stay closed," someone growled in a raspy baritone. Judging by the sound of his voice, he was standing just to the right of Alvarez, in front of the second cabinet.

A squeal next to his right ear sent a spike through his head. Alvarez removed the gun, gripping it tightly in both hands. The proximity of the door prevented him from leveling the muzzle, and he held the Browning pointed straight down between his feet.

He inhaled slowly, trying to quiet his frazzled nerves while he waited for the door to swing open. He could feel the hair on the back of his hands and neck standing on end, the tingle in his nerves like thousands of small electric shocks. The door handle rattled, and he felt the lock bar brush the back of his wrists.

"This one's okay," the voice said. "Check the others."

"Want me to padlock 'em?" The second voice, a mellow tenor, sounded slightly slurred, as if the speaker had been drinking. Alvarez caught a sudden whiff of alcohol, and he realized the second man must be right in front of the cabinet.

"Nah . . . fuck 'em. If they're closed, they'll be all right."

The voice retreated, and the second man rattled several more handles before announcing, "They're okay now."

The first voice, now some yards away, seemed impatient. "Come on, Carmine, we're already late. That ain't going to make us popular with Harlow."

"The hell with him. Son of a bitch has some kind of Napoleon complex. Thinks he's God, or something." The snarl of a laboring servo put an end to the exchange, and Alvarez could feel the motor's vibration through the soles of his shoes. When the shuddering stopped, the conversation was picked up as smoothly as if it had never been interrupted.

"J. P. Morgan's more like it. To hear him, you'd think he hung out with the Rockefellers. What an asshole."

"He's all right."

"Long as the checks don't bounce."

"You got that right." The cockpit door slammed off to the left, and Alvarez exhaled thankfully.

THE SUN FINALLY, thankfully, descended. Mack Bolan stood at the window, watching the last red streaks darken to purple then to bluish gray. He slapped carelessly at the window screen, angering a hundred flies. To retaliate, they buzzed the screen like drunken barnstormers, diving recklessly toward the wire, and sometimes losing control long enough to slap themselves silly on the metal grid.

As he watched the bugs, he wondered just how much difference there really was between a mindless insect and a man who did exactly as he was told. The line—if there was one—was not one he could see clearly.

The sky was almost completely dark, and small points of light sparkled in the tiny squares defined by the screen. He moved closer, expanding each square to a universe, and watching other stars blossom in each space formerly reserved for a single fire. Examined so minutely, in such an oppressive air, the light seemed so cold, and far more distant than usual. He fastened his gaze on Betelgeuse, the red giant in Orion, and slowly, like a blind man reading his first Braille, moved his fingertips from square to square, until the colossal star vanished.

He scratched his fingers down along the wire, raking them like a lion's claws and leaving thin lines of pared nail etched across the screen. He turned suddenly and walked back to his bunk, where he sat down heavily. He dropped his head to the air pillow but couldn't find a comfortable position. He was too restless. He knew too much about which he could do too little.

Lucien Picard lay on his side on his own bunk. He held a skin magazine before his face, but Bolan could see by the steady, motionless focus of the eyes that he wasn't reading. He sat up abruptly, tossing the magazine to one side and grinning at Bolan. "Hey, you want to take a walk?"

Bolan shook his head, but Picard insisted. He stood reluctantly while Picard waited for him at the door. When he stepped through the screen door, held wide by Picard with exaggerated graciousness, the Frenchman followed immediately.

Picard lit a cigarette and tossed the match aside, watching it trail a thin plume of gray smoke as it fell to the sand. The farmhouse where they were staying was isolated, but the sound of the night was more natural than that of the desert. Off in the distance, animals of rich voice and nocturnal habit argued with one another and with the night itself.

Picard dragged on the cigarette and walked toward a low, split-rail fence behind the farmhouse. Way off in the distance, nearly forty miles away, N'Djamena was a low, wide smear of light on the horizon. Its glow arched up like a pale rainbow, dislodging the darkness and swallowing the stars.

Picard leaned on the fence and said, "I'm leaving. I just wanted you to know."

"You can't. What about tomorrow?"

"That's exactly why I have to leave. It is not an easy decision. I know what we had agreed, but that was before I knew what I know now."

"I understand...."

"No, I don't think you do. I know that if I leave, an innocent man may be murdered tomorrow. But if I don't, if I stay here knowing what I know, it is possible that others, perhaps hundreds of others, of my countrymen may die. It is not an equation, I know. But I am not a mathematician, either. I am a Frenchman first, an indifferent spy second and only lastly a moral philosopher. Perhaps that is why I do it so badly, and why I can't see any other choices."

"What are you going to do?"

"I have to get to N'Djamena, to the French embassy. They have to be warned about the assassination and the armor attack. You can come with me. If you talk to your embassy, you can head off the assassination."

"But Harlow and the others will get off scot-free. If I go with you, he will dig himself a hole. I can't take that chance."

"And suppose you fail? Suppose you don't get the chance to take out the shooters. The president of this country will be dead, and you will still lose Harlow. Come with me. We'll sound the alarm and then we'll go get Harlow together."

"I don't think so, Lucien. I have to stay, to see it through."

"I understand. Look, I'll meet you at the chopper tomorrow, if I can. But don't wait for me."

"When do you plan to leave?"

"After midnight."

Bolan nodded. He clapped Picard on the shoulder. "I'll
see you tomorrow."

"I hope so."

"I'm counting on it."

CHAPTER THIRTY-NINE

The Sauer was right where it was supposed to be. Bolan saw it from the open door. Slipping inside, he closed the door behind him and walked to the window. He leaned close to the dusty glass and rubbed the inside of the pane with his fingertips, leaving a small patch of relatively clean glass behind.

The clear area was just large enough for him to make out the width of the plaza, already lined with expectant crowds. President Joseph M'tele was due in just over an hour. Every avenue leading into the open square teemed with celebrity watchers and vendors.

The day was destined to be a landmark in the history of an independent Chad. Fresh from negotiating his first major international agreement, M'tele, like any politician, was interested in waving a few flags, calling a little attention to himself and making as much hay as possible from his newly minted global credibility. That the U.S.-Chad mutual security pact was only an agreement in principle seemed not to matter a bit to the anxious throng. They all wished their young president well.

But Bolan knew that somewhere on the periphery, there were three men who were less sanguine about the achievement. And all Mack Bolan had to do was find them. Crossing his fingers and making a wish wouldn't cut it. Bolan had sixty minutes to track them down and kill them. Anything less would be a disaster, and with the Libyan armor poised for a quick strike over the border, a successful assassination would signal a war that could envelop the continent.

In the past the superpowers had come to the brink of war over much less. Africans of every political stripe and every color had already been choosing sides for two dozen years.

Now, with suspicion a new American virtue, and face a major Soviet preoccupation, the likelihood that Africa would boil over from Cape Town to Cairo was all but a certainty. Vietnam and Afghanistan were lessons apparently unlearned.

Bolan opened the canvas bag draped over one shoulder and pulled a pair of compact binoculars from a leather box. He brought the glasses close to the windowpane, trying to compensate for the smeared glass with a twiddle of the focus knob. The blurred grime hampered his visibility a bit, but he was still able to get a clear look at the borders of the plaza. Unfortunately he didn't know what he was looking for. He didn't even know whether he would recognize it if he found it.

He swept the margin of the plaza, moving his head instead of simply turning it. The narrow angle of coverage afforded by the clean spot in the center of the pane was all he had to work with. By the time he'd covered the left half of the plaza, familiar images kept slipping into the edge of his consciousness, crying out for recognition. Gritting his teeth and cursing softly to himself, he pushed both needles and haystack out of the way.

Bolan was getting nowhere fast. He slipped the glasses back into their case and walked to the desk to retrieve the Sauer. Five shells sat in a box alongside the rifle. Bolan smiled. He loaded the rifle, then reached into his bag and groped around until he found the box of ammunition. His rummaging in the warehouse had paid off handsomely. In addition to the extra ammo for the Sauer, he had secured two boxes of 9 mm NATO rounds for the Beretta, and a standard issue Colt .45 automatic and plenty of rounds. The AutoMag was on short rations, but he would have to make do.

The biggest prize though—other than the block of C-4 and a detonator—was an Ingram sound suppressor. The Sauer wouldn't take it, of course. At least not straight. But necessity, as they say, is a mother. He had already stripped the inside of the suppressor, reaming it out with a long, narrow blade. And now he knew why he had always loved gaffer's tape. Working quickly, he cut several strips of the shiny, silver vinyl tape and tacked a row of four-inch hunks on the edge of the desk.

The Sauer was scoped, so he used a coarse file and the knife blade to scrape away at the front sight, smoothing it down enough to accommodate the suppressor. He wrapped a tape strip around the barrel and tried the suppressor. It slipped on too easily, and he yanked it off again then wrapped a second piece of tape around it, doing his best to preserve the contours of the barrel. This time the suppressor resisted, and he screwed it gently back and forth, taking care to keep the tape intact.

Holding the rifle at arm's length, he assessed the alignment, made a couple of slight adjustments, then secured it with a couple of quick tacks of tape. He checked the alignment again, keeping one eye on his watch while he worked. He set the rifle down, keeping the muzzle in the air, and hauled eighteen inches of the tape from the roll, severed it neatly and wrapped the entire half yard around the joint.

It looked like hell, the bulky suppressor even more bulbous now, like a mummy wrapped in Bloomingdale's best. He checked the alignment a final time, then sprayed the tape with flat black Krylon paint, to minimize the glare. It was crude and as ugly as sin, but it would work.

And the Executioner knew, better than anyone else, that no matter how ugly the tools, the death they brought was uglier still. Somebody once said that form followed function. If that was true, then the muzzle of an assassin's rifle ought to look like the very mouth of hell itself.

While he waited for the paint to dry he went back to the window, this time tugging the sash upward a half foot, to let the others, wherever they were, know he was in place.

What they didn't know was that he wouldn't be there for long.

Bolan ripped a thick drapery from the front window, then wrapped the tools of his trade in the dusty cloth. He picked up the whole bundle and stepped to the door. Listening for a moment, he turned the knob and pulled the door inward, opening it three or four inches. A thud echoed at one end of the hall as a door closed, and Bolan waited to see whether someone had entered it. When the echo died without further noise, he pulled the door all the way open and stepped onto the slick tile. He debated for a moment whether to go right or left. It was a toss-up.

Left won.

At that end of the hall a fire door led to the stairs. It creaked when he opened it, but moved easily enough, and he closed it behind him, tugging impatiently against the reluctance of the pneumatic hinge. The stairwell was red lit and dusty. He started up the gray painted concrete, taking the steps two at a time. By his watch he was down to forty minutes.

Six stories above he found the roof door held shut with a thick iron bar. He set his package on end in the corner and removed the bar as quietly as he could. Exchanging the bar for the rifle, he pushed the door open and felt an immediate surge of cool air flow out around him, then change quickly to a wave of hot air swirling in, smelling of melted tar as it slipped through the crack. The breeze turned into a brisk wind that died as soon as the door was fully open.

Bolan stepped cautiously out onto the roof, laying his rifle just under the doorsill. He pulled out the binoculars and hung them around his neck by the vinyl strap. Hoisting them, he checked nearby roofs for security and, seeing none, walked to the parapet. A chest-high wall, broken in places with loopholes like a medieval fortress barricade, ran the entire perimeter of the roof. The wall gave him some cover, but it also restricted his movement.

Bolan sprinted back to the door, reached inside for the bar and jammed the door shut by wedging one end in the sticky tar and the other under a strap hinge. He jerked the rifle from under the sill and carried it to the center of the wall on the plaza side.

At the wall he knelt down, the glasses in his hand. From far below, a jumble of sound wafted across the plaza, spilling up and over the surrounding buildings. Bells and gongs, a dozen kinds of drum. The shifting rhythm, accented in every conceivable meter, accompanied the steady hum of fifty thousand people.

Bolan's only hope was to figure where he would be if he were each of the three remaining shooters. And if one of them was on the same side of the plaza, either in this building or an adjacent one, he could be out of luck. The glasses picked out the incongruous figure of Carter, languishing against a low wall at the edge of the fountain. Bolan watched the man for thirty seconds before it hit him. Since he had to raise the window to signal he was in position, and he didn't know what to look for from the others, then possibly Carter was the key. By watching him, Bolan might be able to pick out the other three shooters.

At the edge of his field of vision, the waters of the fountain bubbled like liquid silver. Bright flashes of pure white light stabbed at his eyes, and he closed them to near slits to ward off the glare.

Carter kept fidgeting on the rock wall, and Bolan pinned the glasses to him. A short black strand dangled from the man's rear pocket, and Bolan zeroed in on it. Even through the glasses, it could have been anything from a short-range antenna to a loose thread.

"Come on, Carter," Bolan muttered, "do something. Give me a break!"

Carter stood and cupped a palm over his eyes, looking toward the parliament wing of the presidential palace. Bolan scoped the left half of that building but saw nothing that interested him. Then, casually, almost too casually, Carter turned to stare at the wall of the building right below Bolan.

"That's it, Carter, that's the way. See the open window? Now, give me a clue!"

Carter turned back to look into the center of the plaza. He climbed up on the stone wall, about three feet above street level, and stood on the mortared rock. Gradually, with a studied nonchalance, he tilted his head to the side, still shading his eyes, and stared into the mouth of the Boulevard de Bastille. A tall, needlelike office building, twenty stories crammed into a tiny lot in the best urban fashion, towered over two- and three-story buildings on either side. Its black glass facade sparkled with hundreds of suns, a mirror image in every pane. A slender gash in the center ripped the facade from top to bottom. A string of terraces nestled in the heart of the gash.

Carter stared at the building for several seconds, and Bolan swept its face with the binoculars. He started at the top and worked his way down, but saw nothing. Carter glanced away just as Bolan put the glasses back on him, then looked back at the same building. Bolan followed suit.

A flash of white light winked on the fifth floor, and Bolan fixed the glass on the spot. For a long moment he saw nothing, then he saw what had caused the flash: a terrace door yawned open to the rising heat, and its movement must have reflected the sun for a moment as it opened. Boring in through the doorway, Bolan caught a shadow—a man in a dark shirt.

Carter was staring directly at the terrace, then turned abruptly, as if suddenly aware he was being careless. Spinning on his heel, he watched a small group of drummers dance by, breaking like a wave on the fountain and dividing in two. They flowed effortlessly past the low stone and regrouped on the far side.

Blaring horns funneled out of the mouth of Boulevard de Bastille. The motorcade was approaching. Bolan checked his watch, and had less than ten minutes to find the other two shooters. Carter seemed jittery and had begun to pace back and forth on the wall. He glanced at Bolan's open window, several floors below, then off to Bolan's left. He had done that before, but Bolan had seen nothing when tracking the man's glance.

On a hunch the warrior sprinted to the left parapet and looked out over the wall. A row of small office buildings, the tallest no more than six stories, stood in a ragged phalanx far below. Bolan left the glasses on his chest as he scanned the nearest roof, then the next and the third. On the fourth roof he got lucky. An elevator shaft, its tower rising fifteen feet above the roof, stood near the front edge of the building. Its skylight was a pyramid of glass, and the front face of the pyramid was open.

Bolan brought the glasses to his eyes and twirled the focus knob back and forth, trying to resolve a shadow in the glass box. But the glass was covered with fine yellow dust. It reflected too much light and he couldn't see through it. Watching the open face for a minute, he finally got what he needed. Like a tentative antenna, a slender shadow slipped through the open glass. The binoculars told him all he needed. The muzzle of a Sauer wavered in the open air, like a fern in a gentle breeze.

That made two. But where was the third?

He had ten minutes to find him.

CHAPTER FORTY

The landing took Alvarez by surprise. He had been prepared for a long flight, but three hours later his stomach
turned inside out and climbed halfway up his esophagus.
The familiar constriction in his chest had him gasping for
air. The plane dropped quickly, and Alvarez tried to put
himself on the outside, watching the precipitous descent as
if from a great distance, minimizing his involvement with
the aircraft. It was the only way he could get through it.

When the landing gear scraped along the airstrip, he held
his breath for a long moment, then took the Browning out
of his shirt. He gripped it tightly and imagined his knuckles
white-hot, ready to explode into small stars. His eyes were
closed to concentrate all his attention on sound. This had to
be the last stop.

As soon as the plane stopped rolling, he felt it shift,
braking in a gentle turn, and then even that motion ceased.
The engines died and the cockpit door banged open. The
barbershop duet returned, their distinctive voices in mumbled counterpoint growing louder as they approached the
metal cabinets, then receding. The men stopped talking, and
all Alvarez could hear was their footsteps ringing on the
wooden floorboards of the cargo bay.

The servo hummed, laced with the metallic whine of
pneumatic rods sliding through greased bushings, and a
hard thud made the plane tremble as the cargo door touched
down. Alvarez waited impatiently. Every instinct screamed
for him to open the cabinet and slip out into the hold, but
he was so damn close, and to lose it all now would be crim-
inal.

More footsteps, this time receding and finally dying away
altogether, and he realized they must have left the plane. His

eyes were still closed and he focused every sensory synapse on sound. The plane was silent except for the ping of contracting metal as the engines cooled down after the long flight. The cabinet was getting uncomfortable. Alvarez couldn't stand the smell of his own breath, and blew it down and away through tensed lips. The scent of garlic from the stolen pita filled the coffin like a liquid. The atmosphere was oppressive, and his nostrils were offended by the odor of his own body.

An avid reader, as a teenager he had worshiped Poe. Now he remembered "The Premature Burial," and began to understand it for the first time. What nightmare must the author have lived to render the sensations of entombment so faithfully? He shrugged his shoulders to release the building tension, but the movement just reinforced his sense of confinement. Somehow he had controlled his anxiety during the interminable flights, but now that he had finished the journey, every nerve cried out for satisfaction, every brain cell screamed for him to do something, anything, to end the claustrophobic torture.

Alvarez started counting, not knowing why or how far he would count before he would stop. The gesture seemed foolish to him, as if he were using it to postpone some inevitable thing. And there was only one thing certain—he would have to leave the safety of the cabinet sooner or later. At seventy-five he cursed, then pushed on to one hundred. That was enough, he thought, and let go of the Browning with his right hand. He grabbed the lock bar and pushed it to the side. The swivel squealed, then gave with a sharp clank.

Carefully pushing the door open a few inches, he waited for a long count, then opened the door all the way, stepping through while still holding on to the bar. The door bumped the adjacent locker, then stayed still. He let it go, opening a palm toward it as if to beg its cooperation. It swung back as he bent to retrieve his parka, bumping against his elbow and tolling softly.

Holding the parka by its collar, Alvarez closed the door again and looked toward the open cargo bay. Behind the lip of the plane, he saw a dark sky, the clear, hard points of the stars twinkling slightly against the indigo-tinged coal of the heavens. He rubbed his sore shoulder, his fingers stumbling over the thick wrapping of the sling wound over his upper arm. The shoulder didn't hurt as much, and for that he was grateful.

He was walking toward the stars, almost at the head of the ramp, when he heard voices again. He rushed backward, nearly stumbling over some coiled canvas straps on the deck, and dropped down behind one of the pallets. A powerful diesel roared like a starving lion, and the plane rocked as something hit the foot of the ramp. The yawning bay grew suddenly darker as the uprights of a forklift bobbed into view, then grew longer. Framed between them, like a shadowy field judge behind a goalpost, the driver turned his head to holler at someone still on the ground.

"Get the lights, will you, Carmine? Harlow ought to have his head examined. Why should we have to unload this bastard all by ourselves?"

The question hung unanswered in the air while the forklift hovered at the ramp head, the throb of its chugging engine making the plane tremble. Running footsteps rocked the ramp again, and Alvarez huddled behind the pallet, the Browning braced against one corner of the rough canvas.

Carmine appeared alongside the forklift like a shadowy egret, a collection of slender angles, all arms and legs. He stepped past the forklift, moving across the ramp for a switch bank. Alvarez felt his finger tense on the trigger. The checkered grip tingled in his palm, and he drew a bead on the center of Carmine's chest. If he put on the lights, it was all over, and Alvarez knew it.

He fired once, the Browning spitting through its suppressor. The 9 mm slug slapped the flesh and broke a bone with an audible crack. Carmine spun to his right, propelled by the impact, and Alvarez fired again, this time catching the birdlike shadow high and to the left. Carmine fell, his groan punctuated by the smack of his forehead on the edge of the cargo bay just before he toppled out of sight.

"What the fuck...?" Baffled, the man on the forklift seemed momentarily paralyzed. Alvarez shifted his aim and scored with a quick shot through the uprights, catching the driver in the center of his face. He flew backward, and without his feet and hands at the controls, the unbridled forklift turned, its engine stuttering as the clutch was released without a foot on the gas. It chugged and died, then followed the law of gravity and began to roll backward.

It hit an obstacle Alvarez couldn't see, and only when he heard the man scream did he realize it had rolled over on the driver. The cry gurgled to an end, and the forklift fell off the edge of the ramp. Alvarez stepped out cautiously, the Browning squeezed in both hands.

He stopped at the mouth of the cargo hold. Carmine lay on the sandy ground, pinned to it through the abdomen like a butterfly to a corkboard by one prong of the fork. His head and shoulders were hidden by the engine housing, his legs stuck out at awkward angles.

The driver lay on the ramp, his head downward. In the indifferent light, a dark ooze of liquid shadow flowed from his mouth and up one cheek to disappear in the tangled hair above his shattered forehead. Alvarez felt a twinge of nausea and turned away for a moment until it passed.

He shuddered, then stepped past the dead man, squeezing his parka to his chest as if for consolation. He ducked his head behind the bundled coat to keep it between himself and the motionless driver. He felt, rather than saw, the ground, as his feet scraped on the sand. The mottled warehouse loomed to his left, and he realized where he was. It was, it had to be, the same encampment he had seen so long ago, when it seemed this interminable nightmare had begun.

Alvarez scooted down the ramp, trying to muffle his footsteps on the planking. He sprinted toward the open warehouse door. It was dark inside and no one seemed to be about. If he took the forklift driver at his word, there wouldn't be. Ducking through the door, he stumbled backward, then leaned against the inner wall to catch his breath. The exertion made his shoulder throb, and he clutched it while his breath came in spasmodic gasps.

Under the rasp of his own ragged breathing, he heard distant voices, somewhere deep inside the building. A dim light was on in the far corner. He was torn between the desire to see who it was and to run into the desert to find some cover. He did neither.

He knew the Browning was empty, and he had only two clips remaining. The Coonan carried only what was left in the magazine. Alvarez skipped into the nearest aisle, the voices a dull monotone in the background. He strained to read the markings on the crates, which were stacked on the floor and cramming the shelves. Working his way deeper into the building, his back to the dim light, he found several crates of ammunition, but none suited his weapons.

Cartons of .45-caliber shells, and 7.62 mm ammo for AK-47s stood cheek by jowl with dozens of crates marked "5.56 mm" for the M-16 and Colt Commando assault rifles stacked alongside them. He made mental notes as he moved, realizing that he might have to work with whatever fortune threw his way.

At the first intersection, he found an open crate of Ingram MAC-10s. He grabbed two of the submachine guns and draped them over his shoulder by their leather slings. They were perfect—if only he could remember where he had seen the .45-caliber ammo. He stuffed the heavy Coonan between two crates, tucking it out of sight. It slipped out of his hand and dropped to the metal shelf with a dull clang.

Alvarez held his breath, straining to hear the voices. They muttered on, and apparently the speakers had heard nothing. He worked his way back toward the ammunition and found what he wanted. Three cartons, the top one open, sat by themselves on a shelf. He pulled back the cardboard flap and groped inside for some smaller boxes. Grabbing three, he stuffed them into the pockets of his parka, put another one in his pants pocket and shuffled back along the aisle, keeping one eye on the dim light and reading the dark, smeared lettering stenciled on rough wood boxes with the other. He backed past a crate of 9 mm rounds and grabbed a box for the Browning.

Now, all he had to do was find Bolan, if he was even here. And if he was still alive.

As Alvarez reached the front wall of the warehouse, the light in the rear went out. A door slammed, shaking partitions in the back of the building, and the voices grew suddenly nearer. He was too far from the door to make a break for it, so he scurried into a crevice against the front wall.

As the voices drew closer he realized with astonishment that one of them was a woman. He flattened himself against the wall, crouching behind some stray cartons. The beam of a flashlight danced in a narrow aisle, casting shadows on the ceiling and flashing whenever it caught a gap between stacks of crates.

They were still talking, but the man had dropped his voice to a whisper. The woman's musical alto seemed unconcerned. "I still don't see what all the cloak-and-dagger stuff is about."

"Shh. Keep your voice down," the man barked, his own voice momentarily rising above the rasping buzz it had been.

"What's the big secret? Everybody here works for you, don't they? Why should you have to hide?"

"Dammit, Marielle, I told you. This is some dangerous shit we're doing."

"What exactly *are* you doing?"

"I already told you, don't ask me about business now. You already know too much. I knew I shouldn't have brought you here."

"Well, it's too late for that, isn't it?"

"Just shut up, will you?"

They were only a few yards away now, and Alvarez listened to them bicker, but he wasn't sure what the argument was about. Their shoes scraped on the concrete, the brittle sand crunching now and again under their hard soles. The light swerved around a corner, spearing just above his head, and the agent pressed himself into a compact ball.

A moment later they were gone.

They were almost certain to see the corpses lying at the open cargo hold of the plane, and he wished for a moment he had dragged the bodies out of sight, then remembered the pinioned Carmine and knew he wouldn't have been able to do anything about him, even if he had thought to.

He stepped to the door, the boxes of bullets making him feel clumsy, the shells grinding against one another as his movements twisted the flimsy cardboard containers in his pockets. He watched the couple angle away from the plane. Their backs were to him and he slipped through the doorway on tiptoe. The woman seemed to sense something and turned to look over her shoulder.

For an eternal second her eyes were fixed on him, and he brought up the Browning. But she smiled a crooked smile, tossed her long red hair with her head and leaned in to take Harlow by the upper arm.

Alvarez slid like a lizard along the edge of the wall, his feet grinding in the dry soil. He was fifty yards from the door when the man pulled free of the woman's grasp and turned to look at the plane. They stopped, and Alvarez froze in his tracks.

He was not in a direct line of sight, but if the man turned back toward the warehouse, he was a goner. Two jeeps were parked just ahead, and he sprinted for them, ducking behind the front bumper of the nearer one just as the man called, "Hey, Carmine. What's the holdup?"

Feet crunched on the sand, and the next thing Alvarez heard was a shout. "Jesus Christ. Sadowski! Sadowski, get out here."

Running footsteps receded, and Alvarez peeked out from behind the jeep. The woman stood alone. She turned her head slightly, as if looking for something. Then she smiled.

CHAPTER FORTY-ONE

Mack Bolan bent below the wall and unwrapped the Sauer with its makeshift suppressor. He blew some dust off the scope and crept to the first loophole on his left. He sat on his haunches, propping the muzzle of the rifle on the mortar at the bottom of the loophole. He peered through the scope and sighted on the side window of the glass pyramid. The shadow inside was probably displaced, and he used the end of the hidden man's rifle as a rough index of his location.

With the suppressor in place, there would be a loss of muzzle velocity, but he wouldn't know how much until he fired the first shot. He was shooting down at an acute angle, and that, too, would affect the trajectory of the bullet. Aiming slightly high, he watched the shadow wavering in its crystal palace, and he thought about the old adage concerning glass houses and throwing stones.

The carnival sounds from the street below swelled into a rhythmic thunder, and the sirens of the motorcade grew shrill, their pitch slowly rising as they approached. The sound was compressed, massing in front of the vehicles and echoing off the walls of the stone-and-glass canyon of the Boulevard de Bastille. The shadow stopped moving, and Bolan knew the hidden assassin was getting ready. There were two others to take out, and there was no more time to waste.

Bolan gauged the shot again, aiming for a spot about three inches above the apparent crown of the gunman's head. He drew a deep breath, steadied the rifle and squeezed. The muffled report of the Sauer was like the pop of a half-empty balloon. The slug slammed into the metal frame of the window just above the ledge. Bolan saw a puff of rock dust and heard a ping as the slug glanced away. The impact spun a web of glittering cracks in the glass, a semicircular spiral radiating out from its focus at the frame. The refracted light of the sun painted the cracks with every color in the spectrum.

Bolan adjusted his aim quickly and squeezed again, this time shooting for a spot near the top edge of the window. He knew that aiming a little higher might expose him to the risk of overshooting the mark, but time was virtually nonexistent.

The glass collapsed inward, and through the scope Bolan saw a startled face looking up at him for just an instant. Bolan fired again, and this time the head of the assassin seemed to come apart like a pomegranate. Through the powerful scope Bolan saw the splattered wall on the far side of the shaft.

The assassin's rifle teetered for a second on the window ledge, then seemed to tip in slow motion. The weight of the stock carried it back into the shaft, the muzzle flashing by as it picked up speed. Bolan backed away from the scope, his mouth set in granitic repose.

Sprinting across the roof in a tight crouch, he skidded to a halt at the corner closest to the opening of the boulevard. Just to the left of where he stood, another loophole afforded him the clearest sight line to the assassin in the terrace door. He pulled three more shells from his pocket and reloaded the Sauer. There was no time to adjust the sight.

His third shot had been louder than the first two, but time was too short to retape the improvised suppressor. He squeezed the gaffer's tape to reseal it as best he could and held the rifle at arm's length to make sure it was still properly aligned.

Backing away from the wall, he watched Carter through the scope. The man seemed to be unaware that anything had happened. Bolan knelt again, slipping the Sauer onto the ledge. The terrace door was still open, but there was no one in it. The terrace itself was deserted.

Leaning far to the left, Bolan could just make out the pair of motorcycles at the head of the motorcade. The sirens were growing louder, and people along the route were beginning to press against the barricades. In two or three places the line bowed out into the street. Policemen stood with their backs to the crowd, their linked arms straining to hold back the crush.

The terrace door was still vacant, as if the shooter were waiting to make a grand entrance. Bolan didn't blame him. Closer to the ground than the others, he was the most easily seen. The policemen lining the edge of the plaza had their hands full, but a stray glance was all it would take. The gunman had wisely elected to stay well back from the door until the last possible minute.

Using the scope as much to see what he could inside the door as to sight on the as yet invisible target, Bolan could see the dim outlines of furniture against a light-colored wall. The lights in the apartment were out, but the bright sun was pouring through the open door. Directly behind the warrior, it beat down on his shoulders and head. He was aware of a thin trickle of sweat beginning to work its way down his spine, rushing from vertebra to vertebra, stopping at each one for a second to replenish itself and compensate for the sheen of perspiration left behind.

Every nerve in his body seemed to vibrate, and he wondered whether anyone nearby might hear him humming like a high-tension wire. Suddenly an almost indiscernible pale shadow splashed on the gray wall behind a sofa. Bolan watched the outline move slowly to the left. He couldn't determine the source of the light throwing the image on the wall, and he scanned left and right, trying to gauge the location of the figure.

A broad, high window to the left of the terrace door, perhaps that of a bathroom or kitchen, was the only spot that made sense. Bolan shifted the scope to the window, but the nearly opaque glass was impenetrable.

Staring again through the open doorway, he began to wonder whether his eyes were playing tricks on him. There were only two minutes to go now, and he still had two shooters to take out. For one crazy instant he thought about putting a shot through the doorway as a deterrent, but passed on it, knowing he risked drawing return fire. He couldn't afford to be seen by anyone, especially when there was still the possibility the assassination might be successful.

The blob of darkness on the wall began again to move, first to the left and then to the right, as if it had a will of its own and was undecided which way to go. And then the shadow grew darker and larger. Bolan watched it for a moment, then realized someone, possibly the shooter, had drawn close to the high window.

Then he realized why. The recessed terrace door gave the shooter an angle only after the motorcade had passed the building. In order to see where it might be, he had to use a window on the front wall.

Bolan glanced to the right and could see the open limousine now, its fender pennants fluttering in the backwash as it nosed through the throng. Beyond the car people had spilled out into the boulevard and fallen in behind it in an impromptu parade. The crowd on the leading edge pressed forward as the car came abreast of it, as if drawn forward magnetically.

Bolan turned back to the terrace doorway. The shadow vanished and a gray shape took its place. Through the scope Bolan could see a black man in jeans and work shirt. He held a rifle in his hands. Bolan panned up with the scope as the figure stood motionless about five feet inside the door. The warrior tightened his finger, felt the nerves grow hot and the muscles begin to contract when the man stepped aside.

Bolan cursed softly. The shadow reappeared, then contracted and vanished. The man was back. Bent over at the waist, he seemed to be struggling to move a piece of furniture. His head kept bobbing up and down, and his shoulder was almost beyond the doorframe, affording Bolan virtually no target at all.

The sirens grew shrill as the motorcycles began to sweep into the plaza. Bolan caught the lead cycle out of the corner of his eye, losing his concentration for a second, and when he looked back to the doorway, the man stood there, his head and shoulders above the lintel and out of sight.

Standing on a wooden table to get himself a better angle, the assassin now presented Bolan with no margin of error for his own shot. He drew the scope upward, following the line of buttons on the work shirt. The dark blue blobs of plastic against the washed-out denim already looked like bloodless bullet holes. Bolan moved the scope higher, the black bricks of the wall above the door now filling the field. Estimating the height of the bricks to be two inches, he counted up three rows of the dark stone, letting the horizontal cross hair coincide with the mortar. He dropped the scope a bit to make sure he was centered, then raised it again and held it steady.

The crowd below began a rhythmic clapping, thousands of hands striking in unison. A chant began, too distorted by the thousands of voices for Bolan to make out the words. There was something in the compelling sound that made the words unnecessary.

The hair on the back of his neck tingled, and Bolan found his heart racing to get in sync with the tempo below. Squeezing once, he dropped the scope for a second. He no longer saw the denimed figure. He waited patiently. Then Bolan saw him, sprawled across the sofa, his neck bent at a crazy angle. Aiming now just below the lintel, Bolan fired a second time, and then again. In the bottom half of the lens he saw the third shot strike home, the body jumping, then lying still.

And then there was one.

The third had been the hardest to find. Even once he had made the assassin in the third perch, he wondered whether he was right. It kept gnawing at him. The third was the easiest target for him, the shortest shot, and he turned reluctantly to the task. At the back of his mind he puzzled over the reluctance, wondered if he was somehow kidding himself. Deep in his soul he knew he wasn't, but he couldn't shake the depression beginning to sweep over him.

Two men were already dead at his hands. He had done it before. So many times he had lost count. He remembered each one, and each one ran in his head on those dark nights of the soul that seemed to come more and more often. But he never counted. This wasn't about numbers. It was about justice. Human life was not something to be taken easily, not even for The Executioner. But he had done it before. Already that day he had snuffed out two lives, and the men who died had been prepared to take an innocent life. But an eye for an eye was no solace.

On the other hand, it was all too easy to walk away from the violence, to say no one had the right, for whatever reason, that two wrongs didn't make a right. But Bolan knew, as most of those fainthearted apologists for the perfectibility of man in an imperfect world did not, that turning the other cheek did nothing except get you a second black eye.

So, he had killed two men.

And now he had to kill a woman.

She was still there on the balcony, still in her bikini. The tanning oil gave her flesh a luster, and the sun seemed to splinter on the sheen, then slide off, torn to colored ribbons. The chaise lounge was still where it had been, and she still lay upon it, her slender legs bent at the knees. But the rifle was no longer under the chaise. It was in her lap, covered with a towel. Bolan could just make out the muzzle between her feet. The tented cloth covered the weapon but gave her access to the scope.

She had propped up the back of the chaise and sat erect. Her body canted to the left, the left arm extended to steady the rifle. Bolan brought his own rifle around and aimed for the top of her head, knowing the slug would drop a bit and rip through the back of the chaise. The halo of bright blond hair rippled, filling the spaces between the curls with reflected light.

The presidential limo was just entering the plaza. Bolan squeezed the trigger twice, emptying the magazine. He dropped the scope slightly and saw the pair of ragged holes in the back of the lounge. He knew he still had to get Carter, and make it to the chopper if he wanted to shut this thing down completely. He wanted to feel empty. But he couldn't. He couldn't feel at all. And there was no time for self-indictment.

That would come later, in the heart of some other dark night.

CHAPTER FORTY-TWO

Lucien Picard snaked through the tall hedge. The rough branches stabbed at his exposed skin, and the sharp-edged leaves slashed at his neck and arms. It was hot in the open field behind him, and the sweat on his neck seeped into the cuts and scratches, making them sting and burn. The hedgerow was more than five yards deep and as dense as any jungle. Ants dropped onto his exposed skin as he shook the leaves, and flies, drawn by the sweat, buzzed him incessantly.

After several minutes of worming and burrowing, taking a few detours to avoid the thicker growth, he managed to reach the inner perimeter of the green barrier. He pulled some branches aside just far enough to peer through into the cloistered garden behind the house. His watch told him he had less than a half hour to do what he had come to do.

The brief visit the day before had given him no sense of the complexity of the layout. Seen from the front, the house was large, but relatively ordinary. But the rear view was something else entirely. Involuted folds of low hedge, meticulously sculpted into perfect geometrics, wound maze-like through the garden. The hedgerow itself was on a landscaped ridge, elevating it several feet above the level of the garden. He found himself looking straight at the second story of the house, with the garden spread out below him.

But as complicated as the garden was, he had a more serious obstacle to overcome. A wire fence, nearly eight feet high, ran the entire perimeter of the garden. Getting over it without being seen was not going to be easy. If it was wired in any way, it might prove altogether insurmountable. But that wasn't the worst of it.

The home of Adrian Caprieaux was no longer deserted. The vice president was scheduled to arrive within a half hour, and the veranda at the rear was now well guarded. Picard counted no fewer than four men on the veranda itself, and the smoky glass of the rear wall, overlooking the garden from both the first and second floors, could conceal a few more. At least a similar number would be posted on the front portico, and the attack team totaled six, counting the three men on the security team who were supposed to be on Harlow's payroll.

The assassination was supposed to be carried out by Picard, Tony Masseria and the flaky kid, Rogers. No direct assistance was to be expected from the three men on the security team who had been bought, paid for and presumably delivered. They were simply to interfere with any attempts that might be made to protect Caprieaux if the assassins were discovered before they had completed their mission, and to ensure confusion in the aftermath of the shooting, to allow unhampered escape.

The hitch was that no one but Sadowski knew which men they were, and he refused to identify them. "When the time comes, you'll know," he'd said, an infuriating smirk twisting his porcine features into a cartoon villain's disfigured grin.

Picard was between the devil and the deep blue sea, and he knew it. Unbidden, the words of the old tune started running through his head. Not knowing which of the bodyguards had been turned, he was trapped between Harlow's killers and bona fide security people who would blow him away on sight.

To complicate matters still further, his mind kept drifting. Unconsciously he was listening for some evidence that his warning to the French ambassador had come in time. The Libyan armored division poised for its strike from Koufey in Niger, just across the border from Lake Chad, had been spotted by French air reconnaissance, but nothing had been made of it. The SDECE chief of station in the capital had told him that because the Libyans were so often poking around in the wastes of central Africa, it was assumed that this was just one more such excursion.

Lulled by the general perception of Libya as an over-armed dwarf, run by a village idiot, the French had given no thought to the armor's proximity to N'Djamena. It was too late to maneuver ground forces to the northern edge of the lake, leaving an air strike as the only possible counter. And that was something that would require clearance from Paris.

Picard shook his head to toss off the speculative cobwebs. He drew back into the shrubbery and looked at his watch. He had a half hour, give or take a few minutes. The center door on the veranda was to be opened as soon as Caprieaux was in the house. At that point the assassins were to rush the veranda, where the three traitors were to be posted. The plan was half-assed, and Picard crossed himself in a silent prayer of thanks.

He had said nothing at the briefing, and now realized he had been lulled by the plan's stupidity because his fondest wish, in any case, was for it to fail. That it probably would seemed likely. That it might succeed in spite of itself was a possibility he didn't care to consider.

Taking care not to rustle the branches of the dense foliage, he backed away from the fence and started to work his way parallel to the wire. Picard realized that either Sadowski or Harlow must have known about the wire. If he could find the point at which Masseria's team planned to enter the garden, he could use the same route. That assumed, of course, that this wasn't one more of Harlow's ill-planned adventures. He heard a whisper sift through the leaves ahead of him and realized that Masseria and his team had still not crossed the wire. That gave him a slight edge, but he'd have to act fast.

Pausing to get a better fix on the location, he leaned into the greenery, ignoring the bugs swirling around his head and the stinging of his shredded skin. A flash of blue winked at him, and he turned his head in time to see a denim-clad figure crawl through a thin patch of shrubbery. A moment later another man followed him. Picard's view was too frag-

mented for identification, but he didn't think either man was
Masseria.

Picard edged forward, carefully moving each branch and
guiding it back into place as he moved past. The shrubbery
seemed to be thinning a bit, but the going was painfully
slow. Suddenly he found himself staring into a green tunnel. On all sides the raw ends of recently severed branches
jutted out into the open space.

Looking to the left, he saw a green wall, flush up against
the wire fence. Someone had hacked away at the shrubbery
in the past few days, cutting his way toward the house from
the open field, and leaving just enough greenery at either
end of the tunnel to conceal his handiwork from someone
in the garden or the open farmland. Picard felt the raw ends
of three or four branches and noticed they weren't sticky.
The sap had already had time to dry.

He slipped through the last few branches into the tunnel
and moved toward the fence. He kept one eye over his
shoulder in case someone else might enter from the outside. At the wall, he pushed a few leaves to one side and
peered through the fence. Directly in front of him, a tall
shrub of some kind marked the limit of the garden. A neat
two-foot hole had been hacked in the fence, and a disk of
severed wire lay like an abandoned barbecue grill on the
ground in front of the hole.

Picard moved to one side to see around the obstacle. Near
the center of the garden, concealed behind the sculpted
hedgerows, two men were crawling on hands and knees.
Tony Masseria was right behind them. The guards on the
veranda seemed unaware of the intruders as they sat on
white patio furniture, talking among themselves.

His first reaction was to crawl through the hole himself
and follow the assassins, but if he did that, he would lose
sight of them, possibly until it was too late. Armed only with
a handgun, opening fire from behind the fence was out of
the question.

He watched Masseria closely, looking for any indication
that his attempt to dissuade the young man from partici-

pating had made an impression. Masseria seemed nervous, but that was hardly inappropriate. The other two kept looking back to Masseria for guidance. He motioned for them to stay put, and looked at his watch.

Picard checked his own. Caprieaux was due in ten minutes. Taking a deep breath, he dropped to his stomach and slithered through the fence. He climbed back to his feet right behind the tall shrub and looked for the hit team. They were where he had last seen them, crouching in a tight row at the center of a corridor in the sculpted hedge. Resisting the impulse to get closer, Picard took the safety off and cocked his automatic pistol.

His nerves were on fire, and the forced inactivity heightened the irritation of the bugs and burning scratches on his neck and arms. He took a deep breath and let it out slowly, trying to restore some sense of equilibrium, but he couldn't shake the disturbing sensation of being a helpless observer. He felt as if he were watching a movie played out on a three-dimensional screen. He had the impression that he could insert himself into the action, but would have no effect on its outcome.

He waited helplessly for the three men to do what they had come to do. Off to the right, he heard a low roar, and looked involuntarily in that direction. A small cloud of dust rose and fell over the roadway, and he realized that Caprieaux was going to walk into the house any minute. He kept his fingers crossed, waiting for an opportunity to toss a monkey wrench.

He glanced at Masseria again, hoping to see some sign that he was wavering. He'd worked on Masseria all the night before but had gotten nowhere. The kid's conscience was bothering him, there was no doubt about it, but he was too scared to know what to do.

A car door slammed in front of the house, followed quickly by three more. Adrian Caprieaux was about to walk into his house for the last time, unless someone did something. Picard started to creep down the slope in front of him, reached the bottom of the garden and stopped to get his bearings.

Looking through a fringe of leaves at the top of a hedge, he could see the roofline of the house. As near as he could tell, he was about ten feet to the left of the center door to the veranda, and just to the right of the three-man hit squad, who were several yards closer to the house.

He raised his head a little higher and could just make out the hairline and forehead of one guard. If his memory was accurate, he was the man posted on the right corner of the veranda. He raised his head higher still, just as the veranda door swung open. The guard he could see turned toward the door, and muffled greetings were exchanged in rapid French.

It was now or never. Picard squeezed off a shot, aiming his pistol in the air. He saw the three hidden shooters pop up like shooting gallery ducks. The Frenchman rose in time to see Caprieaux thrown to the veranda by one of the bodyguards, who promptly covered the prostrate vice president with his own body.

Masseria brandished a .45 automatic; the two men with him carried submachine guns. All three charged toward the veranda, the lead man spraying its width with random fire. The smoky glass starred and cracked as the SMG swept across and back, the web of fissures glittering brilliantly with refracted sunlight.

The bodyguards dived to the pavement, struggling to pull their own weapons. Picard planted himself and aimed at the lead assassin. He fired two quick shots, but both missed the charging gunner. Masseria heard the gunshots behind him and turned, just as Picard fired again. This time he found his target. The bullet struck the lead gunner squarely between the shoulder blades, just as he reached the veranda. The impact of the slug slammed him forward, and he tripped over the top step, landing facedown on the stone. His gun clattered on the pavement and slammed into the wall just to the left of the veranda door.

Masseria raised his own gun, but a shot from the veranda caused him to turn. He dived to the ground as one of the bodyguards began to return fire, emptying a handgun in the general direction of the charging assassins. When the magazine was empty, the security man hurled his pistol at the second gunner and dived for the SMG lying against the wall.

The gunner was faster. He opened fire with the Uzi on his hip. The guard's dive carried him through the center of a tight figure eight. Picard closed his eyes, unable to bear the sight of the body jerking as it tumbled, bright red stars painting the pale night of the guard's light blue jacket.

The corner guard raised his own gun from his position flat on the veranda, his feet at the apex of wall and porch railing. Masseria swung his pistol around and fired. The shot slammed into the left shoulder of the second gunner. Stunned by the impact, the surprised man turned to look at Masseria. His lips moved, but no sound came out as he mimed his final thought, "What did you do?"

Picard, taken by surprise, froze with his own gun aimed at Masseria. Tony tossed him a thumbs-up and turned back toward the porch. The fourth bodyguard, a toadlike man in a dark pin-striped suit, snared the abandoned Uzi from the doorway. He swept it across the porch in search of a target, before settling on his colleague, still pressing Caprieaux to the ground.

The fat man fired a short burst, but the gun was nearly empty. He tossed it aside in disgust and reached for his own side arm. Picard fired twice, catching the butterball in the shoulder with his first shot. The impact had tilted the man away from Picard, and he started to fall sideways.

The second shot grazed the fat man's shoulder, which sprouted a bright puff of padding as the stitches parted, then bored in through the lower jaw and splattered a bright halo of blood and shattered teeth as it exited to slam into the glass of the door. As he fell, he got off a wild shot. Picard watched in frozen horror as Tony took the shot in the back of the head. The young man's smile of satisfaction exploded outward, leaving a bloody void where his face had been.

The veranda door flew open, showering slivers of loose glass in a semicircle before it slammed against the wall. Six men in dark suits poured through, each armed with a submachine gun. In the sudden silence, Picard heard the buzz of flies swarming around his sweat-soaked shoulders and naked neck.

And in the distance, a helicopter.

CHAPTER FORTY-THREE

When Bolan looked over the wall, the limousine had just entered the plaza. Carter was looking expectantly over his shoulder, back at the fifteenth-floor window. Bolan left the empty Sauer on the roof and sprinted for the stairs, the canvas bag over his shoulder slapping his hip. He tossed the steel bar aside and yanked the door open.

Inside, his eyes struggled with the absence of sun, and he nearly stumbled at the first landing. The heavy bag threw his balance off, and he swung his shoulders to get the weight behind him, where he would have better control. Grabbing on to the railing to keep his descent under tight rein, he took the steps one at a time, his legs pumping like anxious pistons. Each gray plateau loomed up ahead of his foot like a ghost ship coming out of the fog, and he cursed the darkness.

By the seventeenth-floor landing, his eyes had adjusted and he increased his pace. Taking the steps two at a time now, he spun around each landing like a mad dervish, plunging into the next staircase without breaking stride. The combination of sudden turns and oxygen debt made him light-headed, but there was no time for hesitation.

As he entered the last staircase, he could hear his footsteps bouncing off the roof of the stairwell. The hollow thuds seemed to have a dozen echoes, each reinforcing the others as his heavy boots slammed into the concrete. On the ground floor he flung open the fire door and skidded into the polished stone lobby. The revolving door was blocked by a dozen onlookers too self-aware to join the crowd in the plaza, and he shoved them aside to slip out onto the pavement.

Someone hollered after him, but the thick glass of the door swallowed the sound, and he spilled outside into the mob. He could see the stone wall to the left of the fountain statue, but Carter was gone. He stepped into the street, now jammed from curb to curb with shouting, clapping people, and pushed his way through to the fountain. Most of the fountain wall was lined with people, parents hoisting their children up for a better view and those who had had difficulty seeing over the throng.

Bolan stepped onto the wall, squeezing in between a short man with his daughter on his shoulders and a fat woman who was as wide as she was tall. He nearly knocked the woman into the splashing fountain, grabbing her by the flab on her upper arm just as she was about to pitch forward.

She turned to curse him, but the look on his face told her she shouldn't. Mumbling under her breath in some language Bolan didn't understand, she glared at him, then turned back to the open car, now making a sweeping right and heading into the long, flower-lined approach to the presidential palace. Standing on his toes, Bolan scanned the crowd, but there was no trace of Carter. He grabbed the binoculars and turned them on the milling mob, looking for those few white faces in a sea of black. Carter's clothing was nondescript, no doubt by design, and it was by color only that he would stand out.

The few Westerners in the mob seemed less passionate, drawn more out of curiosity than enthusiasm. Bolan bounced from one fair head to the next, spotting a pale neck here and a raised white arm there. No Carter.

Swinging the glasses up Boulevard de Bastille, he spotted a shock of dirty blond hair. He turned the focus knob, trying to resolve the image when the man turned to look over his shoulder. Bolan had found his man, nearly a block away and moving fast. He must have sensed that something had gone desperately wrong and was running for his life. The crowd down the boulevard grew progressively thinner as it trailed after the motorcade, and Bolan had to hurry if he wanted to beat Carter to the chopper.

He jumped off the wall, the shock of his landing jarring loose something that had been tugging at his memory since he'd entered the stairwell. That black strand trailing out of Carter's pocket. If it was a transmitter antenna, Carter could radio ahead. It wouldn't stop Bolan, but it would sure make his job a lot tougher. He wished to hell Picard had hung in.

Bolan barreled into the mob, slowly picking up running room as people realized he wasn't going to slow down. People stared at him as he rushed by, parting like water ahead of a speeding boat and turning to look after him. Carter was nearly a block away, and he was going to get into the clear long before Bolan. The gap would widen, and if he got to the jeep six blocks away, there would be hell to pay.

It was too risky to stop and try to get a fix on the fleeing man, so Bolan just buried the needle and put his shoulder into the charge. Two blocks away from the plaza, the police lines were already dissolving. Most of the pedestrian traffic was confined to the broad sidewalks. Scattered groups still lingered on the roadway, but the police were trying to herd them back onto the pavement.

Bolan could catch a glimpse of Carter now and then. He was just about to enter the bazaar, where a different kind of tangle would intervene. The sidewalk shops and tented vendors were getting ready for business, and some of the crowd had begun to mill around, waiting for the shops to open.

Bolan stayed in the street, and Carter did the same. The gap was beginning to narrow, but not quickly enough for Bolan. Carter obviously thought otherwise. He stopped and turned, planting his feet wide apart. Bolan zigged, and the first shot splattered the pavement, spraying chips of broken concrete in a sharp fan. Carter fired a second time, and this one went high. Bolan heard a window behind him go out, the sharp crack of the impact followed by a sudden avalanche of sound as the shattered glass cascaded onto the sidewalk.

People screamed and fell to the ground all around him. The unarmed police were at a disadvantage, and Carter knew it. One officer ran toward Carter, waving his arms over his head. For a second the merc paused and looked at Bolan. He raised the pistol again and fired twice more. The first shot went wide, slamming into a brick wall behind the Executioner. The second caught the defenseless policeman in the side, and he fell, writhing in pain.

Carter turned to run, firing once more over his shoulder at the wounded man. The bullet struck him in the chest and he lay still. Bolan scrambled to his feet and raised his own gun, but the zigzagging Carter kept charging through small knots of confused onlookers. His feet pounded on the pavement as Bolan drew closer. Carter seemed terrified now, and turned once more to toss a shot at the demon pursuing him.

The gun didn't go off, and Carter looked at it for a second as if surprised. He wheeled again to flee, and Bolan could see his quarry struggling to reload the apparently empty automatic. The crowds had all but vanished now, as people took refuge in every available alleyway and open door. Half a block later Bolan kicked an empty clip lying in the gutter where Carter had dropped it.

Twenty yards farther on another clip—this one loaded— lay in the middle of the street. Carter fumbled with the flap on his rear pocket and hauled out a small black box. Even without binoculars Bolan was now close enough to see the small black strand dangling from its bottom. He dropped to one knee and aimed carefully. The Beretta hissed, and Bolan heard the 9 mm slug strike home. The box tumbled from Carter's hand and he rushed on, glancing at it over his shoulder as if it, too, were chasing him.

At the next corner the merc ducked behind a wheeled cart, its square awning supported by four metal rods. The crossbars flapped with a blizzard of brightly colored scarves and kerchiefs. He peered through the garish screen and squeezed off three quick shots. Bolan returned two, one narrowly missing Carter as he ducked behind the cart again. The second ripped two scarves from their crossbar and snapped the bar in two. The lowest rung of the display was now gone, leaving a foot-high gap across the width of the cart.

Bolan reached into the canvas bag for Big Thunder and slipped the Beretta back into its sling under his half-open shirt. He dropped to his stomach and brought up the big .44-caliber automatic in a two-handed grip. Carter popped up and down, then up again behind another part of the cart.

The cart itself was low slung, and Bolan could see nothing beneath it to gauge Carter's location. He took a guess and fired once. The big gun slammed a shot through the left corner of the cart, but Carter popped up on the other end almost immediately and fired twice. Bolan didn't wait. He banged a second shot, then a third, through the right end of the cart. The impact of the heavy projectiles made the thin veneer of painted tin ring, and Carter pitched to the side and lay still.

Bolan scrambled to his feet and charged toward the wounded man, whose head lay at a peculiar angle, supported by the curb. His eyes were open but unblinking as Bolan cautiously approached. A thin trickle of blood spilled from the lower corner of the man's half-open mouth. A small pool had already collected in the gutter.

Bolan knelt and checked the fallen man's pulse. He felt nothing under his fingers. Quickly he searched Carter's pockets for the keys to the jeep, found them on the second try and stood up. Looking back toward the plaza, he noticed people beginning to leave their shelters. Some, now more curious than frightened, had even begun to push forward, for some reason walking on tiptoe in exaggeratedly slow movements, their arms at awkward angles to keep balance in their unnatural gaits.

Leading the way, three policemen, walking quietly but with no trace of fear, formed a wedge in the center of the street. The lead officer waved his hand as though asking if the coast was clear, and Bolan nodded.

Bolan tucked the keys into a shirt pocket and slipped away from the cart, angling through a broken field of tent shops on the front edge of the bazaar. A halfhearted shout for him to stop drifted to him as he dodged stalls and wooden display tables. A brief flurry of footsteps stopped almost immediately, as if the police were less than serious about catching up to him. He didn't blame them. He didn't bother to turn around.

The chopper behind the vice president's residence was scheduled for takeoff in less than thirty minutes. He needed the jeep, and more than a little luck. Even then, it would be too close for comfort.

The bazaar seemed strangely quiet as he ran through its winding alleys. His neck prickled, as if someone were watching him from behind every canvas flap. The bright colors and the overwhelmingly present olfactory assault of food and spices made the silence all the deeper. It seemed unnatural that the ear would be denied the same riotous diversion as the other senses.

For a moment he heard only the sound of his feet on the soft, dry earth, and it seemed to come from a great distance, as if he were watching someone else, his size, dressed as he dressed and driven by identical fears. The detachment at first fascinated him, and he watched his own feet as they struck the earth, tossing up small puffs of dust that vanished almost instantly.

It reminded him of watching television when he was a child, seeing the silent footage of aerial bombardment. Everything was visual, the feathery halos of whirling B-29 propellers, an occasional cloud of flak off the wing, the sticks of bombs tumbling out of the bays with strange grace before blossoming into giant silent flowers of gray and white, all without a sound.

When he reached the jeep he felt better. Driving would give him something to focus on, something to engage his concentration. But even as he climbed into the driver's seat his mind kept drifting back to the shadow behind the glass in the elevator shaft.

The detachment of such a death had given him a new perspective on what lay ahead, perhaps unpredictably soon, for himself.

CHAPTER FORTY-FOUR

From the road, the Mi-16 was an oblong speck on the horizon. It kept low, just skirting the occasional trees dotting the bleak savannah. Carter's jeep bounced unmercifully, and Bolan pushed it as fast as he could over the pockmarked road without losing control. He watched the chopper dip and soar as it grew slowly larger, its eight-bladed rotor just a gray blur in the air, like a disk of smoke following along in its wake.

Bolan was getting closer to Caprieaux's estate, but the chopper was a hell of a lot faster. He rode the brake to ease over a twenty-yard stretch of potholes in the fractured asphalt, then swerved to his left, narrowly avoiding a wheel buster of a caldera at the last second. The speedometer needle hovered around fifty as he pushed the cumbersome jeep toward its upper limit in second gear, and worried that the transmission might give out. But the lower gear gave him better control, and it was worth taking the risk.

A dark line on the left side of the horizon was the tree-lined avenue leading to the estate, and he stepped on the gas, shifting to third as the chopper was now clearly visible over the flat fields along the road. The temperature gauge on the dash was near the red zone, and the oil pressure light stuttered a tentative warning.

The avenue of trees seemed to grow before his eyes as he approached. Across the middle of the road, just before the entrance, he noticed a pair of jeeps were parked bumper-to-bumper. Something had happened, that was plain enough. It was also obvious the security men would never let him through. With just a quarter mile to go, Bolan swung the steering wheel for a hard left, and the jeep soared over a weed-clotted ditch, landing with a scream of protesting springs.

Half a dozen figures scurried around behind the pair of jeeps blocking the road, and a third barreled out of the trees and angled toward him. The driver obviously planned to intercept him, and if possible cut him off. Bolan floored the jeep, kicking it into fourth and ignoring the foot-high bushes sprinkled randomly through the tough, dry grass. He could hear nothing over the roar of his own engine. A dim flash, washed out by the harsh sun, winked at him from the front of the oncoming interceptor, and his windshield suddenly grew translucent as a fine web of cracks spread out from the upper left.

Bolan took his left hand off the wheel, trying to keep the jeep steady with his right as he leaned forward to release the windshield then shoved it forward over the hood, where it landed with a smack. A second shot from the jouncing defender glanced off the hood, its whine immediately drowned by the roaring of his engine. Two men sat in the front seat of the pursuer, and Bolan guessed them to be security men assigned to Caprieaux. Their zeal was a hopeful sign. Men seldom exerted such energy in defense of a dead man.

The security man in the passenger seat began waving his arms over his head, and he looked almost comical as he bounced high in the air, then slammed down on the hard bench seat of the jeep. He struggled to keep his balance without using his hands, and nearly toppled out after a particularly vicious dip.

Bolan had no desire to exchange gunfire with men who were just doing their job, but he knew, as they did not, that the struggle was far from over. The speeding jeeps were fewer than a hundred yards apart now and the gap was closing rapidly. The warrior pointed toward the chopper, but neither guard bothered to look.

Bolan held a steady course and calculated a very near miss at best, if neither jeep changed direction. The passenger stopped waving his arms and grabbed the back of his seat with one hand, bringing his other down to rest on the top edge of his windshield.

The man's hatchet-thin face was expressionless, and the Skorpion in his hand was definitely serious. At twenty yards Bolan guessed a short burst from the machine pistol was imminent, and yanked the wheel hard to the right. His jeep rose up on the two wheels, perilously close to flipping over as its big tires churned the dry earth into arid, weedy clods and a thick plume of dust.

Bolan braked sharply, spinning the wheel hard left and kicking the transmission into neutral, as the jeep slammed to a halt. While it still rocked on its hard-pressed suspension, Bolan jerked the .45 Colt from his shirt and spun in his seat. He fired twice, taking out both rear tires of the interceptor, then popped the clutch and started digging. He bent low over the steering wheel as a burst of fire rattled off the rear of his jeep.

He didn't dare look back, but the straining of his pursuers' engine told him they were trying to continue the chase on two flat tires. The blowouts would have ruptured the tires, and fifteen or twenty yards should be enough to strip the rubber right off the rims.

The chopper was less than a quarter mile away, and Bolan could see the tall savannah grass bending beneath its rotorwash as it roared toward the rear of Caprieaux's estate. The dark green of the tall hedge around the rear garden looked almost black against the expanse of bleached-out grass beyond it. Bolan steered for the rear corner of the hedge, beginning to ease up on the gas as he drew closer.

The Mi-16 swooped toward the back line of the hedge, hovered for a moment, then dropped down like a hungry predator. Bolan leaped from the jeep and grabbed the canvas bag from the passenger seat. He sprinted along the hedgerow, taking the corner at full tilt. The side door of the chopper was open, and four men jumped to the ground, each armed with an AK-47 assault rifle.

It suddenly became clear. The chopper was never intended to airlift the assassins at all. It was there to blow them all away, effectively erasing any connection to Mason Harlow. Bolan slung the bag over his shoulder and chambered a round in the .45. The big Colt felt solid in his hand, its weight like an unpleasant fact.

The leaves fanned outward halfway down the hedgerow, and someone stepped into the open. Bolan didn't recognize Picard until the Frenchman saw the Kalashnikovs and turned back toward the fragile protection of the foliage. At almost the same instant he spotted Bolan and waved toward the hedge.

The gesture alerted the riflemen, one of whom began to swing his AK-47 in Bolan's direction. The big guy reacted as if the two of them ran on a single circuit, swinging up the automatic and planting his feet to squeeze off a shot. The report of the Colt was blown away by the swirling wash of the chopper, and Bolan barely heard it himself. He reacted to the kick of the powerful pistol, and the recoil seemed to travel back up his arm to bury itself deep in his gut.

Renowned for its firepower—and notorious for its lack of accuracy—the Army-issue Colt was, to some people's way of thinking, a better paperweight than it was a weapon. But as long as Bolan had it, he knew he was going to use it. He fired a second shot, this time finding the mark, though high and to the right. The heavy slug slammed into the target's shoulder, spinning him in a clumsy 180.

The wounded man opened his mouth in a silent howl of pain as he staggered in a half circle and let go of the Kalashnikov. The rifle pitched downward, only to be arrested in midfall by a heavy leather sling. Bolan dropped to one knee and braced his shooting hand with his left arm, emptying the magazine in a near-silent burst. The pistol hammered against his thumb, trying to ride up and away from the falling target.

Bolan nailed him twice more, leaving bright stains on the front of a beige Windbreaker. The man collapsed on wobbly knees, then fell facedown. The back of the light jacket was a scarlet mess, ragged flaps of cloth forced outward by the passage of shattered bone and deformed bullets.

Bolan dived into the hedge just as a second Kalashnikov sought him out. The Mi-16 droned on, wrapping every noise in its own thunder, and the warrior only realized how close a call it had been by the rain of broken twigs and leaf fragments cascading over his head and shoulders.

The wiry branches of the hedge clawed at his face as he squirmed toward the spot where Picard had disappeared. Intermittent bursts of fire hammered in the open field, the telltale racket of the AK-47s reduced by the chopper's engine to short sharp pops. As he twisted and turned his way through the tangle, Bolan slipped a new clip into the Colt and tucked it in his shirt, replacing it with the .44 AutoMag.

Bolan crept at an angle now, moving closer to the open field. He swept branches aside with one arm, but the gunners were too far forward. He didn't want to risk revealing himself without making sure he could reduce the odds by one. He crawled a few more feet and tried again. This time he could see the nose of the chopper, and he knew he was getting close.

Ducking his head and creeping forward as close to the ground as he could, he managed to avoid the worst of the clinging vegetation. He reached out with his left hand, supporting the full weight of his upper body on his right elbow, and his hand seemed to enter a vacuum. He groped from side to side without encountering a branch or leaf. Scooting ahead, his shoulders emerged into the green tunnel.

Picard was lying just inside the mouth of the opening, his head against the green wall. He was bleeding heavily from an ugly wound in the left leg where a stray round from a Kalashnikov had ripped through his thigh.

Bolan hauled himself clear of the tangle just as a head appeared in the upper reaches of the wall. The warrior's weight was on his gun hand, and he swung the big .44 awkwardly, pivoting on his elbow. He squeezed off a shot just as the man spotted him, his eyes widening in what could have been either surprise or fear.

The mop of dark curls vanished almost immediately, and Bolan didn't know whether he'd scored or not. Either way, his location was no longer a secret. He grabbed the semiconscious Picard by the ankles and started to drag him backward with one hand, training his weapon on the end of the tunnel.

Like a swarm of killer bees, a rain of fire ripped at the leaves just over his head. Bolan ducked instinctively, losing his grip on the helpless Frenchman. He bent forward to get a better grip, moving to the right, flush up against the foliage. Slipping into a break in the thicket, he tugged Picard after him, fighting gravity, deadweight and grasping greenery all at the same time.

When Picard was out of harm's way, Bolan shucked off the canvas bag and tucked it under the Frenchman's head. Then he dropped to the ground and moved parallel to the tunnel, squeezing through narrow openings between clumps of roots. Two men stood between him and the helicopter, and an already scarce amount of time had turned from gold to platinum. Any scarcer, and it would cease to exist at all.

At the very edge of the matted vegetation Bolan paused, hoping to hear some sound giving away the gunmen's location, but the chopper was just too loud. He slid forward, feeling more like a cruising python than a man, the AutoMag hampering his movement. He bent his legs then dug his feet into the dry soil and pushed, helping his progress by tugging at a cluster of thick roots just above ground level.

As he emerged into the sunlight his eyes burned with sweat from his brow. Momentarily blinded, he blinked away the perspiration and a slight movement to his left caused him to turn. He swung the .44 up and fired even before the image resolved itself.

The shot went wide, but the man staggered backward, his feet catching in the weeds and lagging behind his center of gravity. He jammed the AK-47 in his hands toward the earth, using it as a deadly crutch, but he was too far off balance. He landed heavily on his butt, one arm tangled in the rifle's sling. Bolan fired again, catching him this time in the throat. The heavy slug severed the spinal cord on its way out, causing the lifeless head to wobble, then roll to one side like a broken toy.

The last man—apparently the chopper's pilot—dropped his rifle. He turned toward the aircraft and started to run, his headset cable trailing behind him in the dust. Bolan fired twice more, aiming low to spare his life. The first shot missed, but the second buried itself in the pilot's left calf, smashing the shinbone and knocking the man to the ground. He writhed in agony, gripping the wounded leg in both hands.

Ducking back into the tunnel, he found Picard sitting up and knotting a bloody strip of his shirt around his wounded leg.

"You okay?" Bolan shouted.

Picard shook his head, then tried to rise. He got to his knees and started to topple. Bolan grabbed him by the collar and heaved the man to his feet. Picard clenched his teeth in pain, throwing his weight on the warrior and starting to hobble. Picard fluttered a hand to get Bolan's attention, then put his mouth to the taller man's ear.

"We have to get the hell out of here. Caprieaux's security people are shooting at anything that moves."

"Tell me about it."

CHAPTER FORTY-FIVE

Picard slumped in the co-pilot's chair, a headset sitting crookedly over his ears. Bolan thanked his stars he knew some Russian, and opened the throttle. He'd logged some time in helicopters, but the Mi-16 was a new one for him. The big chopper lifted away sluggishly, sideslipping just a bit as Bolan tried to get used to the controls. They weren't as sensitive as those he was used to, and he kept overcompensating out of frustration.

As he cleared the top of the hedge a jeep full of security men careered around the end of the garden. Armed with rifles, they threw up a hail of fire, but the few hits they managed glanced harmlessly off the armored skin of the Soviet chopper. Bolan looked through the broad, high cockpit window and watched the jeep shrink rapidly away.

A final flurry of rifle fire drummed against the bottom of the helicopter as the men below one by one emptied their weapons. They continued to stare up at the rising bird until Bolan swung it around and lost sight of them. Without charts, and over unfamiliar terrain, the flight to Waw al-Kabir promised to be interesting.

Bolan scanned the console for a compass, finally locating a digital at the center of a wilderness of dials and gauges. He brought the nose around until he found due north and swung his mike into place. "Look for some charts, will you? I have to figure out these damn controls."

Picard adjusted his headset. "Check that screen on the right."

Bolan glanced at a blank rectangle of thick glass mounted on the lower edge of the console. A bank of toggles and a digital keypad were set in a black metal panel just above it. "What about it?"

"Bet you a yard it's an electronic atlas. All we have to do is make it work."

"A *yard*? Where the hell did you learn to speak English, especially that kind of English?"

"Two years at Berkeley, postgraduate sociology. It just seemed to be there by the time I left. Osmosis, maybe."

"See what you can do with those switches."

Picard nodded and Bolan turned his attention to visual navigation. A thin haze loomed ahead of them, and the warrior took the chopper up a little higher, leveling off when the altimeter read one thousand meters. The fuel gauge, at least, was easy to read, and the chopper's tanks were more than half-full, the needle sitting just under three-quarters.

Picard flicked each toggle over the dark screen. The first threw a bright smear of green across the glass, but it quickly faded. The second brought the green back, this time to stay, and the third superimposed a grid of bright white lines.

"Now we're getting somewhere," Picard shouted. He turned his attention to the keypad, tapping hesitantly at it, then depressing a wide key marked with a red arrow. A swirl of contour lines was etched against the grid. "All right. Almost there."

Picard drummed his fingers thoughtfully, then slapped the control panel. He punched a number in, depressed the arrow and shouted, *"Voilà!"*

"What have you got?" Bolan asked, casting a sidelong look at the screen.

"An index. How's your Russian?"

"It's been better."

"Well, brush up in a hurry or this thing won't help us."

Bolan watched the foggy smear ahead and slightly to the left grow more sharply defined, and he realized they were heading for Lake Chad. Picard stumbled through the index in stilted phonetic Russian until Bolan recognized something.

"Try that one," he suggested.

Picard punched the corresponding numbers in, and the screen fluttered briefly, then glowed with the outline of the huge lake they were speeding toward.

The two men played hide-and-seek with the pattern of the numbers, finally putting it together well enough to make some limited use of the topographical charts stored in the on-board computer. After thirty minutes they were over the center of the lake.

Bolan said little as he watched the digital chronograph click through its interminable cycle. Picard seemed preoccupied, and made no attempt to break the silence. The lake fell away behind them as Bolan kept the throttle out almost all the way. They were in Niger now and Bolan kept a weather eye out for airborne reconnaissance. If a fighter jumped them, they were in trouble. He didn't feel comfortable enough with the alien chopper even to consider anything but an immediate touchdown, assuming he would be given that chance.

The Mi-16 throbbed and Bolan could feel the power plant through the soles of his boots. On the horizon, several plumes of black, oily smoke towered over the desert waste. He nudged Picard and pointed to the canvas bag on the floor of the cockpit.

"Get the binoculars and check that out, will you?" He pointed toward the columns of smoke.

"No need to. I already know what that is. That is Colonel al-Hassan's armored column, after the French air force took issue with him."

"How do you know that?"

"Why the hell do you think I had to get to the embassy? They were waiting for clearance from Paris when I left. I got the impression it was just a formality. Something to satisfy the government of Niger. Not that it would have made any difference if the request was denied." Picard snapped his jaw shut and swung the glasses around to survey the desert.

He dropped the binoculars for a second and punched some numbers into the computer. Craning his neck to see behind them, he compared the topography below to the squiggly line on the computer screen. "Yeah, that's it, all right." He stabbed a finger in front of Bolan's face, pointing toward a gray huddle just beyond the smoke. "That's Koufey. Looks like al-Hassan didn't get very far."

Bolan smiled grimly. "So, that leaves us with Sadowski and Harlow."

"That should be fun. I can't tell you how much I am looking forward to taking those bastards down. But we have to watch out for Marielle."

"So, you *do* know her. I thought so. One of yours?"

"No," Picard said. "Nothing like that."

"What, then?"

"It's a long story."

"Make it shorter. Just tell it."

Picard sighed. "Three years ago a terrorist bomb exploded in the terminal at Orly, killing her husband and two of her three children. She had taken her daughter to the rest room. It saved both their lives."

"I don't see the connection."

"I was the SDECE liaison with the Sûreté. I talked to her and I did some digging. I told her what I learned. I shouldn't have, but..." Picard shrugged. "What could I do? It was horrible for her. She was so angry. She wanted to work for us, but it was out of the question. So..."

"So she went out on her own."

"Yes. I hope to God that she... I feel responsible. I..." He seemed unable to confront the possibility that Marielle might become yet another victim.

Bolan tried to get Picard's mind off the unsettling possibility. "And what exactly was it that you told her?"

"That the bomb was planted by Black September."

"But...?"

"But that the materials to make it had been furnished by someone else. An American. She didn't want to believe that at first, but there was no other possibility."

"Mason Harlow."

"I didn't know that at the time, but, yeah, Mason Harlow."

"What the hell is she doing with him in Africa?"

"I guess she plans to kill him."

"She's had plenty of chances."

"Maybe she wants to take the whole network down with him."

"Don't we all?"

THE SETTING SUN smeared the horizon with red and purple, masses of thin clouds gradually turning a dark gray, then disappearing as the sun sank out of sight. Leon Alvarez lay flat in the desert, watching the search teams comb the warehouse and the surrounding buildings. Brilliant yellow light poured out of the open door, splashing a tall rectangle on the ground, occasionally broken by a darting shadow.

Harlow paced anxiously back and forth near the open door, shouting orders, but he seemed to be losing his enthusiasm for the search. Alvarez was grateful the woman had not turned him in—for whatever reason—but the suspicion that he had gotten his last break was chipping away at his confidence. Things had been going well, and he now realized that they had gone all too well. You had only so much luck, and this time out he had caught his breaks early.

Occasionally using the binoculars lying next to him in the sand, he had tried to find Bolan among the searchers, but the big guy wasn't there. Alvarez screwed his courage up a notch, realizing he was on his own. In the dark it was unlikely they would come looking for him out in the desert, but when morning came they would be hard on the heels of the sun. Even if he could manage to evade them, dying of thirst was a virtual certainty. That left him only one option. He would have to take the offensive, and he would have to do it that night.

The milling search teams had made it difficult to calculate the odds but he had seen enough to know they weren't good. A dozen men straggled out of the warehouse door, drifting toward the barracks in twos and threes. The interior lighting started to dwindle, and the long row of windows grew steadily dimmer. Mason Harlow now stood in the center of the doorway, talking to a short, dark man in a Libyan army officer's uniform.

Alvarez watched them closely through the binoculars, wishing he could hear what they were saying. He tried to read their lips, but they kept turning their faces to peer into the warehouse, and the bits and pieces of the conversation he managed to get were too disjointed to tell him anything he couldn't have guessed. A small group of men—five or six, he wasn't sure—stepped into the block of light outside the doorway, and vanished as the lights went out altogether. A few seconds later exterior lights went on in clusters, strings of floods bathing the warehouse wall and a narrow strip adjacent to it with yellowish light.

The small group stood outlined against the glare, and another man joined them as the warehouse door slowly closed. Harlow's Libyan companion waved his arms stiffly, and one by one the members of the small group dispersed as they took up their appointed positions. Evidently Harlow wasn't going to take chances during the night, posting a heavy guard around the perimeter of the warehouse. But they had neglected one thing in the frenzied activity. The C-47, still wide open, and still full of plastic explosive, sat unwatched.

Alvarez scanned the compound with the glasses, trying to fix the sentry locations. The one of most immediate concern to him stood alongside the warehouse door. Two more, one at each barracks door, sat on folding chairs, rifles cradled across their knees. The others were nowhere to be seen. But what gave him hope was the fact that each of the sentries he could see was stationary. That gave him a bit of an edge. But unless he could get to the plane, it wouldn't mean a damn thing.

The sentries quickly settled down for what promised to be an unnecessarily long and uncomfortable night. Alvarez watched patiently from the shadows and kept the glasses trained on the man by the door. The band of light from the floods reached halfway from the warehouse to the C-47. If he stayed low and kept the low-slung transport between him and the guard, he could make it to the plane. Getting up the ramp would be harder, but unless he could think of something else, it was his only chance.

Alvarez started to creep forward, his stolen weapons and ammunition like the weight of the world pressing on his shoulders. He crawled slowly, pausing every few yards to listen. It was only two hundred yards to the plane, and another hundred to the sentry, whose shadowed face seemed to droop a little toward his chest as Alvarez painstakingly closed the gap.

As he started to move closer after a short pause, the sentry moved suddenly, shaking his head from side to side in an exaggerated fashion. Alvarez held his breath and pressed himself into the earth. He thought for a moment the guard might have heard his body scraping over the sand. Flush against the wall, the guard's face was shrouded in shadow, and it was difficult to see where his attention was directed. Alvarez tapped his fingers on the sand impatiently.

And then he heard the chopper.

CHAPTER FORTY-SIX

Picard saw the lights first. "Over there," he said, pointing to the left. "That's it. It has to be."

Bolan grunted his agreement and banked slightly, until the lights low on the horizon were dead ahead. The big Mi-16 was getting low on fuel, and he had started wondering whether they were going to make it.

"You got that C-4 wired?" Bolan asked.

"All set. Four small blocks. I still don't see how we get to use it. We can't bomb the place. And if we hit the ground, we better be running."

"We have a better chance if we take out the Libyan barracks. If you drop two blocks on each roof, they'll stay put. Then we blow them. Cuts the odds way down."

Picard didn't say anything. He didn't have to. Bolan already knew what the Frenchman was thinking, and some things didn't have to be said. Some things were so incontrovertible, they made your mind up for you. All you had to do was stand back and let reality take charge.

"I guess you're right," Picard finally conceded. "But I don't like it."

"You got any better ideas, I'd love to hear them."

"No...I don't."

Bolan nodded. He could see his own reflection on the inside of the cockpit windshield, his skin glowing a pale green, hovering in the glass like a genie in a magic mirror. Only this genie didn't know any more than he did. There was a questioning face in the glass, but no answers.

As the chopper drew closer the outlines of the buildings began to materialize as if out of nothing. They were shadowy, and seemed to appear in bits and pieces, like a developing photograph. With less than a mile to go Bolan spotted a bulky shadow short of the warehouse.

"What's that?" he asked. "Put the glasses on it, Lucien."

Picard brought the binoculars up and peered through the glass. "Looks like a plane, a big one. C-47, I think. You thinking what I'm thinking?"

"What if more Libyans are sitting there, the whole bunch of them waiting for us?"

"Yeah, that's what I'm thinking."

"If the pilot was supposed to radio in, we could be in big trouble. I'm hoping the chopper is no big deal. They have to be expecting it, and maybe nobody will care."

"I got a news flash for you. We're already in big trouble, regardless."

"Maybe . . . maybe not. We'll see."

"I thought that's what you'd say."

"Look, Lucien, we're almost out of fuel. We don't have any choice."

"I know, but I don't have to be happy about it."

As the camp assumed a sharper definition, Bolan wheeled the chopper wide to the right. He came in from the left and passed over the warehouse while Picard cranked open his door.

Banking slightly to give Picard a better angle, he dropped his airspeed and passed over the first barracks. The Frenchman leaned far to the right, a cube of C-4 in his hand, the short transceiver wire jutting stiffly out of the puttylike explosive. He snapped his wrist sharply and watched the cube slam into the barracks roof and flatten under the impact. Bolan nudged the chopper forward and Picard tossed the second block, this time letting gravity do most of the work.

The chopper slid sideways and Bolan held it steady over the second barracks. When the last block of explosive was in place Picard yanked a slender whip antenna out of a small handset. Bolan swung the chopper in a tight circle, then zipped toward the warehouse. "I'll tell you when," he said, easing the controls forward and letting the chopper drop the rest of the way to a landing.

Bolan left the pilot's chair and climbed into the rear of the chopper, slipping the canvas bag over his shoulder. Sliding the side door open, he glanced toward the nearest barracks. So far no one seemed to have taken notice of their arrival.

The helicopter was only lightly armed, but they had to play the cards they'd been dealt. Picard limped out of the cockpit and joined Bolan at the door. Keeping one eye on the compound, Bolan quickly unlimbered a .50-caliber machine gun on a swivel mount just inside the door. He fed an ammo belt into the big gun and jumped to the ground. "You stay here. Watch the barracks."

"Where you going?"

"I'm going to rig the warehouse." He sprinted toward the huge storage complex, one of Picard's stolen Uzis in his hand, a spare clip in his pocket. The canvas bag flapped hard against his hip as he ran.

He was halfway to the door when he spotted the guard in the shadows. Bolan swung the Uzi around, but the guard made no move to stop him. The warrior stopped in front of the motionless figure, who had an AK-47 balanced precariously on his knees. Bolan leaned forward, and now he knew why. The front of the man's shirt was soaked with blood, the ugly stain already darkening in a stiff fan around the handle of a switchblade planted just above the heart.

Bolan frowned. Something was out of kilter. He stepped away from the dead man, shifting the Uzi from his right hand to his left. He grasped the knob of a small entry door to the left of the main door, turned it and tugged outward. The door opened easily. A sudden flash, like that of a firefly in a shoe box, winked at him from the interior, then was gone.

Bolan stepped through the door and pulled it closed. He stared at the darkness for a long time, trying to place where he had seen the light. As his eyes adjusted to the gloom, he took a few tentative steps, then stopped to listen. A soft rasp in the darkness caught his ear, and he instinctively dropped to his stomach. He had his own light in the sack, but he knew it would give him away. He didn't want to use it unless he had to, so he took it out of the bag and stuck it in his belt, where he could reach it in a hurry.

He wormed forward, his clothes unavoidably scratching the concrete floor. A sudden hiss, a few yards in front of him and a few feet in the air, froze him in place.

"Bolan, stay there."

"Who is that?" Bolan whispered.

"It's me, Alvarez."

The light returned, its beam wavering a little as Alvarez climbed over some wooden crates. In the backwash of the broad beam Bolan could just discern the man's features. He waited while the agent scrambled toward him, playing the beam ahead of him, then clicking it off when he cleared the last obstacle.

"What the hell are you doing here?"

"The real question is where the hell have *you* been?" Alvarez laughed quietly. "I thought I was going to have to take this whole shootin' match on by myself. Picard still with you?"

"Yeah, he's outside. Got a pretty bad leg, but he can still pitch in. What's the story?"

"I got the warehouse set to blow, but there must be ninety or a hundred men in the barracks. I don't know how we can handle that."

Bolan smiled a tight smile. "We dropped some plastique on two of the barracks. That'll cut the odds a little."

Alvarez waved his arm, then winced with pain. "Geez!"

"You okay?"

Alvarez nodded. He reached into his pocket for another painkiller and swallowed it dry. "I'll be all right as long as we make it quick."

"If we don't, hip boots won't help us breathe."

"Then let's get the show on the road. Where's Harlow?"

"In barracks two, I think. He's got a woman with him, and some big bastard with about as much hair as a cantaloupe. Name's Sadowski."

"We've met," Bolan said.

"I know."

Alvarez flicked his torch along the wall until he found the gray metal box housing the circuit breakers for the warehouse. He opened the squeaky door and popped each breaker into the off position. "Let's go," he said. The two men slipped out of the door into the darkened compound. The chopper sat idly, Picard no longer visible without the floodlights.

Bolan led the way past the C-47 and slipped up alongside the chopper. "Lucien," he whispered. "You there?"

Picard answered from the interior of the helicopter. "Here..." He jumped down from the darkened hold of the Mi-16, wincing as the impact shocked his wounded leg.

It was time to take charge, and Mack Bolan did what he did better than anyone else. "Get that .50-caliber out of the chopper. I'll be right back."

"Where you going?" Alvarez asked.

"To get a jeep. They've got us outnumbered. That means we have to be more mobile than they are." He vanished into the shadows under the big transport. He sprinted through the darkness to the makeshift motor pool. One by one he checked the half dozen jeeps nosed into the L of the warehouse. None of the first few had the keys in their ignitions, but on the fifth one he got lucky.

He left the keys in place and climbed into the driver's seat just long enough to pop the transmission into neutral and take the hand brake off. Jumping to the gritty sand, he started to push the jeep, steering with one hand. He got the blocky vehicle in a slow roll, when someone turned the corner.

"Yo, Francis, what the hell happened to the lights, man?"

Bolan froze for just an instant, then reached into his shirt for the Beretta 93-R. Ducking behind the jeep, he stared into the gloom, trying to pinpoint the man's location.

"Frannie, you there? Quit jerkin' around, will you? Turn the lights on, man."

Bolan spotted a beige phantom against the dark wall. The man's steady footsteps slowed and became irregular, as if he were picking his way through a mine field. Bolan waited until he stopped altogether.

"Francis?" the sentry whispered. "You there?"

Bolan's Beretta coughed a discreet reply. The shot took the unsuspecting guard dead center, and he slumped to the ground with a dull thump. Bolan stepped around the jeep in a crouch. He tiptoed toward the fallen guard and knelt beside him. In the dim light he could see the dark stain over his heart.

He loosened the Kalashnikov from the grip of dead fingers and slung it over his shoulder, then sprinted back to the jeep. He got it rolling again, this time a little faster. When he passed under the wing of the C-47, Alvarez saw him coming and rushed over to lend a hand. Together they maneuvered the jeep up to the side of the chopper.

Picard, leaning against the side of the chopper, worked on the thumbscrews, disconnecting the machine gun from its mount. He hauled the heavy gun out of the chopper, and Bolan grabbed the other end. It took only a minute to fit the gun to the jeep's own mount.

The French agent hauled himself back into the chopper and manhandled a pair of crates to the lip of the hold. Bolan grabbed each crate by its rope handles and lugged the ammunition to the rear of the jeep, dumping each crate on the back seat.

When the second case of belted ammo was in place, he growled, "I guess it's time."

"What's the game plan?" Picard asked.

"First we take out the two barracks and the warehouse. Then we'll have to handle whatever happens."

"Some plan."

"If you got a better idea, I'm all ears," Bolan said.

Picard climbed into the rear of the jeep and swung the .50-caliber weapon around to face the front of the nearest barracks. Alvarez sat behind the wheel, and Bolan was in the passenger seat with the Kalashnikov across his knees.

He nodded and said, "Anytime you're ready."

Picard depressed a red button on the transmitter, and the rear barracks went up in balls of orange flame. Like giant balloons rising, the fireballs climbed over the roof of the closer barracks, expanding and pushing thick black smoke ahead of them until they merged in a wall of flame.

Alvarez triggered his own detonator, and the warehouse seemed to shudder. The ground began to shake, and the walls of the huge building began to fold outward, as flimsy as stage scenery. Great metal panels blown away from their supporting beams toppled like playing cards. The center of the shattered building already glowed with a white light, and explosion after explosion scattered showers of sparks, and comets of flame whooshed and hissed as they flew through the air. The holocaust had an eerie beauty, and the three men watched as if mesmerized, before Bolan shook himself free of the hypnotic trance.

He tapped Alvarez on the shoulder as the screen door of the nearest barracks flew open.

"Let's roll...."

CHAPTER FORTY-SEVEN

The standing barracks was starkly outlined against the harsh orange light. Men started to pour outside, and Picard started hammering out rounds. Bolan felt the whole jeep shuddering beneath his feet, and a jarring rattle shook his spine.

Alvarez moved the jeep at an angle, giving Picard a clear field of fire as he bucked across the open field. The running men, most of them half-dressed, carried rifles and ran in aimless circles. There was little cover and no direction. A handful of the men sprinted barefoot for nearby jeeps. Picard watched and waited, opening up with the .50-caliber weapon when they slowed to scramble into the jeeps. They fell like cordwood, stacked one on another in small mounds around the first jeep.

Alvarez swung the vehicle around as scattered men started to return fire. Bolan had been searching the milling mob for any sign of Sadowski or Harlow. The machine gun fell silent, and Bolan turned in time to see Picard struggling with a second belt. The big guy climbed over his seat and held the belt until Picard was able to lock it in place.

"How's your leg holding up?"

The Frenchman showed a mouthful of teeth that wasn't quite a smile. "I'll be all right as long as I don't have to run."

Bolan slapped him on the shoulder, then jumped back into the passenger seat. He picked up the AK-47 and swept it across the open field, but the men had started to recover from their surprise. Fire sporadically cracked from the barracks windows, the shooters hidden by the darkness, but the moving jeep was not an easy target in the chaos.

A thick pall of smoke hung over the encampment, gradually lowering like a proscenium curtain. Puffs and billows blew across the dry soil, propelled by superheated air pouring from the burning buildings, then spiraled up into the night. Backlit by a hellish orange shading toward white, the smoky clouds turned yellowish gray and swirled in wide circles, picking up dust and sand as they danced like dervishes.

Bolan watched the warehouse for a moment and saw the last of the metal walls cave in. The metal frame of the building had begun to glow at the heart of the inferno, turning red and orange, even white in places. The heavy beams had begun to sag and, as Bolan looked on, the uprights at one end buckled outward, like the legs of a drunken sailor, bowing into a wider and wider O and finally collapsing altogether. The crash sent a column of white sparks towering into the air, where they were ripped into hundreds of small stars by the air currents before raining back down on the blazing ruin.

Picard raked the windows of the barracks with machine-gun fire, chewing through the flimsy wooden walls, sending chips and splinters flying. A huge explosion in the heart of the warehouse sent blazing scraps of wood in a drunken rainbow. Some of the burning junk landed on the barracks roofs, and the dry shingles caught like tinder.

Smoke began to spiral up from the barracks, and Alvarez swung the jeep around to let Picard rake the front of the low building. Men tumbled through the shattered windows, struggling to their feet and running in every direction. Bolan and Alvarez cracked away with their rifles, like kids in a shooting gallery, chasing shadows in their sights and dropping them with deadly precision. The men were too confused to offer serious opposition.

Several men sprinted for the end of the barracks and turned the corner. Alvarez gunned the jeep, nearly pitching Picard over the back end. The Frenchman grabbed the gun mount and struggled back to balance, Bolan holding him by his shirttail until he twisted back into the seat.

Skidding around the corner, the jeep nearly collided with another. Pete Sadowski, his chest as bare as his bald head, was at the wheel. Smeared with orange light and wrapped in tendrils of black smoke, he looked like a fundamentalist's worst nightmare. His lips were drawn back in a horrible grin as he steered with one hand and waved an Uzi in the other. He reached back with the SMG and fired a burst across the rear of his jeep, sending Picard to the floor.

Bolan spun in his seat and fired the rest of his magazine at the huge merc's jeep, but the gun emptied almost immediately. He dropped the Kalashnikov to the floor between the front seat and the fire wall, and switched to Picard's Uzi.

"Hit the brakes, Leon," he hollered. He fired two short bursts at the grinning demon, taking out the windshield of the merc's jeep before it swung around the corner and disappeared. Bolan jumped from his vehicle and chased after Sadowski.

A tight knot of men dead ahead dropped to their knees and began firing sporadically at the onrushing jeep. Picard swung the .50-caliber MG around, and like a modern Alexander undid the knot with slashing lead.

Three men peeled off from the tight cluster, running to the right, and Picard followed them, catching up with them just before they reached the safety of the other standing barracks. Picard looked back over his shoulder, but Bolan had vanished. He turned back as Alvarez reached the end of the barracks and took a sharp right, skidding on the dry sand. As the jeep stabilized, the rear end of a second jeep swept behind the second barracks. Alvarez gunned his engine, speeding after it, but four men materialized out of the smoke, laying down a wall of rifle fire, and the agent dived for the floor. The jeep bucked twice, then stalled.

Alvarez crawled out of the jeep, ducking between its front fender and the wall of the barracks. Picard tumbled over the rear end, then reached back for an Uzi. He sprayed 9 mm hellfire at the phantoms in the smoke while Alvarez reached into the jeep for Bolan's AK-47. He aimed into the smoke and pulled the trigger, not realizing the magazine was empty.

He cursed and searched around on the floor for a full clip, bumping his wounded shoulder on the front seat. The jarring shock knocked the clip from his hands, and it clattered to the floor of the jeep. Two more men joined the original four, and they started to move toward the jeep in a ragged half circle, laying down a steady field of fire as they advanced, still half-wrapped in thick, black smoke.

Alvarez groaned and started groping on the floor for the magazine, closing his fingers over it just as Picard's Uzi went dry. He yanked the old clip out and crammed the new one in as Picard struggled to find more ammunition for his weapon.

Bringing up the AK-47, Alvarez drew a bead on the closest man, smoke-shrouded from the waist down, and fired a short burst. The man dropped into the smoke and disappeared. Moving his aim to the other end of the line, Alvarez fired again. This time he missed, but the advancing gunman dived to the ground, firing blindly out of the smoke.

Picard had his Uzi reloaded, and like an old man watering his lawn, snaked a looping fire line across the four remaining men. The gun bucked in his hands, its muzzle bouncing hard off the tail of the jeep and reducing the minimal accuracy still further. Alvarez aimed low, catching the center man as he dropped to his knees. The man pitched backward, clutching his throat, then disappeared in the black cloud.

"Where's Bolan?" Alvarez hissed.

"He went after Sadowski on foot."

"We have to get this jeep rolling again."

"Not yet. Those bastards are sitting there, just waiting for that."

A sudden thud and rattle in the jeep broke off the conversation. Alvarez hollered "Grenade!" and ran toward the rear of the jeep, bouncing between it and the barracks wall. He grabbed Picard and hurled him to the ground, covering the smaller Frenchman with his body. He felt the shudder as the grenade went off. The jeep was torn apart, its ruptured fuel tank splattering gasoline over the end wall of the barracks and bursting into flame.

The agent rolled off the Frenchman and swung his AK-47 in a wide arc, spraying fire into the smoky cloud a foot above the ground. He felt the searing heat of the blazing barracks through his shirt and scrambled to his feet, tugging Picard by the collar.

SADOWSKI LET GO of the wheel and turned, the rifle clenched tightly in one hammy fist. He fired randomly, and Bolan zigzagged through the smoke like a man possessed. He coughed his way through the oily clouds and circled around the idling jeep.

Sadowski stood in the front seat, bellowing unintelligible profanity, then stepped down to the ground, placing one foot before the other in a grim advance. He whirled once, thinking he'd heard something behind him, and fired a short burst, then spun back. He leaned into the swirling smoke as if it weren't even there.

Bolan crouched, fighting back a cough that would give him away, holding his breath and watching through teary eyes as the shadowy figure moved slowly past him. The roar of an engine startled both men, and a jeep barreled around the corner, its headlights trying to pierce the thick pall. It headed right for Sadowski, and the big man leaped to one side, turning to curse after the vehicle.

Bolan sprang. He charged straight ahead, covering the last five feet in an arcing dive, slamming his shoulder into the larger man just above the waist. The impact knocked Sadowski to the ground and sent his Uzi flying. The warrior landed on the larger man's back, but Sadowski struggled up, throwing off the weight on his shoulders as if it weren't even there.

He spun, snarling like an angry tiger, as Bolan scrambled to his feet. His eyes, too, were stung by the smoke, and he wiped them with a grimy hand, trying to clear his blurred vision. Bolan put his head down and charged straight forward, catching Sadowski with his head and left shoulder in the pit of the stomach. The impact crushed the air out of his lungs, and he grunted but kept his feet.

A blow to the back of the head sent Bolan sprawling and bright flashes danced before his eyes. He shook his head to clear it, and his vision was less blurred, but an ache started at the top of his skull and continued halfway down his back. He circled, trying to buy himself some time.

Sadowski grinned, showing all his teeth in a black, smeared face as he moved forward one step at a time, slowly narrowing the distance between himself and the crouching Bolan. An eerie sound rumbled in his chest, and Bolan thought of a caged animal in a zoo. Only this was worse than a zoo, and Sadowski had nothing to restrain his rage.

Bolan went to his belt and pulled a survival knife. He moved it from hand to hand, its serrated edge glittering with orange light as it reflected the roaring flames surrounding him. Sadowski saw the knife, but it didn't deter him. His grin grew broader and he dropped into a crouch aping Bolan's own. The big man's bald head gleamed in the firelight as he half stepped forward. His close-set eyes, their irises coal-black and shot through with reflected flame, looked as if they burned with their own inner fire.

Bolan feinted to the left and Sadowski bought the fake, shifting his weight just enough to lose his balance as Bolan changed direction. Charging toward the tottering giant, Bolan put his full weight behind the knife. The blade stuttered as its serrated edge repeatedly snagged on bone, then slammed to a halt just beneath the sternum. Bolan twisted the blade and slashed it sideways, skirting the rib cage. Sadowski turned toward his adversary, his eyes uncomprehending.

With a soft "Oh," he sank to his knees and Bolan let him fall, relaxing his grip on the knife. Slowly, like a man in an underwater ballet, Sadowski brought his hands up to grasp the hilt. Blood seeped through his fingers, turning a ghastly orange-red in the light from the roaring blaze.

The big man fell like a tree, small puffs of dust thrown up by the crash of his limp body on the ground. Panting, Bolan snatched the fallen Uzi and stared after the speeding ieep, its taillights bouncing over the desert. He ran to Sadowski's jeep and jumped into the driver's seat, kicking the transmission into first. The other driver had a good lead on him, and Bolan gunned the engine. He had to catch the vanishing lights.

The driver was Mason Harlow.

CHAPTER FORTY-EIGHT

Bolan kicked his jeep, keeping one eye on the assault rifle rattling on the seat beside him. The twin points of red grew clearer as he roared into the smokeless air. Ahead of him a long shadow seemed to race him away from the burning ruins of the camp. The neutral soil was smeared with red and orange. An intermittent rumble rocked the ground as large munitions detonated sporadically. The whole camp was an inferno now as live rounds set off by the intense heat speared out of the flames in every direction.

The earth shook with a terrible rumbling sound, and Bolan looked back over his shoulder. A gargantuan black cloud mushroomed over the orange ruins. It must have been the planeful of plastique, Bolan thought. For a second he watched the roiling black and orange, stunned by its fury, fascinated by the rich play of color and shadow. Then he realized that Picard and Alvarez were still in the camp. He took a deep breath, torn between the desire to go back and to chase after Harlow, already three miles ahead of him in the desert.

Bolan turned away from the flames and fancied he could feel their heat swirling around him as he stepped on the gas. He wondered who had been in the passenger seats of Harlow's jeep. The figures had been shrouded in smoke and huddled down behind the windshield, and it had not been possible to see who they were.

The fury of the explosion died away behind him, and the steady discharge of rifle and pistol ammunition was nothing in comparison, sounding more like a background hiss on an audiotape after a thundering Beethoven symphony had finished. He kept his eyes on the red lights, hoping that Harlow needed the headlights until he could get closer. If they went out, Harlow could shift directions a half dozen times and lose him for good.

His teeth chattered as the jeep rocked and bounced unpredictably over the uneven land. The twin points of red light lured him deeper into the night. The driver ahead of him had begun to angle toward the left, and Bolan plowed straight ahead, hoping Harlow was planning on a wide zigzag to throw him off. Without his own headlights, Bolan knew he was impossible to see, and would continue to be until he was almost on top of Harlow's jeep.

Sure enough, two minutes later the jeep angled back to the right, and Bolan had made up more than a quarter mile of Harlow's lead. The lights began to bob less frequently now, as the desert leveled out a bit. The warrior pressed his foot to the floor, trying to coax every bit of speed out of the cumbersome vehicle. He could feel the engine straining, the floorboards vibrating like a live thing under his heavy feet.

The lights suddenly stopped receding, and Bolan took his foot off the gas and coasted, wondering what Harlow was up to. He rolled on, trying not to use his engine, closing the gap a little more, until his momentum dwindled away to nothing. He stopped to listen but heard nothing but the constant crackle of the burning camp a mile behind him. The ammunition was almost exhausted, and the sharp cracks came farther and farther apart, like the last few kernels of popcorn in the bottom of the pan, holding on for dear life, defying the heat until the very last moment, then surrendering to the fire with an arrogant energy.

Bolan shifted down, still leaving the engine at idle. He had heard nothing significant in the darkness ahead but wondered why Harlow would have stopped so suddenly. Then with a sound all the louder for being unexpected, a series of sharp cracks sounded from the direction of Harlow's jeep. It was gunfire, there was no doubt about that, but who was shooting? And at whom?

The lights lurched, and the whine of an extended lower gear, protesting with every turn, ripped across the sand. Bolan popped his clutch and sped after the twin rubies, winding his own engine flat out. The gap continued to narrow as Bolan handled his jeep expertly and Harlow fought the terrain instead of going with the flow. Bolan was within a mile of him now and threw caution to the winds. He clicked on his headlights and picked his way among the rolling mounds of sand, wrestling the steering wheel to skirt them instead of taking them head-on. A quarter mile later, he knew why Harlow had stopped.

A half-dressed figure, clad only in fatigue pants and boots, lay facedown in the sand. An ugly pool of blood lay under the head, the face flattened where it pressed into the sand. The body lay with one hand just above its broken head, as if trying to catch the missing skull and brain tissue broken away by the gunshots. Bolan didn't slow down. He knew there was no point.

Dave McNally was as dead as you can get.

Leaning on the accelerator and holding on for all he was worth, Bolan pushed the jeep still harder. As long as his quarry kept moving, there was nothing to worry about. It was impossible to shoot accurately from the bouncing jeep, let alone steer it at the same time.

Bolan was close enough now to hear the whine of Harlow's engine, a high-pitched snarl over the roar of his own. Close and closer, he pushed the jeep beyond its limits. The engine began to rattle, and he backed off a bit, giving it a breather. Harlow, too, was pushing his engine past its tolerance. Bolan dropped down a bit, staying on Harlow's trail. The gap, now less than half a mile, stayed steady.

The blasts caught Bolan by surprise, and he ducked instinctively, tucking his head down into his chest and leaning as far forward as he could before he realized Harlow wasn't shooting at him. They weren't gunshots at all. He had heard the sound of repeated backfires. The red lights staggered to a halt, and Bolan leaned on it. He covered the half mile in nothing flat.

Harlow was already out of the jeep, the hood above his head as he peered in at the engine. A burst of flame scorched the open hood, and Harlow moved away from the engine compartment. The bright light threw his figure into sharp relief against the dull monotony of the desert behind him. He was backing away from the jeep and turning to run when he saw Bolan.

His eyes flicked back and forth between Bolan's face and the Uzi in his hands. Even now Mason Harlow was calculating the odds. They weren't too good, and he knew it. Backed into the tightest corner of his life, he reverted to form and did what he did best.

He bargained.

"Belasko, I'm sure as hell glad you happened along. The fucking jeep threw a rod or something. The damn engine blew up on me."

"That's too bad."

"We were lucky as hell to get out of there, huh? Geez, I thought I was a goner."

Bolan just stared at him.

"Listen, why don't we just pile my stuff in your jeep, and we can get the hell out of here. I got extra gas and some food and water. We can make it to Tmassah in a few hours. Be there before sunrise."

"No way, Harlow."

"Mason, call me Mason. Listen, I can make it worth your while. I've got all the money either of us will ever need. What do you say?"

"Is that what you told McNally? Before you blew his brains out and left him for the vultures?"

"No, nah. Hell, that isn't how it was. He tried to kill me. I didn't have any choice."

"It's all over, Harlow. Finished. Can't you see it, even now?"

"You're making a big mistake, Belasko. I can make you a rich man. Richer than you ever dreamed."

"Harlow, you don't have a thing that I want. Nothing."

He watched Harlow carefully, waving him toward the jeep with the Uzi. "Walk over there real easy and get in the jeep. I'm going to see to it that you get what you deserve. You'll be locked up for so long your grandchildren will die of old age before you're even eligible for parole."

"No you won't." The voice came from behind him, near Harlow's jeep, and Bolan whirled. The gun went off at the same time, three quick shots, and then clicked.

Harlow fell as if he'd been poleaxed. Bolan rushed to his side and knelt in the sand. Harlow had no pulse. His chest, sporting a short line of dark holes, seeping blood but making no sound, lay still. Mason Harlow had cut his last deal.

Marielle Trebec let the .45 automatic curl around her trigger finger, then drop to the ground with a heavy thump. She collapsed in the sand, her breath coming in short, sharp gasps, broken by sobs.

Bolan walked over to kneel beside her. He reached out a hand, much as he had done to Alison Brewer so long ago it might have been in another lifetime, and tilted her face upward. Great shimmering globes trembled in the corner of each eye but refused to fall. She reached up with one slender hand to wipe them away, smearing the tears under her eyes and sniffling.

"I suppose I have to pay for that, don't I?" she asked, nodding her chin toward Mason Harlow's body.

"I don't think so," Bolan said quietly. "There were no witnesses."